LEGO NINJAGO™

Masters of Spinjitzu

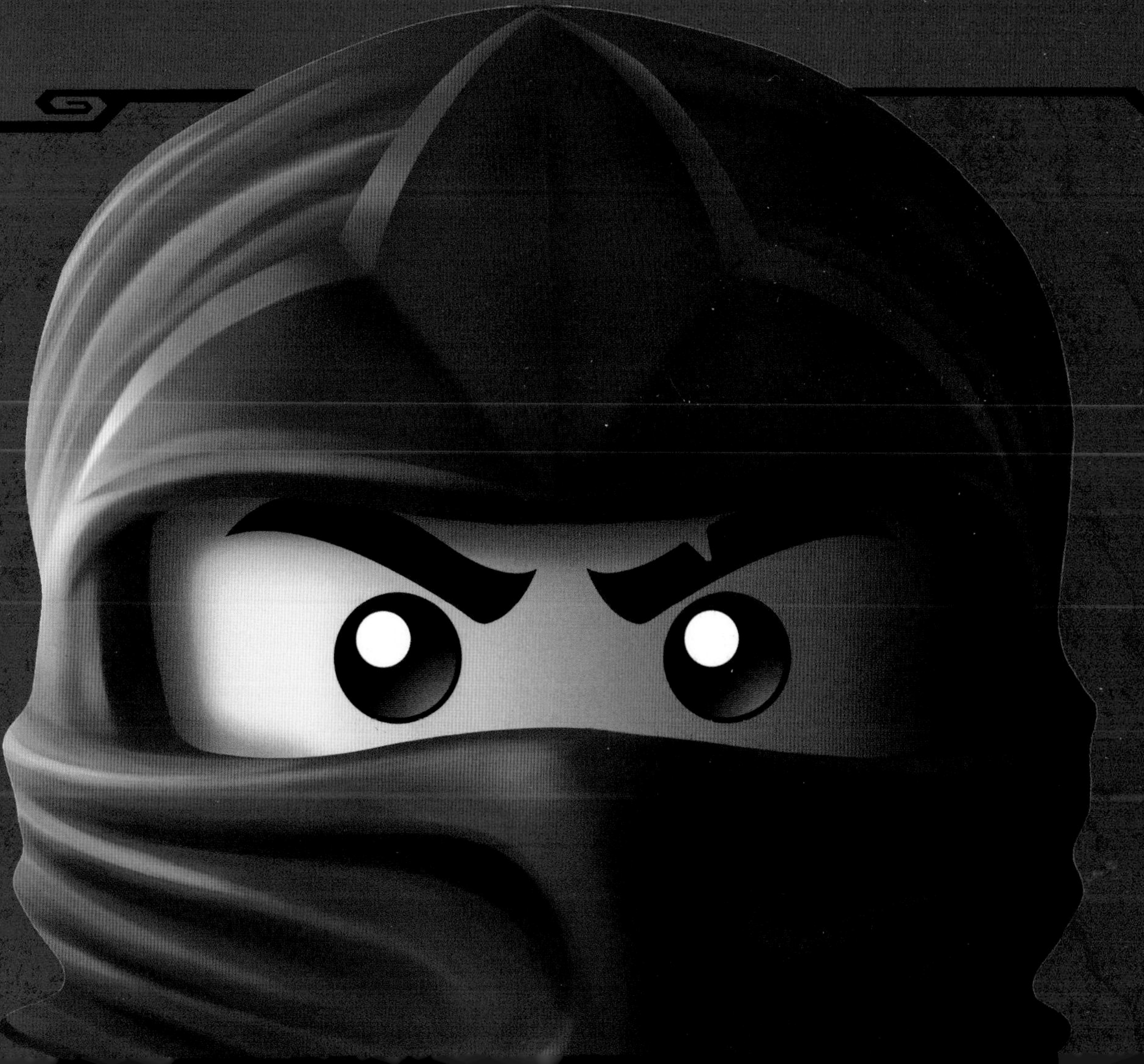

GAMES, GHOSTS & PIRATES
COLLECTION

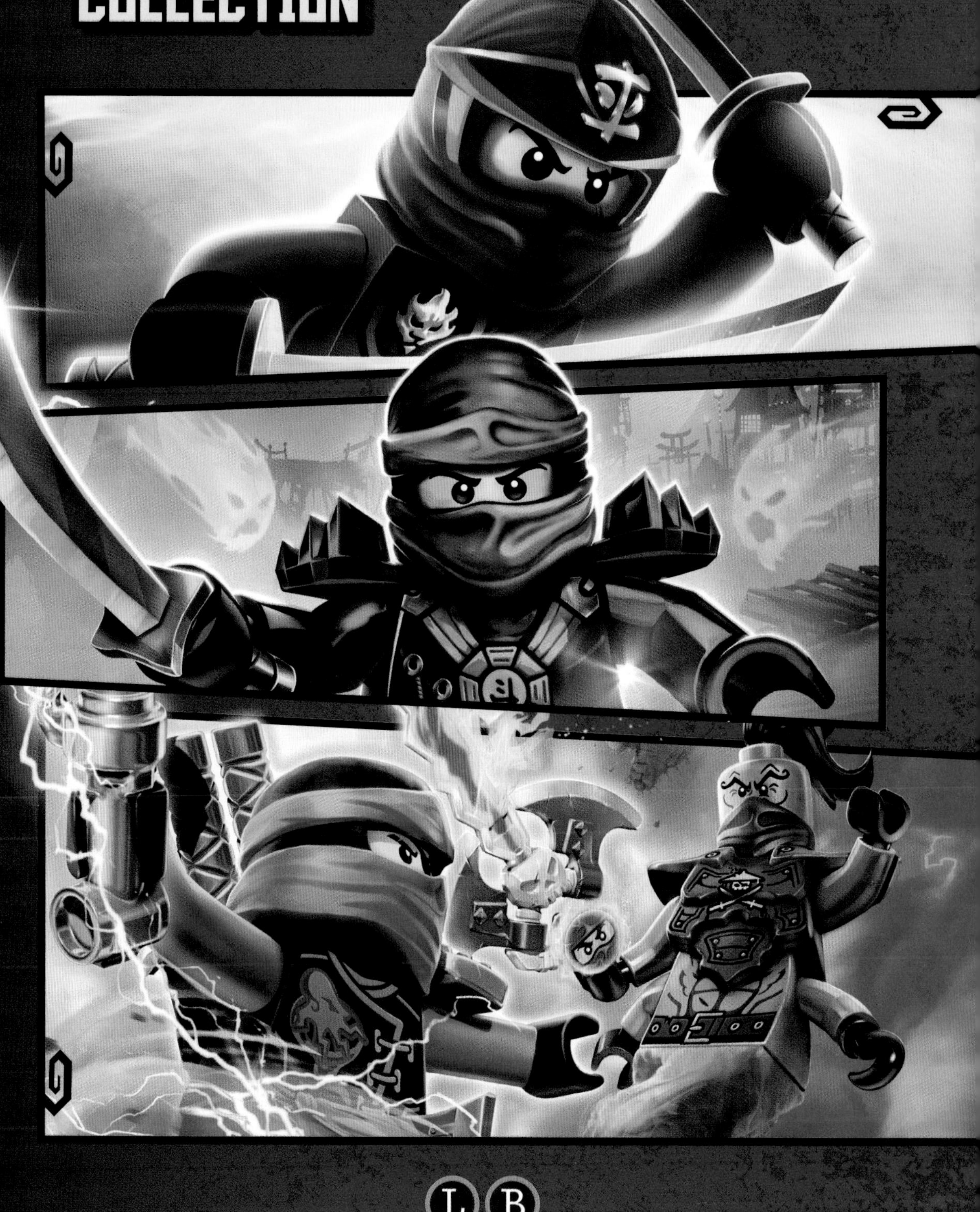

LB

Little, Brown and Company
New York • Boston

LEGO, the LEGO logo, the Brick and Knob configuration, NINJAGO, the NINJAGO logo and the Minifigure are trademarks of the LEGO Group. © 2015 and 2016 The LEGO Group. All rights reserved. Produced by Little, Brown and Company under license from the LEGO Group.

Comics artwork © 2015 and 2016 by Blue Ocean Entertainment AG, Germany.

Stories written by Christian Hector, Clemens Frey, and Tine S. Norbøll
Pencils by Jon Fernandez
Inks by Ivan Solans
Colors by Oriol San Julina & Javi Chaler
Pages 53-54 art by Caravan Studio: Hendy Setiawan (inks) & Felix Hidayat (color)
Page 198 art by Caravan Studio: Hendy Setiawan (inks) & Indar Gunawan (color).

Little, Brown and Company
Hachette Book Group
1290 Avenue of the Americas, New York, NY 10104
Visit us at lb-kids.com

Little, Brown and Company is a division of Hachette Book Group, Inc.
The Little, Brown name and logo are trademarks of Hachette Book Group, Inc.

The publisher is not responsible for websites (or their content) that are not owned by the publisher.

First Edition: November 2016

LEGO Ninjago: Tournament of Elements originally published in
September 2015 by Little, Brown and Company

LEGO Ninjago: Ghost Ninja originally published in
March 2016 by Little, Brown and Company

LEGO Ninjago: From Ghosts to Pirates originally published in
November 2016 by Little, Brown and Company

ISBN 978-0-316-26628-4

Library of Congress Control Number: 2016932979

10 9 8 7 6 5 4 3 2 1

APS

Printed in China

TABLE OF CONTENTS

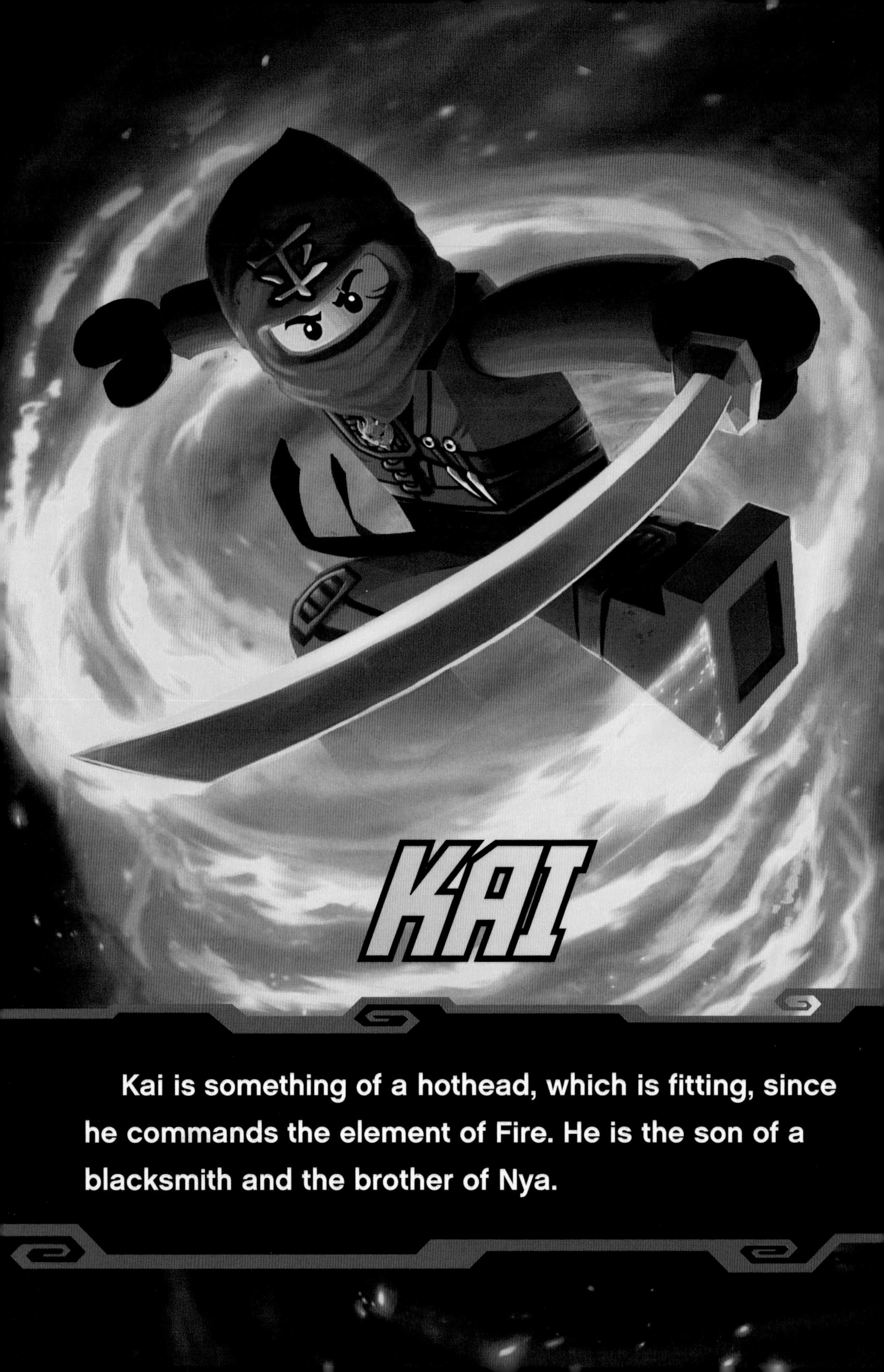

KAI

Kai is something of a hothead, which is fitting, since he commands the element of Fire. He is the son of a blacksmith and the brother of Nya.

COLE

Cole is a very calm and intelligent member of the ninja. He commands the element of Earth, giving him great physical strength and durability.

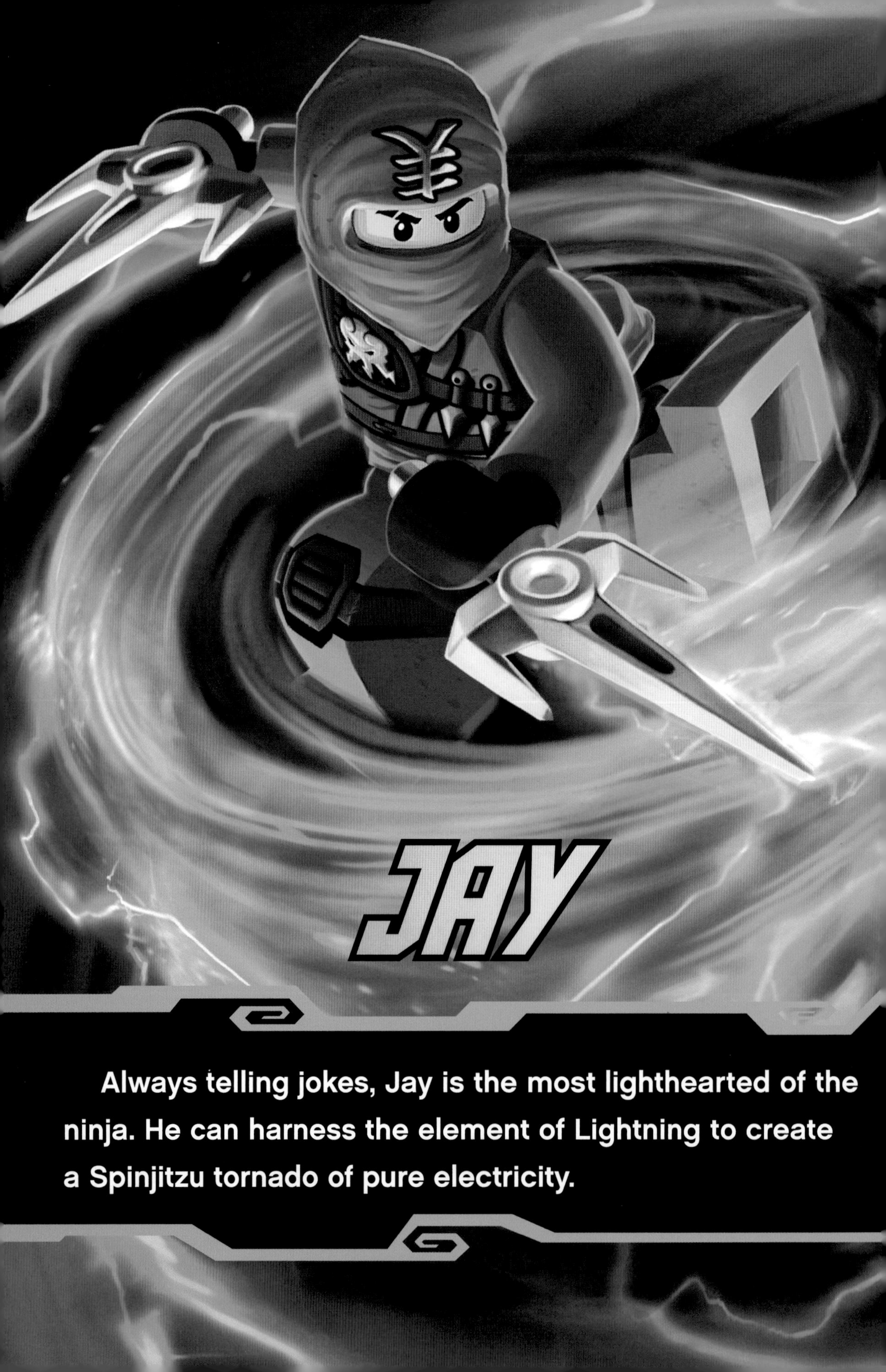

JAY

Always telling jokes, Jay is the most lighthearted of the ninja. He can harness the element of Lightning to create a Spinjitzu tornado of pure electricity.

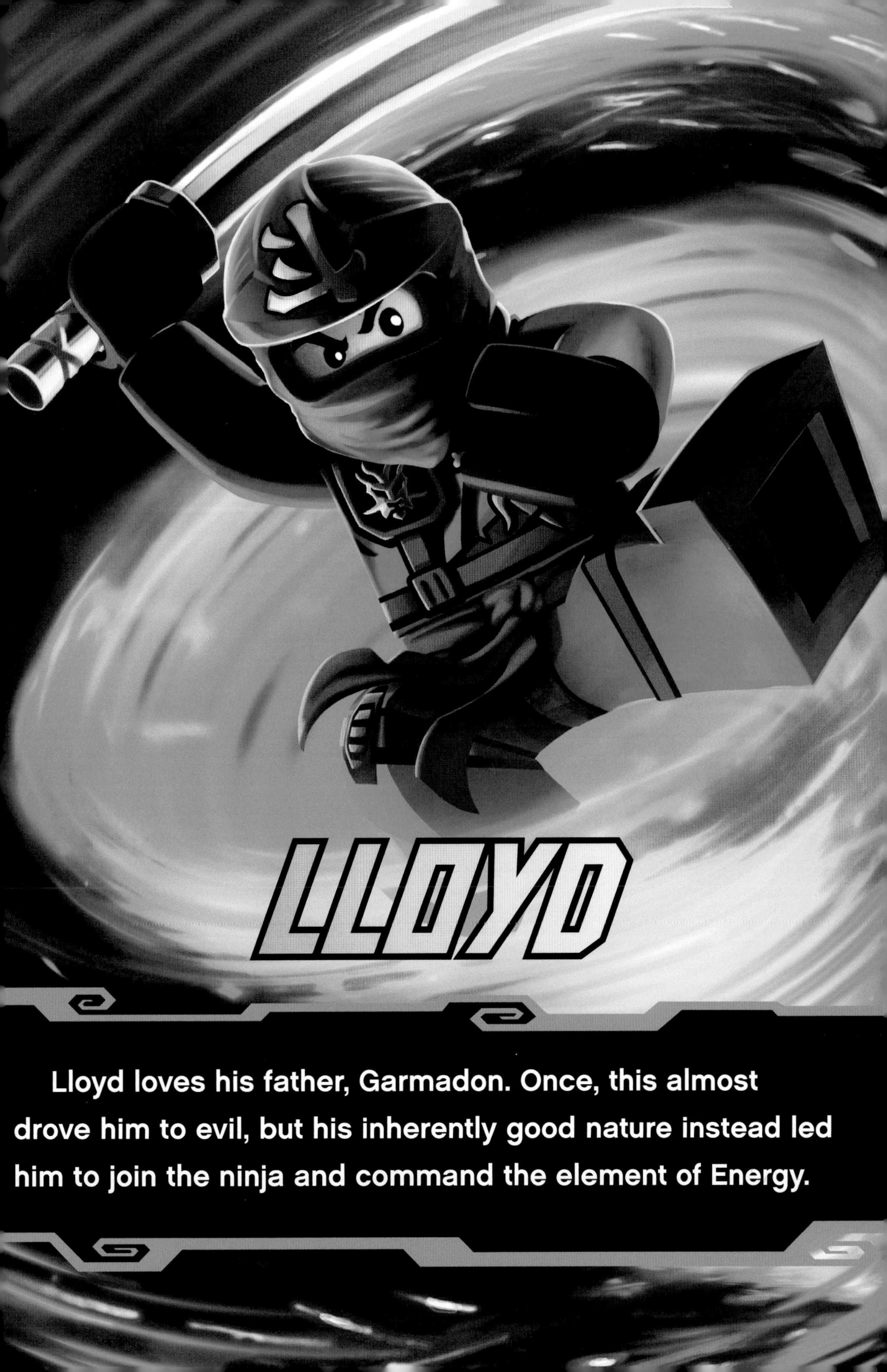

LLOYD

Lloyd loves his father, Garmadon. Once, this almost drove him to evil, but his inherently good nature instead led him to join the ninja and command the element of Energy.

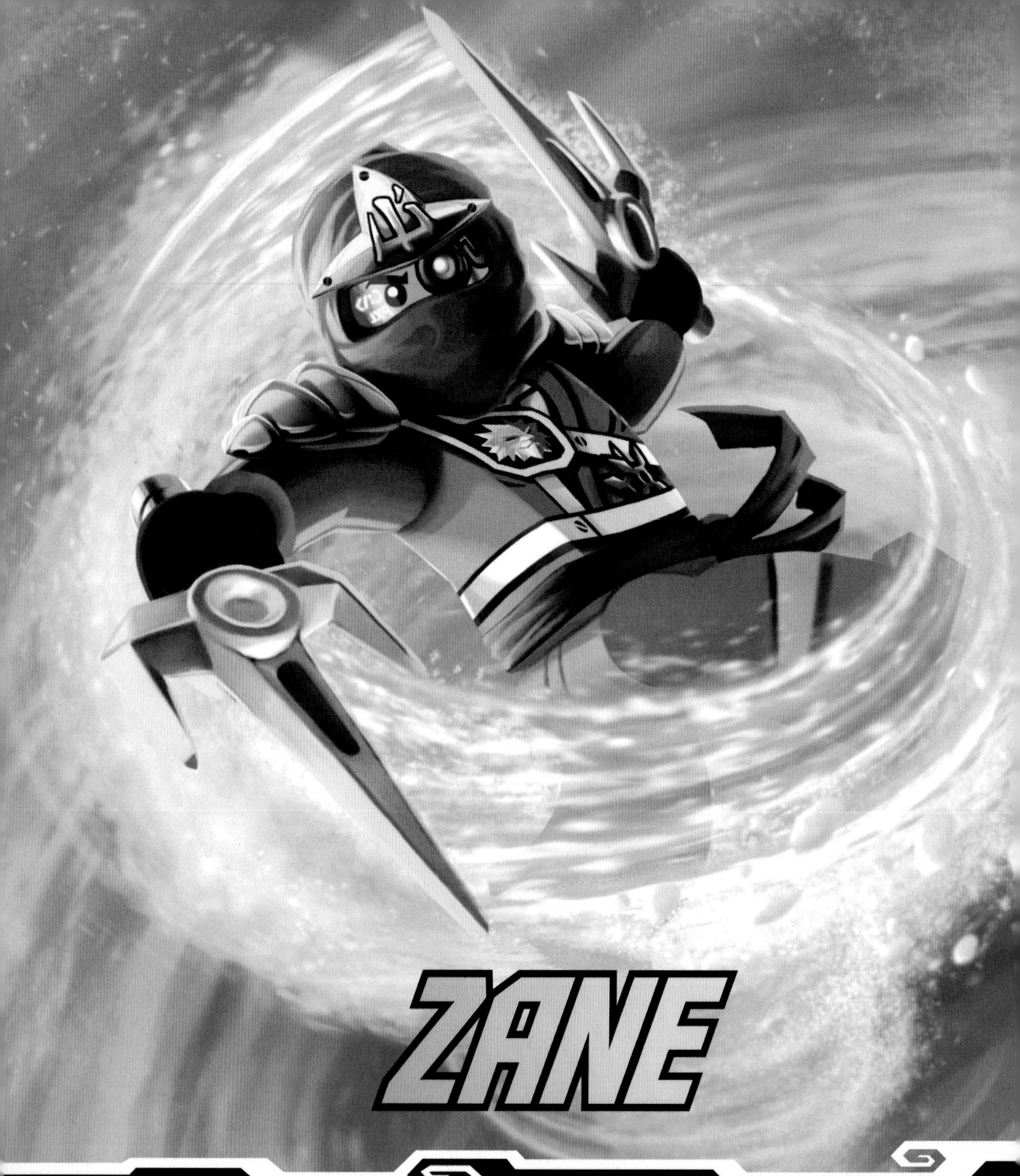
ZANE

Zane is the most reserved and serious of the ninja, but he is also the most respectful. His affinity for Ice allows him to freeze objects and perform a chilly Spinjitzu attack.

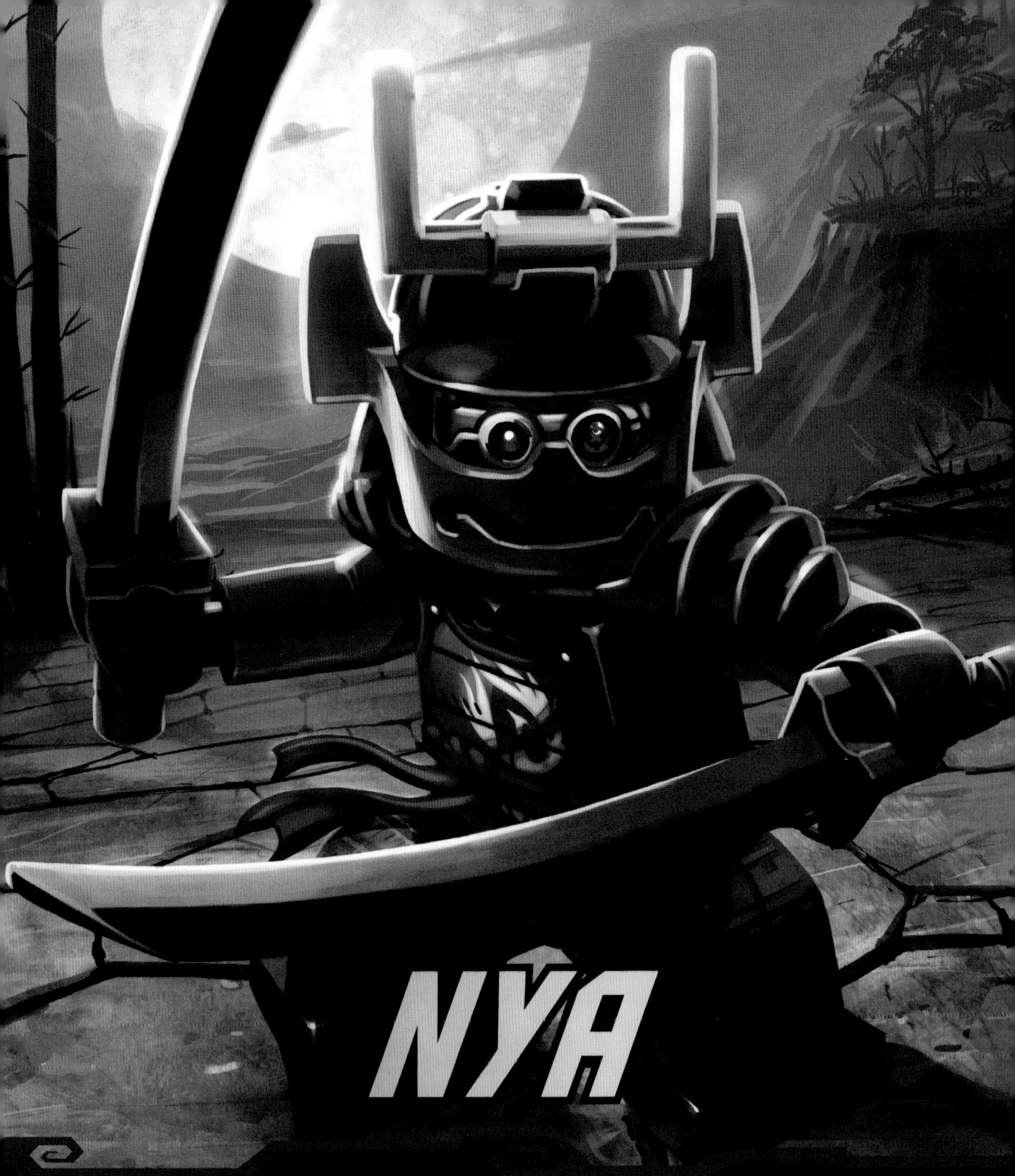
NYA

Besides Cole, no one goes through a bigger change than Nya. After being told she can't go on the quest, she learns she could become the most powerful weapon against the ghosts—as the Water Ninja. But does that mean she can't be Samurai X anymore? After her initial reluctance, she'll have to learn to go with the flow.

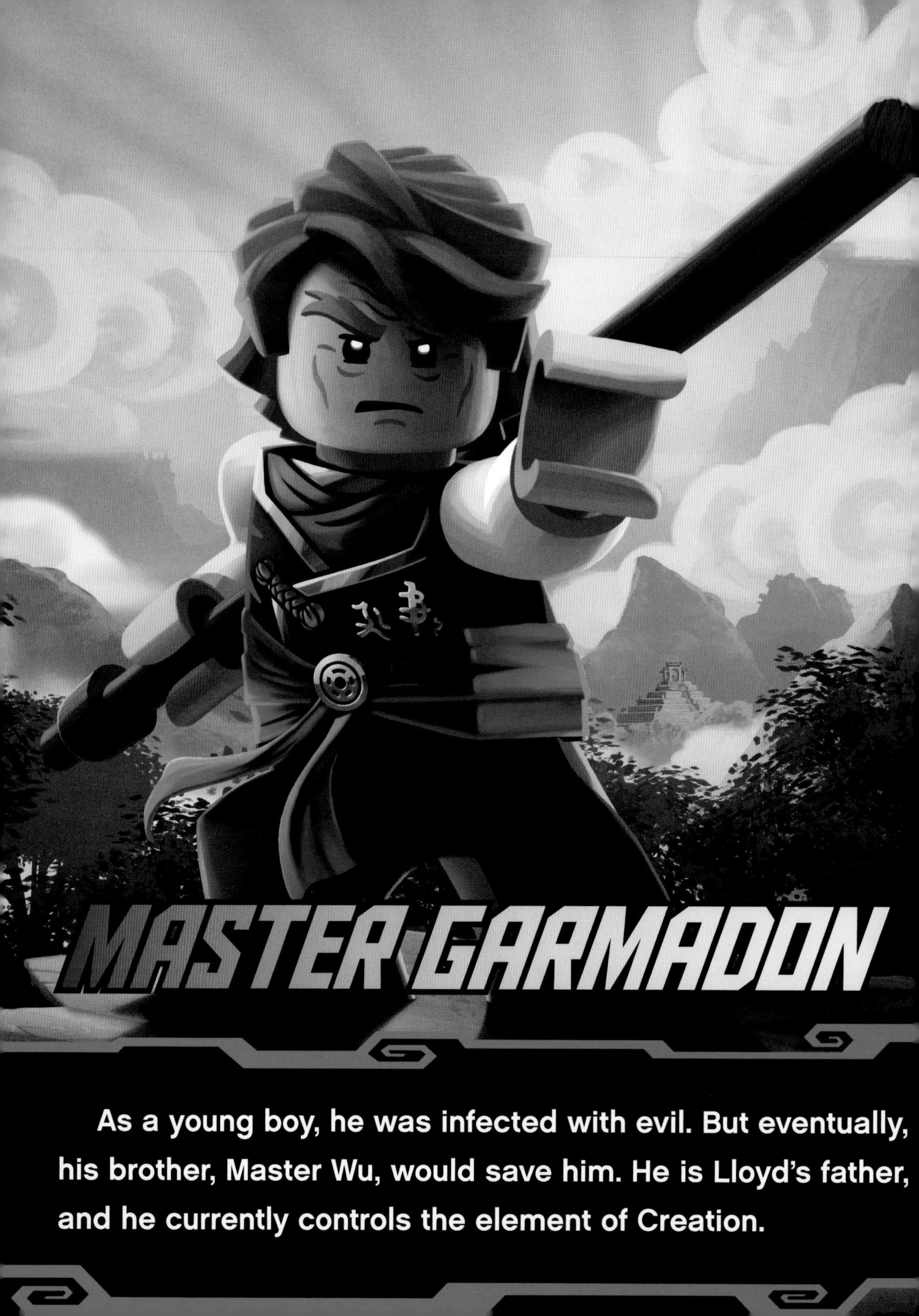

MASTER GARMADON

As a young boy, he was infected with evil. But eventually, his brother, Master Wu, would save him. He is Lloyd's father, and he currently controls the element of Creation.

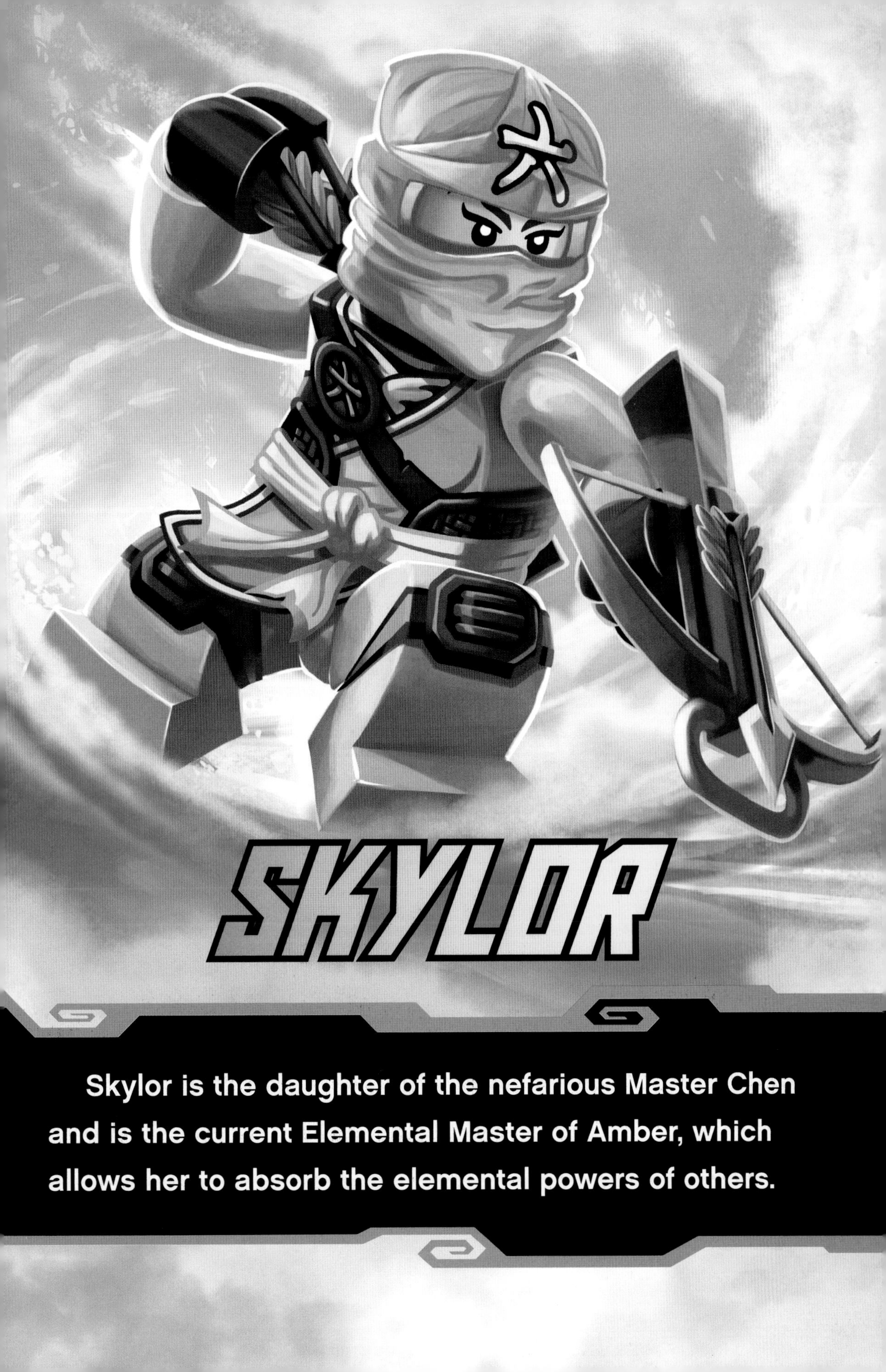

SKYLOR

Skylor is the daughter of the nefarious Master Chen and is the current Elemental Master of Amber, which allows her to absorb the elemental powers of others.

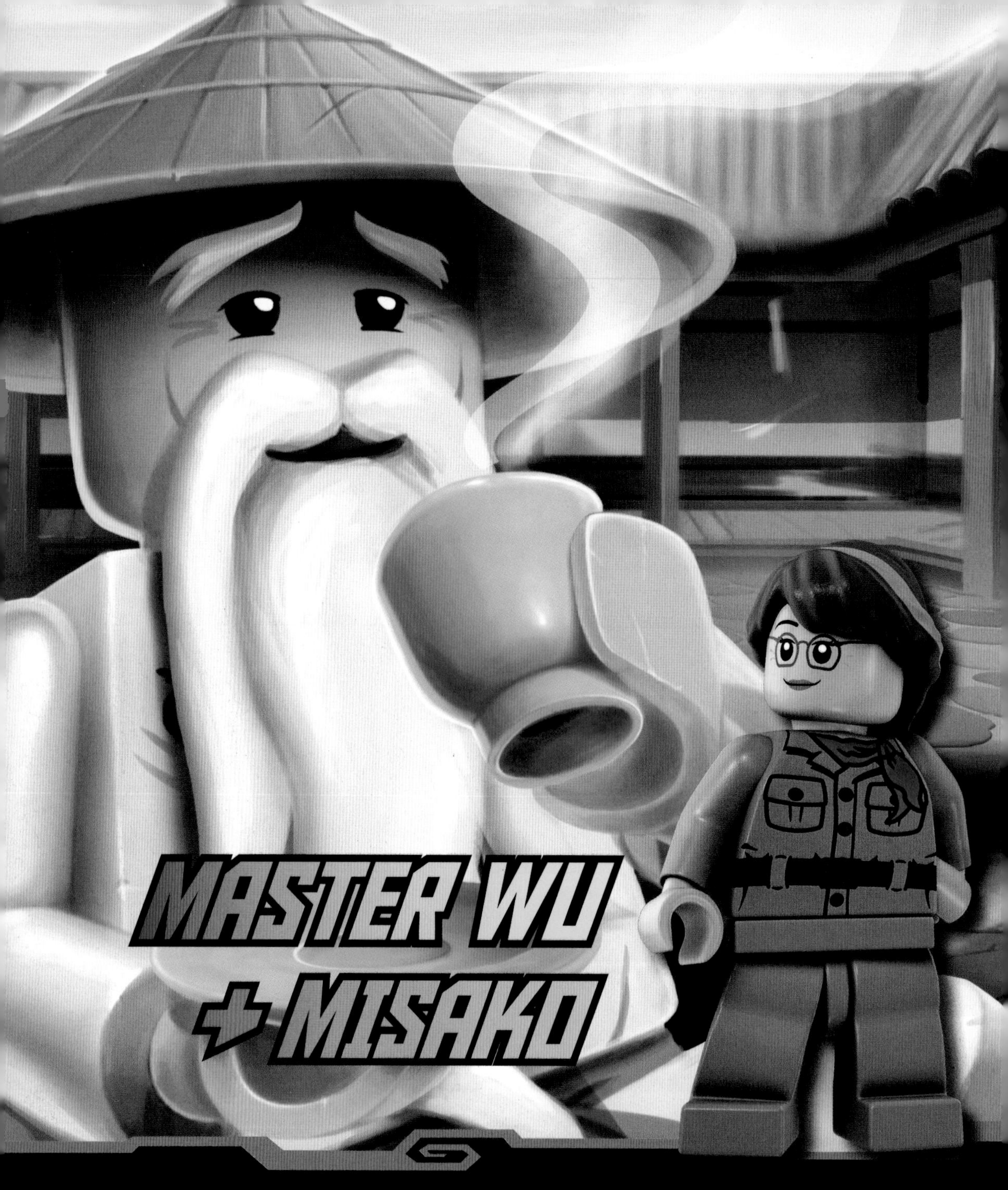
MASTER WU
+ MISAKO

With an eye toward retirement, Master Wu and Misako have purchased a tea farm with the hope of starting a business. But when things get rough, they'll need everything including the kitchen sink, to survive to see retirement.

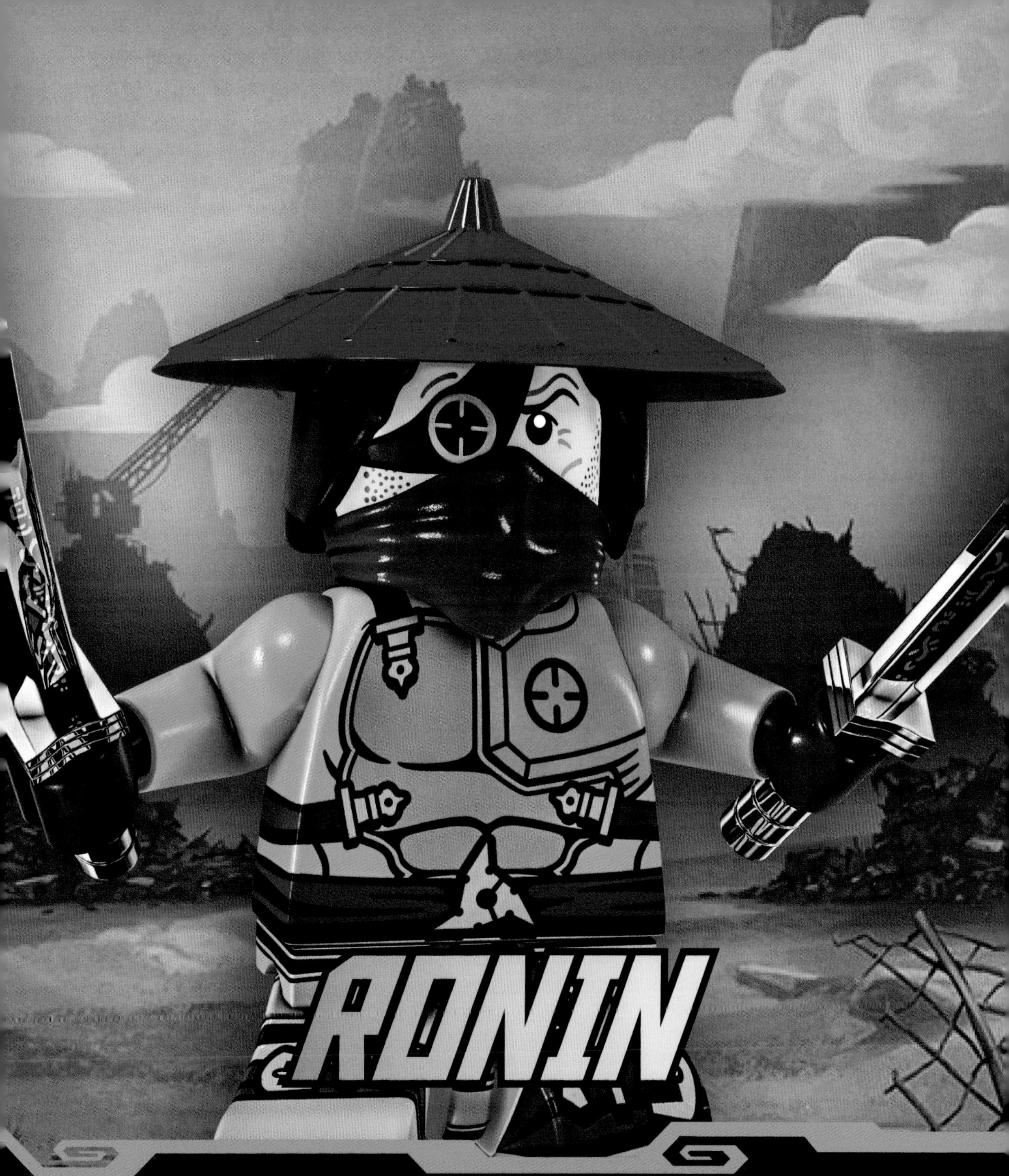
RONIN

The only master Ronin serves is money. Yet this retired thief is trying to make a second chance for himself—as part owner of Master Wu's tea farm.

LEGO NINJAGO™ Masters of Spinjitzu

TOURNAMENT OF ELEMENTS

Story and art by Blue Ocean Entertainment AG
Additional art by Caravan Studio

"Lost Scrolls of Spinjitzu"
written by Greg Farshtey

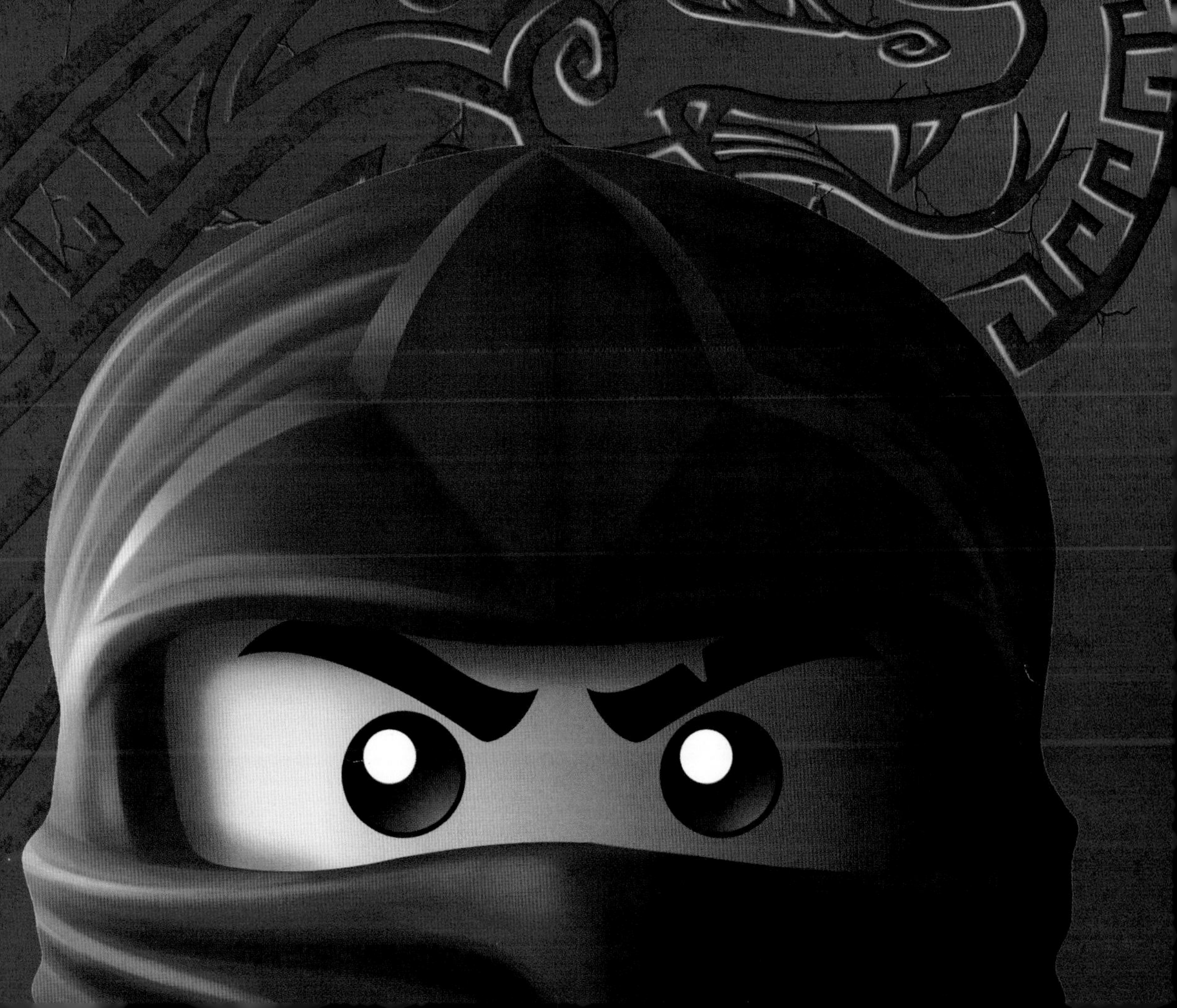

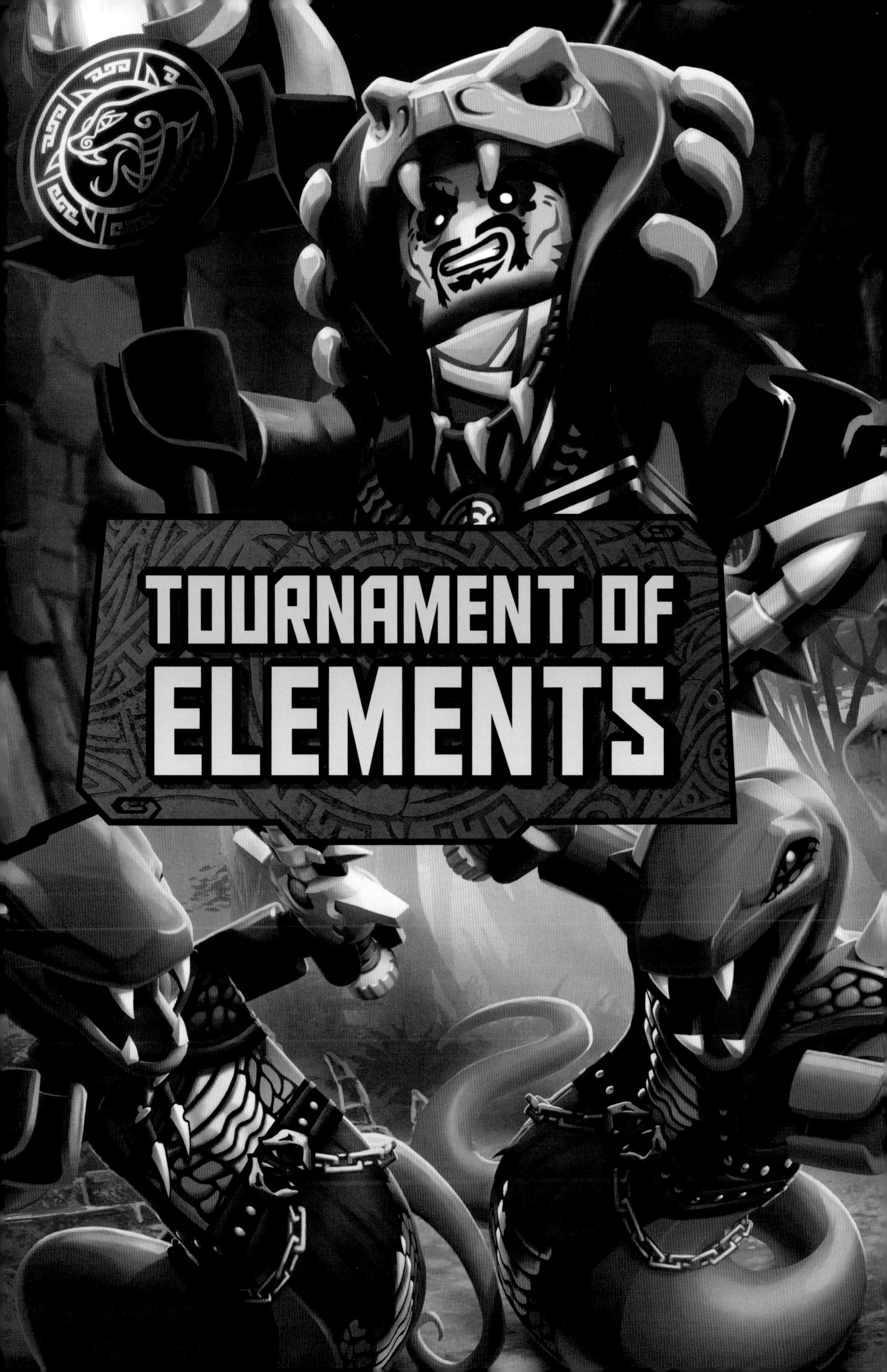
TOURNAMENT OF
ELEMENTS

What came before...

The ninja were involved in an epic battle with the Golden Master. When everything else failed, Zane sacrificed himself to defeat the Overlord. After the battle, Zane was honored with a titanium statue in the center of Ninjago City. Devastated by the loss of their friend, Kai, Cole, Jay, and Lloyd disbanded the ninja team.

But soon after, the team discovered there was a possibility that Zane was still alive. In order to find out for sure, the ninja must travel to a mysterious island and enter the dangerous Tournament of Elements, arranged by Master Chen. But is Master Chen all that he seems, or is he connected to the most feared warriors in the history of ninja: the Anacondrai?!

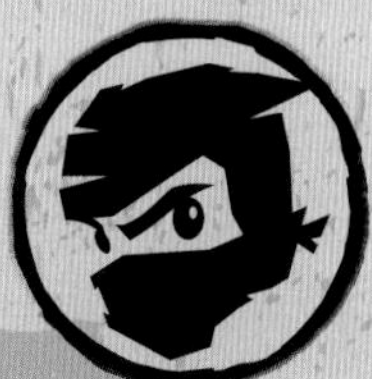

CHAPTER 1

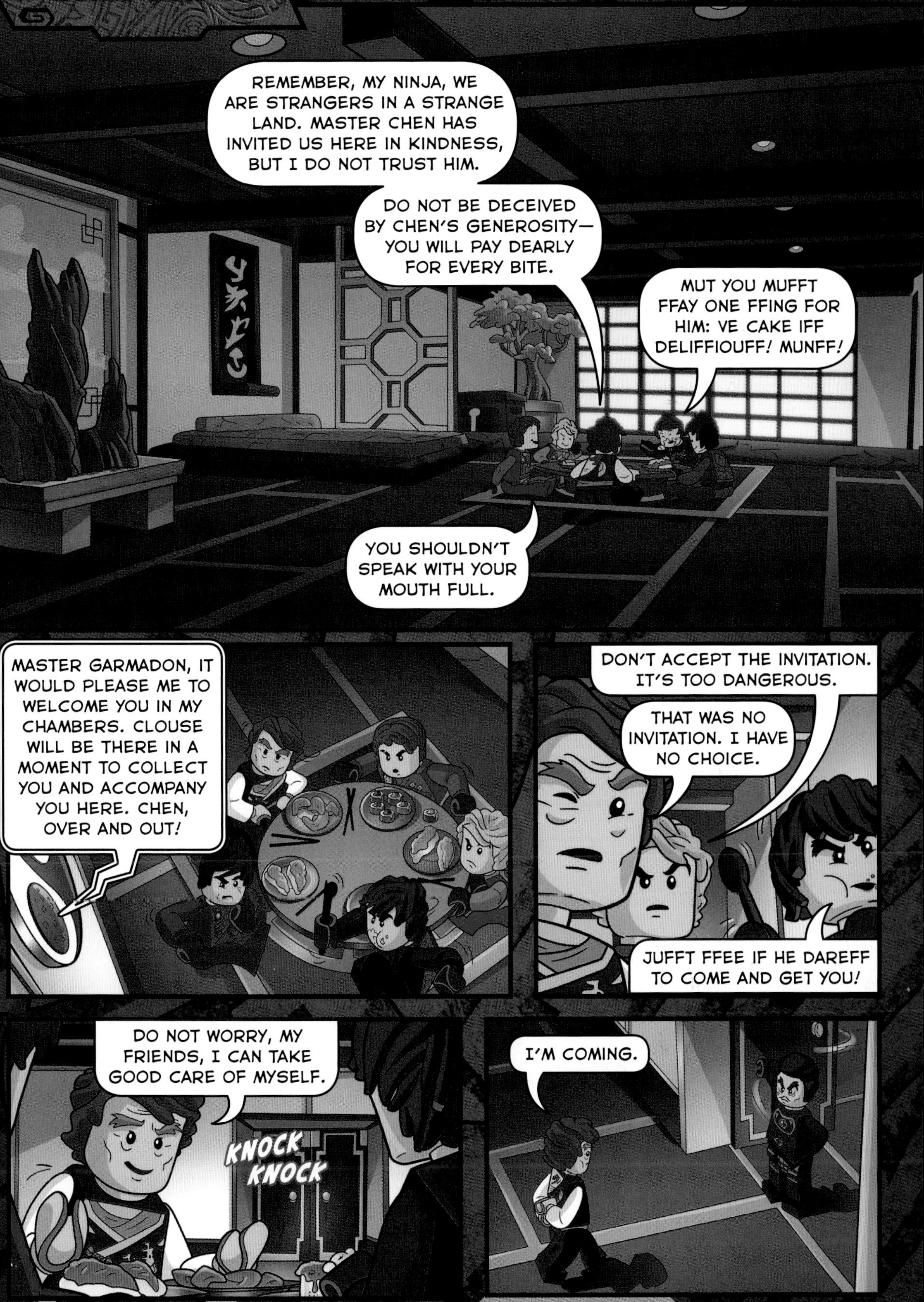

REMEMBER, MY NINJA, WE ARE STRANGERS IN A STRANGE LAND. MASTER CHEN HAS INVITED US HERE IN KINDNESS, BUT I DO NOT TRUST HIM.
DO NOT BE DECEIVED BY CHEN'S GENEROSITY—YOU WILL PAY DEARLY FOR EVERY BITE.
MUT YOU MUFFT FFAY ONE FFING FOR HIM: VE CAKE IFF DELIFFIOUFF! MUNFF!
YOU SHOULDN'T SPEAK WITH YOUR MOUTH FULL.
MASTER GARMADON, IT WOULD PLEASE ME TO WELCOME YOU IN MY CHAMBERS. CLOUSE WILL BE THERE IN A MOMENT TO COLLECT YOU AND ACCOMPANY YOU HERE. CHEN, OVER AND OUT!
DON'T ACCEPT THE INVITATION. IT'S TOO DANGEROUS.
THAT WAS NO INVITATION. I HAVE NO CHOICE.
JUFFT FFEE IF HE DAREFF TO COME AND GET YOU!
DO NOT WORRY, MY FRIENDS, I CAN TAKE GOOD CARE OF MYSELF.
KNOCK KNOCK
I'M COMING.

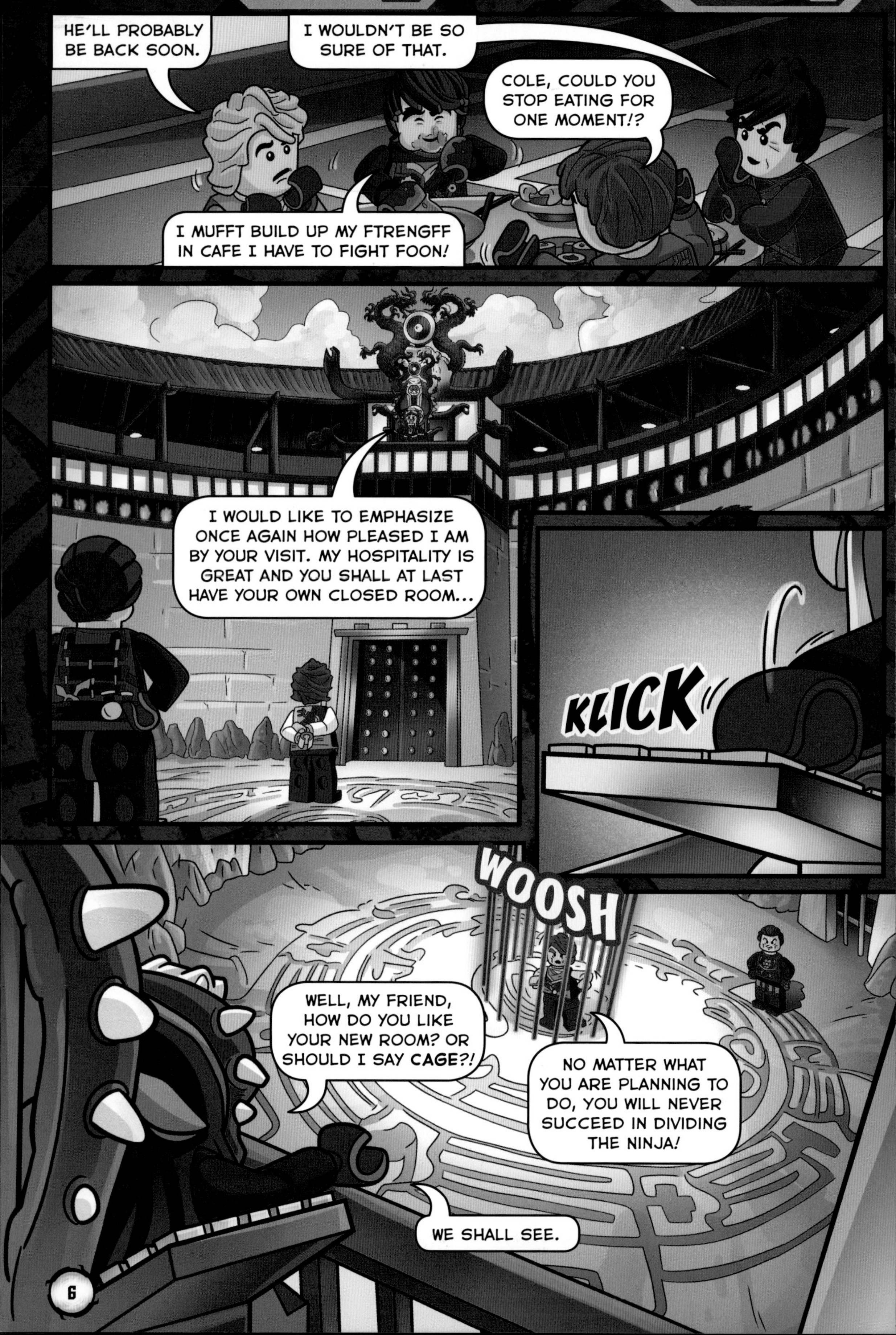
HE'LL PROBABLY BE BACK SOON.
I WOULDN'T BE SO SURE OF THAT.
COLE, COULD YOU STOP EATING FOR ONE MOMENT!?
I MUFFT BUILD UP MY FTRENGFF IN CAFE I HAVE TO FIGHT FOON!
I WOULD LIKE TO EMPHASIZE ONCE AGAIN HOW PLEASED I AM BY YOUR VISIT. MY HOSPITALITY IS GREAT AND YOU SHALL AT LAST HAVE YOUR OWN CLOSED ROOM...
KLICK
WOOSH
WELL, MY FRIEND, HOW DO YOU LIKE YOUR NEW ROOM? OR SHOULD I SAY **CAGE**?!
NO MATTER WHAT YOU ARE PLANNING TO DO, YOU WILL NEVER SUCCEED IN DIVIDING THE NINJA!
WE SHALL SEE.

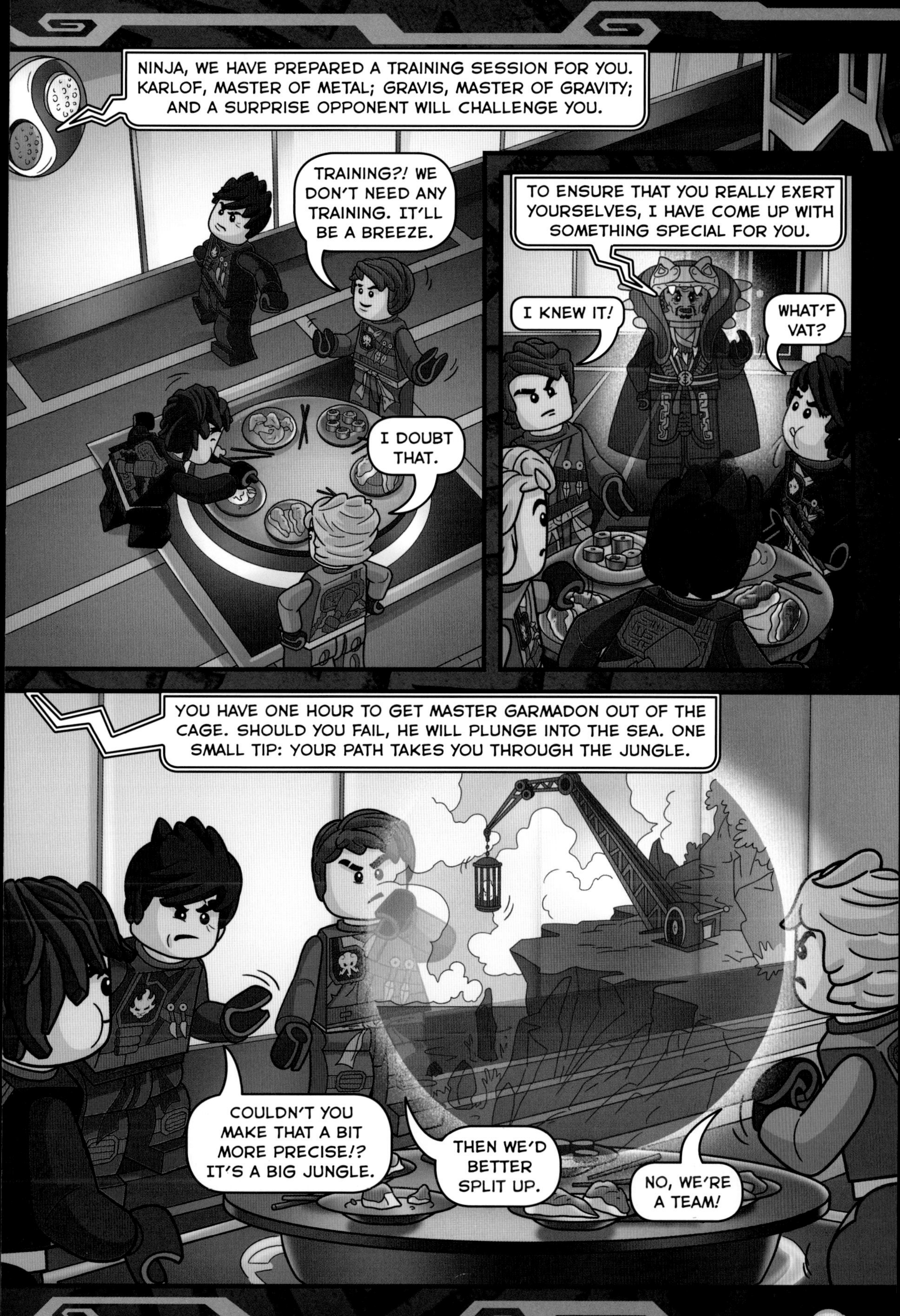

NINJA, WE HAVE PREPARED A TRAINING SESSION FOR YOU. KARLOF, MASTER OF METAL; GRAVIS, MASTER OF GRAVITY; AND A SURPRISE OPPONENT WILL CHALLENGE YOU.
TRAINING?! WE DON'T NEED ANY TRAINING. IT'LL BE A BREEZE.
I DOUBT THAT.
TO ENSURE THAT YOU REALLY EXERT YOURSELVES, I HAVE COME UP WITH SOMETHING SPECIAL FOR YOU.
I KNEW IT!
WHAT'F VAT?
YOU HAVE ONE HOUR TO GET MASTER GARMADON OUT OF THE CAGE. SHOULD YOU FAIL, HE WILL PLUNGE INTO THE SEA. ONE SMALL TIP: YOUR PATH TAKES YOU THROUGH THE JUNGLE.
COULDN'T YOU MAKE THAT A BIT MORE PRECISE!? IT'S A BIG JUNGLE.
THEN WE'D BETTER SPLIT UP.
NO, WE'RE A TEAM!

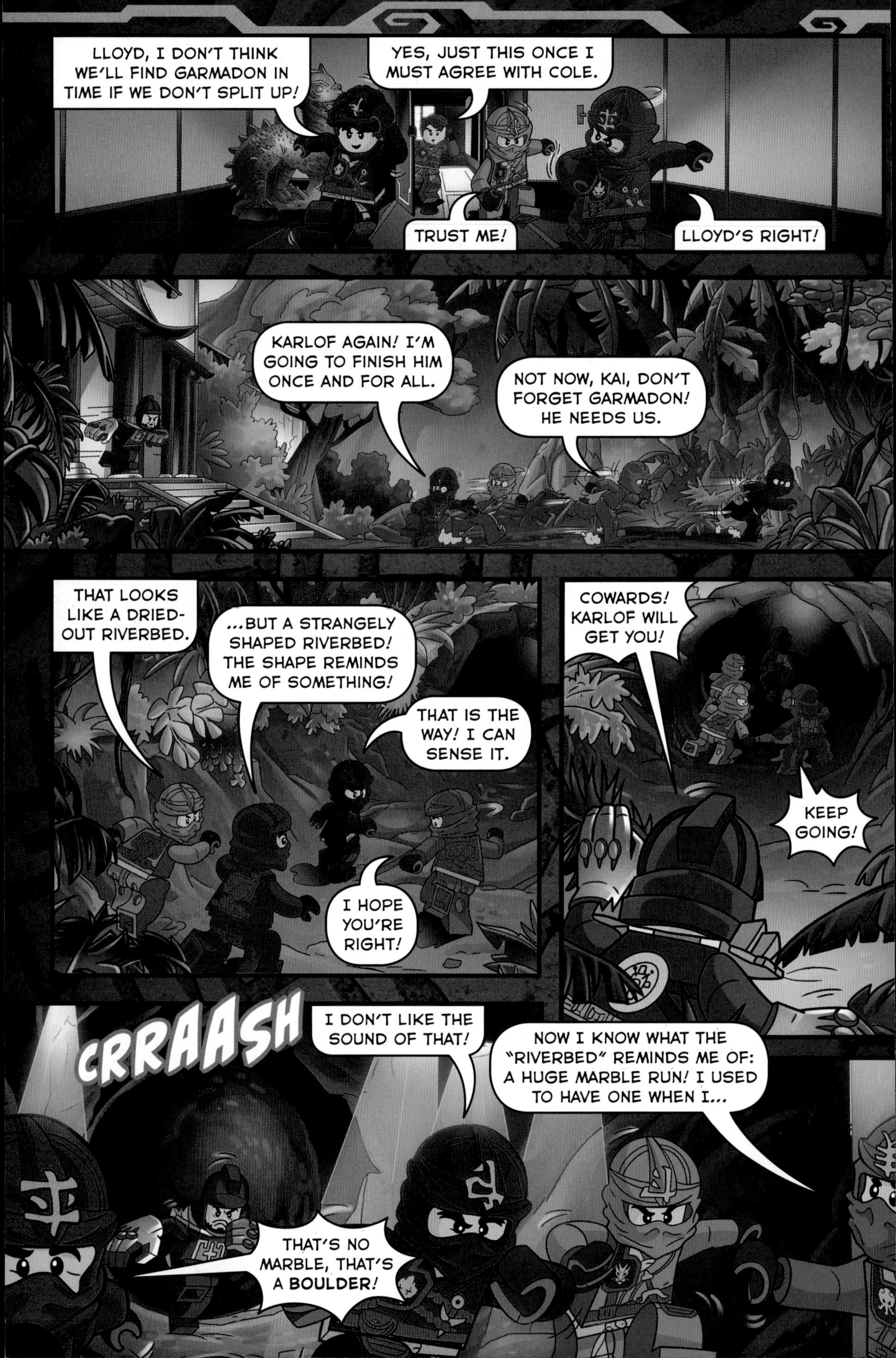
LLOYD, I DON'T THINK WE'LL FIND GARMADON IN TIME IF WE DON'T SPLIT UP!
YES, JUST THIS ONCE I MUST AGREE WITH COLE.
TRUST ME!
LLOYD'S RIGHT!
KARLOF AGAIN! I'M GOING TO FINISH HIM ONCE AND FOR ALL.
NOT NOW, KAI, DON'T FORGET GARMADON! HE NEEDS US.
THAT LOOKS LIKE A DRIED-OUT RIVERBED.
...BUT A STRANGELY SHAPED RIVERBED! THE SHAPE REMINDS ME OF SOMETHING!
THAT IS THE WAY! I CAN SENSE IT.
I HOPE YOU'RE RIGHT!
COWARDS! KARLOF WILL GET YOU!
KEEP GOING!
CRRAASH
I DON'T LIKE THE SOUND OF THAT!
NOW I KNOW WHAT THE "RIVERBED" REMINDS ME OF: A HUGE MARBLE RUN! I USED TO HAVE ONE WHEN I...
THAT'S NO MARBLE, THAT'S A **BOULDER**!

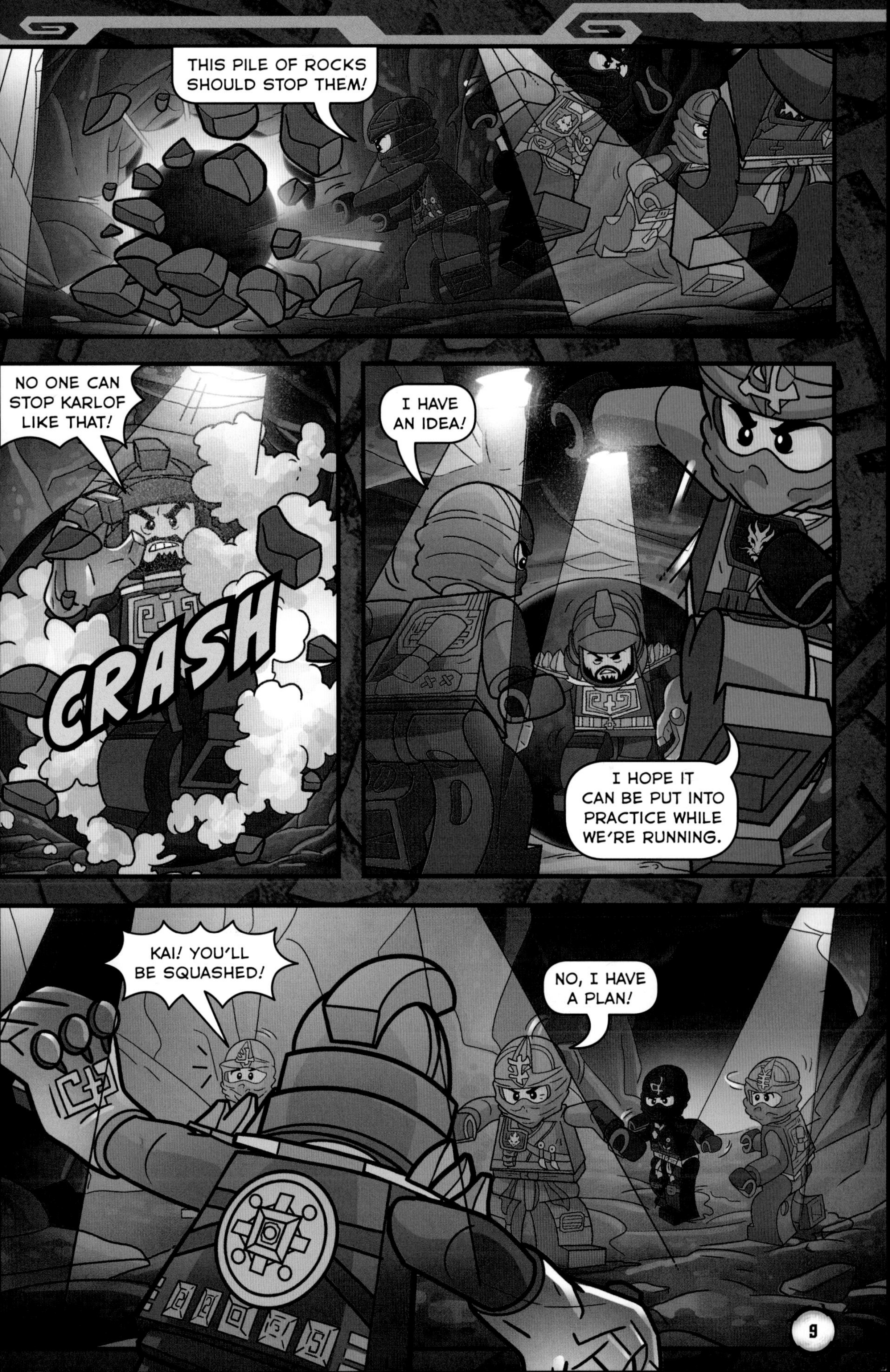
THIS PILE OF ROCKS SHOULD STOP THEM!
NO ONE CAN STOP KARLOF LIKE THAT!
CRASH
I HAVE AN IDEA!
I HOPE IT CAN BE PUT INTO PRACTICE WHILE WE'RE RUNNING.
KAI! YOU'LL BE SQUASHED!
NO, I HAVE A PLAN!

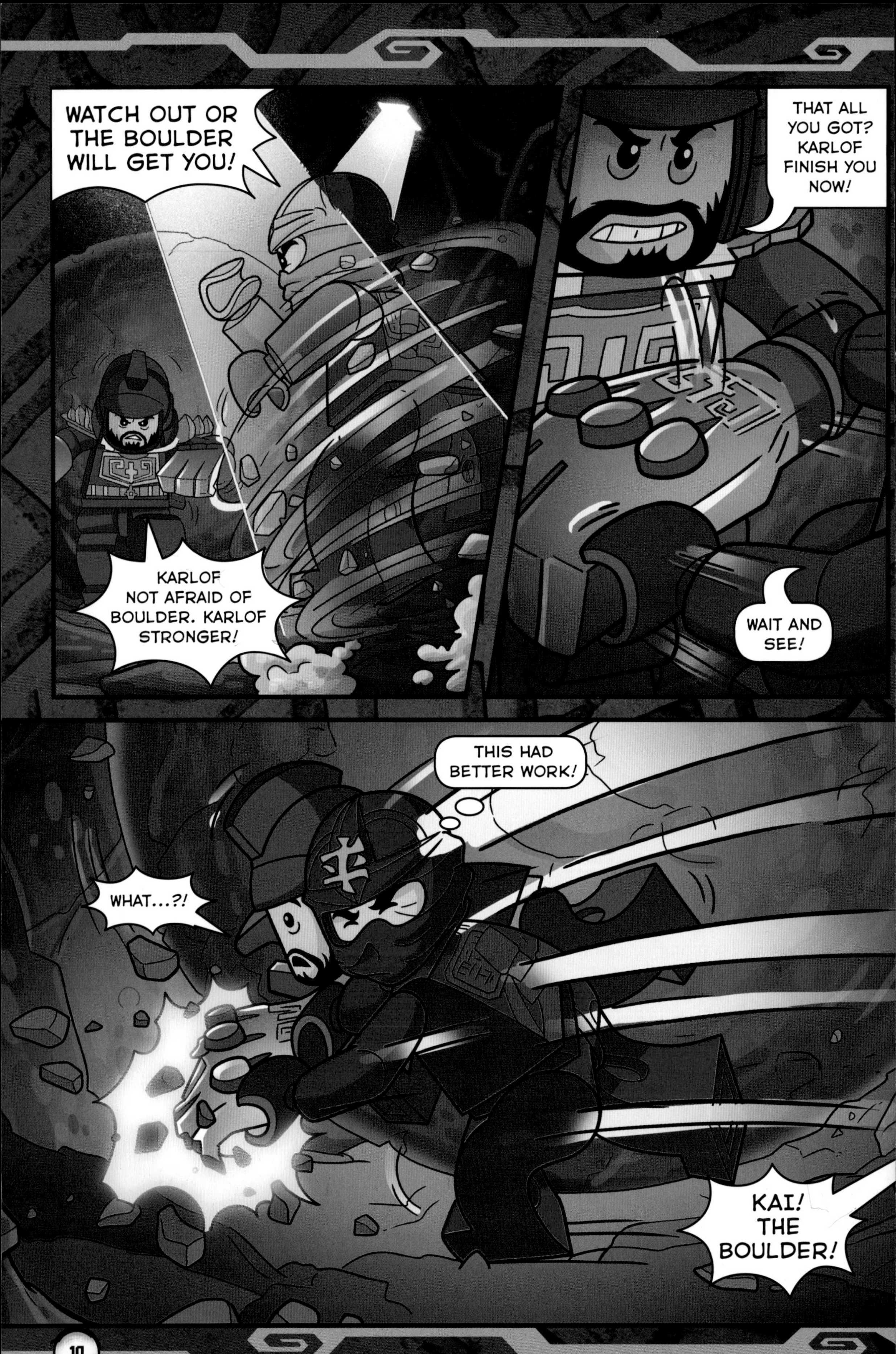
WATCH OUT OR THE BOULDER WILL GET YOU!
KARLOF NOT AFRAID OF BOULDER. KARLOF STRONGER!
THAT ALL YOU GOT? KARLOF FINISH YOU NOW!
WAIT AND SEE!
THIS HAD BETTER WORK!
WHAT...?!
KAI! THE BOULDER!

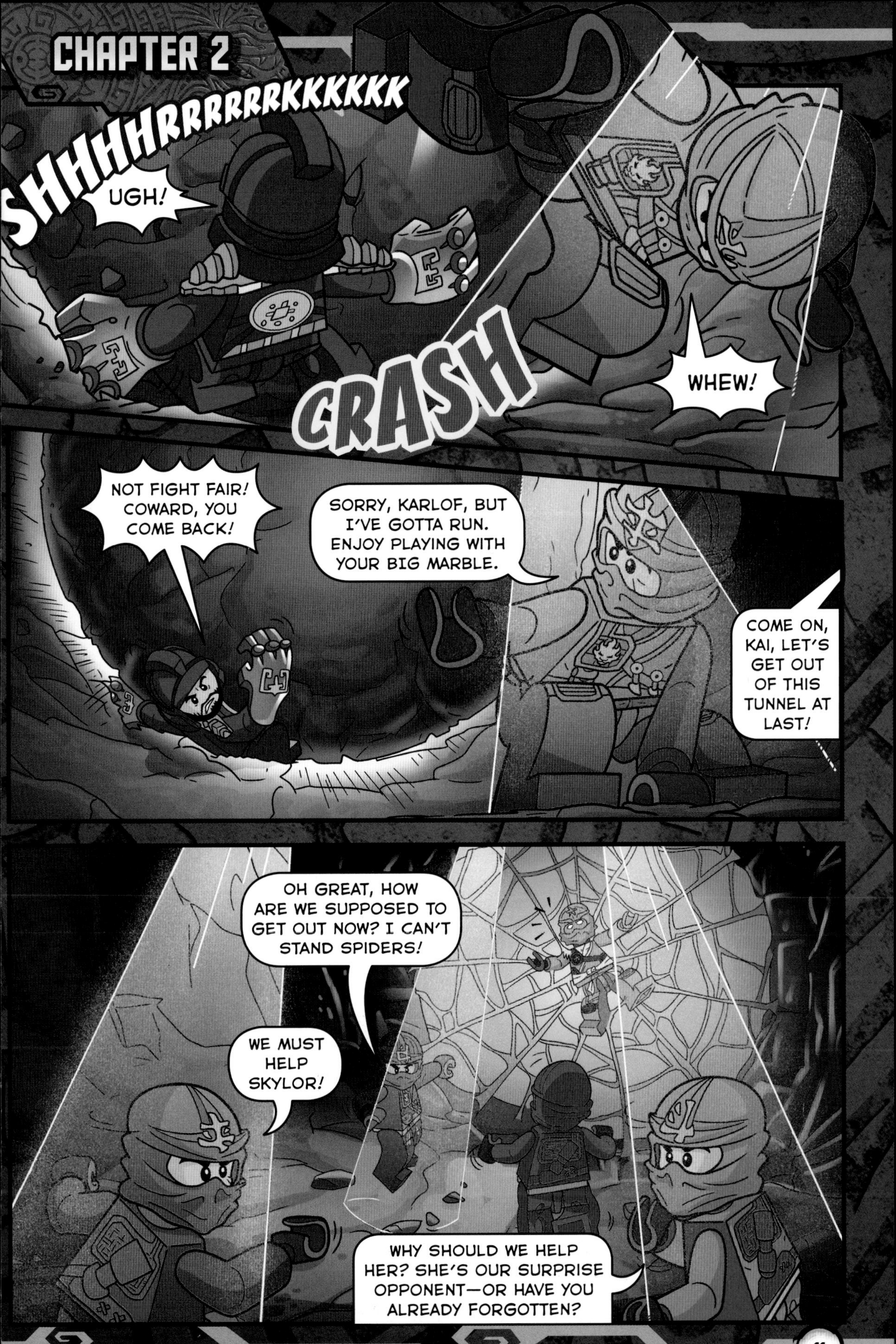
CHAPTER 2
SHHHHRRRRRRKKKKKK
UGH!
CRASH
WHEW!
NOT FIGHT FAIR! COWARD, YOU COME BACK!
SORRY, KARLOF, BUT I'VE GOTTA RUN. ENJOY PLAYING WITH YOUR BIG MARBLE.
COME ON, KAI, LET'S GET OUT OF THIS TUNNEL AT LAST!
OH GREAT, HOW ARE WE SUPPOSED TO GET OUT NOW? I CAN'T STAND SPIDERS!
WE MUST HELP SKYLOR!
WHY SHOULD WE HELP HER? SHE'S OUR SURPRISE OPPONENT—OR HAVE YOU ALREADY FORGOTTEN?

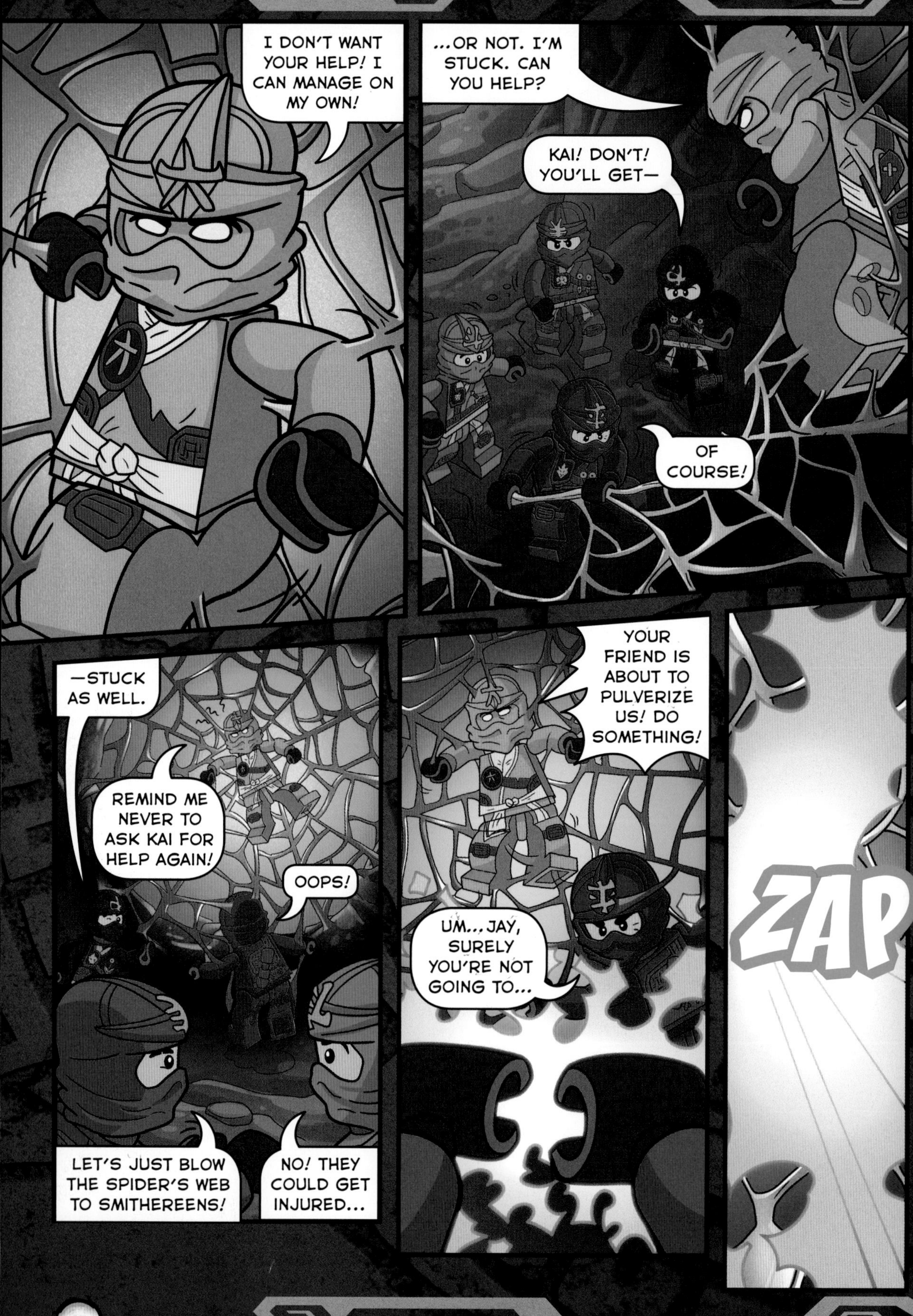
I DON'T WANT YOUR HELP! I CAN MANAGE ON MY OWN!
...OR NOT. I'M STUCK. CAN YOU HELP?
KAI! DON'T! YOU'LL GET—
OF COURSE!
—STUCK AS WELL.
REMIND ME NEVER TO ASK KAI FOR HELP AGAIN!
OOPS!
LET'S JUST BLOW THE SPIDER'S WEB TO SMITHEREENS!
NO! THEY COULD GET INJURED...
YOUR FRIEND IS ABOUT TO PULVERIZE US! DO SOMETHING!
UM... JAY, SURELY YOU'RE NOT GOING TO...
ZAP

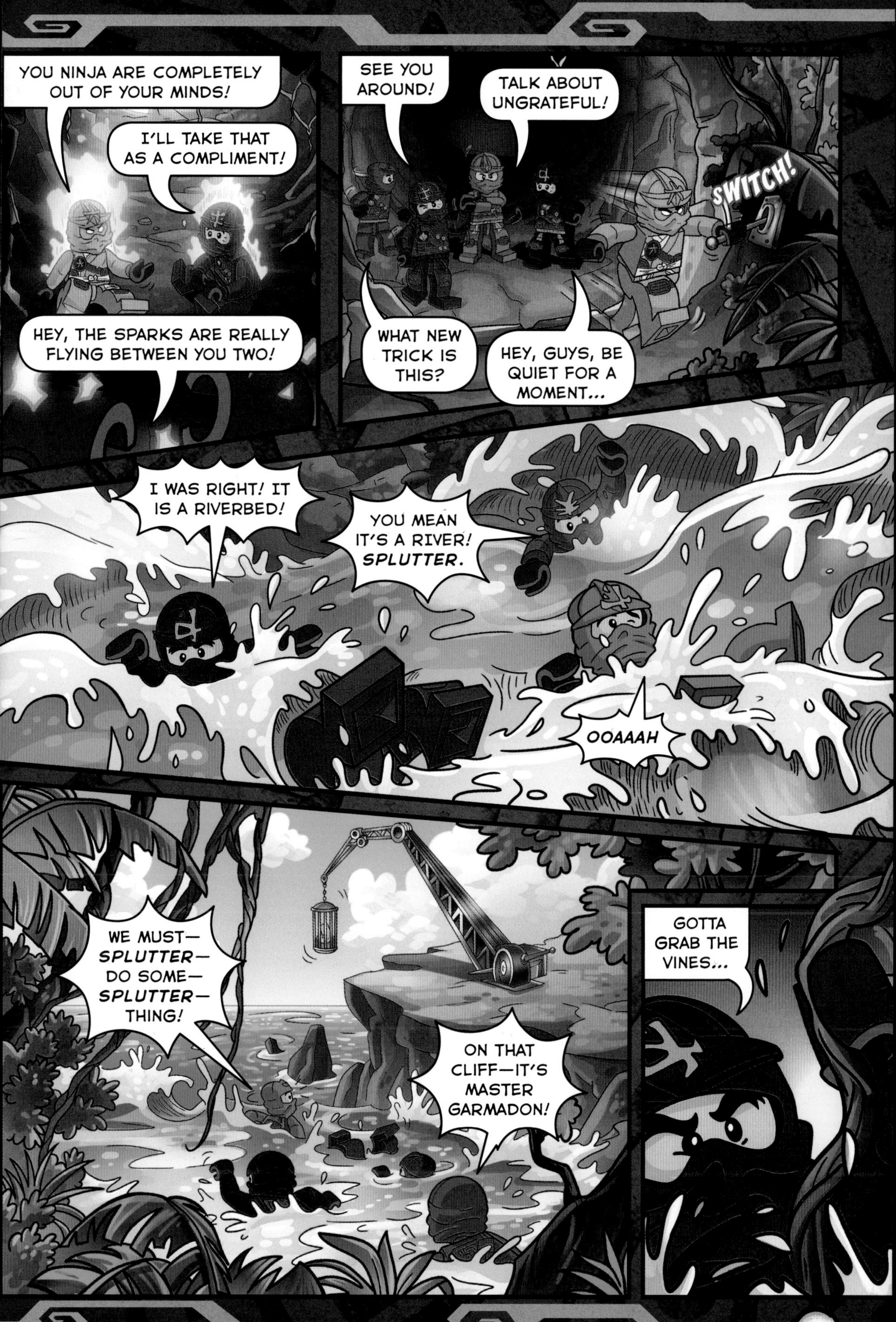

YOU NINJA ARE COMPLETELY OUT OF YOUR MINDS!
I'LL TAKE THAT AS A COMPLIMENT!
HEY, THE SPARKS ARE REALLY FLYING BETWEEN YOU TWO!
SEE YOU AROUND!
TALK ABOUT UNGRATEFUL!
SWITCH!
WHAT NEW TRICK IS THIS?
HEY, GUYS, BE QUIET FOR A MOMENT...
I WAS RIGHT! IT IS A RIVERBED!
YOU MEAN IT'S A RIVER! SPLUTTER.
OOAAAH
WE MUST—SPLUTTER—DO SOME—SPLUTTER—THING!
ON THAT CLIFF—IT'S MASTER GARMADON!
GOTTA GRAB THE VINES...

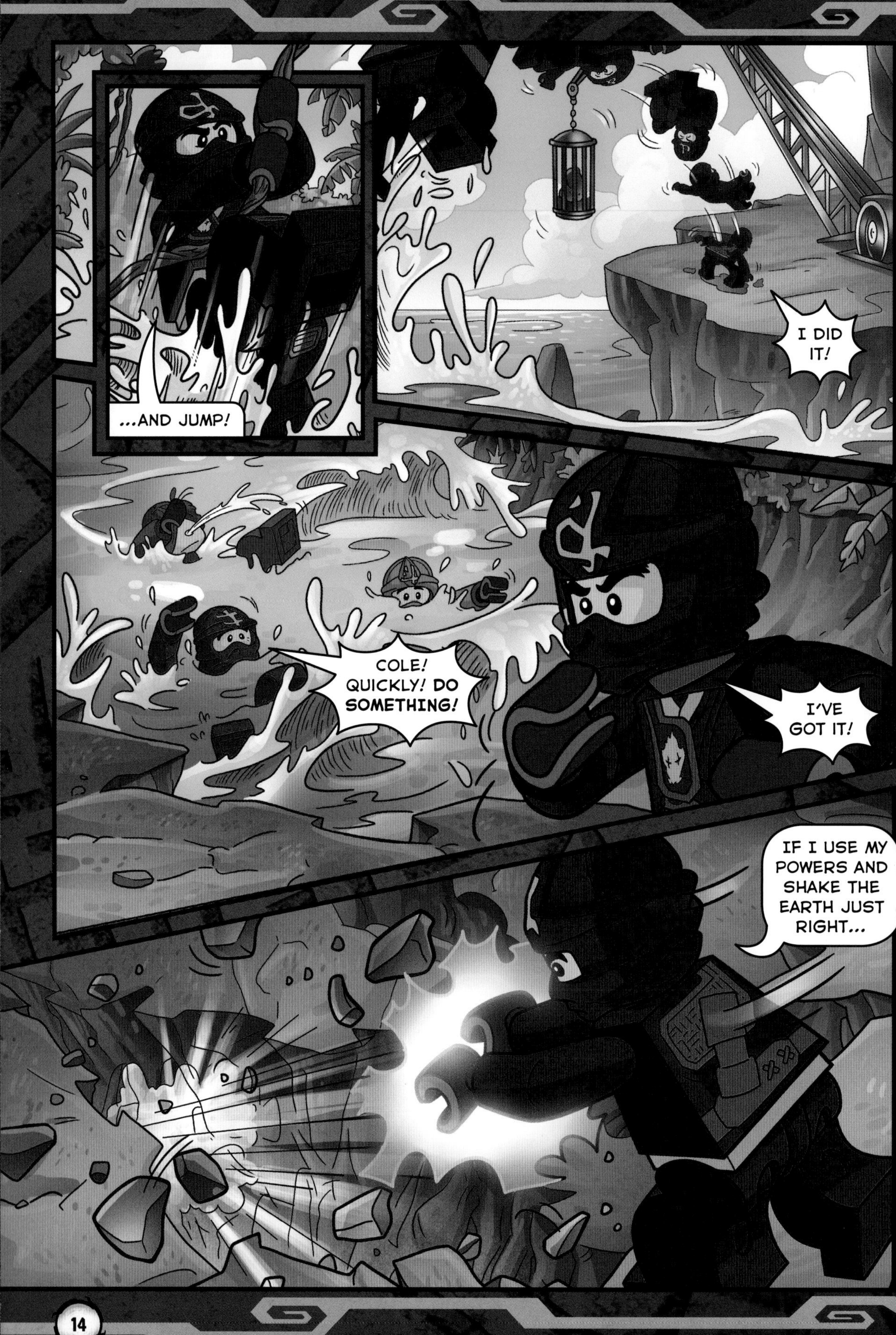
...AND JUMP!
I DID IT!
COLE! QUICKLY! DO SOMETHING!
I'VE GOT IT!
IF I USE MY POWERS AND SHAKE THE EARTH JUST RIGHT...

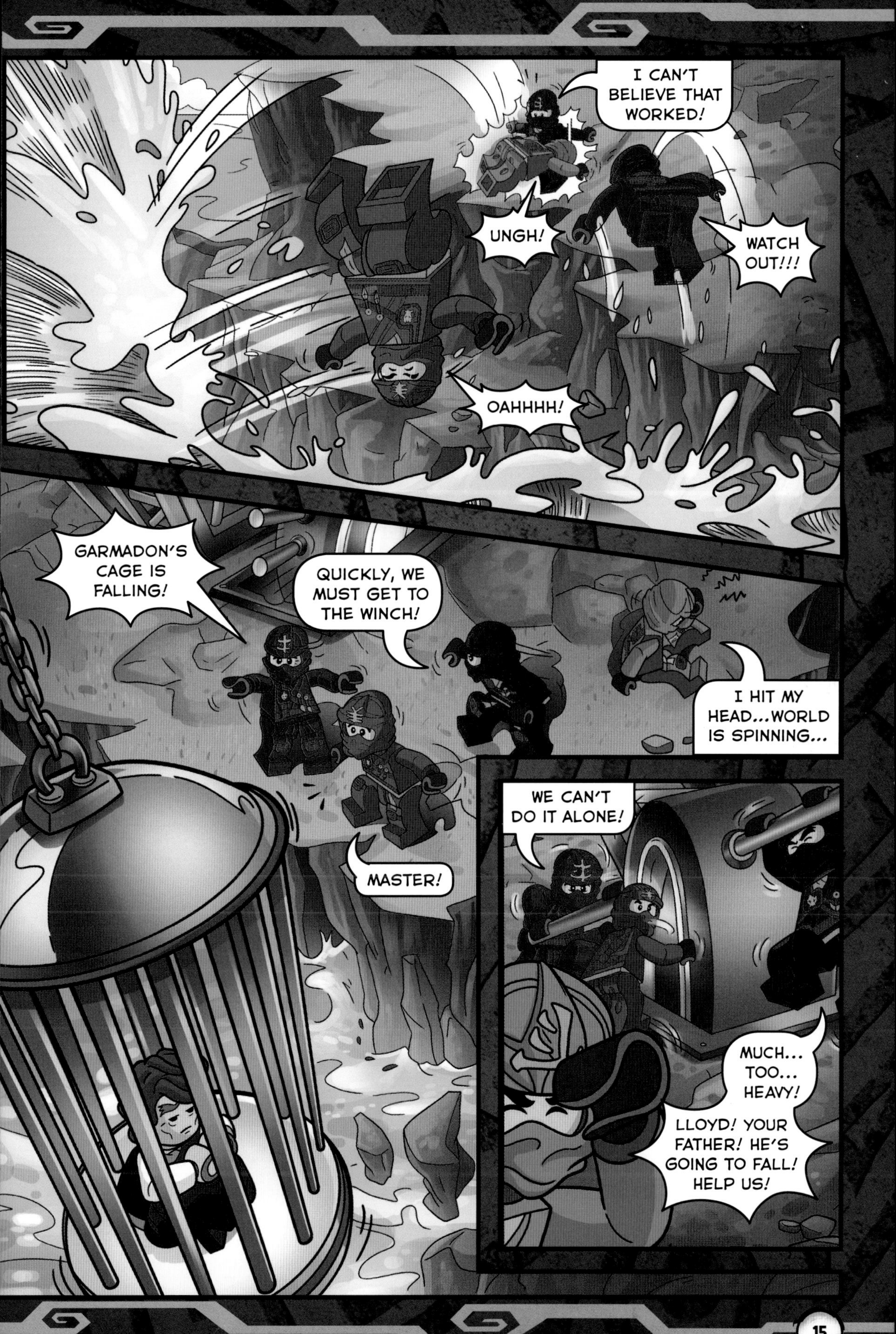
I CAN'T BELIEVE THAT WORKED!
UNGH!
WATCH OUT!!!
OAHHHH!
GARMADON'S CAGE IS FALLING!
QUICKLY, WE MUST GET TO THE WINCH!
I HIT MY HEAD...WORLD IS SPINNING...
MASTER!
WE CAN'T DO IT ALONE!
MUCH... TOO... HEAVY!
LLOYD! YOUR FATHER! HE'S GOING TO FALL! HELP US!

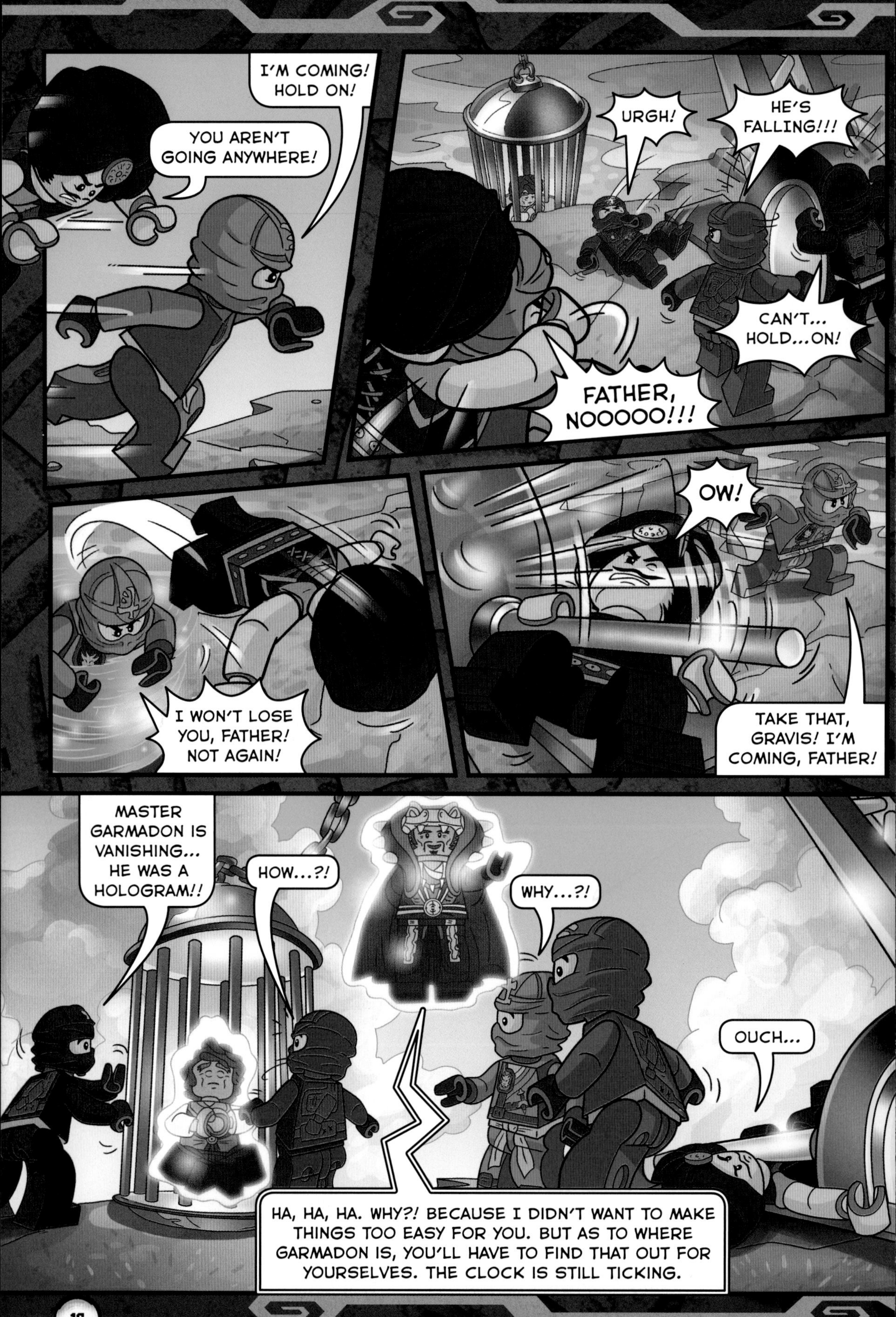
I'M COMING! HOLD ON!
YOU AREN'T GOING ANYWHERE!
URGH!
HE'S FALLING!!!
CAN'T... HOLD...ON!
FATHER, NOOOOO!!!
I WON'T LOSE YOU, FATHER! NOT AGAIN!
OW!
TAKE THAT, GRAVIS! I'M COMING, FATHER!
MASTER GARMADON IS VANISHING... HE WAS A HOLOGRAM!!
HOW...?!
WHY...?!
OUCH...
HA, HA, HA. WHY?! BECAUSE I DIDN'T WANT TO MAKE THINGS TOO EASY FOR YOU. BUT AS TO WHERE GARMADON IS, YOU'LL HAVE TO FIND THAT OUT FOR YOURSELVES. THE CLOCK IS STILL TICKING.

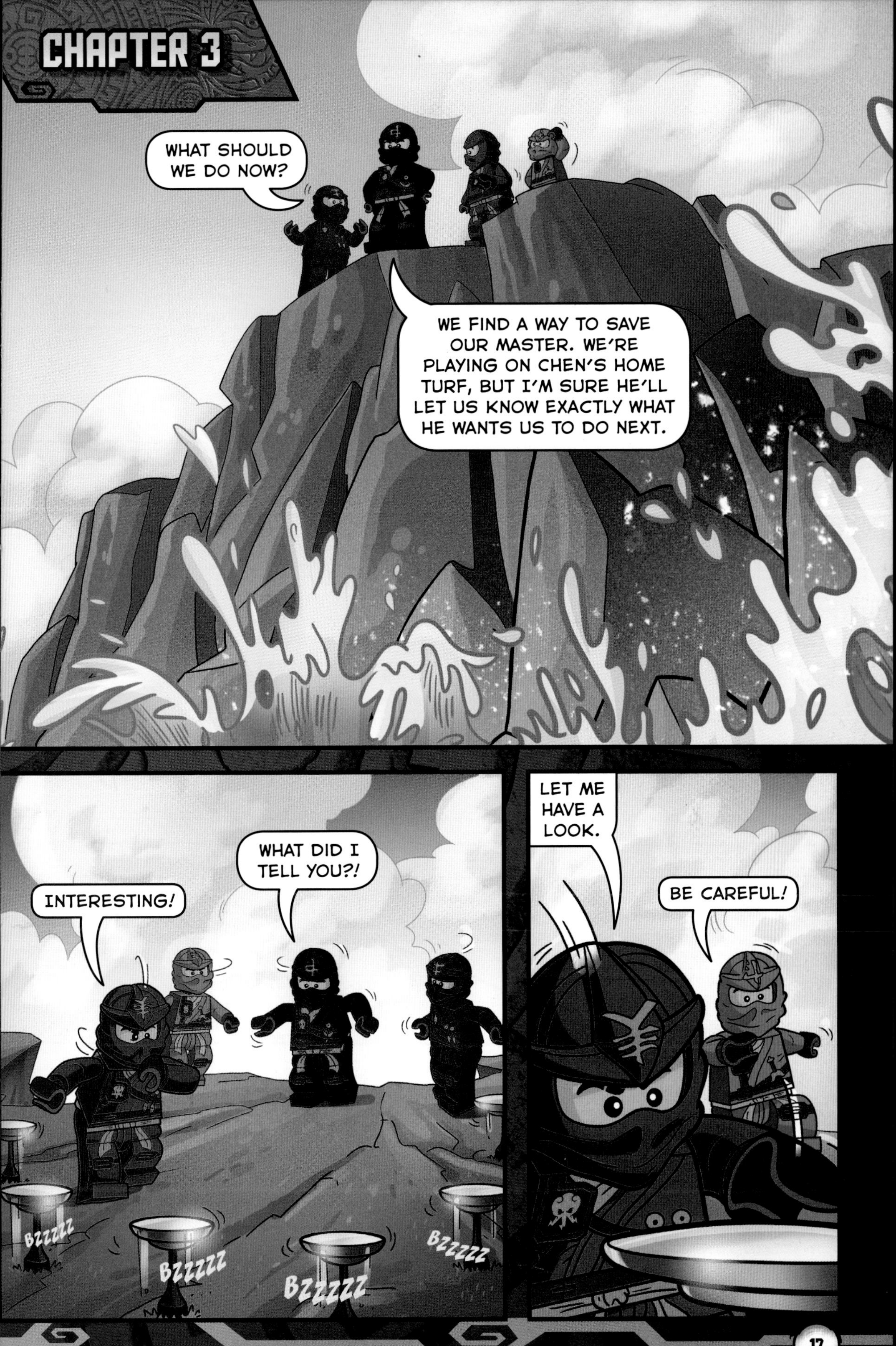
CHAPTER 3
WHAT SHOULD WE DO NOW?
WE FIND A WAY TO SAVE OUR MASTER. WE'RE PLAYING ON CHEN'S HOME TURF, BUT I'M SURE HE'LL LET US KNOW EXACTLY WHAT HE WANTS US TO DO NEXT.
INTERESTING!
WHAT DID I TELL YOU?!
BZZZZZ
BZZZZZ
BZZZZZ
BZZZZZ
LET ME HAVE A LOOK.
BE CAREFUL!

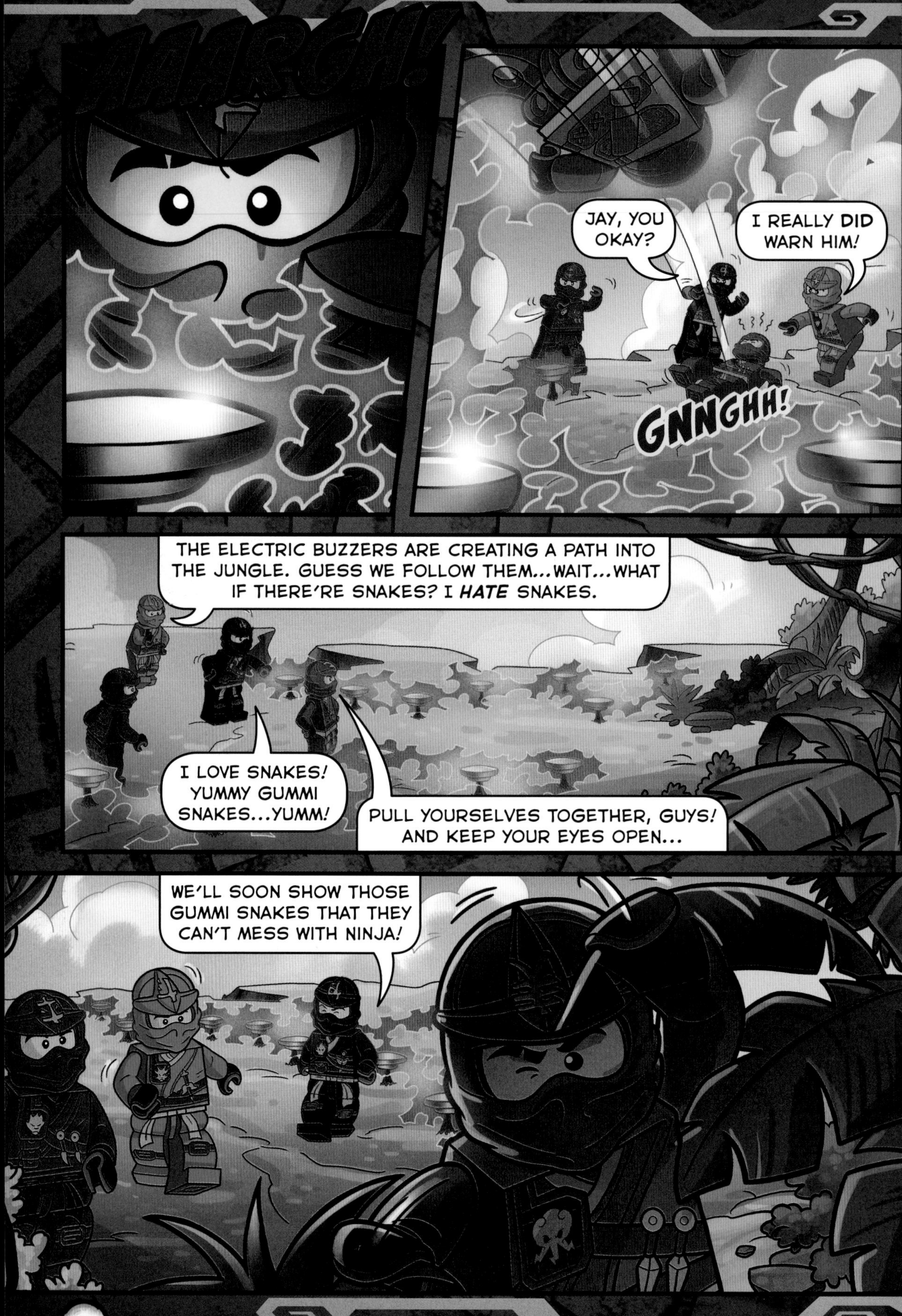
JAY, YOU OKAY?
I REALLY DID WARN HIM!
GNNGHH!
THE ELECTRIC BUZZERS ARE CREATING A PATH INTO THE JUNGLE. GUESS WE FOLLOW THEM...WAIT...WHAT IF THERE'RE SNAKES? I *HATE* SNAKES.
I LOVE SNAKES! YUMMY GUMMI SNAKES...YUMM!
PULL YOURSELVES TOGETHER, GUYS! AND KEEP YOUR EYES OPEN...
WE'LL SOON SHOW THOSE GUMMI SNAKES THAT THEY CAN'T MESS WITH NINJA!

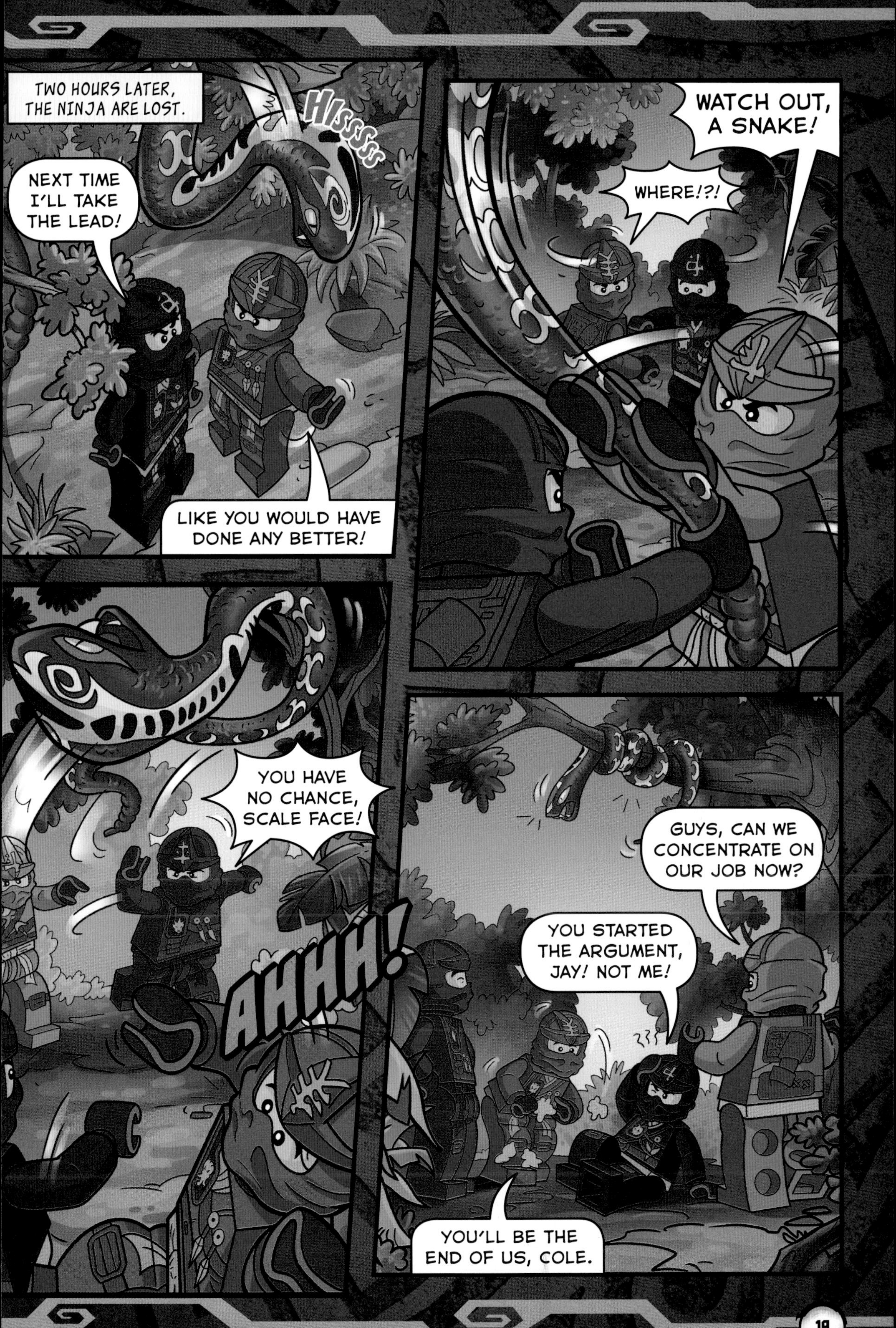
TWO HOURS LATER, THE NINJA ARE LOST.
HISSSSS
NEXT TIME I'LL TAKE THE LEAD!
LIKE YOU WOULD HAVE DONE ANY BETTER!
WATCH OUT, A SNAKE!
WHERE!?!
YOU HAVE NO CHANCE, SCALE FACE!
AHHH!
GUYS, CAN WE CONCENTRATE ON OUR JOB NOW?
YOU STARTED THE ARGUMENT, JAY! NOT ME!
YOU'LL BE THE END OF US, COLE.

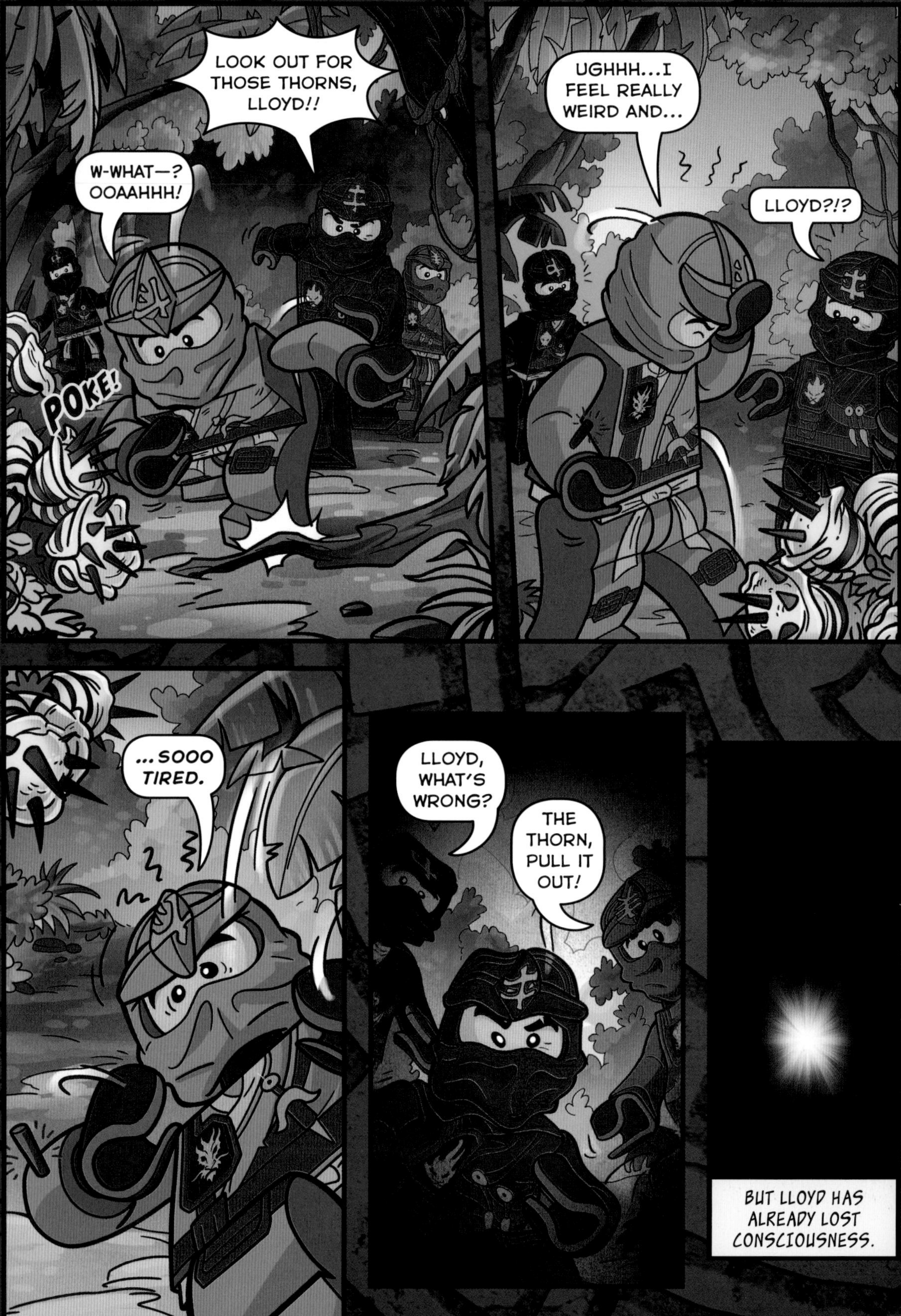
LOOK OUT FOR THOSE THORNS, LLOYD!!
W-WHAT—? OOAAHHH!
POKE!
UGHHH...I FEEL REALLY WEIRD AND...
LLOYD?!?
...SOOO TIRED.
LLOYD, WHAT'S WRONG?
THE THORN, PULL IT OUT!
BUT LLOYD HAS ALREADY LOST CONSCIOUSNESS.

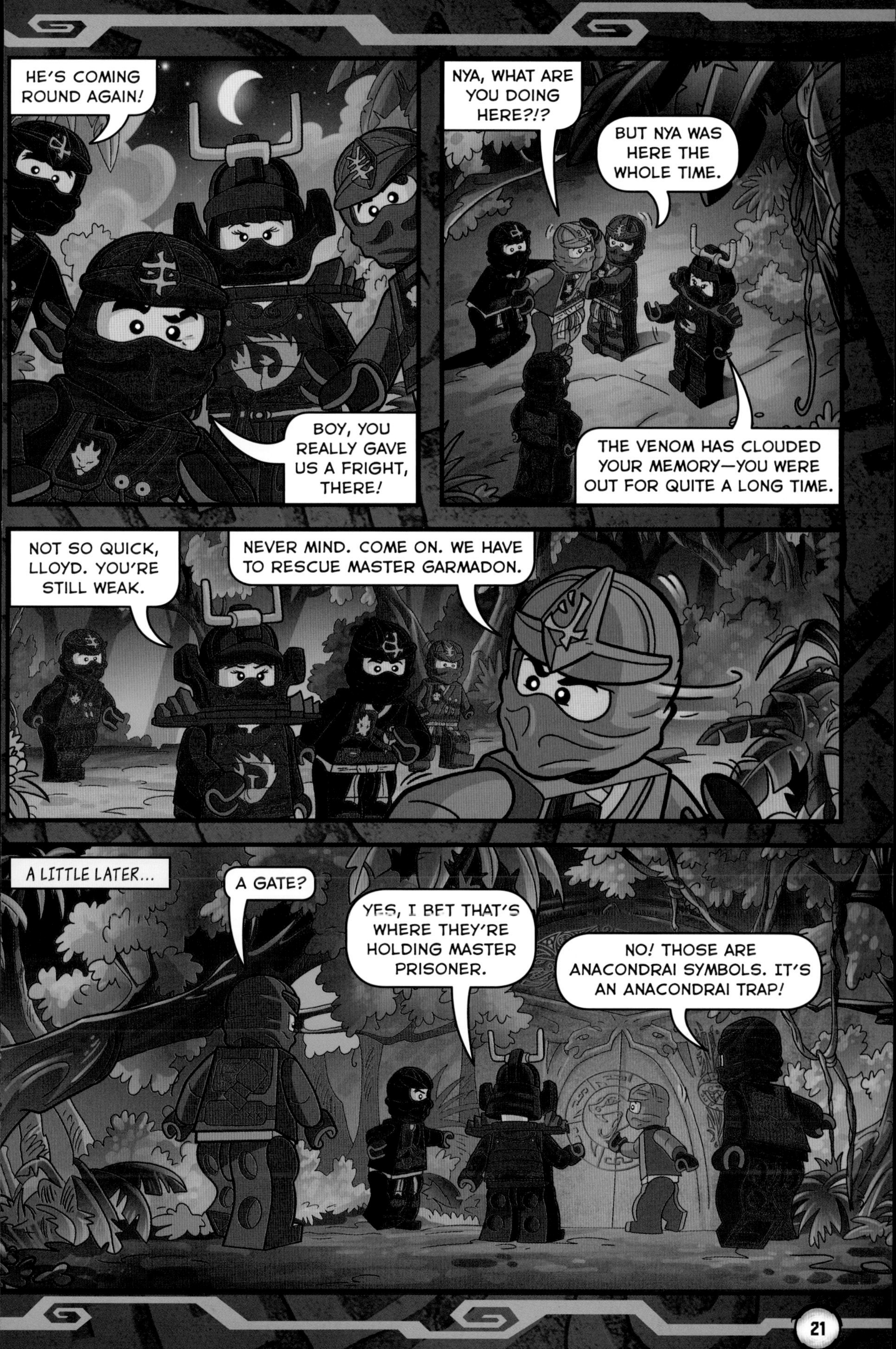
HE'S COMING ROUND AGAIN!
BOY, YOU REALLY GAVE US A FRIGHT, THERE!
NYA, WHAT ARE YOU DOING HERE?!?
BUT NYA WAS HERE THE WHOLE TIME.
THE VENOM HAS CLOUDED YOUR MEMORY—YOU WERE OUT FOR QUITE A LONG TIME.
NOT SO QUICK, LLOYD. YOU'RE STILL WEAK.
NEVER MIND. COME ON. WE HAVE TO RESCUE MASTER GARMADON.
A LITTLE LATER...
A GATE?
YES, I BET THAT'S WHERE THEY'RE HOLDING MASTER PRISONER.
NO! THOSE ARE ANACONDRAI SYMBOLS. IT'S AN ANACONDRAI TRAP!

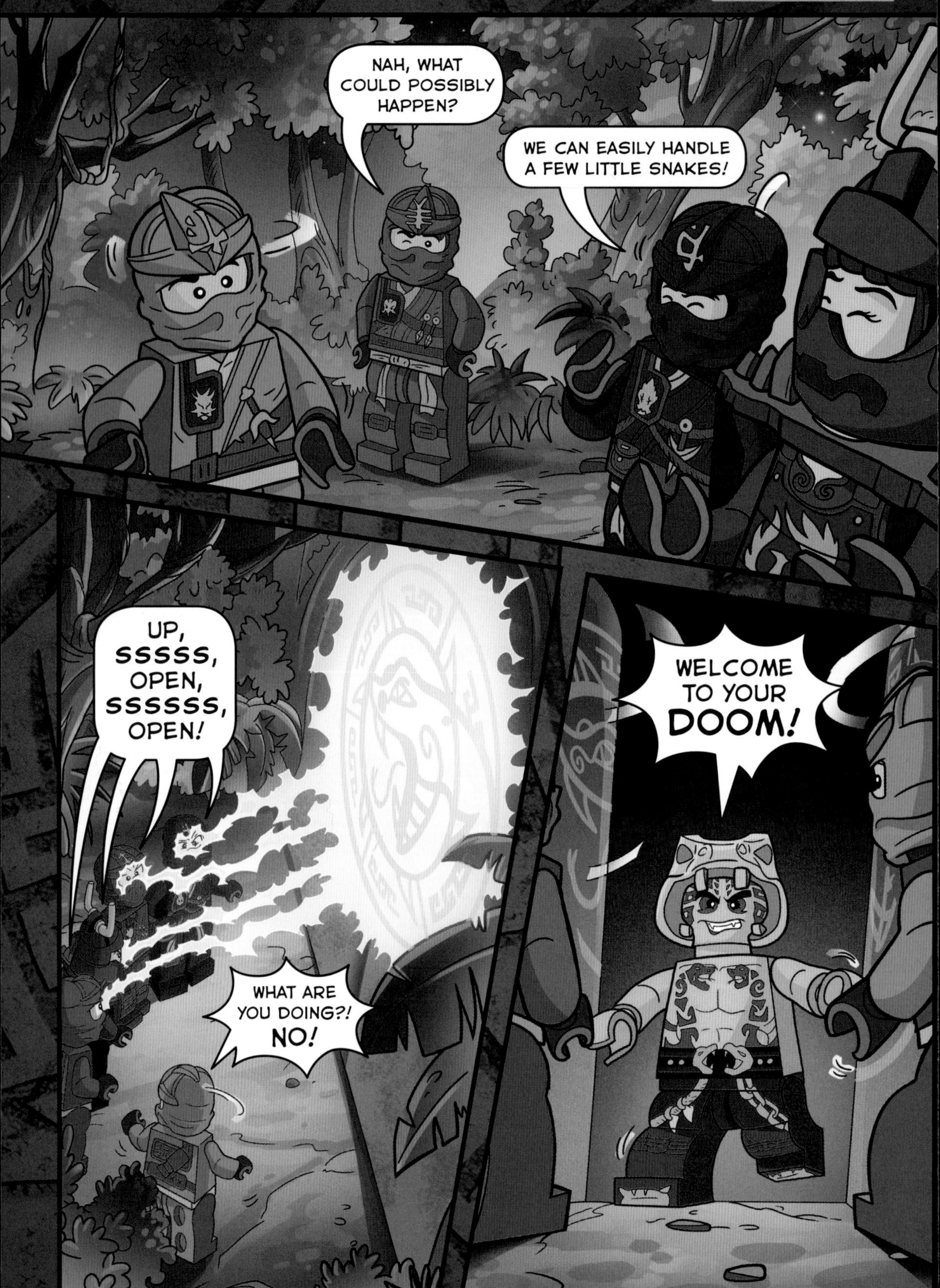
NAH, WHAT COULD POSSIBLY HAPPEN?
WE CAN EASILY HANDLE A FEW LITTLE SNAKES!
UP, SSSSS, OPEN, SSSSSS, OPEN!
WHAT ARE YOU DOING?! NO!
WELCOME TO YOUR DOOM!

CHAPTER 4

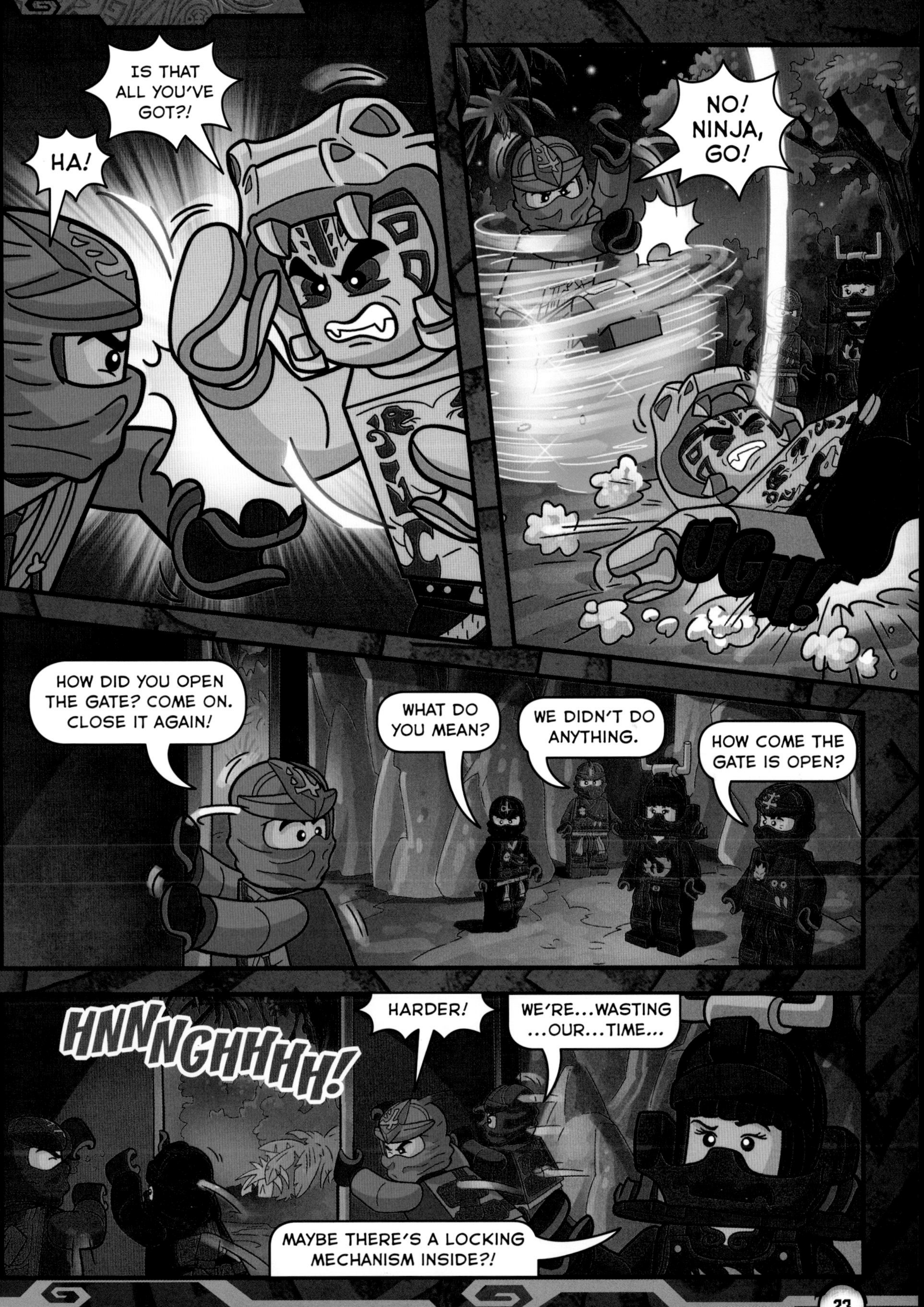
HA!
IS THAT ALL YOU'VE GOT?!
NO! NINJA, GO!
UGH!
HOW DID YOU OPEN THE GATE? COME ON. CLOSE IT AGAIN!
WHAT DO YOU MEAN?
WE DIDN'T DO ANYTHING.
HOW COME THE GATE IS OPEN?
HNNNGHHHH!
HARDER!
WE'RE...WASTING ...OUR...TIME...
MAYBE THERE'S A LOCKING MECHANISM INSIDE?!

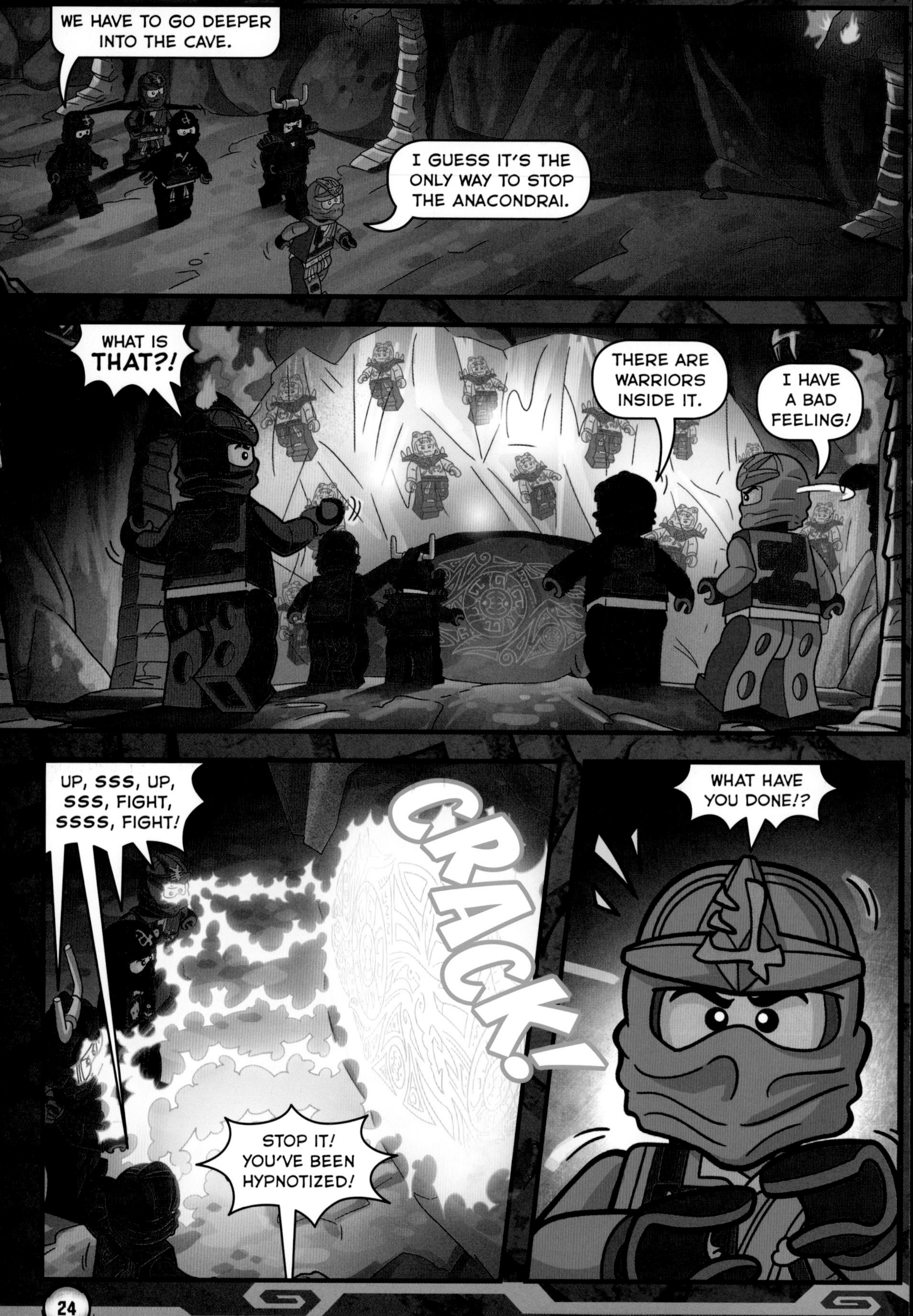
WE HAVE TO GO DEEPER INTO THE CAVE.
I GUESS IT'S THE ONLY WAY TO STOP THE ANACONDRAI.
WHAT IS **THAT?!**
THERE ARE WARRIORS INSIDE IT.
I HAVE A BAD FEELING!
UP, **SSS**, UP, **SSS**, FIGHT, **SSSS**, FIGHT!
CRACK!
STOP IT! YOU'VE BEEN HYPNOTIZED!
WHAT HAVE YOU DONE!?

THAT'S OUR CHANCE!
LET'S GET OUT!
THEY'RE BREAKING FREE!
CRACK!
OUT OF MY WAY!
NINJA-KICK!
NYA, I MUST STOP THE ANACONDRAI!
LLOYD, YOU MUST ACCEPT THAT IT'S TOO LATE! YOU DON'T STAND A CHANCE!

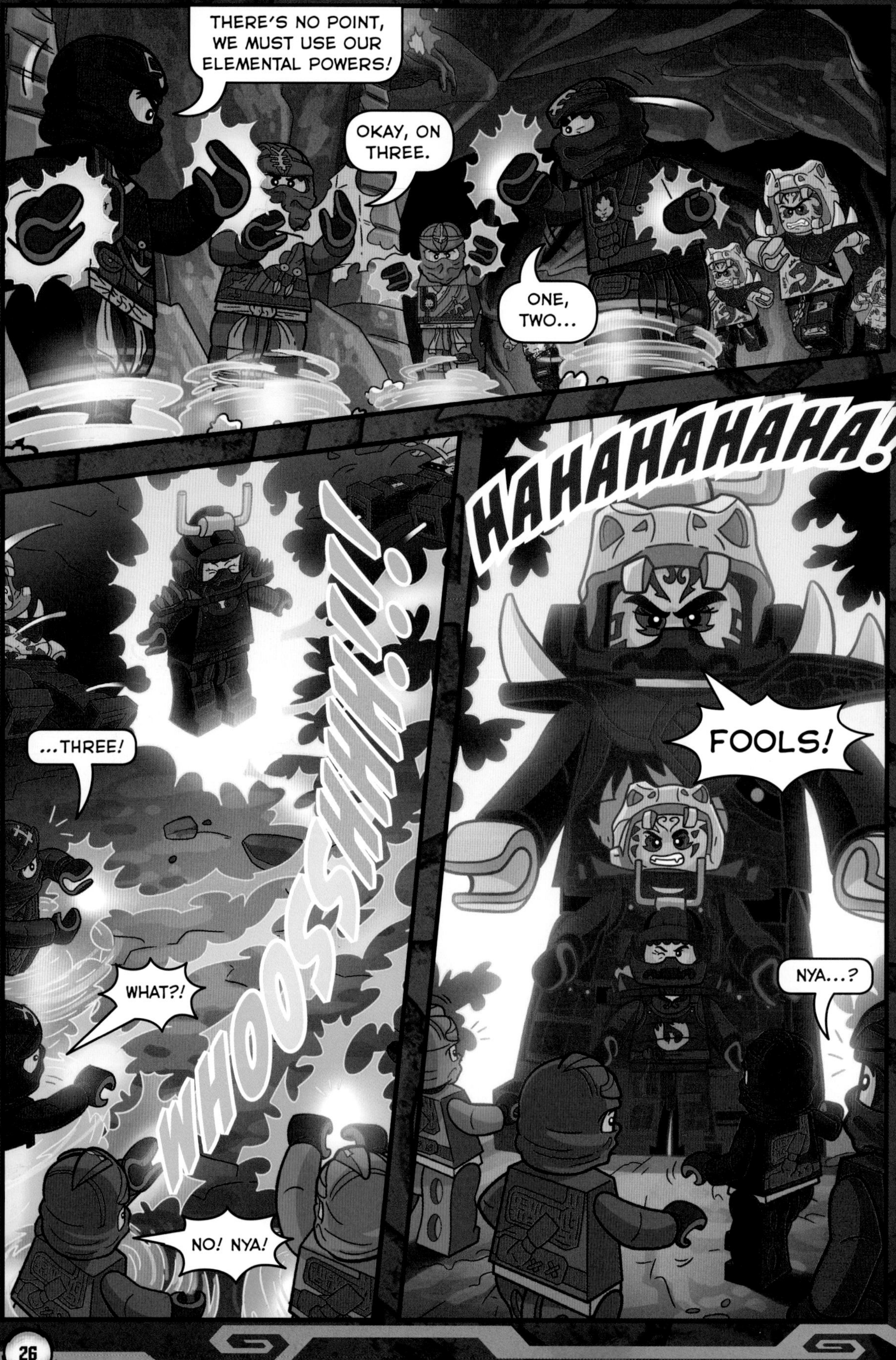
THERE'S NO POINT, WE MUST USE OUR ELEMENTAL POWERS!
OKAY, ON THREE.
ONE, TWO...
...THREE!
WHOOSSHHH!!!
WHAT?!
NO! NYA!
HAHAHAHAHA!
FOOLS!
NYA...?

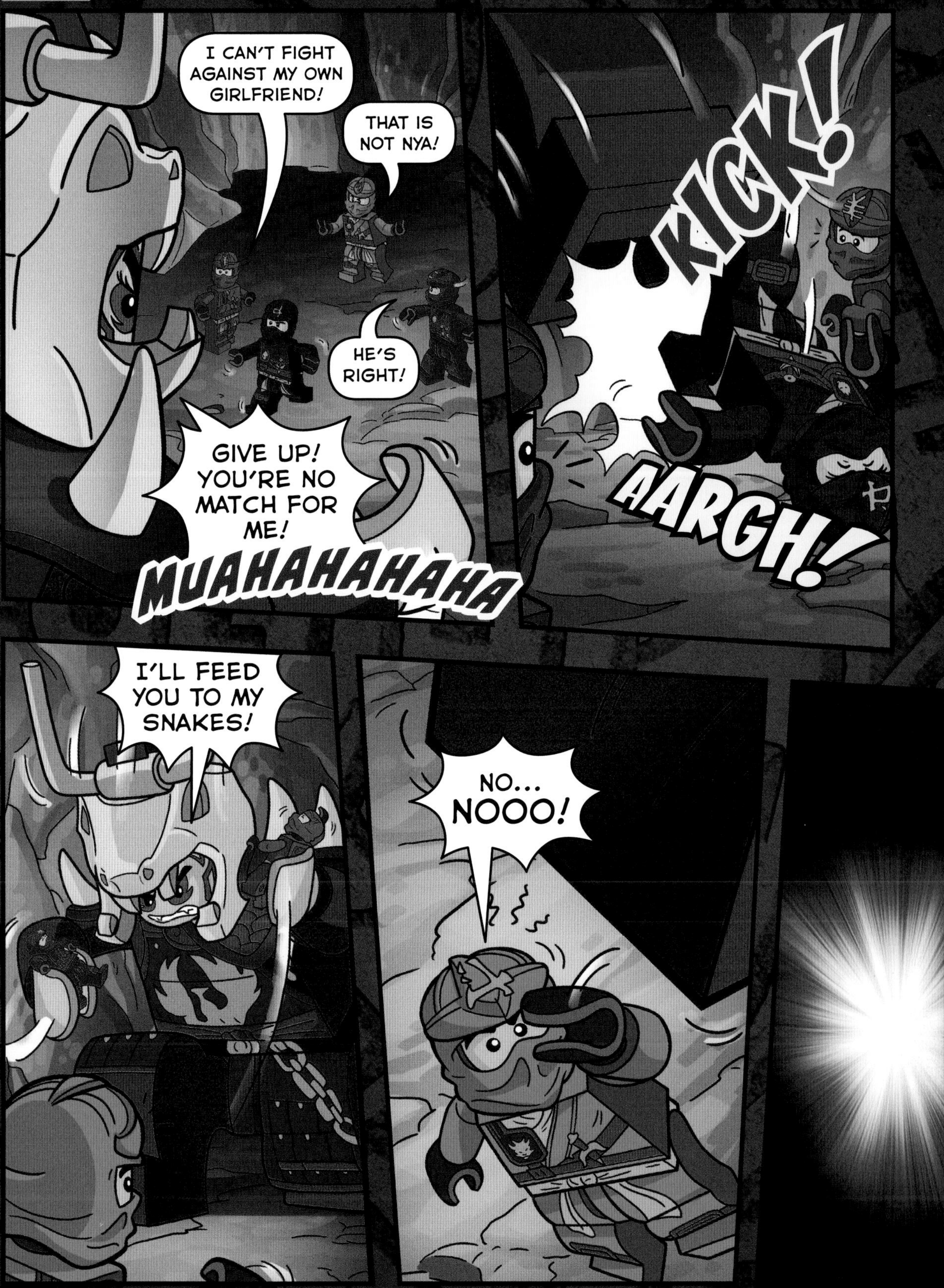
I CAN'T FIGHT AGAINST MY OWN GIRLFRIEND!
THAT IS NOT NYA!
HE'S RIGHT!
GIVE UP! YOU'RE NO MATCH FOR ME!
MUAHAHAHAHAHA
KICK!
AARGH!
I'LL FEED YOU TO MY SNAKES!
NO... NOOO!

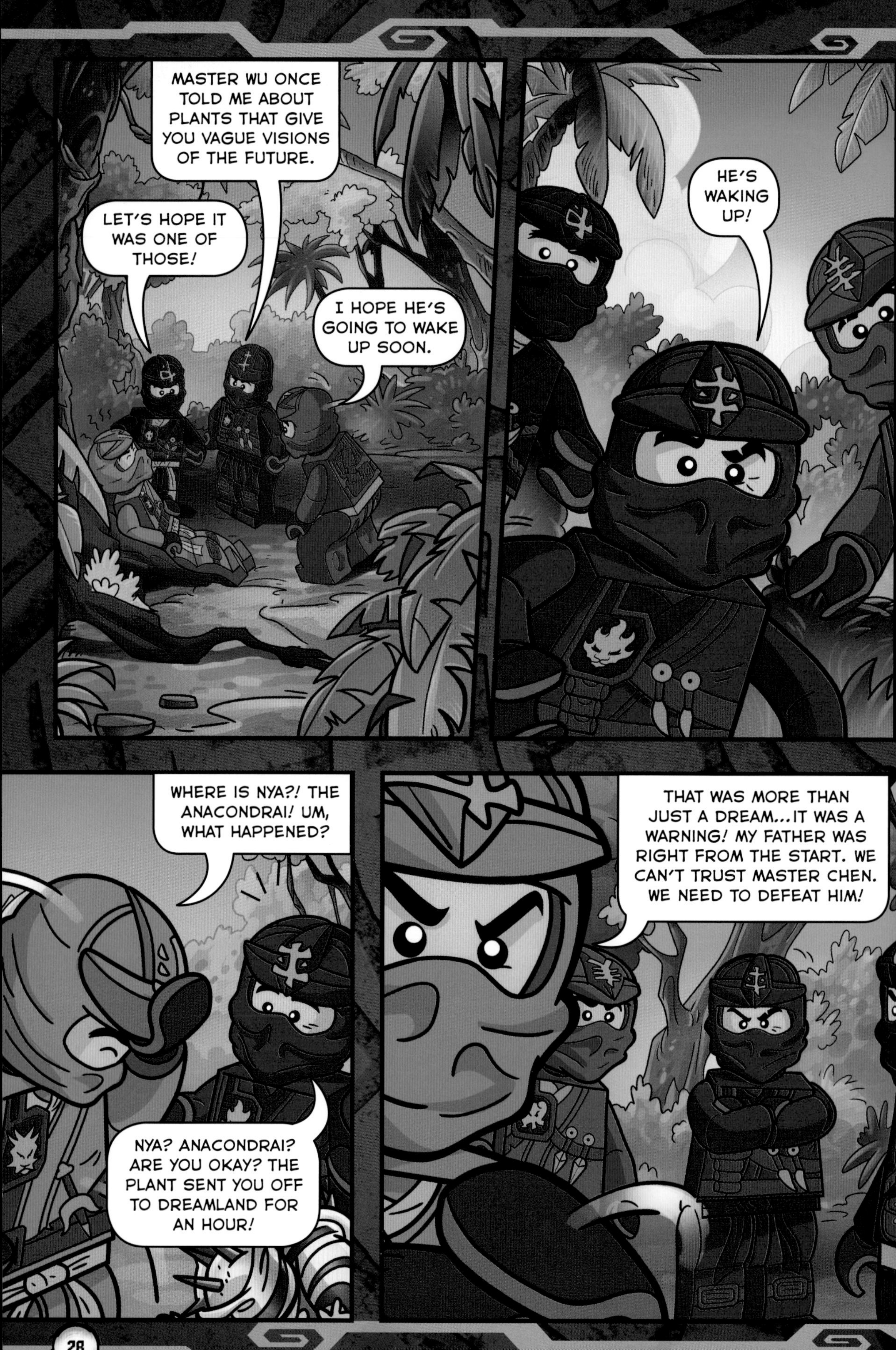

MASTER WU ONCE TOLD ME ABOUT PLANTS THAT GIVE YOU VAGUE VISIONS OF THE FUTURE.
LET'S HOPE IT WAS ONE OF THOSE!
I HOPE HE'S GOING TO WAKE UP SOON.
HE'S WAKING UP!
WHERE IS NYA?! THE ANACONDRAI! UM, WHAT HAPPENED?
NYA? ANACONDRAI? ARE YOU OKAY? THE PLANT SENT YOU OFF TO DREAMLAND FOR AN HOUR!
THAT WAS MORE THAN JUST A DREAM...IT WAS A WARNING! MY FATHER WAS RIGHT FROM THE START. WE CAN'T TRUST MASTER CHEN. WE NEED TO DEFEAT HIM!

CHAPTER 5

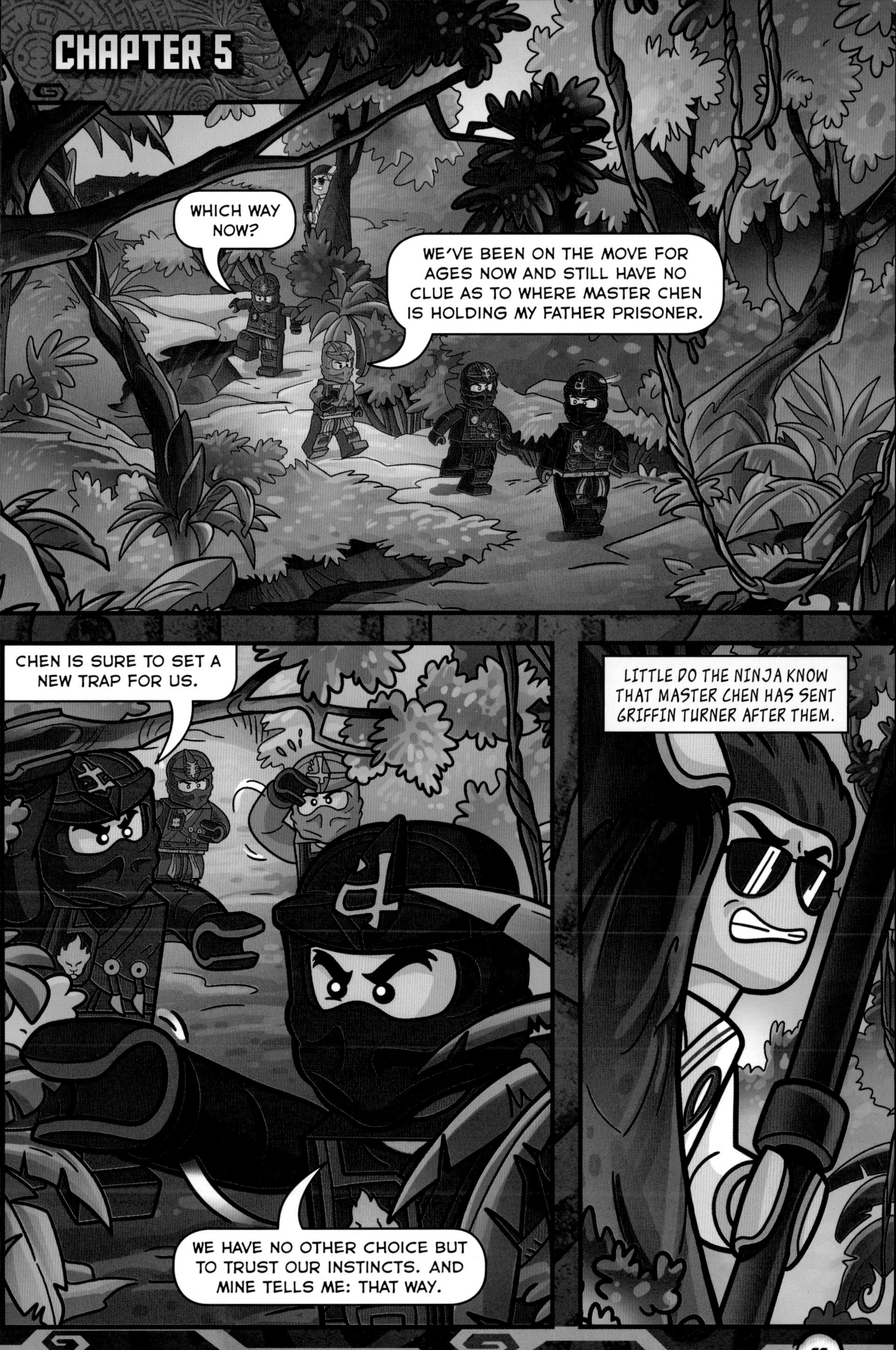

WHICH WAY NOW?
WE'VE BEEN ON THE MOVE FOR AGES NOW AND STILL HAVE NO CLUE AS TO WHERE MASTER CHEN IS HOLDING MY FATHER PRISONER.
CHEN IS SURE TO SET A NEW TRAP FOR US.
WE HAVE NO OTHER CHOICE BUT TO TRUST OUR INSTINCTS. AND MINE TELLS ME: THAT WAY.
LITTLE DO THE NINJA KNOW THAT MASTER CHEN HAS SENT GRIFFIN TURNER AFTER THEM.

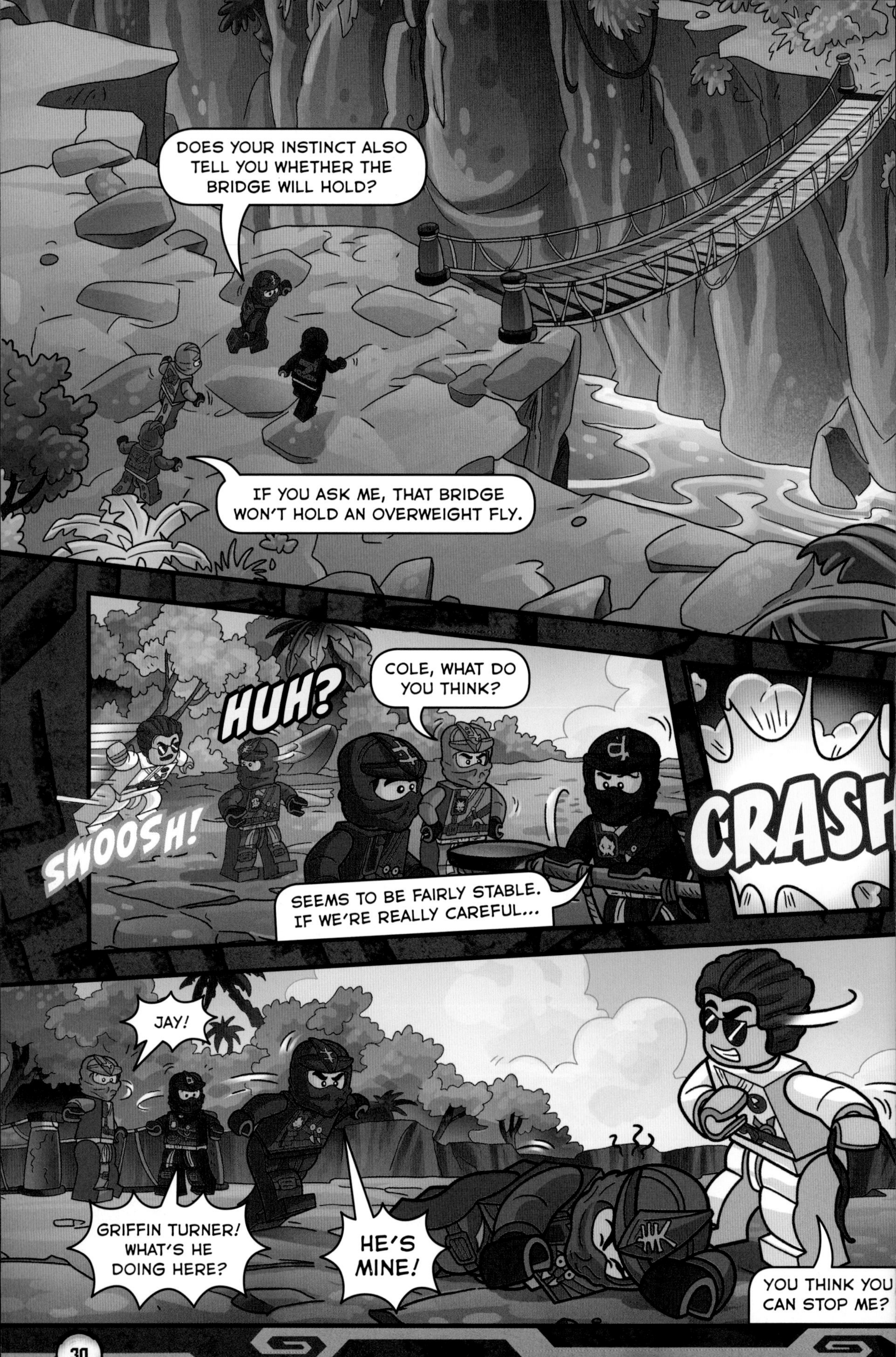

DOES YOUR INSTINCT ALSO TELL YOU WHETHER THE BRIDGE WILL HOLD?
IF YOU ASK ME, THAT BRIDGE WON'T HOLD AN OVERWEIGHT FLY.
SWOOSH!
HUH?
COLE, WHAT DO YOU THINK?
SEEMS TO BE FAIRLY STABLE. IF WE'RE REALLY CAREFUL...
CRASH
JAY!
GRIFFIN TURNER! WHAT'S HE DOING HERE?
HE'S MINE!
YOU THINK YOU CAN STOP ME?

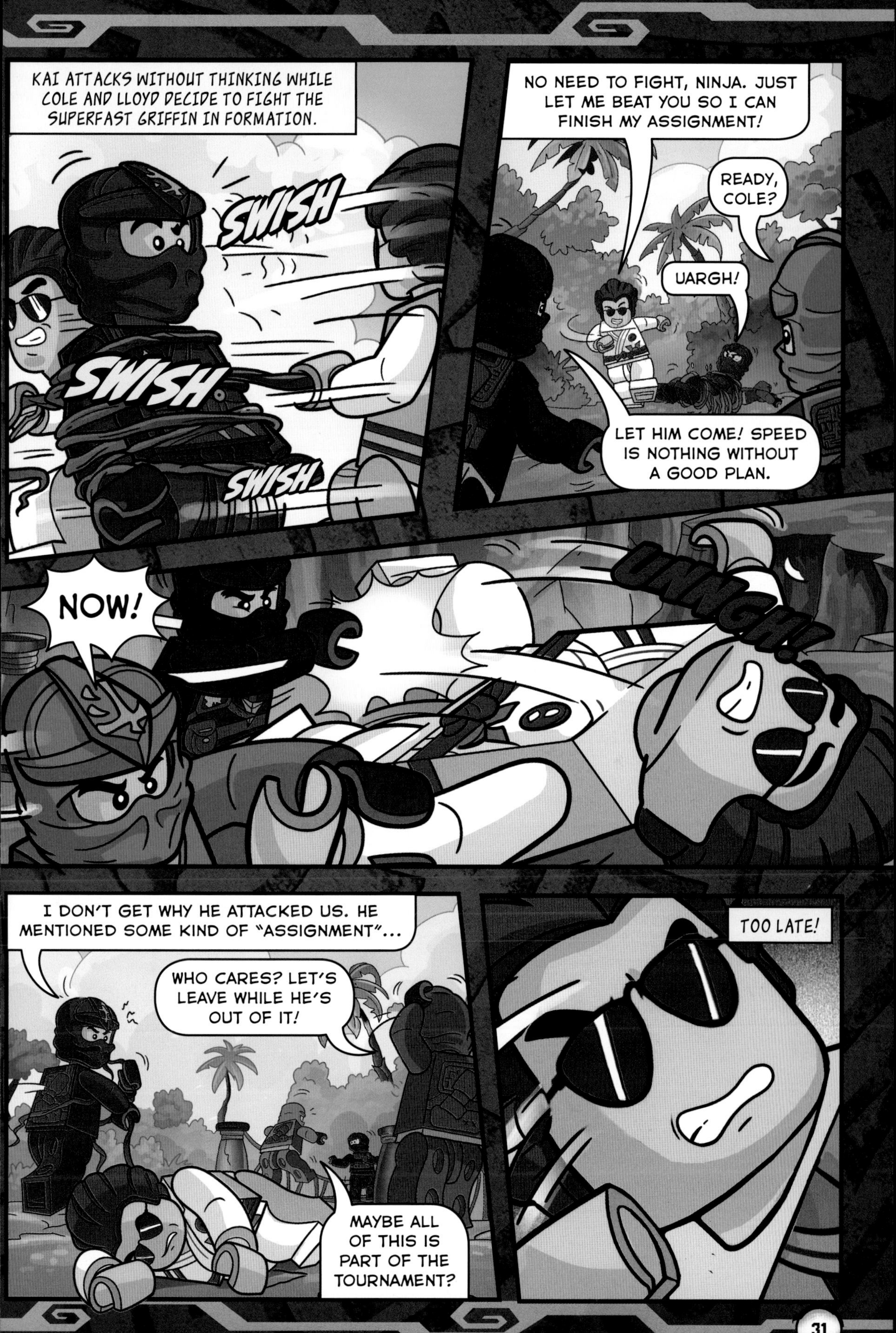
KAI ATTACKS WITHOUT THINKING WHILE COLE AND LLOYD DECIDE TO FIGHT THE SUPERFAST GRIFFIN IN FORMATION.
SWISH
SWISH
SWISH
NO NEED TO FIGHT, NINJA. JUST LET ME BEAT YOU SO I CAN FINISH MY ASSIGNMENT!
READY, COLE?
UARGH!
LET HIM COME! SPEED IS NOTHING WITHOUT A GOOD PLAN.
NOW!
UNNGH!
I DON'T GET WHY HE ATTACKED US. HE MENTIONED SOME KIND OF "ASSIGNMENT"...
WHO CARES? LET'S LEAVE WHILE HE'S OUT OF IT!
MAYBE ALL OF THIS IS PART OF THE TOURNAMENT?
TOO LATE!

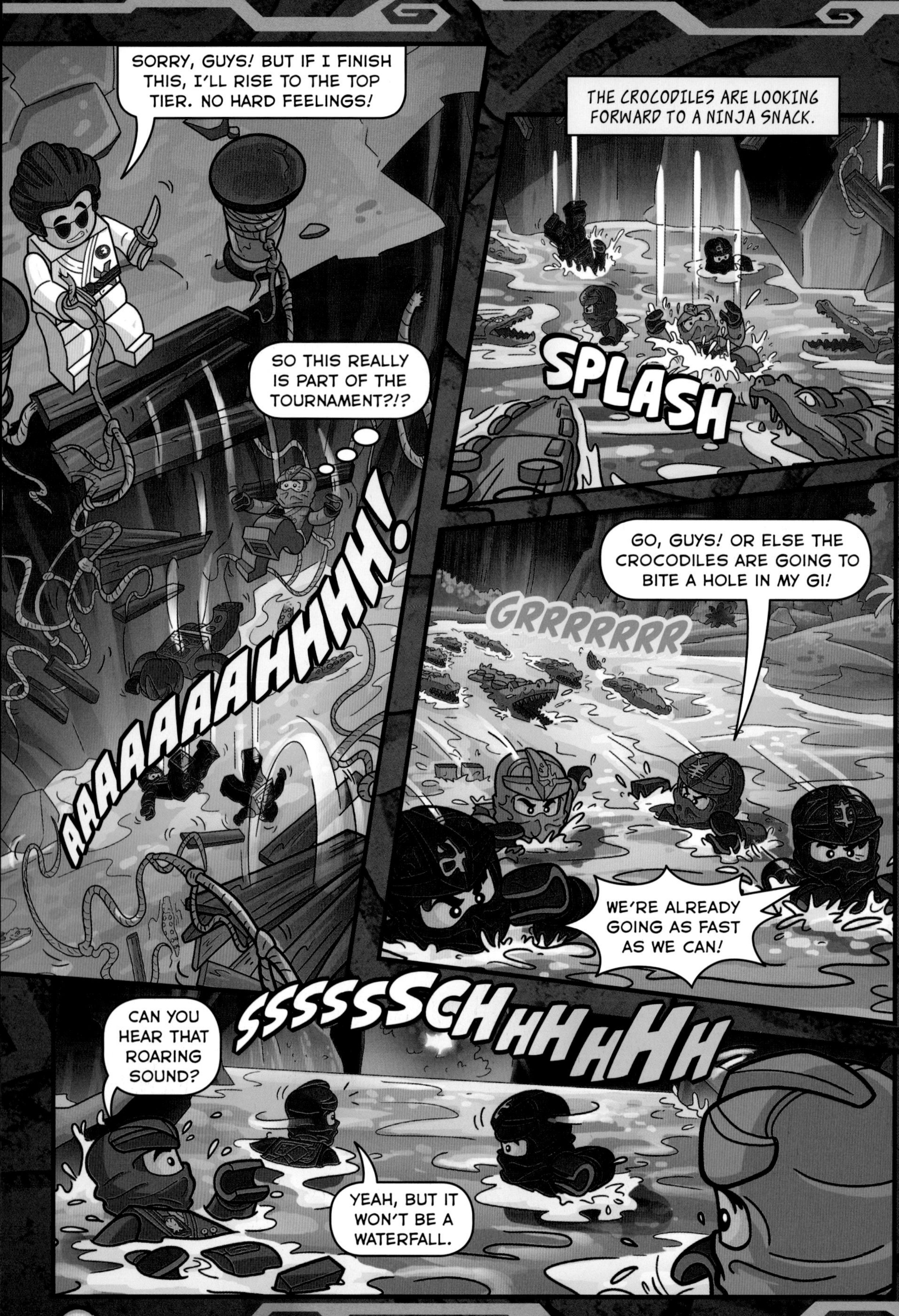
SORRY, GUYS! BUT IF I FINISH THIS, I'LL RISE TO THE TOP TIER. NO HARD FEELINGS!
SO THIS REALLY IS PART OF THE TOURNAMENT?!?
AAAAAAAAHHHHH!
THE CROCODILES ARE LOOKING FORWARD TO A NINJA SNACK.
SPLASH
GO, GUYS! OR ELSE THE CROCODILES ARE GOING TO BITE A HOLE IN MY GI!
GRRRRRRR
WE'RE ALREADY GOING AS FAST AS WE CAN!
CAN YOU HEAR THAT ROARING SOUND?
SSSSSSCHHHHHH
YEAH, BUT IT WON'T BE A WATERFALL.

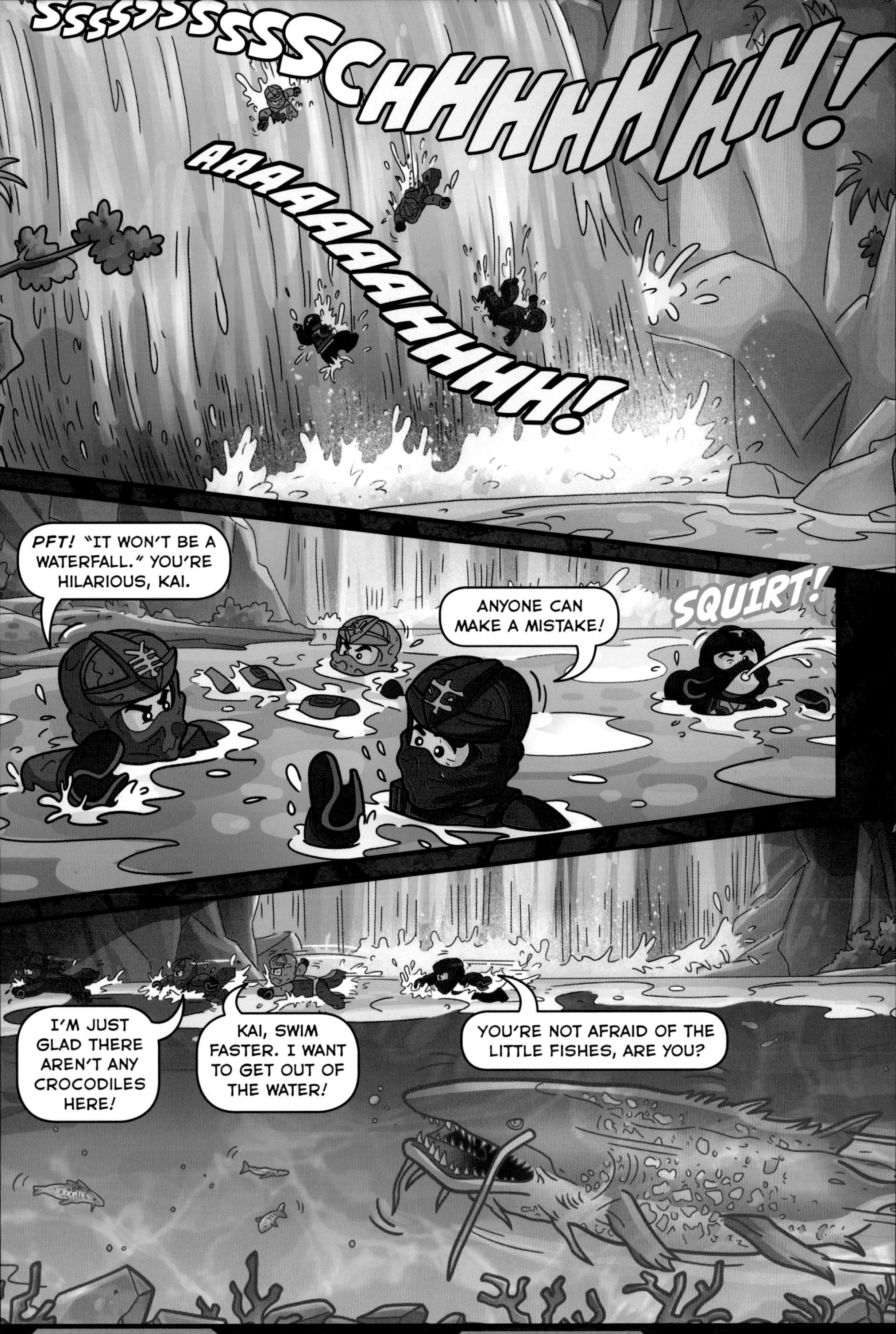
SSSSSSSSSCHHHHHHHHH!
AAAAAAAHHHHHH!
PFT! "IT WON'T BE A WATERFALL." YOU'RE HILARIOUS, KAI.
ANYONE CAN MAKE A MISTAKE!
SQUIRT!
I'M JUST GLAD THERE AREN'T ANY CROCODILES HERE!
KAI, SWIM FASTER. I WANT TO GET OUT OF THE WATER!
YOU'RE NOT AFRAID OF THE LITTLE FISHES, ARE YOU?

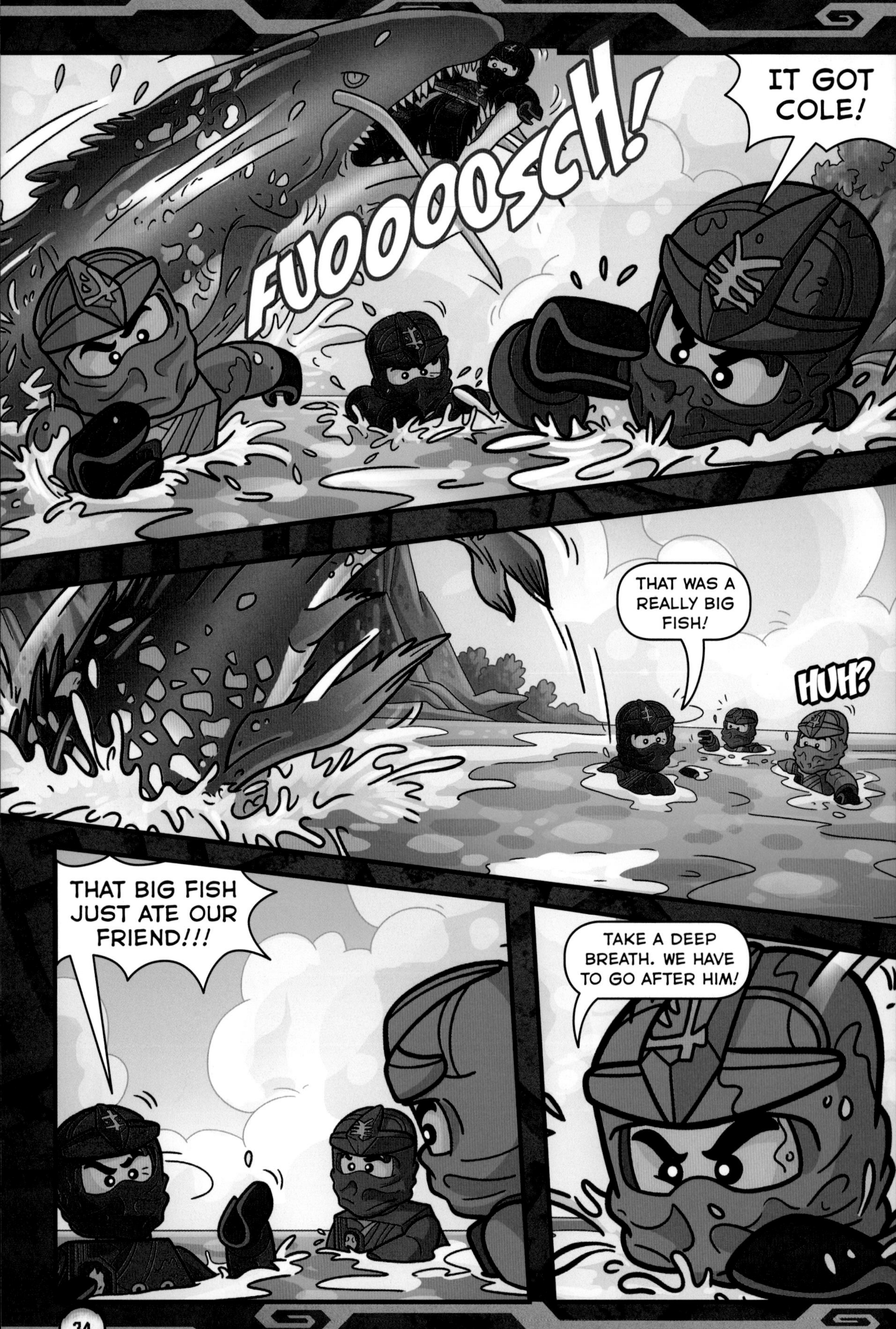
FUOOOOSCH!
IT GOT COLE!
THAT WAS A REALLY BIG FISH!
HUH?
THAT BIG FISH JUST ATE OUR FRIEND!!!
TAKE A DEEP BREATH. WE HAVE TO GO AFTER HIM!

CHAPTER 6

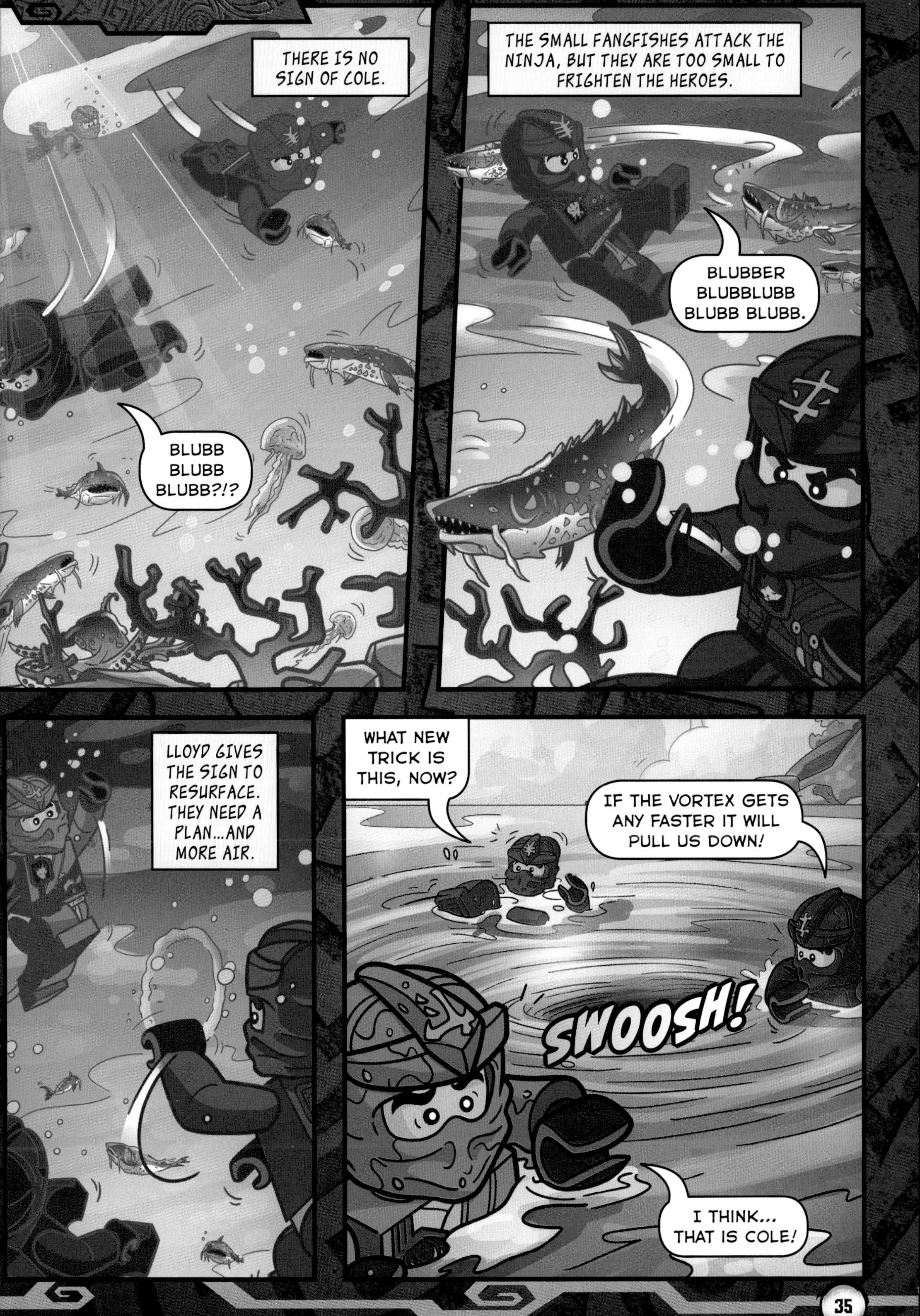
THERE IS NO SIGN OF COLE.
BLUBB BLUBB BLUBB?!?
THE SMALL FANGFISHES ATTACK THE NINJA, BUT THEY ARE TOO SMALL TO FRIGHTEN THE HEROES.
BLUBBER BLUBBLUBB BLUBB BLUBB.
LLOYD GIVES THE SIGN TO RESURFACE. THEY NEED A PLAN...AND MORE AIR.
WHAT NEW TRICK IS THIS, NOW?
IF THE VORTEX GETS ANY FASTER IT WILL PULL US DOWN!
SWOOSH!
I THINK... THAT IS COLE!

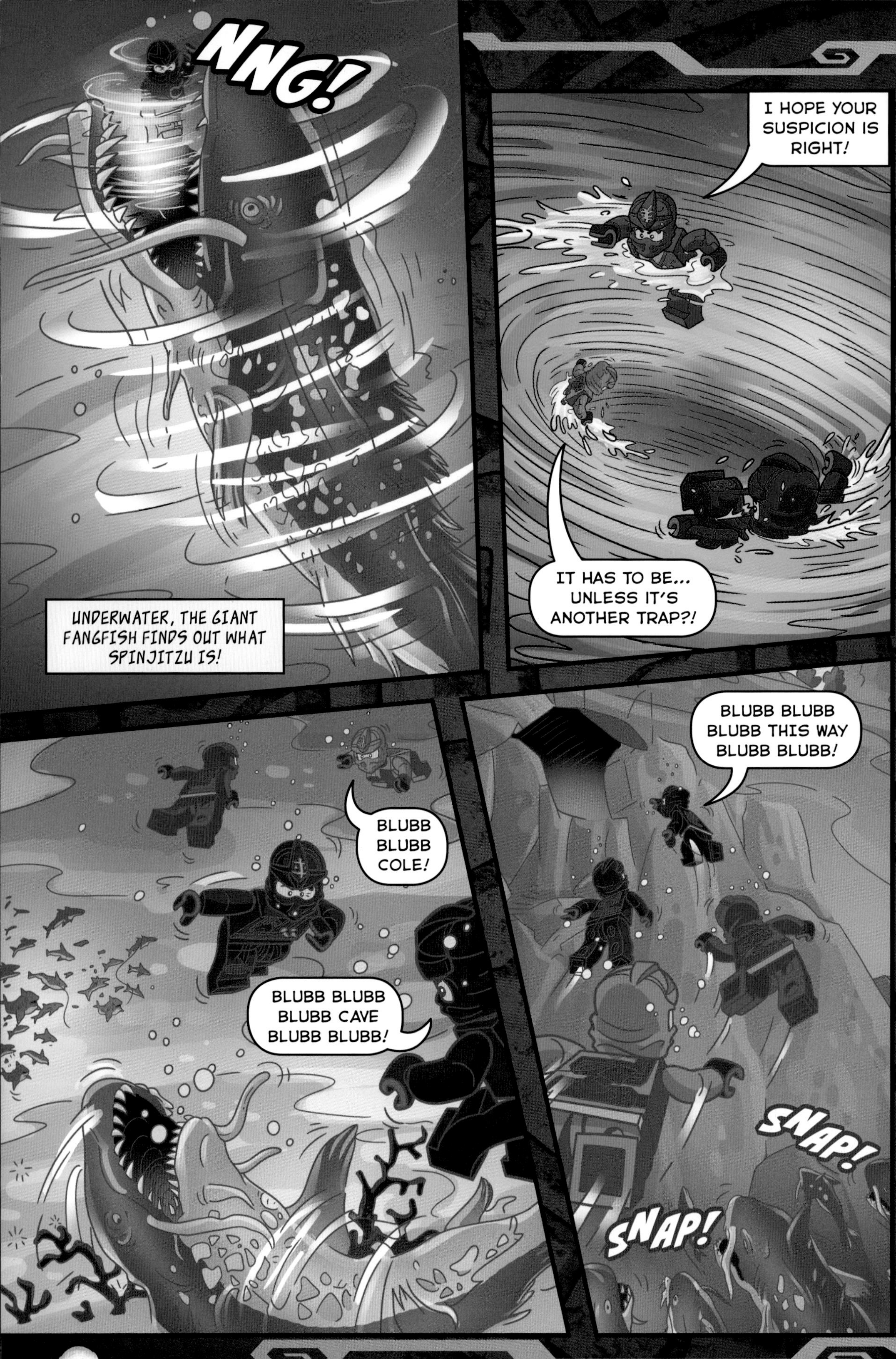
NNG!
UNDERWATER, THE GIANT FANGFISH FINDS OUT WHAT SPINJITZU IS!
I HOPE YOUR SUSPICION IS RIGHT!
IT HAS TO BE... UNLESS IT'S ANOTHER TRAP?!
BLUBB BLUBB COLE!
BLUBB BLUBB BLUBB CAVE BLUBB BLUBB!
BLUBB BLUBB BLUBB THIS WAY BLUBB BLUBB!
SNAP!
SNAP!

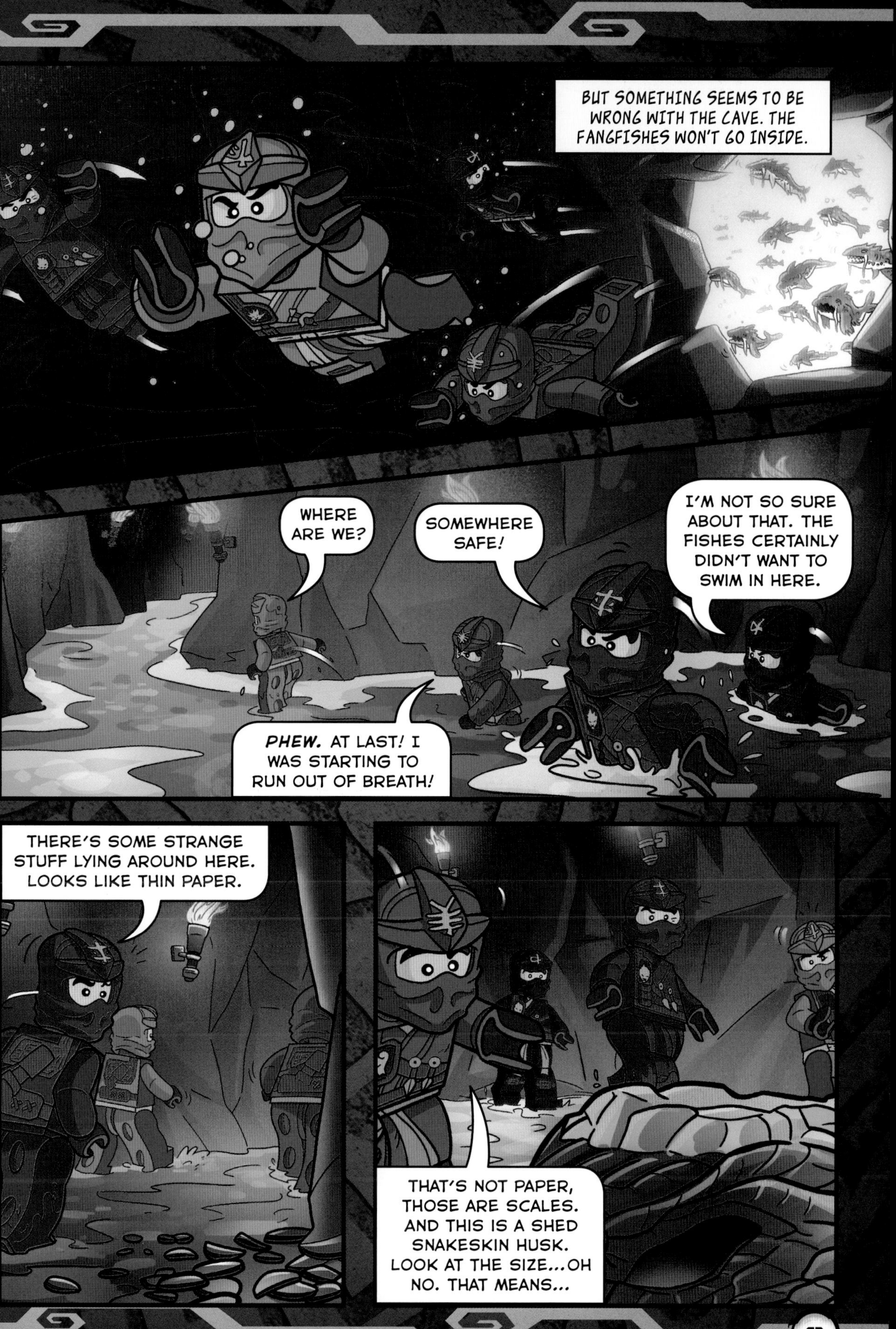

BUT SOMETHING SEEMS TO BE WRONG WITH THE CAVE. THE FANGFISHES WON'T GO INSIDE.
WHERE ARE WE?
SOMEWHERE SAFE!
I'M NOT SO SURE ABOUT THAT. THE FISHES CERTAINLY DIDN'T WANT TO SWIM IN HERE.
PHEW. AT LAST! I WAS STARTING TO RUN OUT OF BREATH!
THERE'S SOME STRANGE STUFF LYING AROUND HERE. LOOKS LIKE THIN PAPER.
THAT'S NOT PAPER, THOSE ARE SCALES. AND THIS IS A SHED SNAKESKIN HUSK. LOOK AT THE SIZE...OH NO. THAT MEANS...

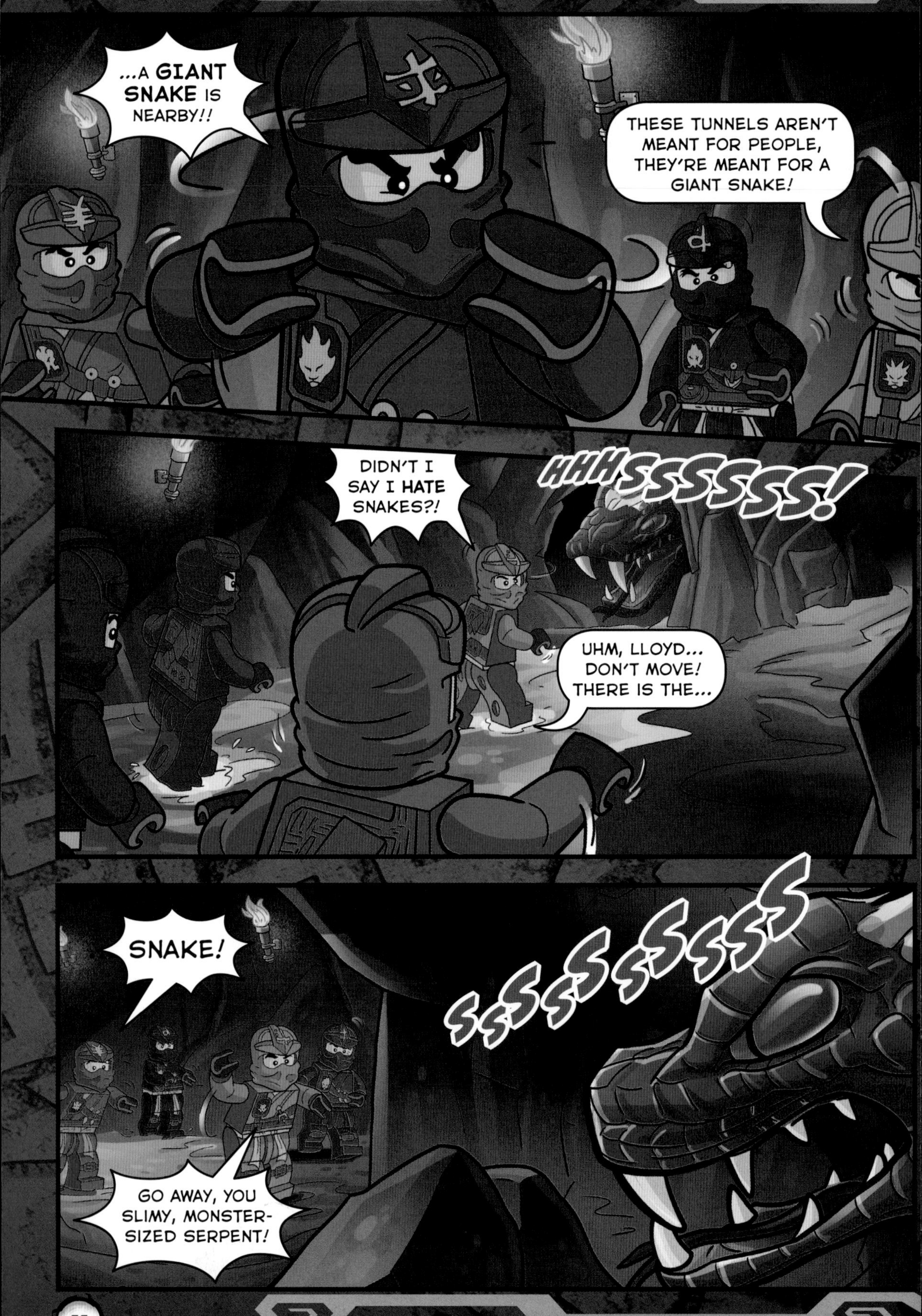
...A GIANT SNAKE IS NEARBY!!
THESE TUNNELS AREN'T MEANT FOR PEOPLE, THEY'RE MEANT FOR A GIANT SNAKE!
DIDN'T I SAY I HATE SNAKES?!
HHHSSSSSS!
UHM, LLOYD... DON'T MOVE! THERE IS THE...
SNAKE!
SSSSSSSSS
GO AWAY, YOU SLIMY, MONSTER-SIZED SERPENT!

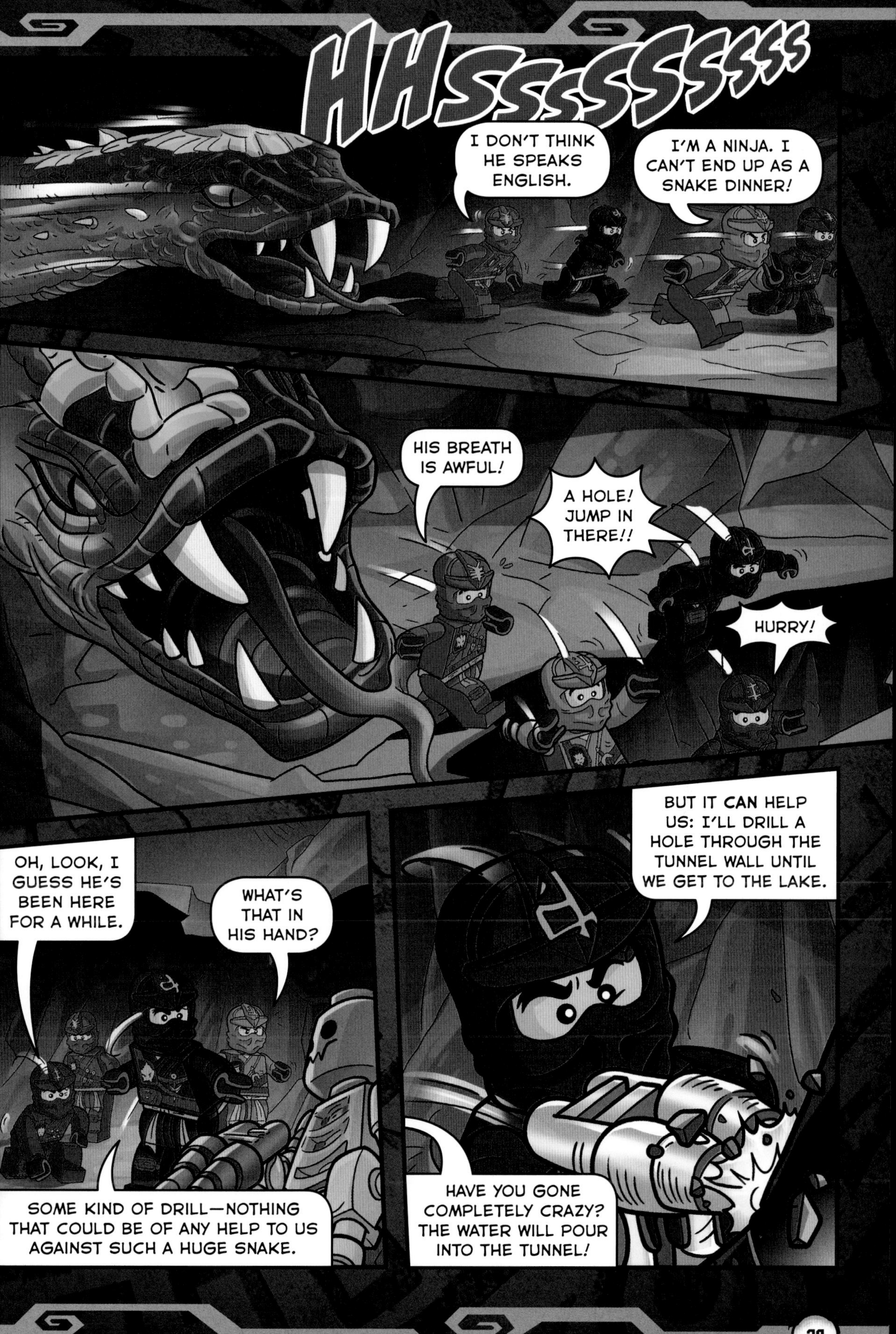
HHSSSSSSSS
I DON'T THINK HE SPEAKS ENGLISH.
I'M A NINJA. I CAN'T END UP AS A SNAKE DINNER!
HIS BREATH IS AWFUL!
A HOLE! JUMP IN THERE!!
HURRY!
OH, LOOK, I GUESS HE'S BEEN HERE FOR A WHILE.
WHAT'S THAT IN HIS HAND?
SOME KIND OF DRILL—NOTHING THAT COULD BE OF ANY HELP TO US AGAINST SUCH A HUGE SNAKE.
BUT IT **CAN** HELP US: I'LL DRILL A HOLE THROUGH THE TUNNEL WALL UNTIL WE GET TO THE LAKE.
HAVE YOU GONE COMPLETELY CRAZY? THE WATER WILL POUR INTO THE TUNNEL!

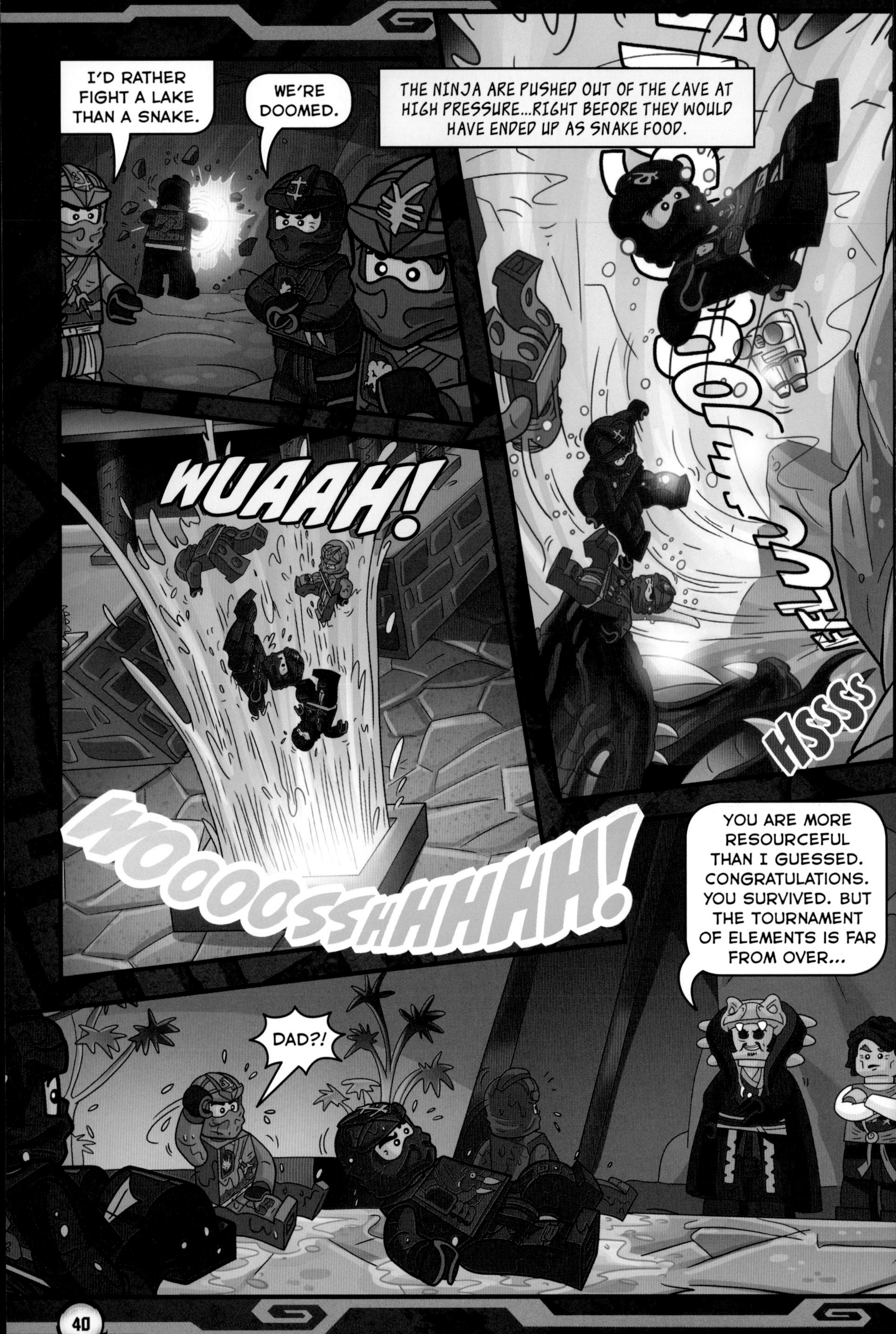

I'D RATHER FIGHT A LAKE THAN A SNAKE.
WE'RE DOOMED.
THE NINJA ARE PUSHED OUT OF THE CAVE AT HIGH PRESSURE...RIGHT BEFORE THEY WOULD HAVE ENDED UP AS SNAKE FOOD.
WUAAH!
HSSSS
WOOOOSSHHHHHH!
YOU ARE MORE RESOURCEFUL THAN I GUESSED. CONGRATULATIONS. YOU SURVIVED. BUT THE TOURNAMENT OF ELEMENTS IS FAR FROM OVER...
DAD?!

CHAPTER 7

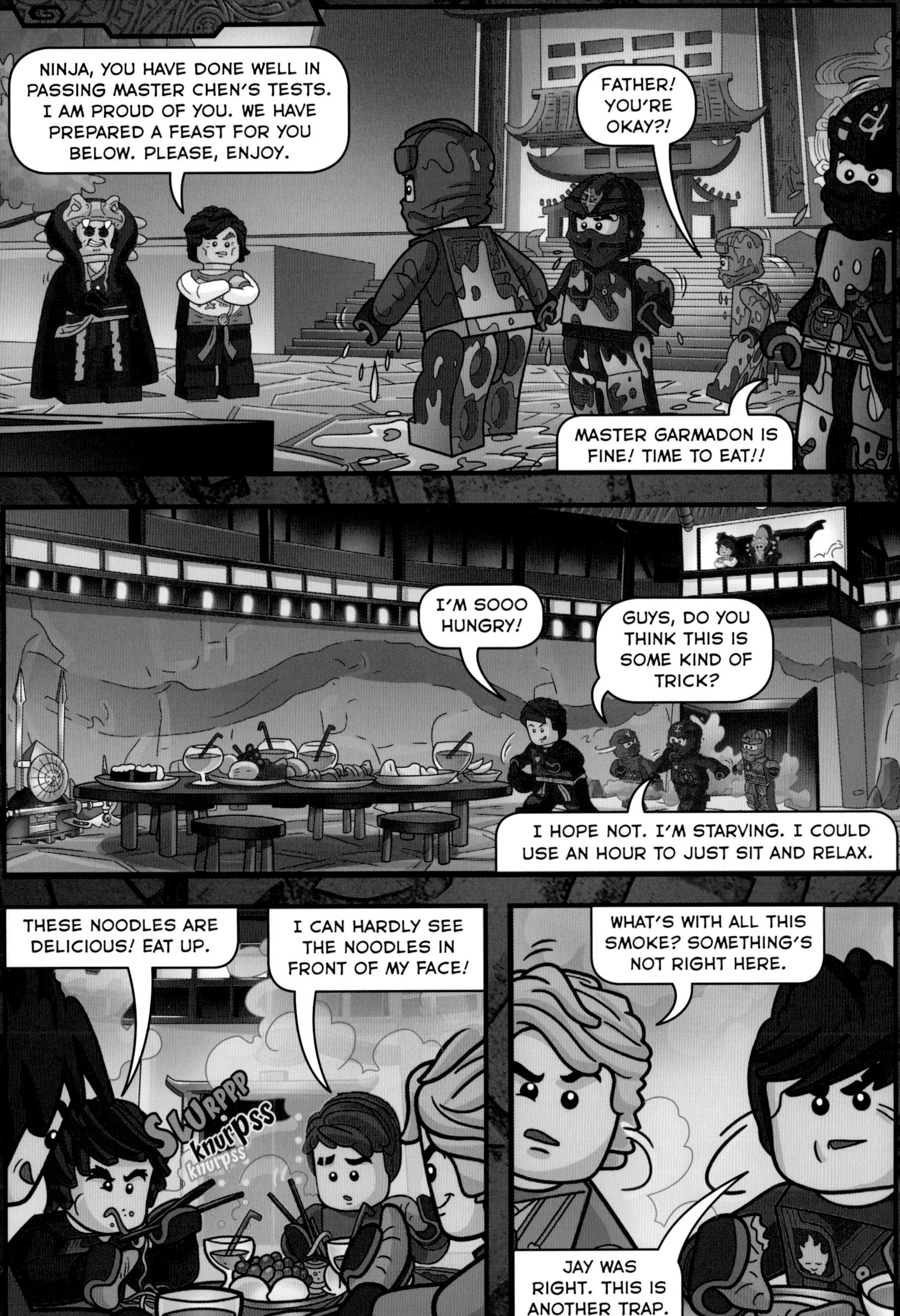
NINJA, YOU HAVE DONE WELL IN PASSING MASTER CHEN'S TESTS. I AM PROUD OF YOU. WE HAVE PREPARED A FEAST FOR YOU BELOW. PLEASE, ENJOY.
FATHER! YOU'RE OKAY?!
MASTER GARMADON IS FINE! TIME TO EAT!!
I'M SOOO HUNGRY!
GUYS, DO YOU THINK THIS IS SOME KIND OF TRICK?
I HOPE NOT. I'M STARVING. I COULD USE AN HOUR TO JUST SIT AND RELAX.
THESE NOODLES ARE DELICIOUS! EAT UP.
I CAN HARDLY SEE THE NOODLES IN FRONT OF MY FACE!
SLURPPP
knurpss
knurpss
WHAT'S WITH ALL THIS SMOKE? SOMETHING'S NOT RIGHT HERE.
JAY WAS RIGHT. THIS IS ANOTHER TRAP.

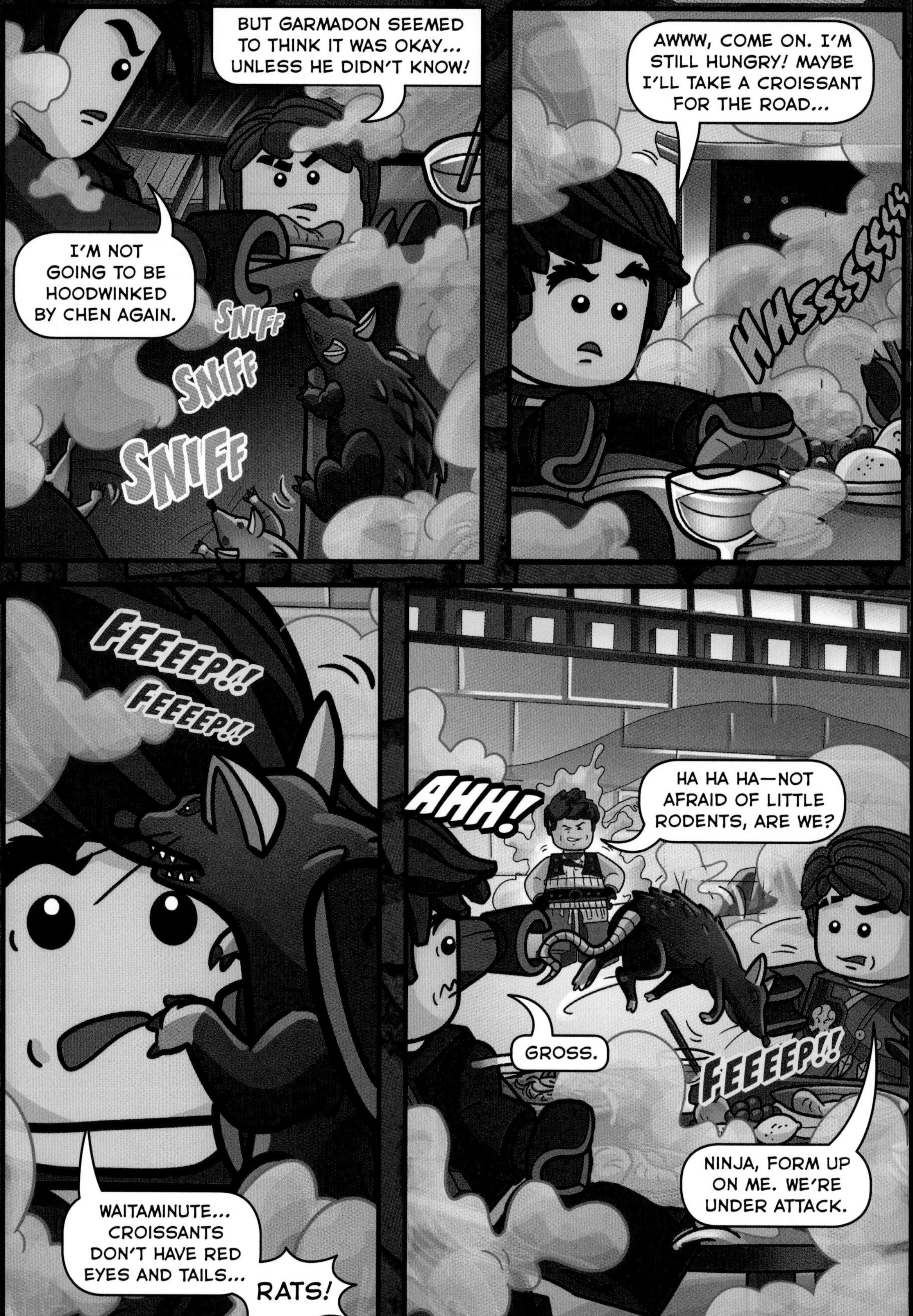
BUT GARMADON SEEMED TO THINK IT WAS OKAY... UNLESS HE DIDN'T KNOW!
I'M NOT GOING TO BE HOODWINKED BY CHEN AGAIN.
SNIFF
SNIFF
SNIFF
AWWW, COME ON. I'M STILL HUNGRY! MAYBE I'LL TAKE A CROISSANT FOR THE ROAD...
HHSSSSSSSS
FEEEEP!!
FEEEEP!!
WAITAMINUTE... CROISSANTS DON'T HAVE RED EYES AND TAILS...
RATS!
AHH!
HA HA HA—NOT AFRAID OF LITTLE RODENTS, ARE WE?
GROSS.
FEEEEP!!
NINJA, FORM UP ON ME. WE'RE UNDER ATTACK.

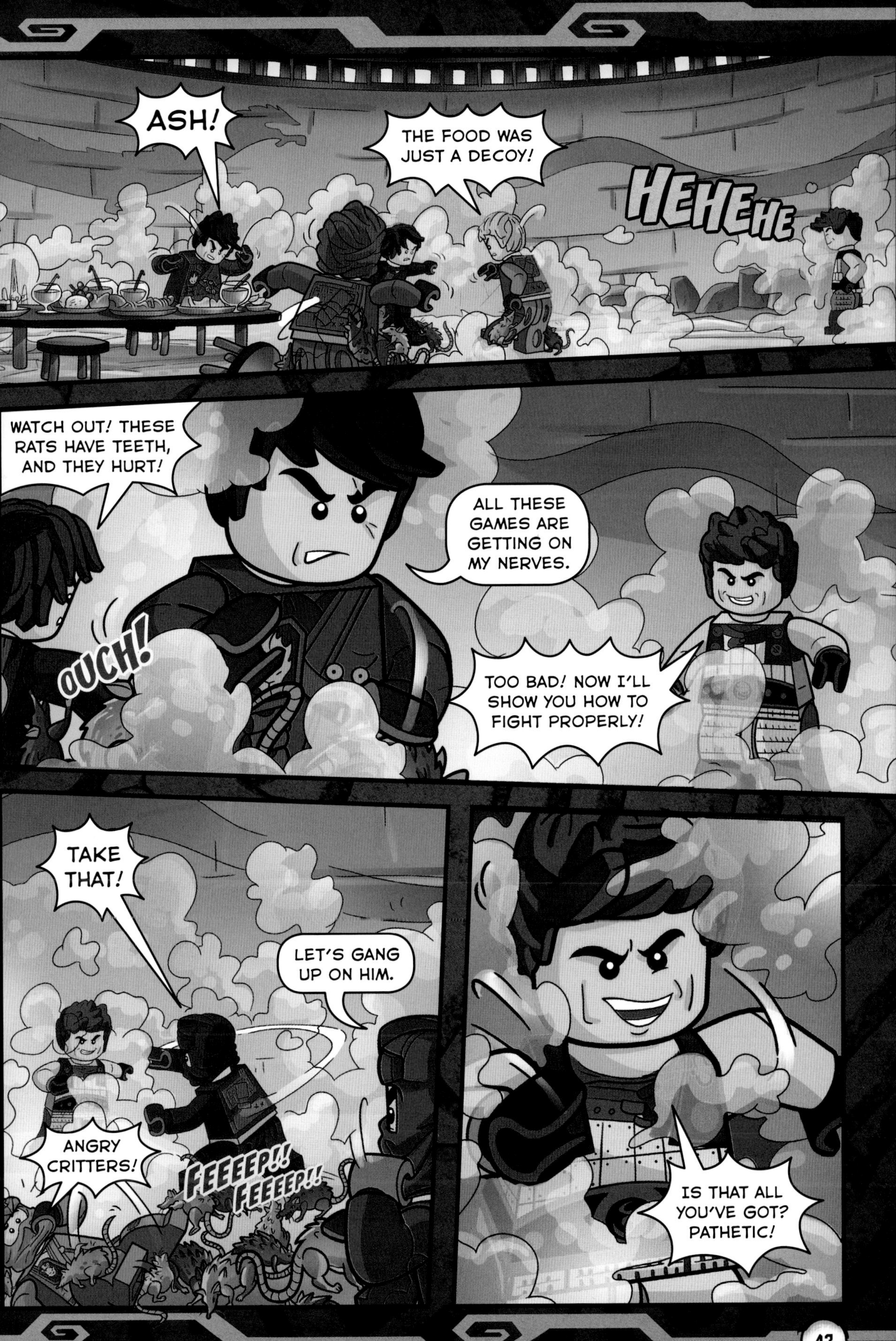
ASH!
THE FOOD WAS JUST A DECOY!
HEHEHEHE
WATCH OUT! THESE RATS HAVE TEETH, AND THEY HURT!
ALL THESE GAMES ARE GETTING ON MY NERVES.
OUCH!
TOO BAD! NOW I'LL SHOW YOU HOW TO FIGHT PROPERLY!
TAKE THAT!
LET'S GANG UP ON HIM.
ANGRY CRITTERS!
FEEEEP!! FEEEEP!!
IS THAT ALL YOU'VE GOT? PATHETIC!

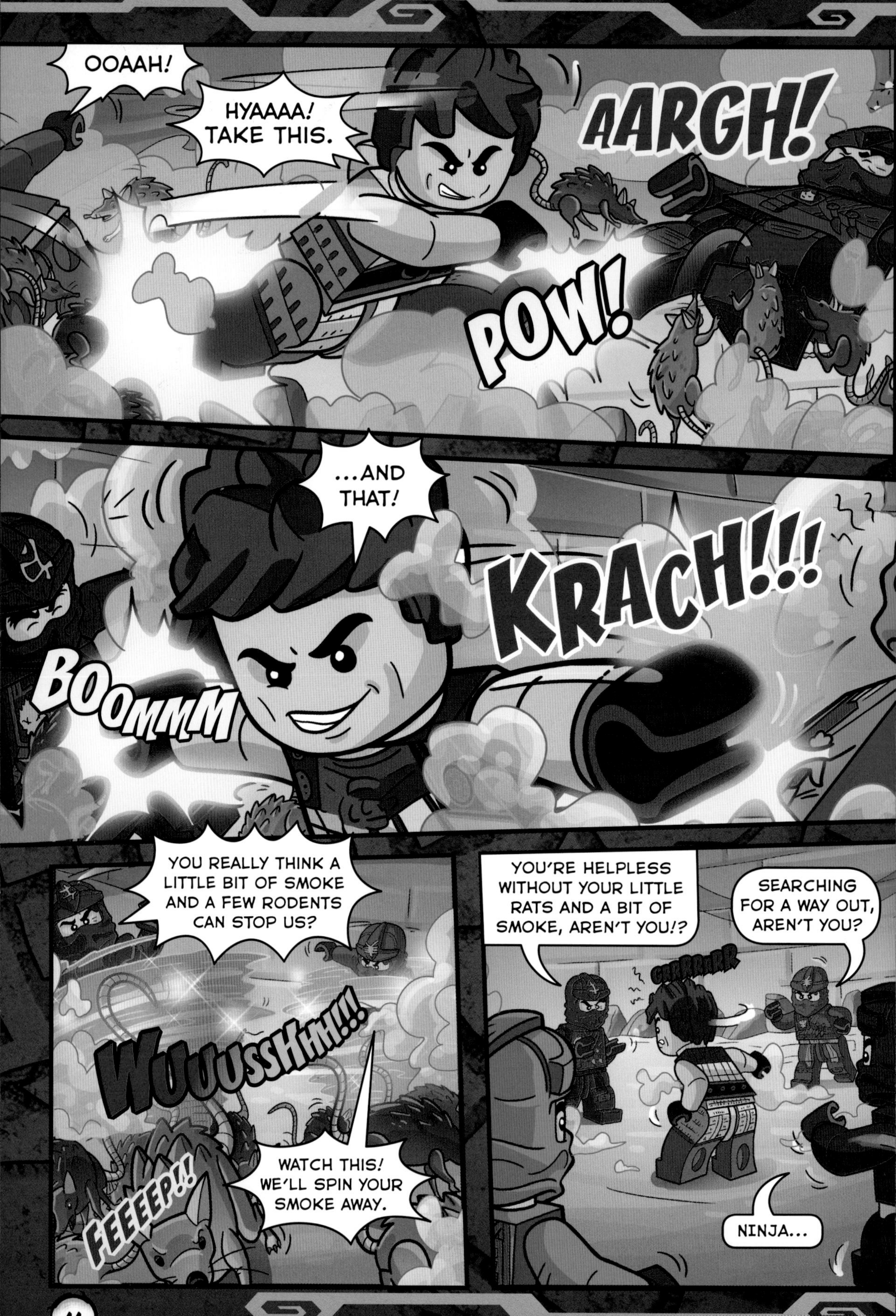
OOAAH!
HYAAAA! TAKE THIS.
AARGH!
POW!
...AND THAT!
KRACH!!!
BOOMMM
YOU REALLY THINK A LITTLE BIT OF SMOKE AND A FEW RODENTS CAN STOP US?
WUUUSSHHH!!!
FEEEEP!!
WATCH THIS! WE'LL SPIN YOUR SMOKE AWAY.
YOU'RE HELPLESS WITHOUT YOUR LITTLE RATS AND A BIT OF SMOKE, AREN'T YOU!?
SEARCHING FOR A WAY OUT, AREN'T YOU?
GRRRRRR
NINJA...

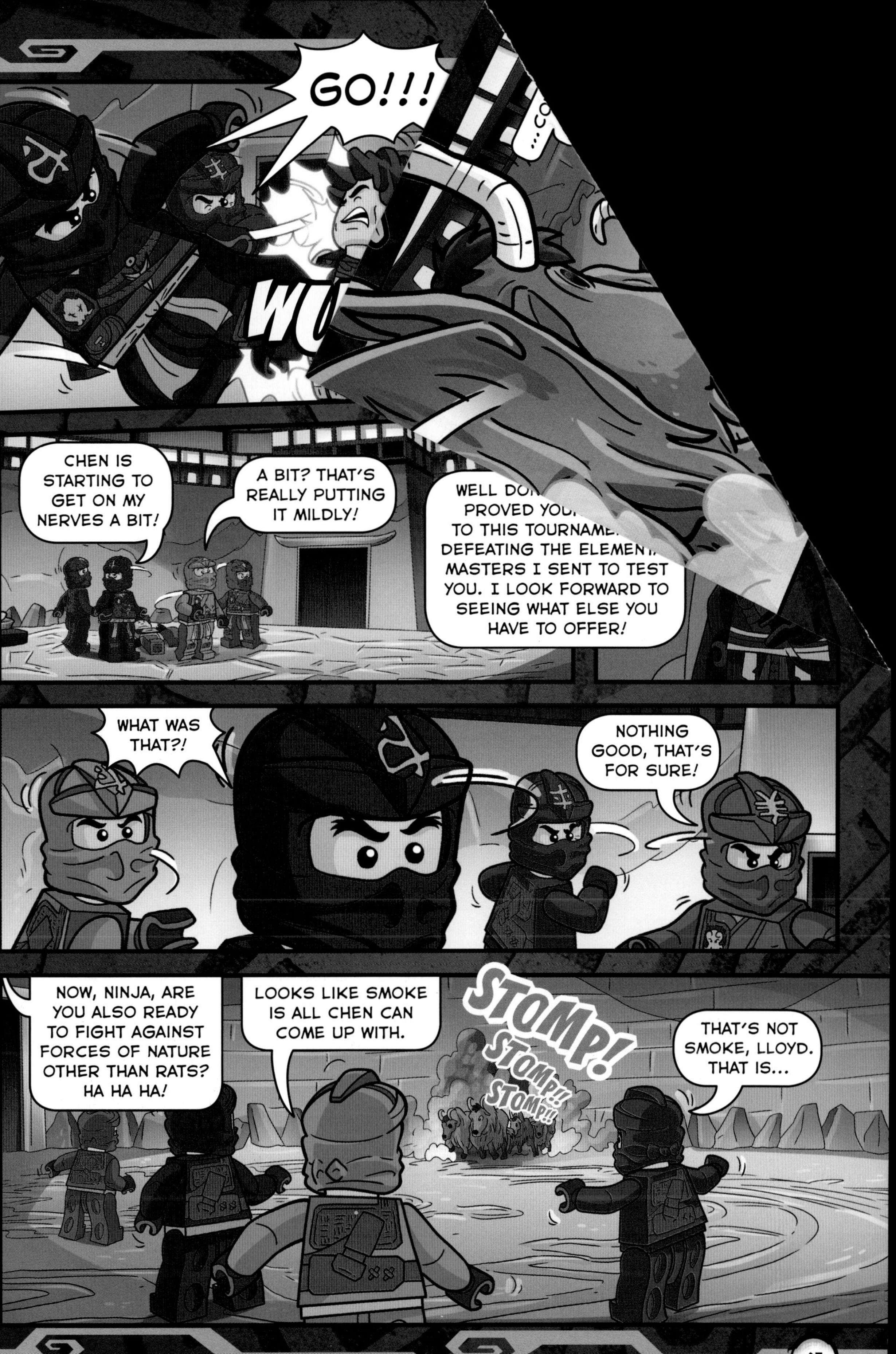
GO!!!
CHEN IS STARTING TO GET ON MY NERVES A BIT!
A BIT? THAT'S REALLY PUTTING IT MILDLY!
WELL DON PROVED YOU TO THIS TOURNAME DEFEATING THE ELEMENT MASTERS I SENT TO TEST YOU. I LOOK FORWARD TO SEEING WHAT ELSE YOU HAVE TO OFFER!
WHAT WAS THAT?!
NOTHING GOOD, THAT'S FOR SURE!
NOW, NINJA, ARE YOU ALSO READY TO FIGHT AGAINST FORCES OF NATURE OTHER THAN RATS? HA HA HA!
LOOKS LIKE SMOKE IS ALL CHEN CAN COME UP WITH.
STOMP!
STOMP!!
STOMP!!
THAT'S NOT SMOKE, LLOYD. THAT IS...

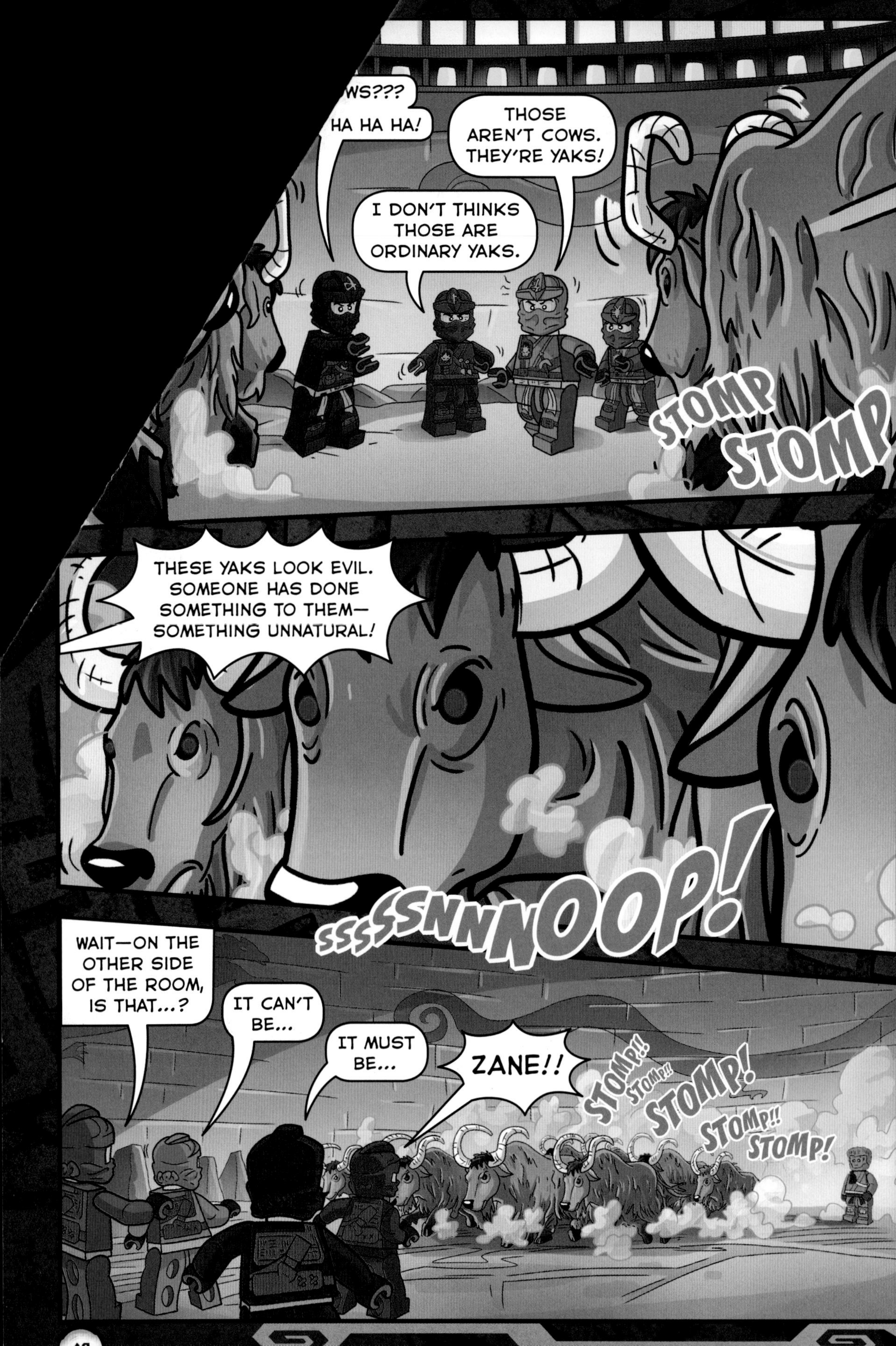
WS???
HA HA HA!
THOSE AREN'T COWS. THEY'RE YAKS!
I DON'T THINKS THOSE ARE ORDINARY YAKS.
STOMP
STOMP
THESE YAKS LOOK EVIL. SOMEONE HAS DONE SOMETHING TO THEM—SOMETHING UNNATURAL!
SSSSNNNNOOOP!
WAIT—ON THE OTHER SIDE OF THE ROOM, IS THAT...?
IT CAN'T BE...
IT MUST BE...
ZANE!!
STOMP!! STOMP!! STOMP!
STOMP!! STOMP!

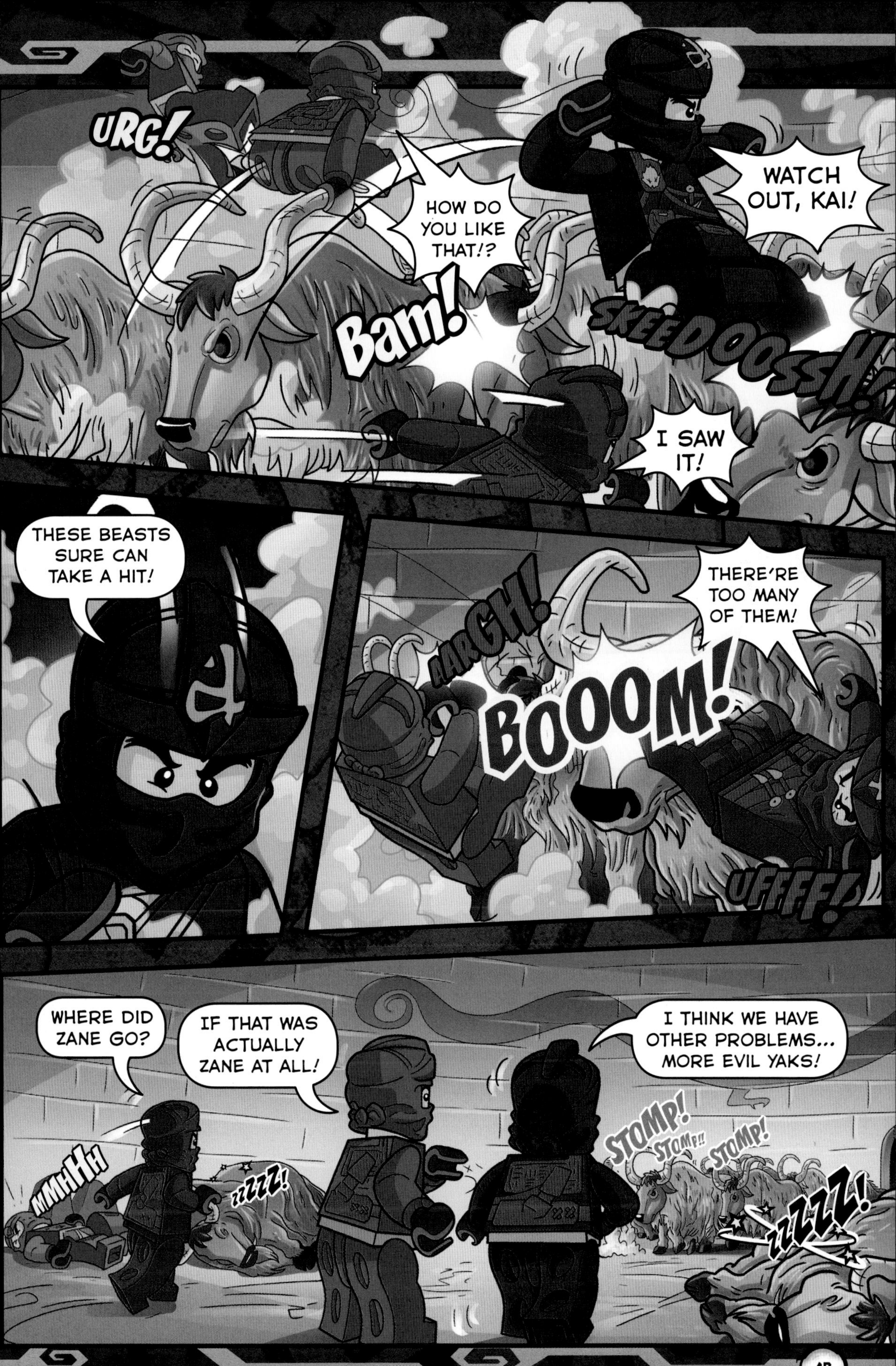
URG!
HOW DO YOU LIKE THAT!?
WATCH OUT, KAI!
Bam!
SKEEDOOSSH!
I SAW IT!
THESE BEASTS SURE CAN TAKE A HIT!
AARGH!
THERE'RE TOO MANY OF THEM!
BOOOM!
UFFFF!
WHERE DID ZANE GO?
IF THAT WAS ACTUALLY ZANE AT ALL!
I THINK WE HAVE OTHER PROBLEMS... MORE EVIL YAKS!
STOMP!
STOMP!!
STOMP!
MMHHH
zzzz!
zzzzz!

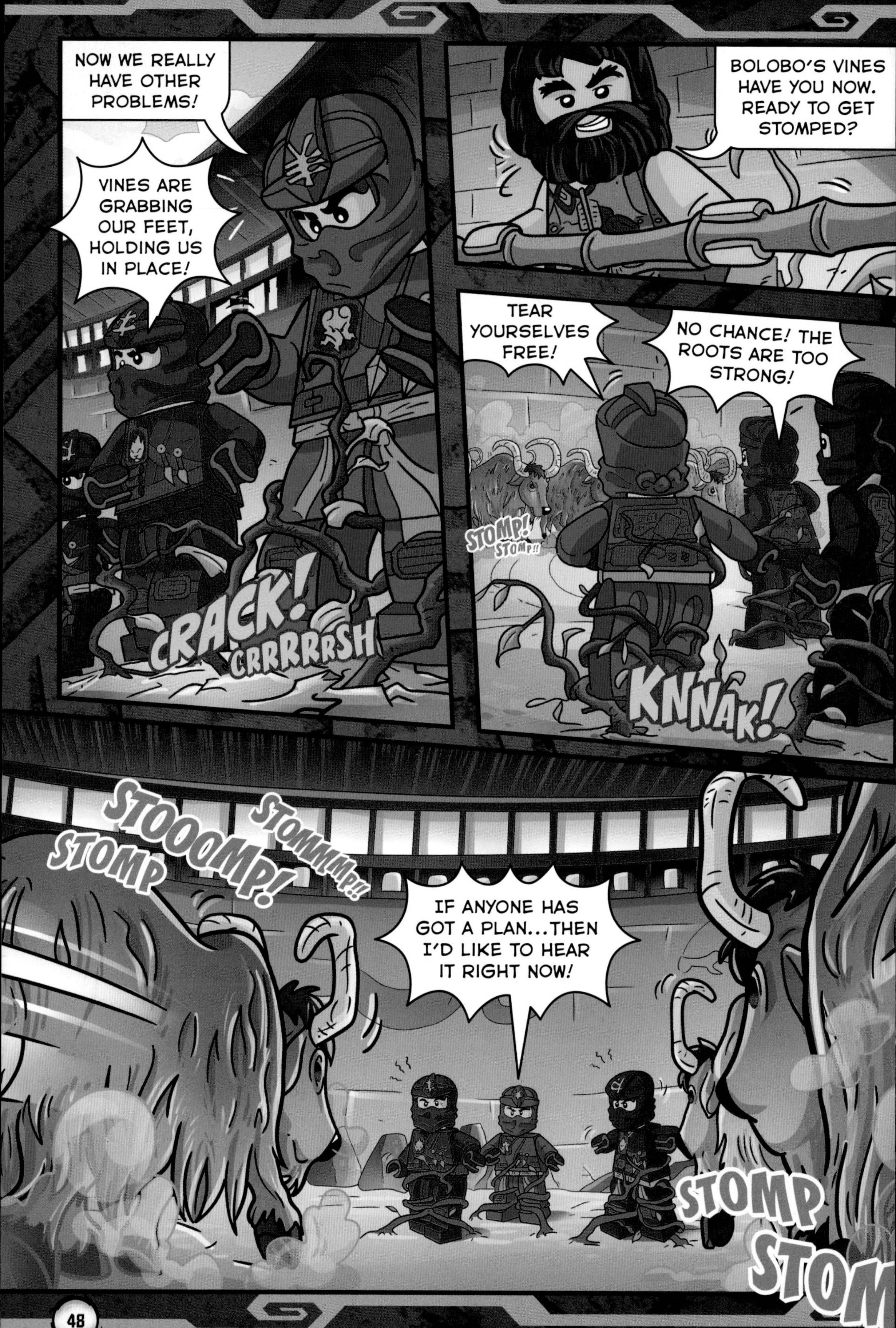
NOW WE REALLY HAVE OTHER PROBLEMS!
VINES ARE GRABBING OUR FEET, HOLDING US IN PLACE!
CRACK!
CRRRRRSH
BOLOBO'S VINES HAVE YOU NOW. READY TO GET STOMPED?
TEAR YOURSELVES FREE!
NO CHANCE! THE ROOTS ARE TOO STRONG!
STOMP! STOMP!!
KNNAK!
STOOOOMP!
STOMP
STOMMMMP!!
IF ANYONE HAS GOT A PLAN...THEN I'D LIKE TO HEAR IT RIGHT NOW!
STOMP
STOM

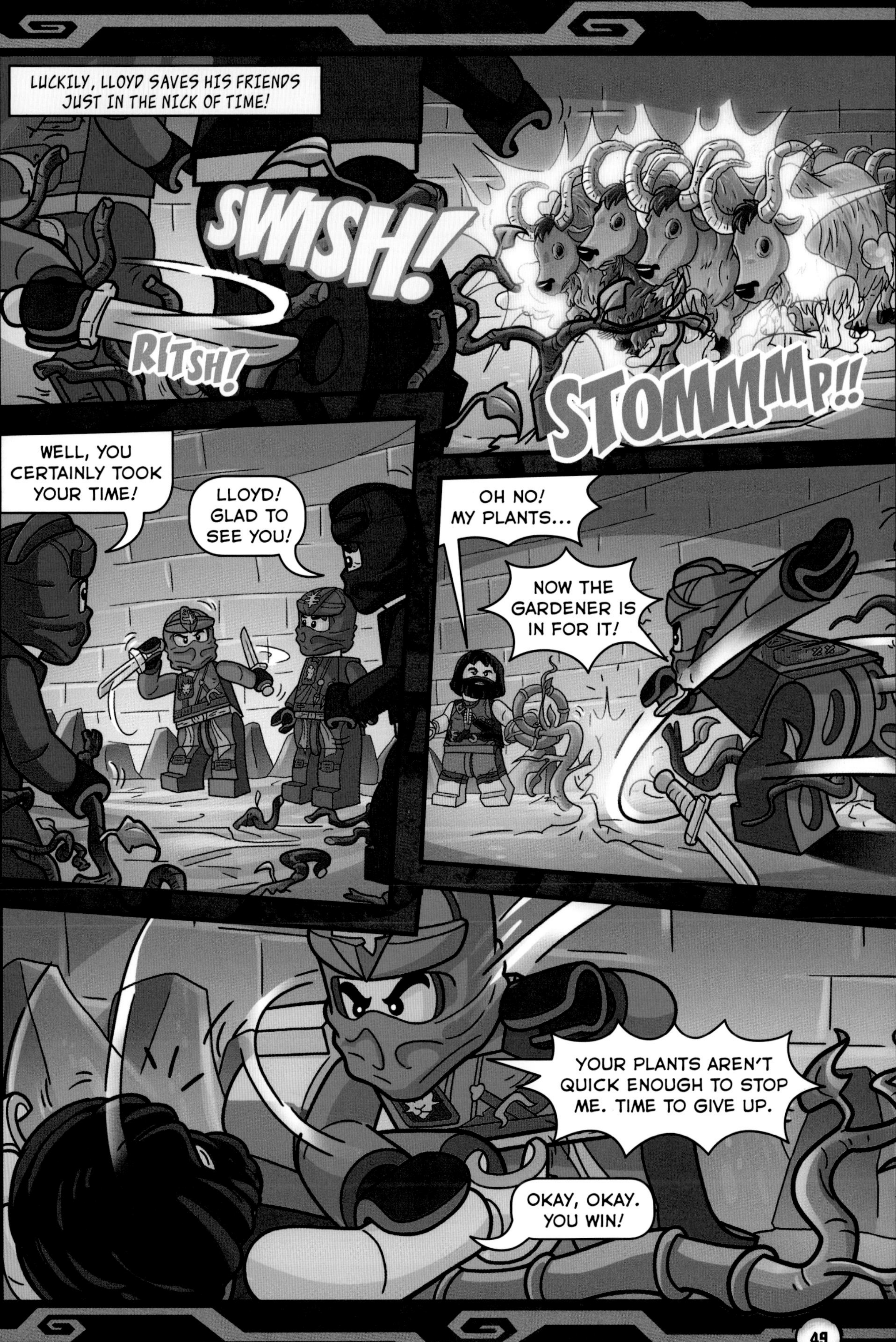
LUCKILY, LLOYD SAVES HIS FRIENDS JUST IN THE NICK OF TIME!
SWISH!
RITSH!
STOMMMP!!
WELL, YOU CERTAINLY TOOK YOUR TIME!
LLOYD! GLAD TO SEE YOU!
OH NO! MY PLANTS...
NOW THE GARDENER IS IN FOR IT!
YOUR PLANTS AREN'T QUICK ENOUGH TO STOP ME. TIME TO GIVE UP.
OKAY, OKAY. YOU WIN!

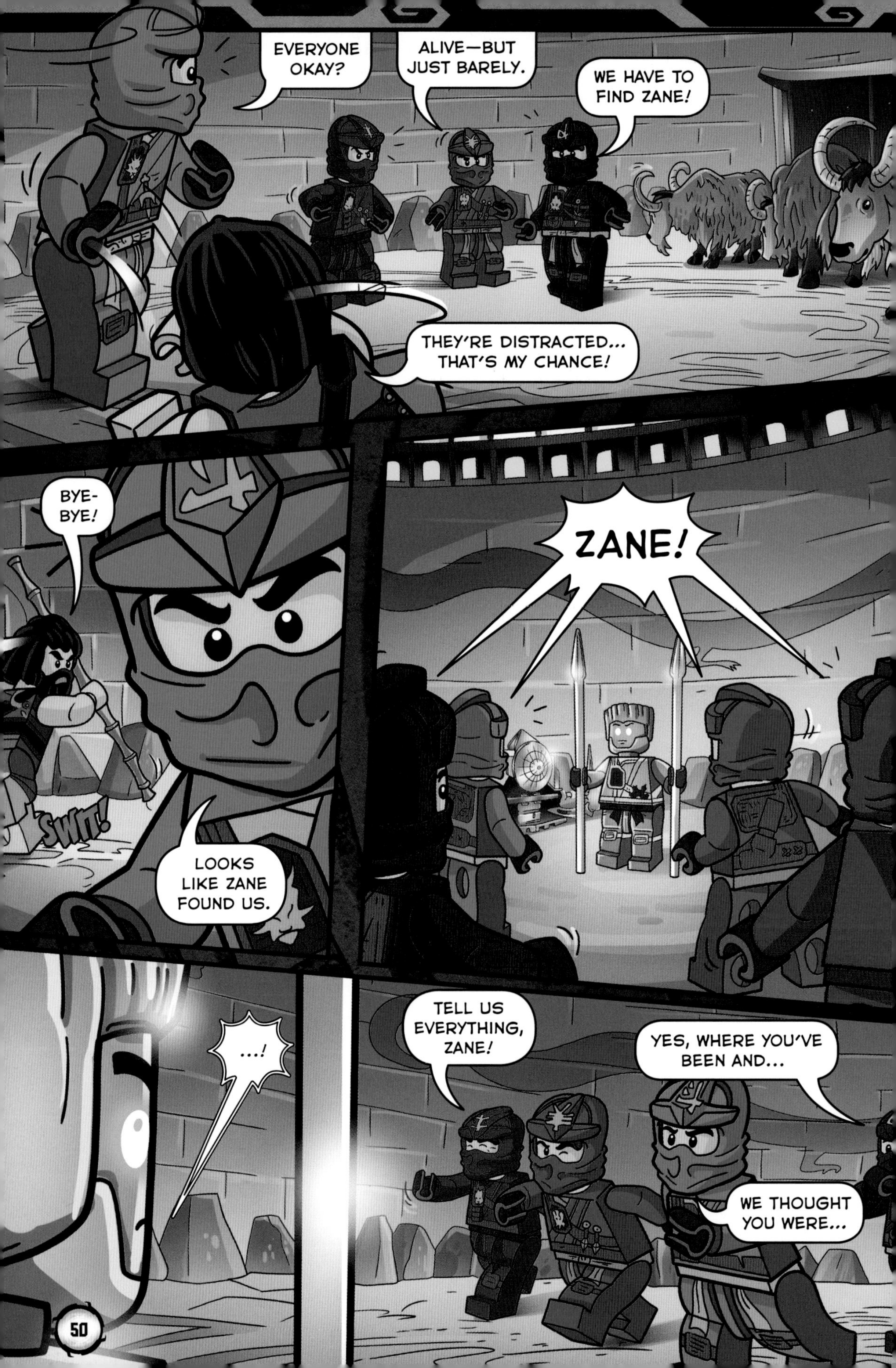
EVERYONE OKAY?
ALIVE—BUT JUST BARELY.
WE HAVE TO FIND ZANE!
THEY'RE DISTRACTED... THAT'S MY CHANCE!
BYE-BYE!
SWIT!
LOOKS LIKE ZANE FOUND US.
ZANE!
...!
TELL US EVERYTHING, ZANE!
YES, WHERE YOU'VE BEEN AND...
WE THOUGHT YOU WERE...

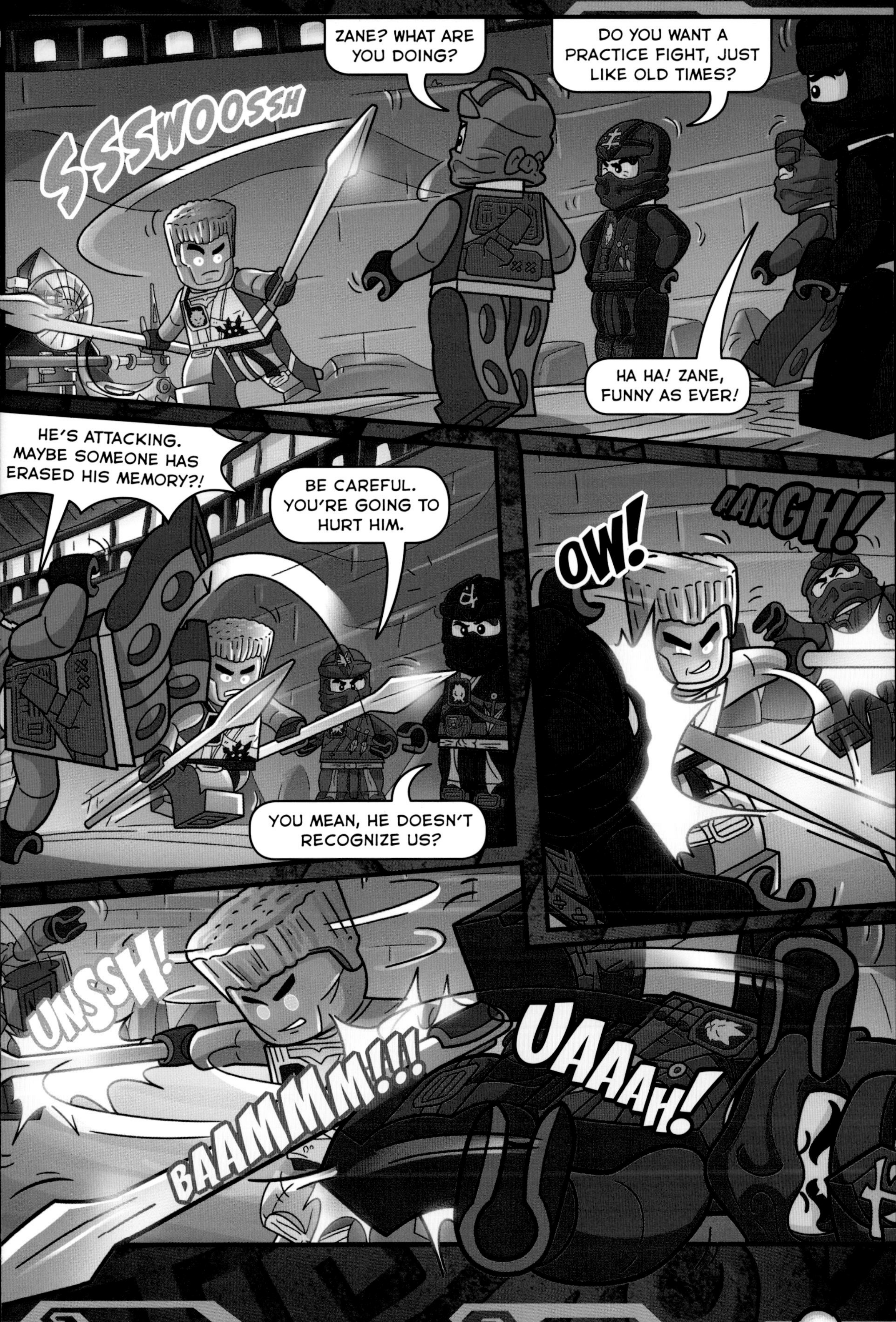
SSSWOOSSH
ZANE? WHAT ARE YOU DOING?
DO YOU WANT A PRACTICE FIGHT, JUST LIKE OLD TIMES?
HA HA! ZANE, FUNNY AS EVER!
HE'S ATTACKING. MAYBE SOMEONE HAS ERASED HIS MEMORY?!
BE CAREFUL. YOU'RE GOING TO HURT HIM.
YOU MEAN, HE DOESN'T RECOGNIZE US?
OW!
AARGH!
UNSSH!
BAAMMMM!!!
UAAAH!

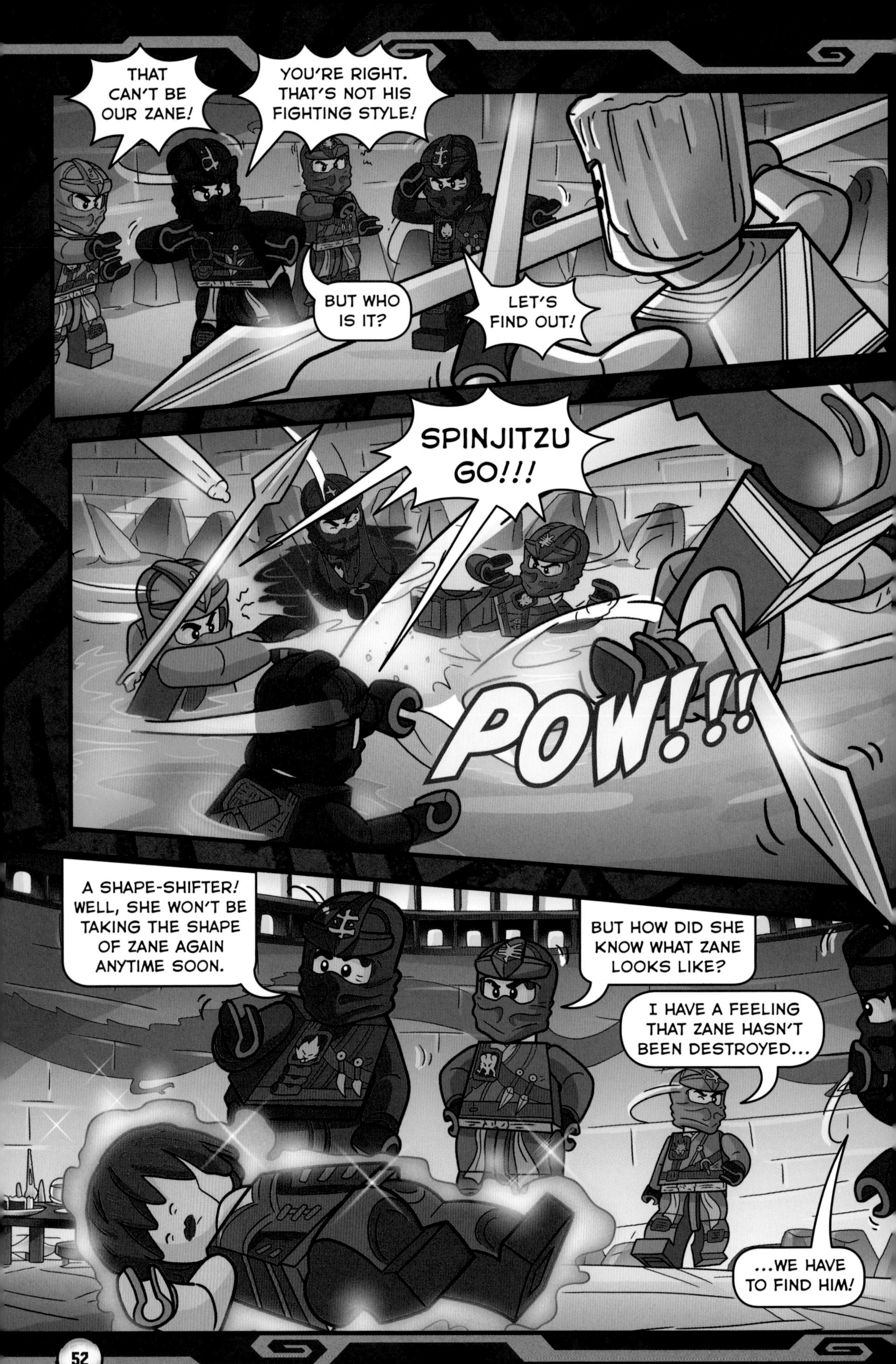
THAT CAN'T BE OUR ZANE!
YOU'RE RIGHT. THAT'S NOT HIS FIGHTING STYLE!
BUT WHO IS IT?
LET'S FIND OUT!
SPINJITZU GO!!!
POW!!!
A SHAPE-SHIFTER! WELL, SHE WON'T BE TAKING THE SHAPE OF ZANE AGAIN ANYTIME SOON.
BUT HOW DID SHE KNOW WHAT ZANE LOOKS LIKE?
I HAVE A FEELING THAT ZANE HASN'T BEEN DESTROYED...
...WE HAVE TO FIND HIM!

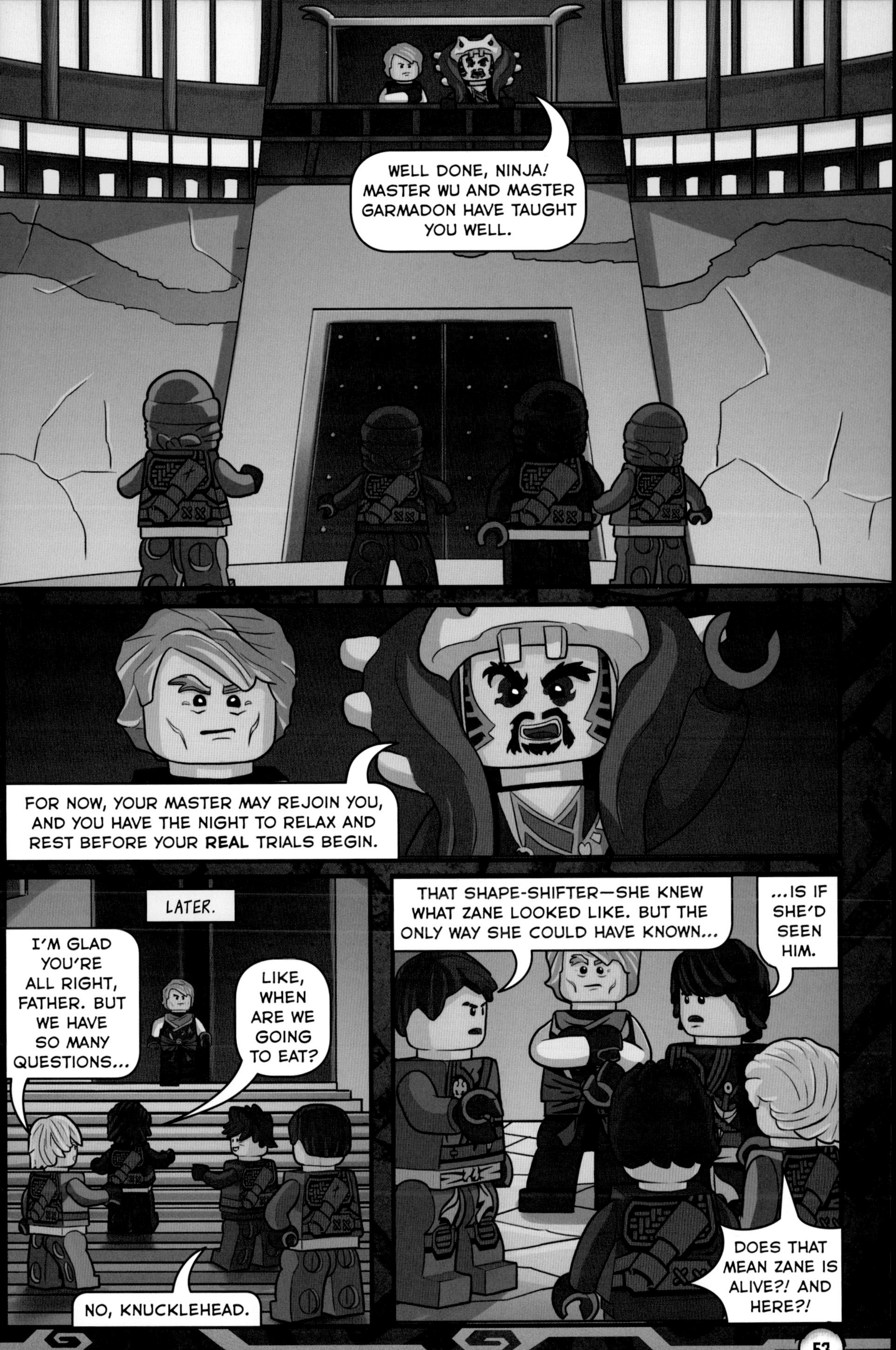
WELL DONE, NINJA! MASTER WU AND MASTER GARMADON HAVE TAUGHT YOU WELL.
FOR NOW, YOUR MASTER MAY REJOIN YOU, AND YOU HAVE THE NIGHT TO RELAX AND REST BEFORE YOUR **REAL** TRIALS BEGIN.
LATER.
I'M GLAD YOU'RE ALL RIGHT, FATHER. BUT WE HAVE SO MANY QUESTIONS...
LIKE, WHEN ARE WE GOING TO EAT?
NO, KNUCKLEHEAD.
THAT SHAPE-SHIFTER—SHE KNEW WHAT ZANE LOOKED LIKE. BUT THE ONLY WAY SHE COULD HAVE KNOWN...
...IS IF SHE'D SEEN HIM.
DOES THAT MEAN ZANE IS ALIVE?! AND HERE?!

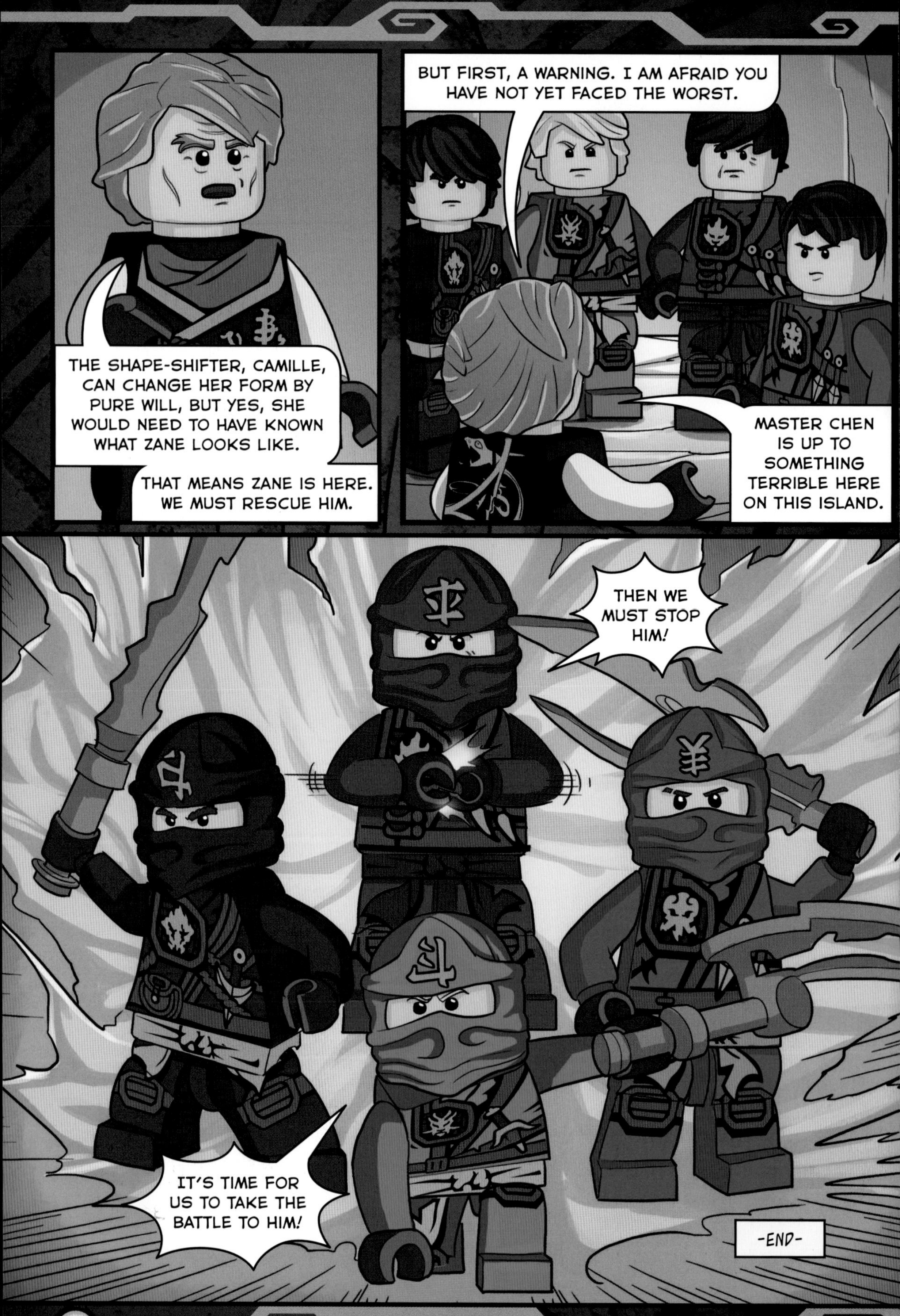
THE SHAPE-SHIFTER, CAMILLE, CAN CHANGE HER FORM BY PURE WILL, BUT YES, SHE WOULD NEED TO HAVE KNOWN WHAT ZANE LOOKS LIKE.
THAT MEANS ZANE IS HERE. WE MUST RESCUE HIM.
BUT FIRST, A WARNING. I AM AFRAID YOU HAVE NOT YET FACED THE WORST.
MASTER CHEN IS UP TO SOMETHING TERRIBLE HERE ON THIS ISLAND.
THEN WE MUST STOP HIM!
IT'S TIME FOR US TO TAKE THE BATTLE TO HIM!
-END-

THE LOST SCROLLS OF SPINJITZU

Welcome to the Ninjago World

Ninjago Island was created long ago by the First Spinjitzu Master, using the power of the Golden Weapons. Although the Ninjago world was initially a place of peace and light, evil arose in the form of the Overlord, who wished dominion over the planet. With no end to the struggle in sight, the First Spinjitzu Master took the drastic step of splitting Ninjago Island in half. The Overlord and his followers were trapped on a portion that came to be known as the Island of Darkness.

This was not the end of threats to the world. The first Serpentine War pitted humans against snake warriors. One of the First Spinjitzu Master's sons, Garmadon, was corrupted by darkness and tried to conquer the world, only to be defeated by his brother, Wu. Master Wu would go on to defend the planet against various menaces for years to come, before eventually recruiting a team of young ninja to help him.

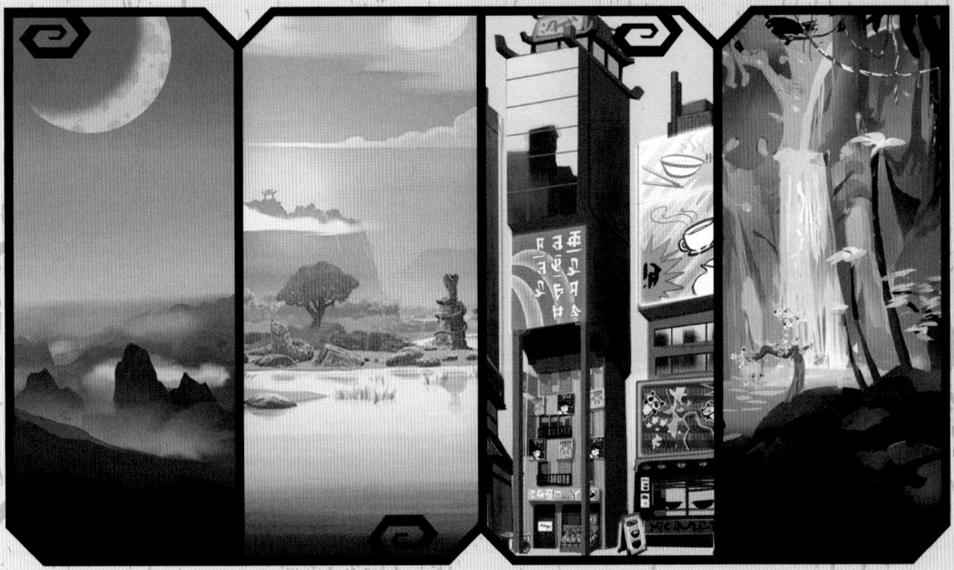

Ninjago is a geographically diverse land, with volcanoes, deserts, ice caps, dense forests and jungles, toxic bogs, and more. Only one city is known to exist—New Ninjago City—but there are long-lost cities dotting the landscape. There are also a large number of villages and farming communities.

The ninja's adventures have carried them all over the land, and they have saved Ninjago Island many times over. Time will tell what excitement the future has in store for them!

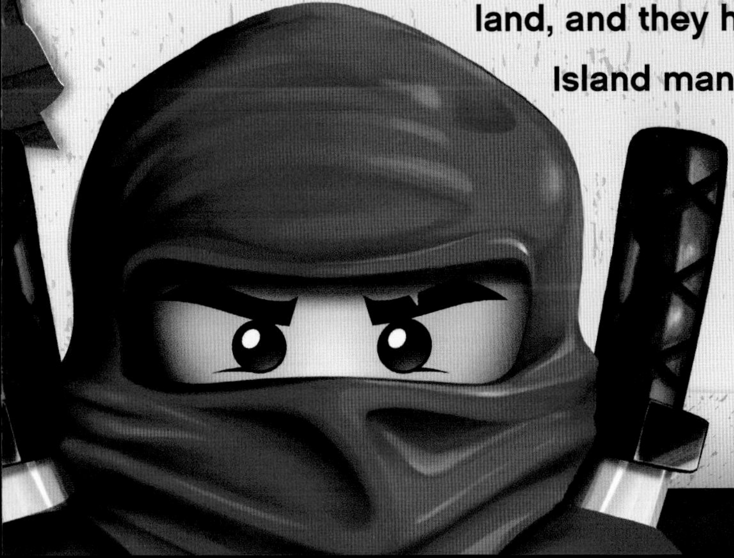

Ninjago map

1. Golden Peaks
2. Master Chen's Island
3. Ninjago City
4. Anacondrai Tomb
5. Samurai X Cave
6. Steep Wisdom Tea Farm
7. Kryptarium Prison
8. Hiroshi's Labyrinth
9. Tomb of the First Spinjitzu Master
10. Tiger Widow Island
11. Temple of Airjitzu
12. Wailing Alps
13. Corridor of Elders
14. City of Stiix
15. Spirit Coves

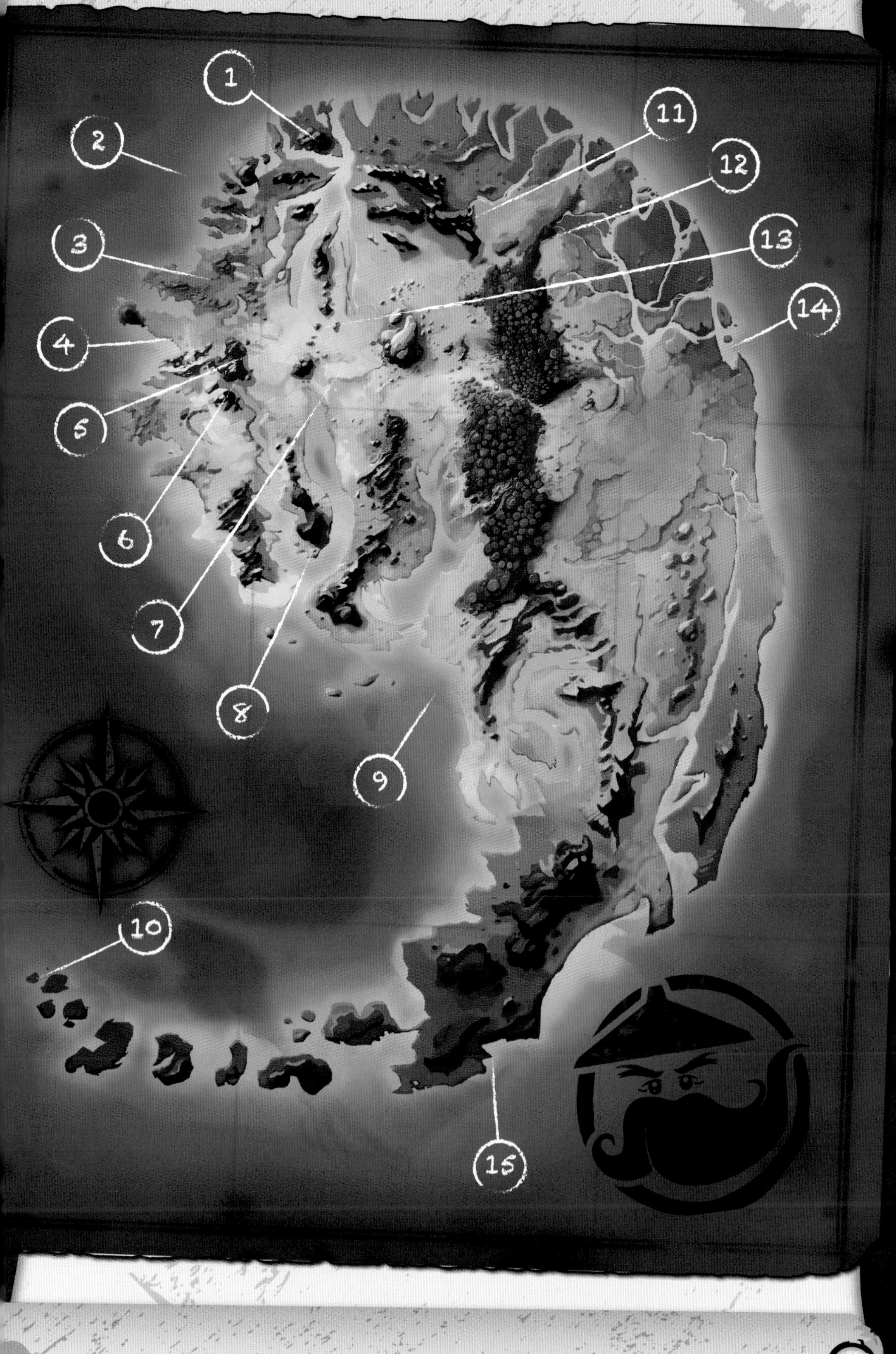
1
2
3
4
5
6
7
8
9
10
11
12
13
14
15

LOCATIONS

Mr. Chen's Noodle Houses

Mr. Chen's Noodle Houses, renowned for their many and varied types of noodle dishes, are the most popular restaurants in the Ninjago world. The diners might not enjoy themselves quite so much if they knew that Mr. Chen is actually Master Chen, an evil genius

planning to conquer the world, and that the noodles

were made by slave laborers. Then again, diners might...those noodles are awfully good.

Underground Noodle Factory

Once elemental fighters lose a match (and their powers), they find themselves trapped in Master Chen's noodle factory. This work camp is heavily guarded by Chen's henchmen. Using giant machinery, laborers work hard to make the noodles. No one had ever escaped from the noodle factory until Cole and Zane led a mass breakout of the workers.

The Corridor of Elders

The Corridor of Elders is a passage in Echo Canyon, the natural landmark that divides Ninjago Island. It is the  quickest route through the canyon and is renowned for the engravings of historical figures etched into its walls. It is the site of the final battle between the ninja and Chen's Anacondrai warriors.

Chen's Fortress

Concealed by Clouse's magic spells, Chen's secret island is home to his fortress and private army. It is considered to be impenetrable and is loaded with trapdoors, booby traps, hidden passages, and other dangers. Catacombs far beneath lead both to Chen's underground noodle work camp and the Anacondrai temple.

Anacondrai Temple

Deep inside Chen's island are the ruins of an ancient Anacondrai temple. This is where Master Chen carries out his dark ceremonies, using his staff to rob the elemental  fighters of their powers. Often, it is the last place the fighters see before they are consigned to labor in the noodle factory forever. It is also home to Clouse's pet Anacondrai snake.

HEROES

Kai

Kai and his sister, Nya, got used to taking care of themselves from an early age, so Kai still prefers to do things on his own. At first, working on a team was a challenge for him. Despite his hot temper, he has grown to become the dedicated young Ninja of Fire and the leader of the team.

Acting first and asking questions later has always been Kai's style. And for him, the lure of this tournament is the chance to prove he is better than all the other fighters. But nothing is more important than his friends. So when push comes to shove, Kai steps up to do the right thing—even when Skylor tries to distract him.

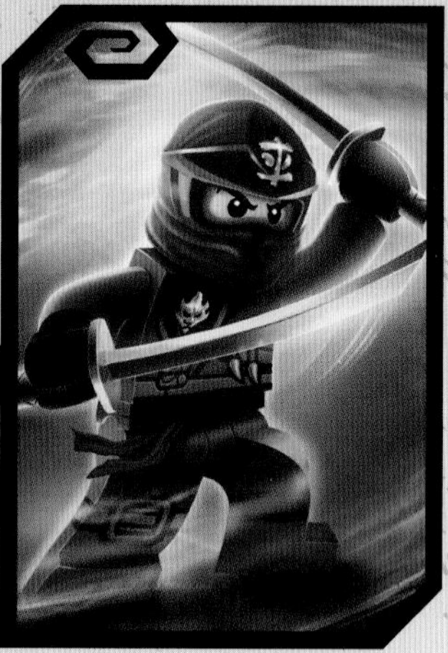

Element: Fire
Color: Red
Home Base: *Destiny's Bounty*
Weapon: Sword
Hobbies: Blacksmithing and cooking

Jay

Jay is a fast-talking, fun-loving, and inventive Ninja of Lightning. His favorite thing about being a ninja is the adventure...well, that and being around Nya, on whom he has a big crush. Jay is best known for his inventions, some of which work, some of which fail spectacularly. More than once, his gadgets have saved the day.

As the ninja head for the tournament, there is a lot of tension between Jay and Cole due to their mutual interest in Nya. Competing in the tournament only makes things worse, but eventually they realize that what they—and the team as a whole—are fighting for is more important than their personal quarrels.

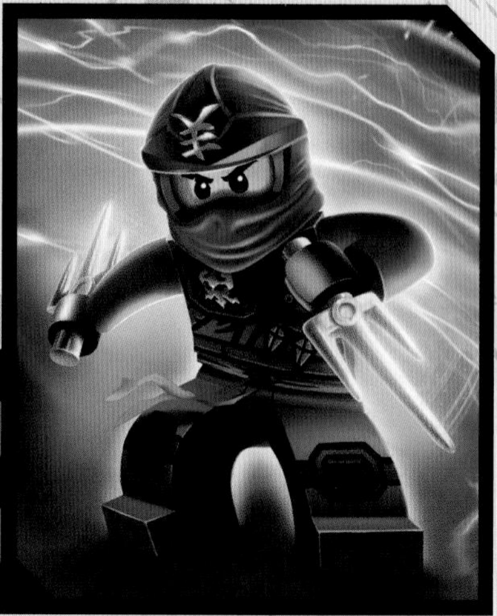

Element: Lightning
Color: Blue
Home Base: *Destiny's Bounty*
Weapon: Nunchakus
Hobbies: Inventing and tinkering

Cole

The Ninja of Earth takes the team's missions very seriously and spends a lot of time planning strategy and tactics. For that reason, he finds the dispute with Jay over Nya to be an annoying distraction at a dangerous time.

Cole has always done his best to come across as serious-minded and fearless. But it didn't take long for his friends to discover that there were things Cole was afraid of, such as dragons. Cole learned to overcome that fear and is hopeful that means he can do the same if he ever again encounters something frightening.

Element: Earth

Color: Black

Home Base: *Destiny's Bounty*

Weapon: Scythe

Hobbies: Rock climbing; dancing

Zane

Zane is a robot called a Nindroid and the Ninja of Ice. He is extremely intelligent but often struggles with things like humor. Despite this, he values his friendships with the other ninja and his relationship with an artificial intelligence named Pixal.

Zane apparently gave his life to defeat the Overlord in an earlier adventure and was believed gone forever. In truth, he was being held captive by Master Chen. By overcoming his own fears and insecurities, Zane emerges stronger than ever before as the Titanium Ninja. Reuniting with his team, he is ready to play an important role in the battles to come.

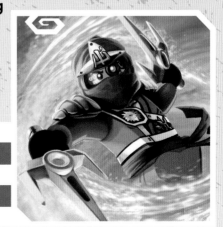

Element: Ice

Color: White

Home Base: *Destiny's Bounty*

Weapon: Shurikens

Hobbies: Working with Pixal

Lloyd

Lloyd is the son of Master Garmadon. When the ninja first met him, he was trying hard to be a villain like his father. But he eventually discovered that it is more rewarding fighting beside the ninja than against them. To Lloyd's surprise, he turned out to be the legendary Green Ninja. For a brief time, he ascended to even greater power as the Golden Ninja, but he gave those powers up for the benefit of his friends.

His age advanced by magic, Lloyd has now become one of the leaders of the team. It is his drive and his belief that Zane is still alive somewhere that keeps the ninja squad from falling apart. He succeeds in reuniting his teammates and taking on the challenge of the tournament, even though he knows that every fighter wants the chance to take down the Green Ninja.

Element: Energy

Color: Green

Home Base: *Destiny's Bounty*

Weapon: Katana

Hobbies: Training; trying to build a relationship with his father

Nya

For too long, Nya has been known as "Kai's sister" or "Jay's girlfriend." She has longed to carve out an identity for herself and be a valuable part of the team. To accomplish this, she secretly built the Samurai X armor and went into action without any of the ninja being any the wiser—at least not until Kai found out.

Nya is both inventive and resourceful. When the ninja disappear on Chen's island, Nya is the one who is able to track down where they are. She even manages to infiltrate Chen's operation for a brief time. Nya hopes that she has proven herself to be considered for ninja training.

Element: None...yet!

Color: Red

Home Base: *Destiny's Bounty*

Weapon: : Golden Nick Daggers; Samurai X armor

Hobbies: Mechanics

Master Wu

One of the two sons of the First Spinjitzu Master, Wu is ancient and very wise. He fought alone for centuries against many terrible villains in order to defend Ninjago. But he eventually realized that he could not continue to do the job alone. He recruited four young men and trained them to be ninja. With his guidance, they not only learned the fighting skills they needed, they also learned how to be heroes.

As time has passed, Master Wu has begun to contemplate retirement. He believes that he can leave the fate of Ninjago safely in the hands of his students. But before he can do so, he has to aid them one more time to defeat a villain as evil as any he has ever faced.

Element: Creation
Color: White
Home Base: *Destiny's Bounty*
Weapon: Nin-jo
Hobbies: Drinking tea

Master Garmadon

The brother of Master Wu, Garmadon was corrupted in his youth and became consumed by evil. He was banished to the Underworld for thousands of years by Wu, but he returned in recent times to battle his brother and the ninja team repeatedly. Finally cured of the darkness inside him, Garmadon took a vow of peace and took over the training of the team. He also worked to rebuild his relationship with his son, Lloyd, although so much time apart made it difficult.

During the battle with the Anacondrai warriors, the spirits of the original Anacondrai had to be freed from the Cursed Realm if the ninja had any hope of winning. Garmadon realized that, in order for this to happen, someone would have to take their place in that otherworldly realm. He made the sacrifice to save his world and his friends. A statue of him now graces the Corridor of Elders.

Element: Creation
Color: Black
Home Base: *Destiny's Bounty*
Weapon: Nin-Jo
Hobbies: Meditation; trying to build a
relationship with Lloyd

VILLAINS

Master Chen

Mr. Chen is best known throughout the Ninjago world as the owner of a chain of successful noodle houses. What few realize is that Mr. Chen is in reality Master Chen, an evil mastermind with plans to start a second Serpentine War.

Ages ago, Chen was a respected master with a "win at all costs" philosophy. His double-dealing led to a war between humans and the Serpentine, which eventually resulted in Chen being exiled to a remote island. There he began to build a criminal empire, using his noodle houses as a front for illegal activities.

Chen's ultimate plan is to transform his followers into Anacondrai warriors and conquer the Ninjago world. To do this, he needs samples of every elemental power. He stages a Tournament of Elements at his island fortress to lure warriors there, only to steal their elemental abilities from them. With those energies, he turns his minions into true Anacondrai serpents.

Leading his army of warriors off the island, Chen succeeds in conquering a large portion of Ninjago, despite opposition by the ninja. He is finally defeated when the heroes succeed in releasing the spirits of honorable Anacondrai from the Cursed Realm. These spirits, angered by Chen's actions, banish him and his followers to the Cursed Realm forever.

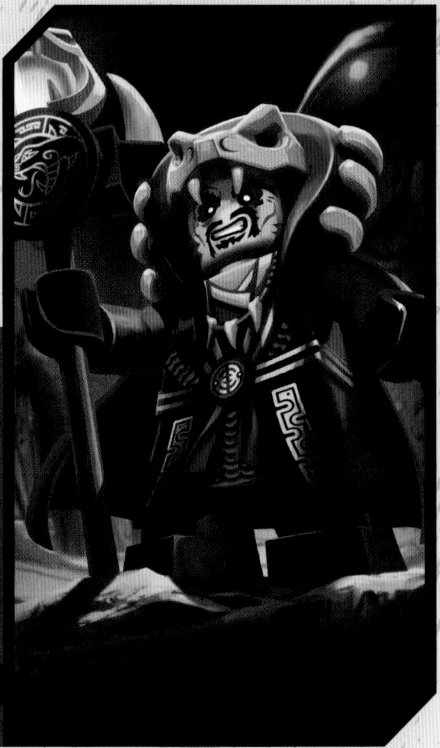

Personality: Chen loves to manipulate others and turns his enemies against each other in order to weaken them. He is ruthless, cunning, and shows no mercy to those who oppose him.

Weapon: Staff of Elements

Hobbies: World conquest

Clouse

Clouse is a powerful sorcerer and Master Chen's second in command. He uses dark magic to keep the ninja from winning in the Tournament of Elements and is completely devoted to the service of his master.

In his youth, Clouse was a student of Chen's, as was Garmadon. Clouse lost out on the chance to be favored by Chen when Garmadon cheated him out of a victory. Clouse has harbored a hatred of Garmadon ever since.

Clouse has been exiled to the Cursed Realm by Garmadon.

Personality: Clouse is bitter, vengeful, and power-hungry. He sees his service to Chen as the best way to achieve what he has always dreamed of.

Weapon: None, but he is an adept spell caster

Hobbies: Studying magic

The Other Anacondrai

Chen's gang of criminals is transformed into Anacondrai warriors as part of the villain's plan to conquer Ninjago. Some of his henchmen include:

Zugu

A former sumo wrestler, later a general in Chen's army. This armored warrior is particularly skilled with a crossbow.

Eyezor

Chen's other general, the one-eyed Eyezor doesn't talk much, but he and his Anacondrai sword are plenty intimidating.

Kapau and Chope

These two best friends don't have much in terms of skill or talent, but they are determined to move up in Chen's army. Kapau and Chope use Anacondrai blades as weapons.

Pythor

In a strange twist of fate, the battle against Chen forced the ninja to ally with one of their worst enemies, Pythor. The last survivor of the Anacondrai tribe, Pythor first met the ninja when he was trying to unite the other Serpentine tribes and unleash the horrible Great Devourer on Ninjago. Later, he allied with the Overlord in yet another plot to conquer the world and destroy the ninja.

This time, though, the hunter is the hunted. Chen needs Pythor to complete his spell to turn his followers into Anacondrai, so Pythor needs the ninja's help to survive. In the end, it is Pythor who discovers that, by releasing the spirits of his deceased tribemates from the Cursed Realm, Chen's false Anacondrai can be defeated. Pythor survives the final battle with Chen, but where he may be now is unknown.

Element: None
Color: Purple and white
Home Base: None
Weapon: Sword
Hobbies: Lying; plotting; betrayal; survival

THE ELEMENTAL FIGHTERS

Master Chen's tournament draws elemental warriors from all over the world to his island. They are all descendants of the Elemental Masters, powerful beings who served as guardians of the First Spinjitzu Master long ago. All of them are stripped of their powers during the tournament by Master Chen with one possible exception: Skylor was turned back into human form, but it is unknown if she still has her powers.

Ash—Master of Smoke

Ash can transform himself into a cloud of smoke at will, appearing and disappearing all over and making it almost impossible to lay a finger on him. His only known defeat was at the hands of Kai.

Skylor—Master of Absorbtion

The daughter of Master Chen, Skylor is able to absorb other elemental fighters' powers. She eventually turns against her father and becomes an ally of the ninja.

Karlof—Master of Metal

Karlof has the power to turn his body into metal and throw powerhouse punches. He is the first fighter to lose in the tournament when he fails to capture one of the Jade Blades needed to qualify for matches.

Griffin Turner—Master of Speed

Super fast, Griffin is one of the more famous elemental fighters and also something of a show-off. He's one of the first to ally with the ninja.

Jacob Pevsner—Master of Sound

Although Jacob is blind, he can use his sound power to "see" the body heat of those around him. He loses to Skylor in the tournament.

Mr. Pale—Master of Light

Mr. Pale can bend light around his body, making himself invisible. Already shy and quiet, most people don't notice him even when he can be seen.

Shade—Master of Shadows

Shade has the power to travel unseen in the shadows. Very much a loner, Shade trusts no one. At one point, he is falsely accused of being a spy for Master Chen.

Tox—Master of Poison

Able to channel various venoms through her system, Tox is definitely a fighter you won't ever forget. She loses in the tournament to Shade.

Bolobo—Master of Nature

Bolobo is a good-natured sort and one of the older fighters in the tournament. His favored weapon is a staff.

Neuro—Master of Mind

Neuro has telepathic powers, allowing him to anticipate an opponent's next move. He can also use his abilities to give his foes headaches.

Gravis—Master of Gravity

Able to control one of the fundamental forces of the universe, Gravis can make objects lighter or heavier, walk on walls and ceilings, and more.

Camille—Master of Form

Camille is a shape-shifter. She was defeated by Lloyd Garmadon in a Thunderblades skating match.

POWERFUL OBJECTS

Jade Blades

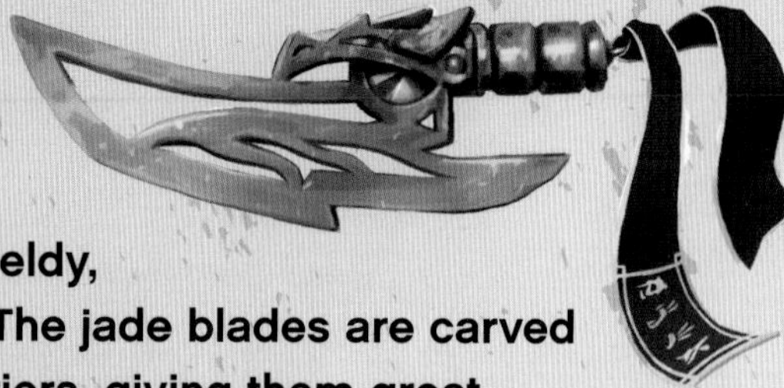

The jade blades are the prizes in the Tournament of Elements. Anyone who wins a match gets a blade. Although they are a bit unwieldy, they are quite useful as weapons. The jade blades are carved from the bones of Anacondrai warriors, giving them great symbolic significance to Master Chen.

The Book of Spells

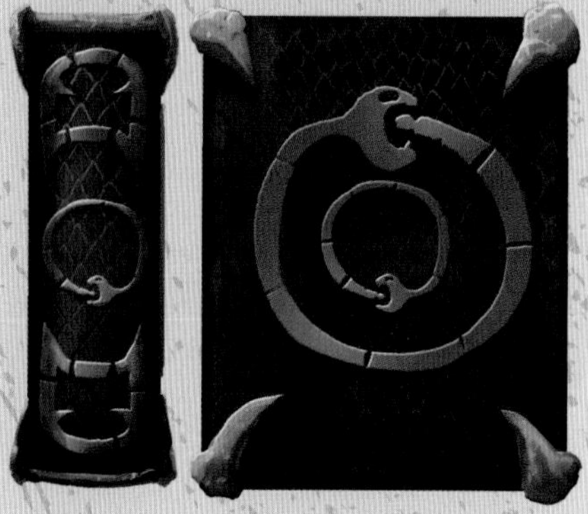

Clouse's most prized possession, The Book of Spells, is a volume of dark magic. The sorcerer uses the spells inscribed on its pages to empower himself and strike at the ninja. The most powerful spell in the book is the Spell of Transformation, which will enable Chen and his followers to turn themselves into Anacondrai warriors.

The Staff of Elements

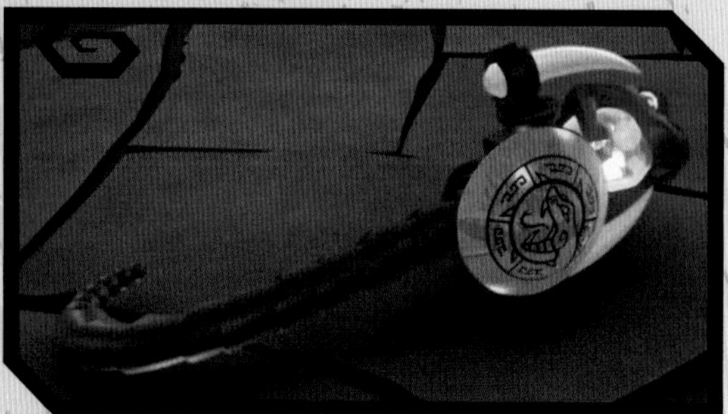

Master Chen's chosen weapon was forged in the Crystal Caves on his island. It has the ability to absorb the elemental powers of each fallen fighter and then unleash them again. It is instrumental in the transformation of Chen and his followers, since a sample of every known elemental power is needed to make the spell work.

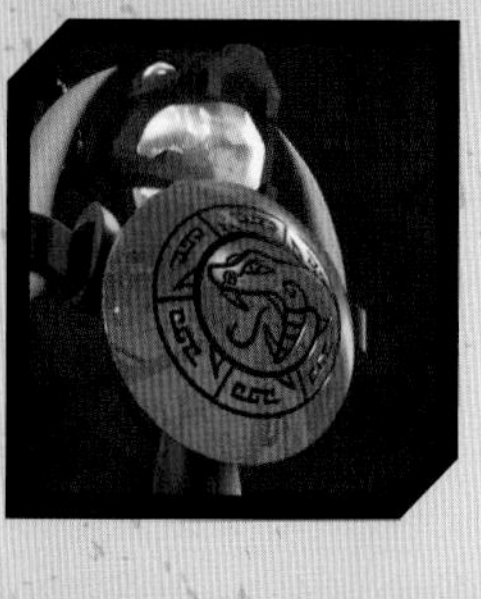

CAN YOU DECODE THE SECRET MESSAGE?

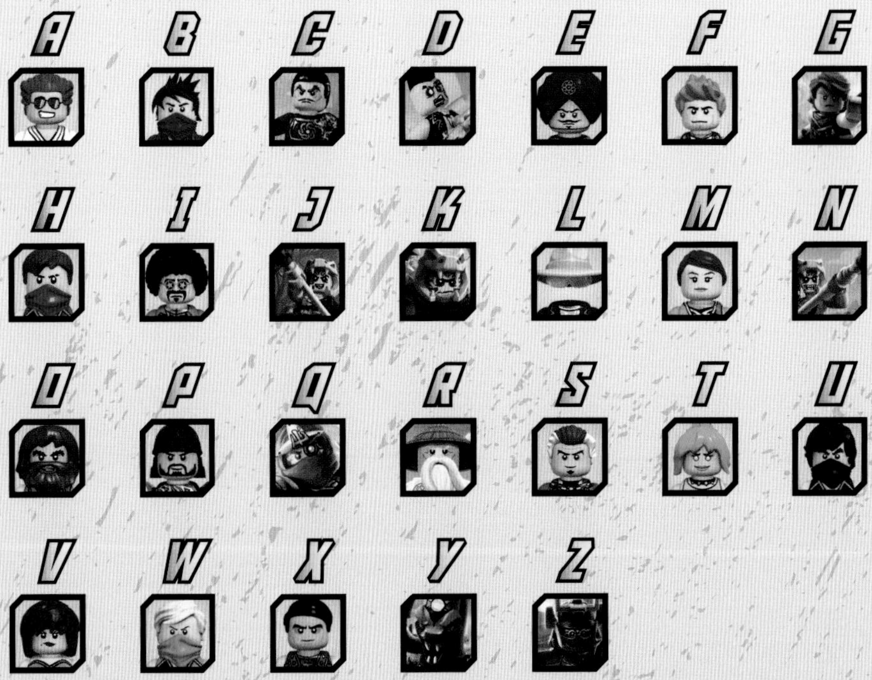
A B C D E F G
H I J K L M N
O P Q R S T U
V W X Y Z

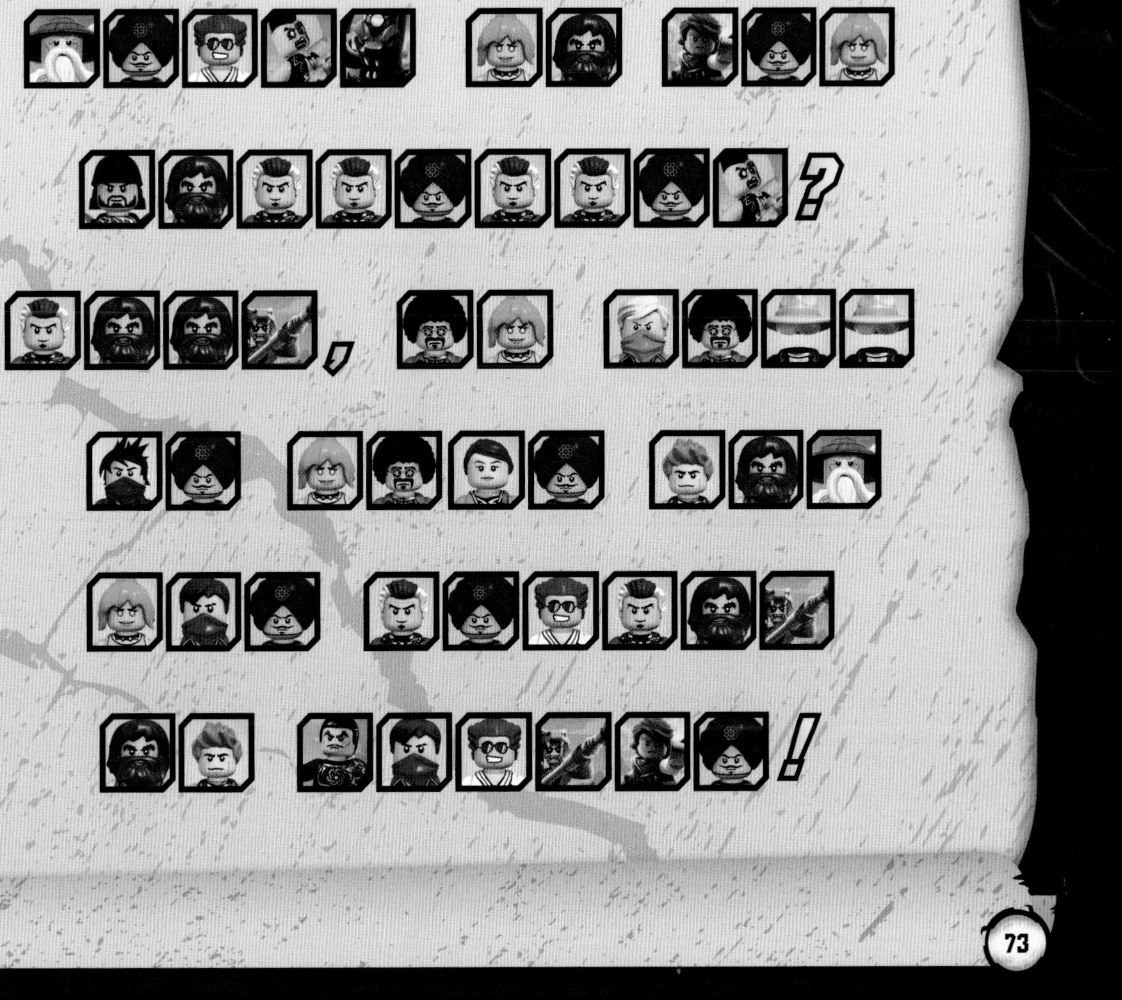

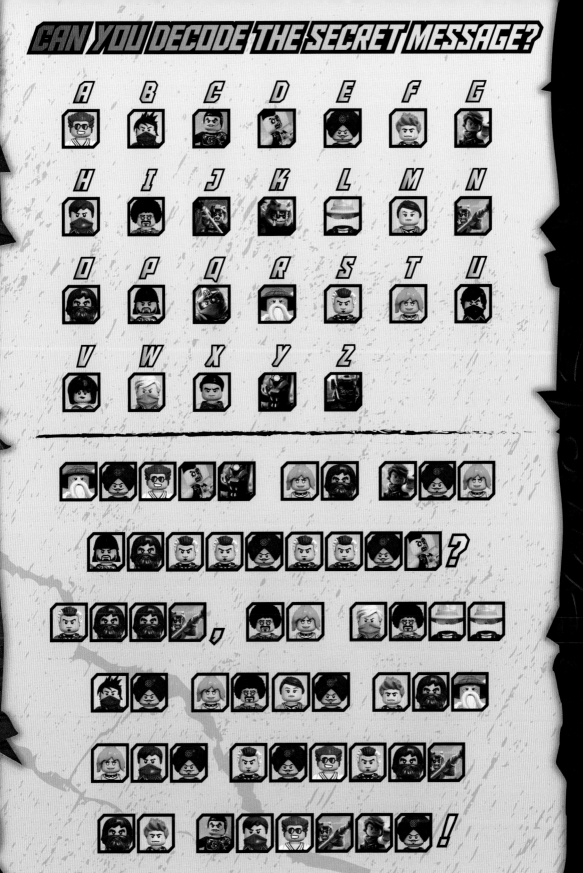

LEGO NINJAGO™

Masters of Spinjitzu

GHOST NINJA

Story and art by Blue Ocean Entertainment AG

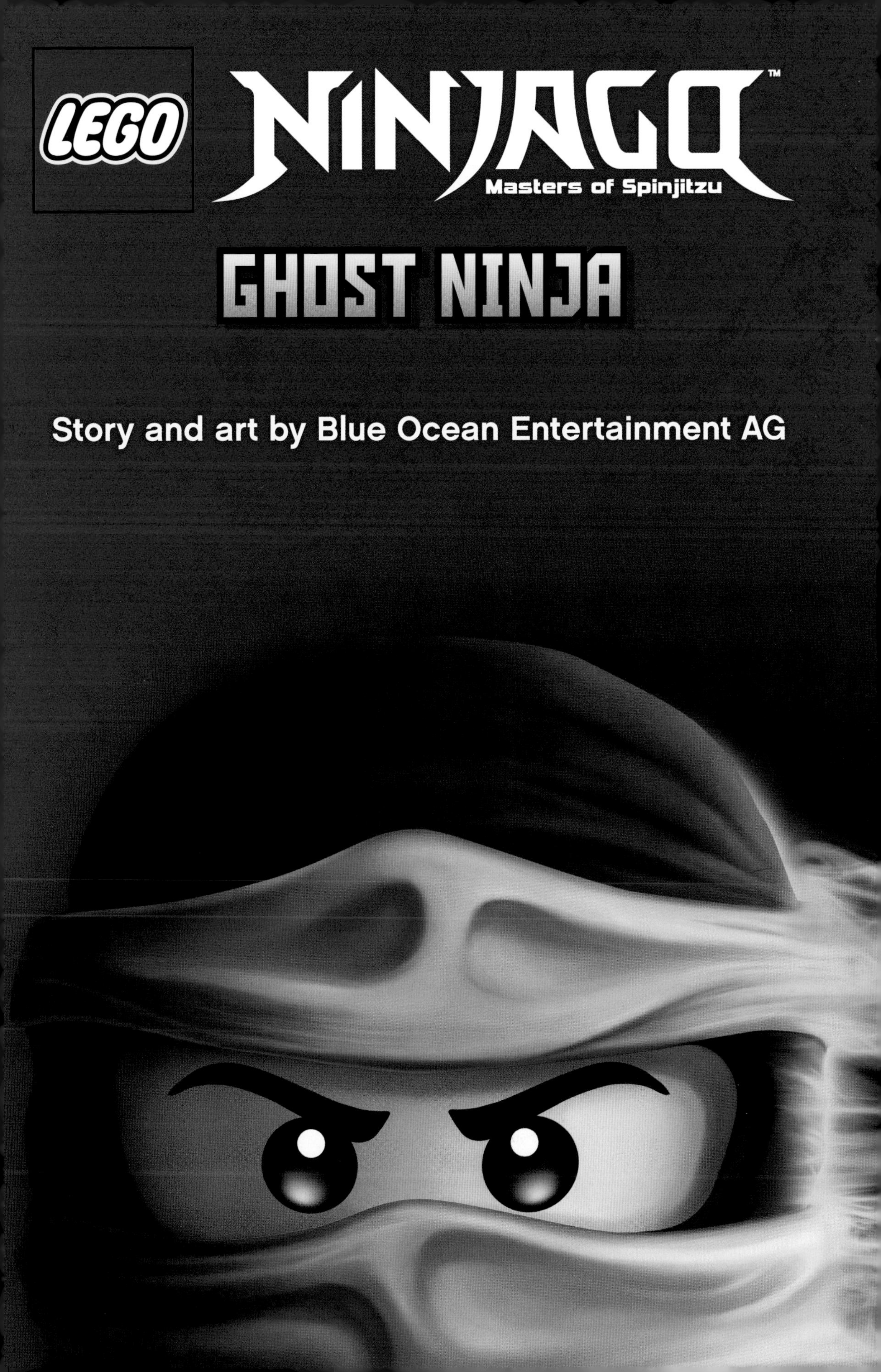

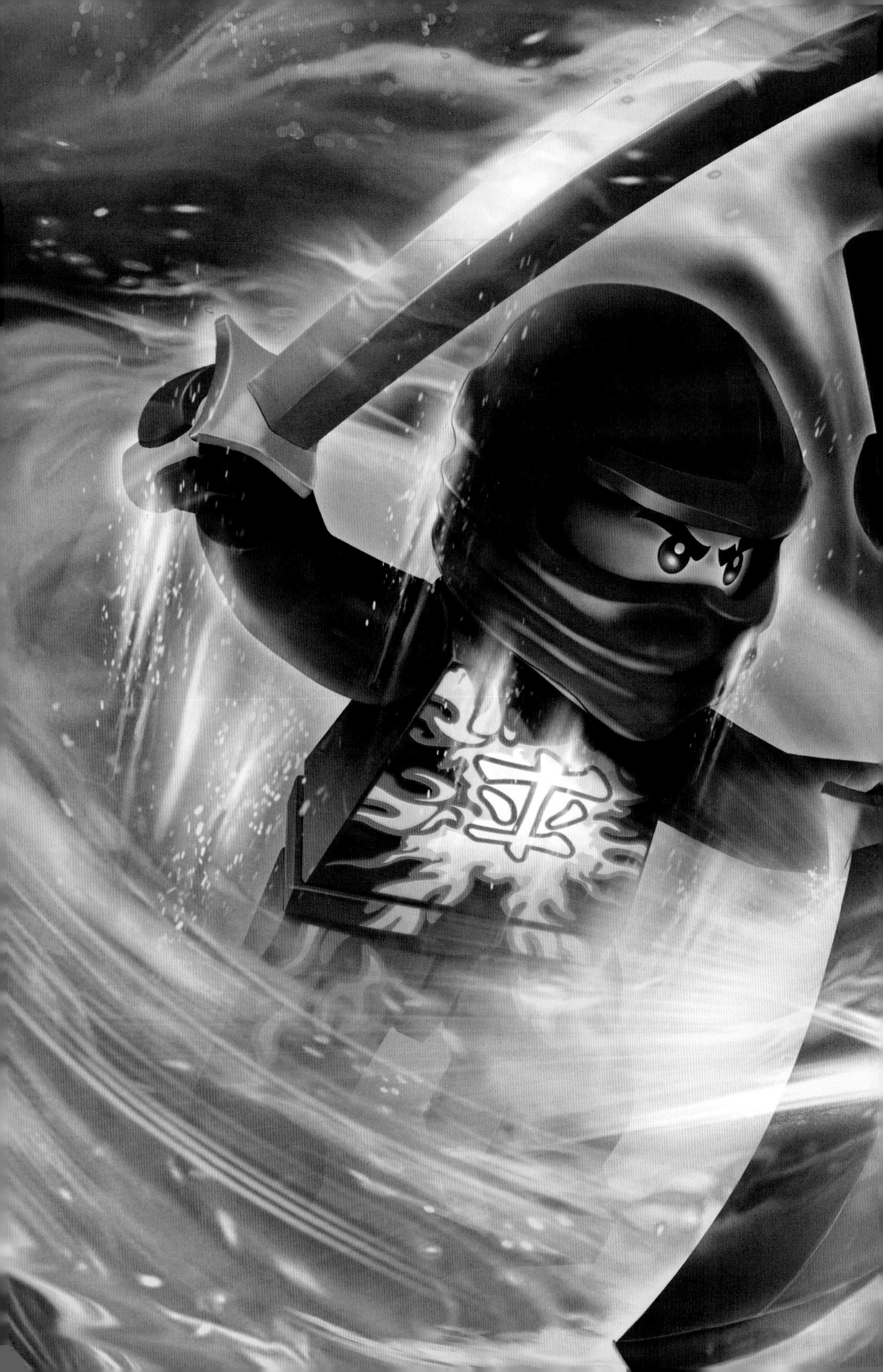

GHOST NINJA

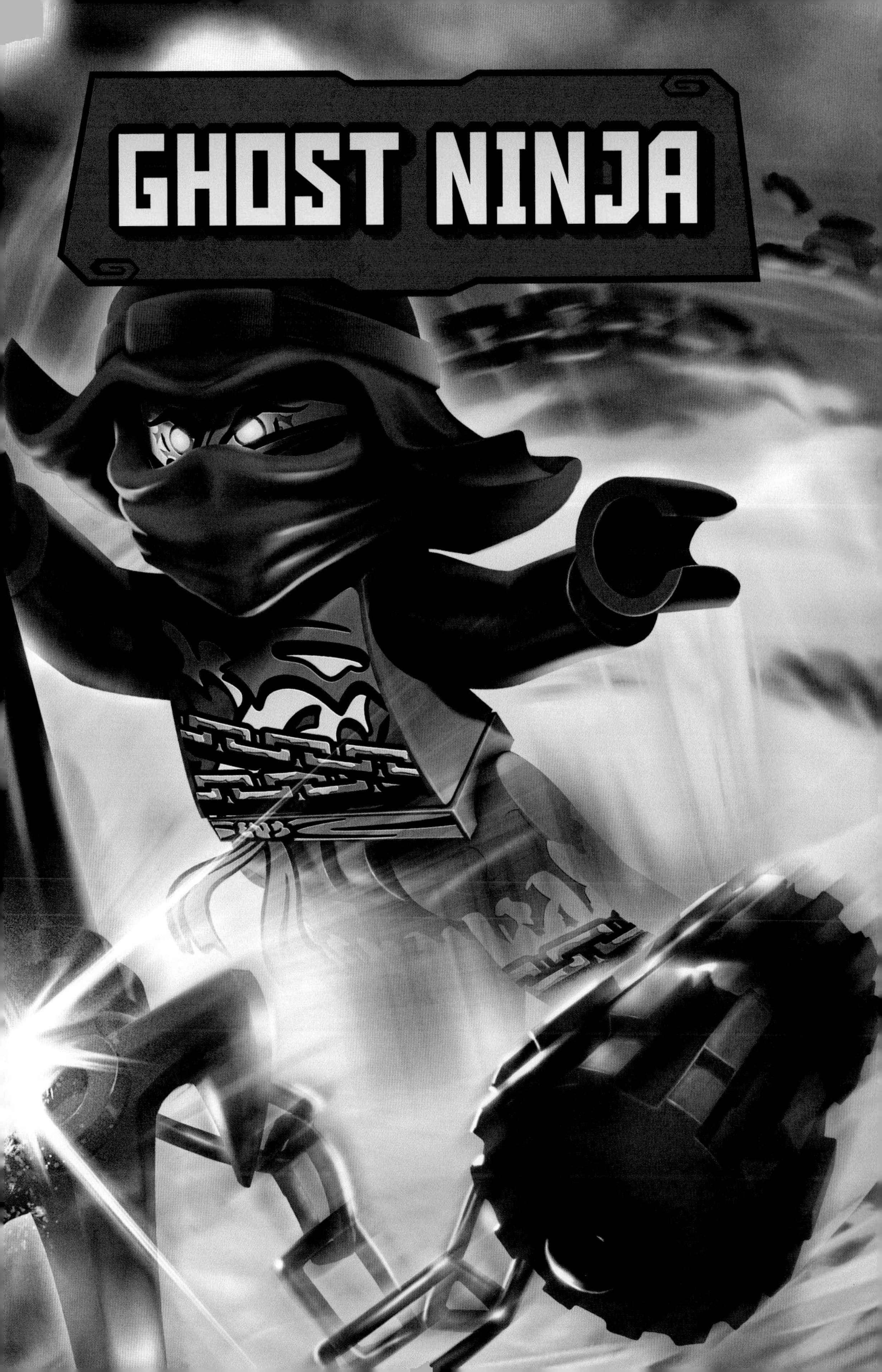

It is a Season of Change...

Since defeating Master Chen and his army in the Tournament of Elements, the ninja have never been more united. Yet Lloyd mourns the loss of his father to the Cursed Realm and questions his path ahead. Kai makes a solemn promise to look after Lloyd, as Nya looked after Kai upon their parents' demise. But that promise is put into jeopardy when a cold wind blows through Ninjago...

The cursed spirit of Morro—the Master of Wind, who also happens to be Master Wu's first pupil—possesses Lloyd. Now, without the aid of their elemental powers, the remaining ninja must square off against their brother, the Green Ninja. The good and the bad race to find the Lost Tomb of the First Spinjitzu Master, which holds a powerful relic called the Realm Crystal, which can not only affect Ninjago, but also other hidden realms the ninja have yet to discover...

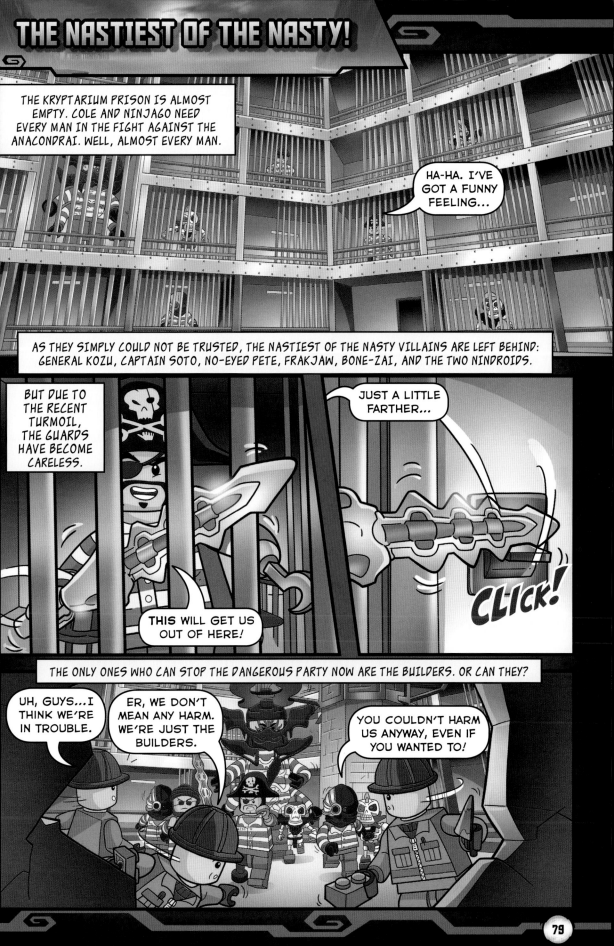

THE NASTIEST OF THE NASTY!

THE KRYPTARIUM PRISON IS ALMOST EMPTY. COLE AND NINJAGO NEED EVERY MAN IN THE FIGHT AGAINST THE ANACONDRAI. WELL, ALMOST EVERY MAN.

HA-HA. I'VE GOT A FUNNY FEELING...

AS THEY SIMPLY COULD NOT BE TRUSTED, THE NASTIEST OF THE NASTY VILLAINS ARE LEFT BEHIND: GENERAL KOZU, CAPTAIN SOTO, NO-EYED PETE, FRAKJAW, BONE-ZAI, AND THE TWO NINDROIDS.

BUT DUE TO THE RECENT TURMOIL, THE GUARDS HAVE BECOME CARELESS.

JUST A LITTLE FARTHER...

THIS WILL GET US OUT OF HERE!

CLICK!

THE ONLY ONES WHO CAN STOP THE DANGEROUS PARTY NOW ARE THE BUILDERS. OR CAN THEY?

UH, GUYS...I THINK WE'RE IN TROUBLE.

ER, WE DON'T MEAN ANY HARM. WE'RE JUST THE BUILDERS.

YOU COULDN'T HARM US ANYWAY, EVEN IF YOU WANTED TO!

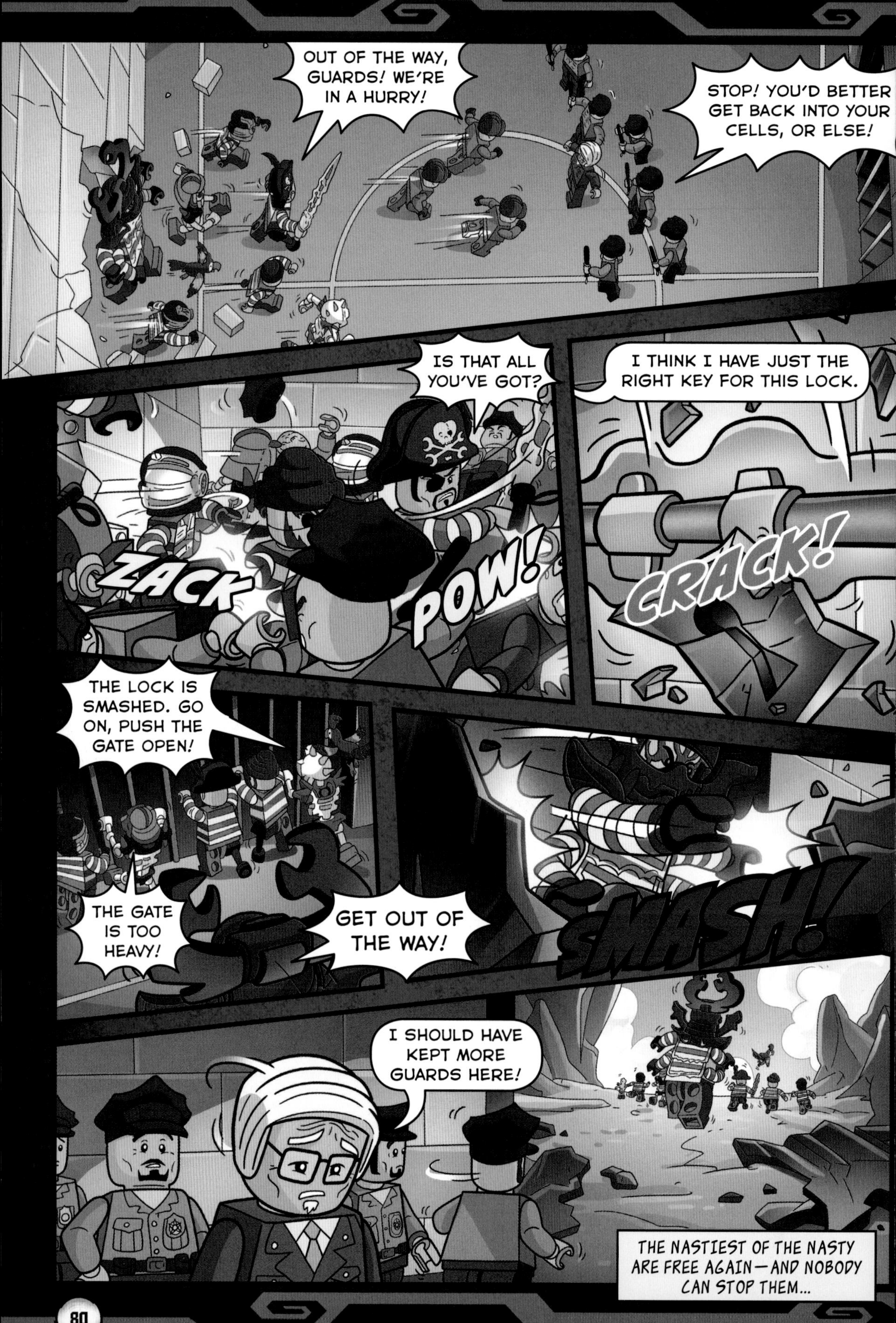
OUT OF THE WAY, GUARDS! WE'RE IN A HURRY!
STOP! YOU'D BETTER GET BACK INTO YOUR CELLS, OR ELSE!
IS THAT ALL YOU'VE GOT?
ZACK
POW!
I THINK I HAVE JUST THE RIGHT KEY FOR THIS LOCK.
CRACK!
THE LOCK IS SMASHED. GO ON, PUSH THE GATE OPEN!
THE GATE IS TOO HEAVY!
GET OUT OF THE WAY!
SMASH!
I SHOULD HAVE KEPT MORE GUARDS HERE!
THE NASTIEST OF THE NASTY ARE FREE AGAIN—AND NOBODY CAN STOP THEM...

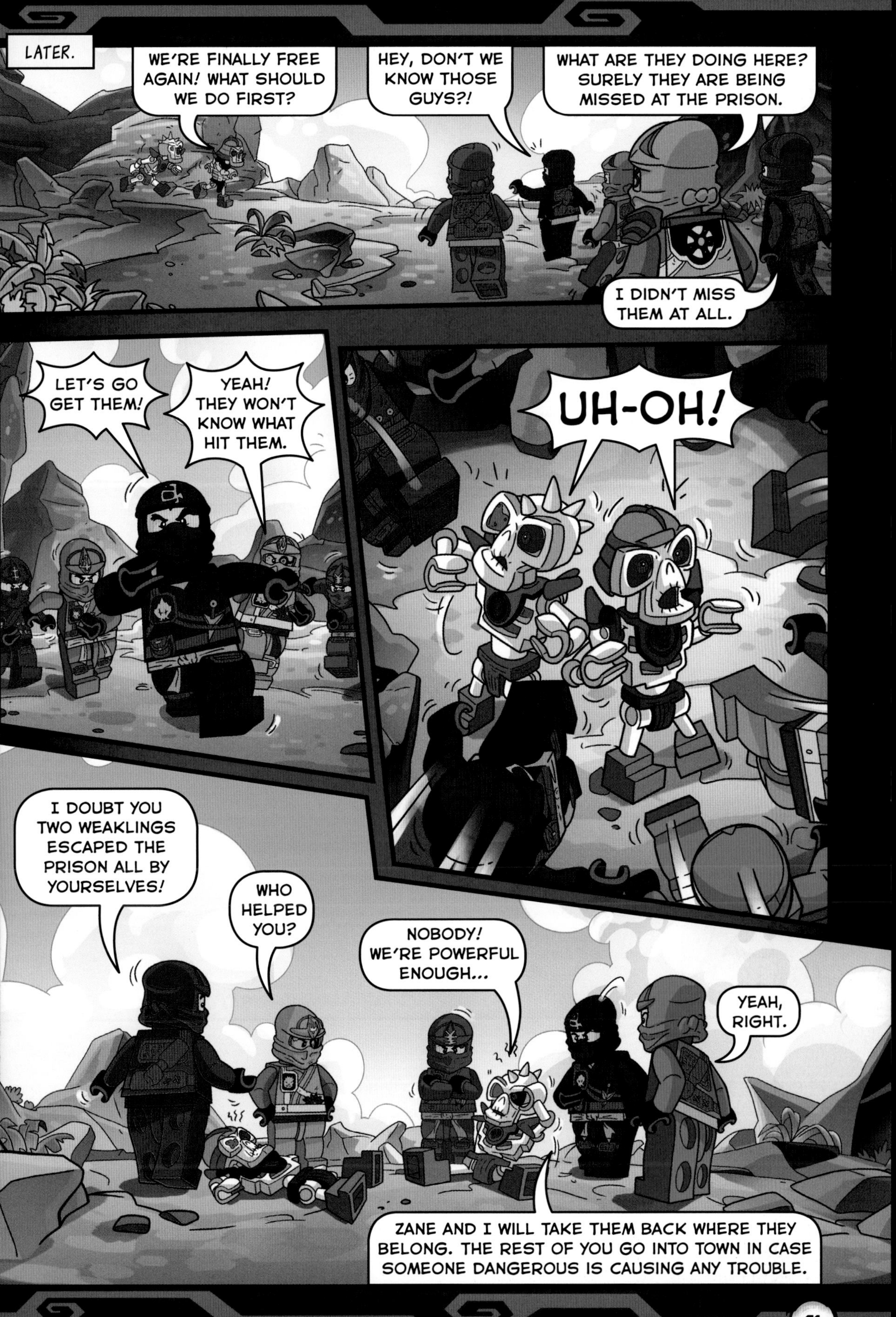
LATER.
WE'RE FINALLY FREE AGAIN! WHAT SHOULD WE DO FIRST?
HEY, DON'T WE KNOW THOSE GUYS?!
WHAT ARE THEY DOING HERE? SURELY THEY ARE BEING MISSED AT THE PRISON.
I DIDN'T MISS THEM AT ALL.
LET'S GO GET THEM!
YEAH! THEY WON'T KNOW WHAT HIT THEM.
UH-OH!
I DOUBT YOU TWO WEAKLINGS ESCAPED THE PRISON ALL BY YOURSELVES!
WHO HELPED YOU?
NOBODY! WE'RE POWERFUL ENOUGH...
YEAH, RIGHT.
ZANE AND I WILL TAKE THEM BACK WHERE THEY BELONG. THE REST OF YOU GO INTO TOWN IN CASE SOMEONE DANGEROUS IS CAUSING ANY TROUBLE.

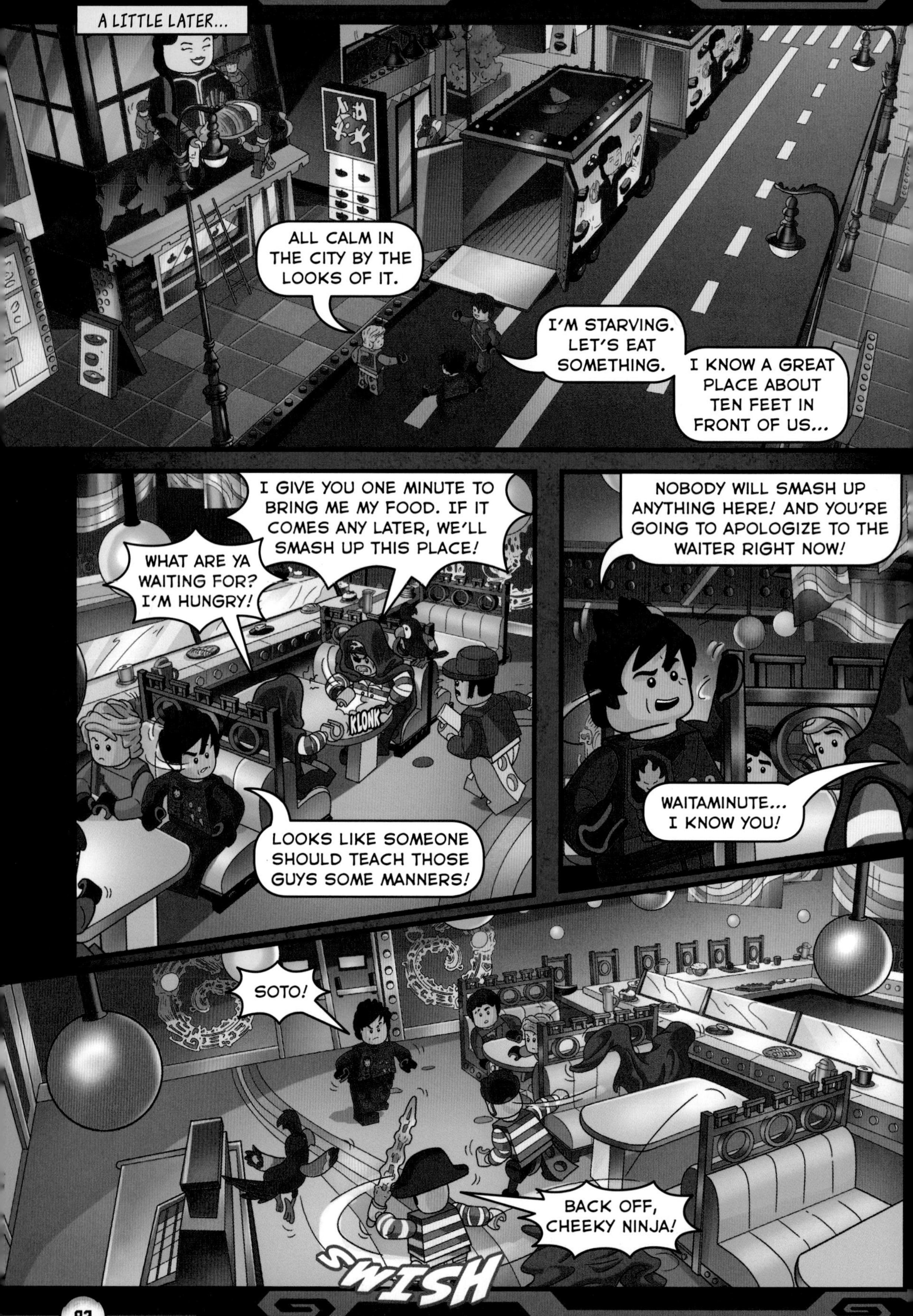
A LITTLE LATER...
ALL CALM IN THE CITY BY THE LOOKS OF IT.
I'M STARVING. LET'S EAT SOMETHING.
I KNOW A GREAT PLACE ABOUT TEN FEET IN FRONT OF US...
I GIVE YOU ONE MINUTE TO BRING ME MY FOOD. IF IT COMES ANY LATER, WE'LL SMASH UP THIS PLACE!
WHAT ARE YA WAITING FOR? I'M HUNGRY!
KLONK
LOOKS LIKE SOMEONE SHOULD TEACH THOSE GUYS SOME MANNERS!
NOBODY WILL SMASH UP ANYTHING HERE! AND YOU'RE GOING TO APOLOGIZE TO THE WAITER RIGHT NOW!
WAITAMINUTE... I KNOW YOU!
SOTO!
BACK OFF, CHEEKY NINJA!
SWISH

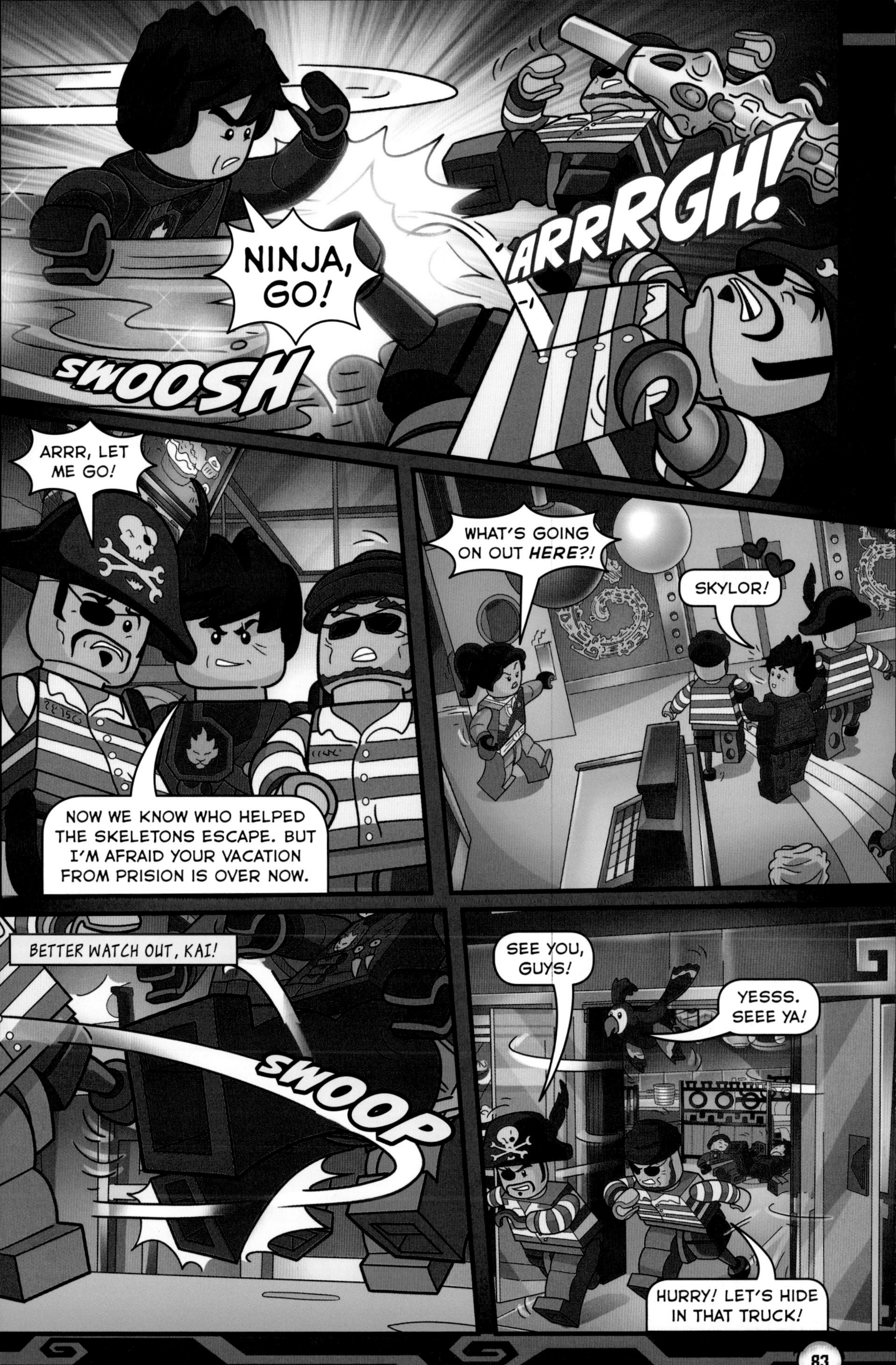
NINJA, GO!
ARRRGH!
SWOOSH
ARRR, LET ME GO!
NOW WE KNOW WHO HELPED THE SKELETONS ESCAPE. BUT I'M AFRAID YOUR VACATION FROM PRISION IS OVER NOW.
WHAT'S GOING ON OUT HERE?!
SKYLOR!
BETTER WATCH OUT, KAI!
SWOOP
SEE YOU, GUYS!
YESSS. SEEE YA!
HURRY! LET'S HIDE IN THAT TRUCK!

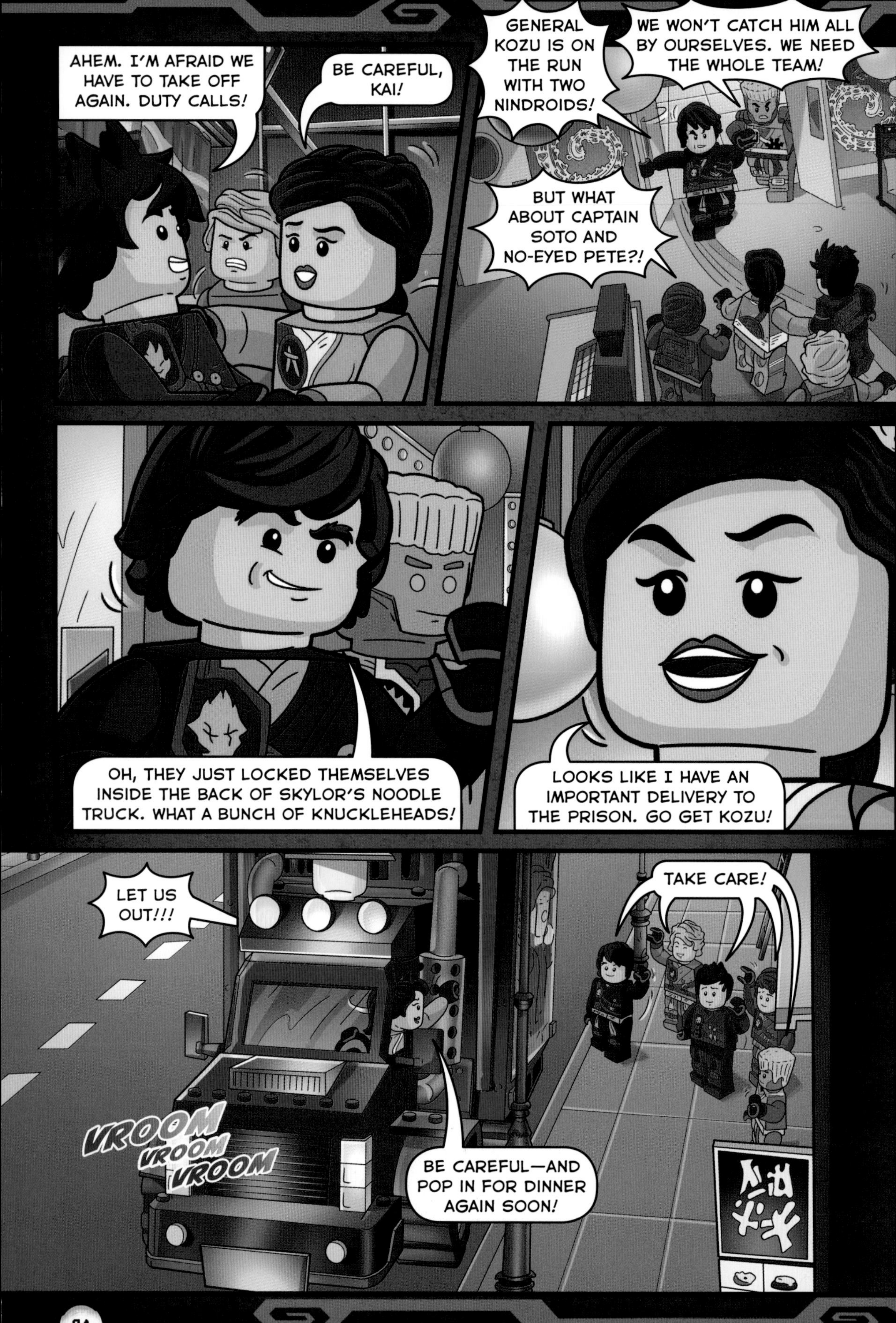
AHEM. I'M AFRAID WE HAVE TO TAKE OFF AGAIN. DUTY CALLS!
BE CAREFUL, KAI!
GENERAL KOZU IS ON THE RUN WITH TWO NINDROIDS!
WE WON'T CATCH HIM ALL BY OURSELVES. WE NEED THE WHOLE TEAM!
BUT WHAT ABOUT CAPTAIN SOTO AND NO-EYED PETE?!
OH, THEY JUST LOCKED THEMSELVES INSIDE THE BACK OF SKYLOR'S NOODLE TRUCK. WHAT A BUNCH OF KNUCKLEHEADS!
LOOKS LIKE I HAVE AN IMPORTANT DELIVERY TO THE PRISON. GO GET KOZU!
LET US OUT!!!
TAKE CARE!
VROOM
VROOM
VROOM
BE CAREFUL—AND POP IN FOR DINNER AGAIN SOON!

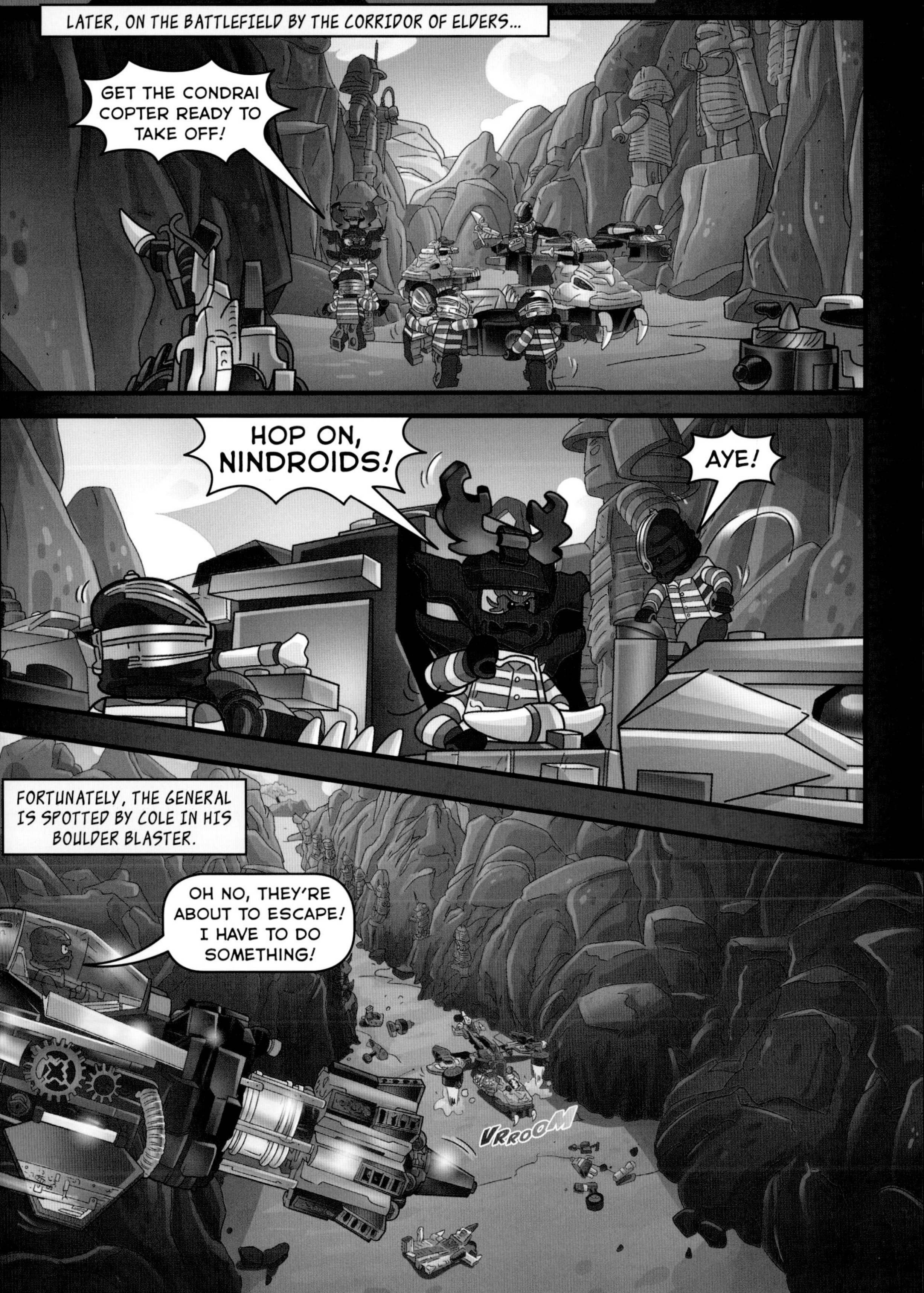
LATER, ON THE BATTLEFIELD BY THE CORRIDOR OF ELDERS...
GET THE CONDRAI COPTER READY TO TAKE OFF!
HOP ON, NINDROIDS!
AYE!
FORTUNATELY, THE GENERAL IS SPOTTED BY COLE IN HIS BOULDER BLASTER.
OH NO, THEY'RE ABOUT TO ESCAPE! I HAVE TO DO SOMETHING!
VRROOM

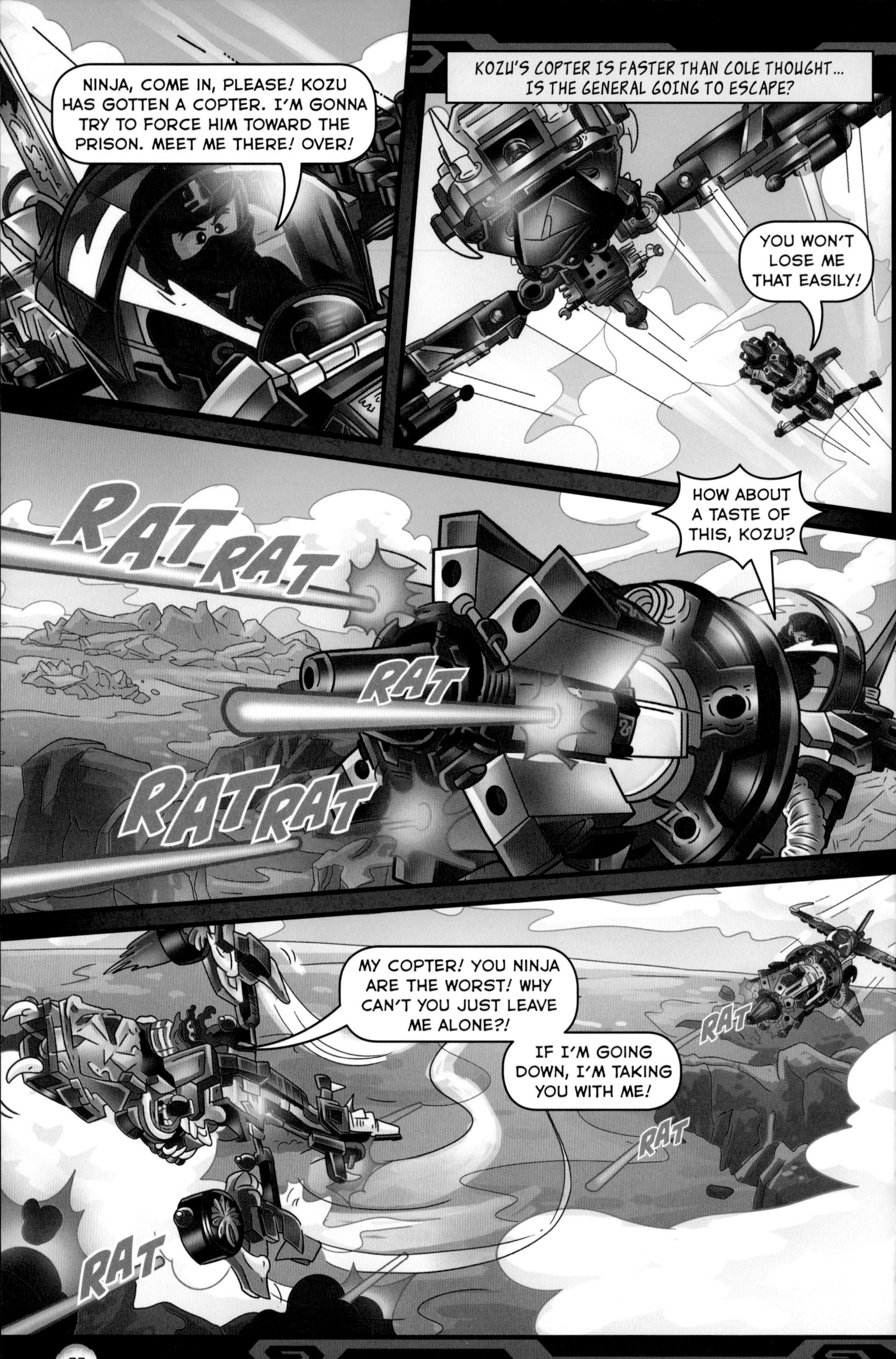
NINJA, COME IN, PLEASE! KOZU HAS GOTTEN A COPTER. I'M GONNA TRY TO FORCE HIM TOWARD THE PRISON. MEET ME THERE! OVER!
KOZU'S COPTER IS FASTER THAN COLE THOUGHT... IS THE GENERAL GOING TO ESCAPE?
YOU WON'T LOSE ME THAT EASILY!
HOW ABOUT A TASTE OF THIS, KOZU?
RAT RAT
RAT
RAT RAT
MY COPTER! YOU NINJA ARE THE WORST! WHY CAN'T YOU JUST LEAVE ME ALONE?!
IF I'M GOING DOWN, I'M TAKING YOU WITH ME!
RAT
RAT
RAT

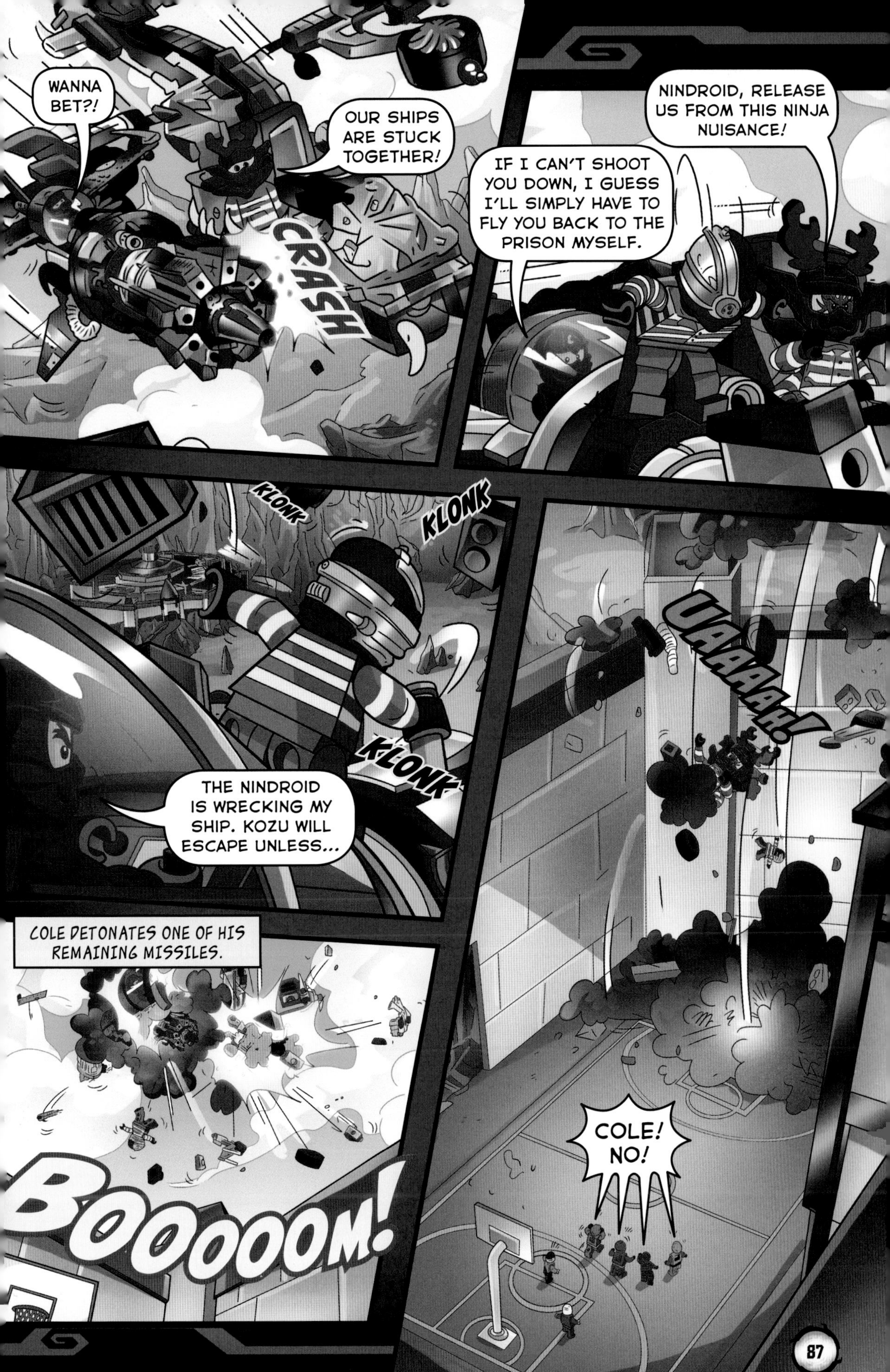
WANNA BET?!
OUR SHIPS ARE STUCK TOGETHER!
CRASH
NINDROID, RELEASE US FROM THIS NINJA NUISANCE!
IF I CAN'T SHOOT YOU DOWN, I GUESS I'LL SIMPLY HAVE TO FLY YOU BACK TO THE PRISON MYSELF.
KLONK
KLONK
KLONK
THE NINDROID IS WRECKING MY SHIP. KOZU WILL ESCAPE UNLESS...
UAAAAH!
COLE DETONATES ONE OF HIS REMAINING MISSILES.
BOOOOOM!
COLE! NO!

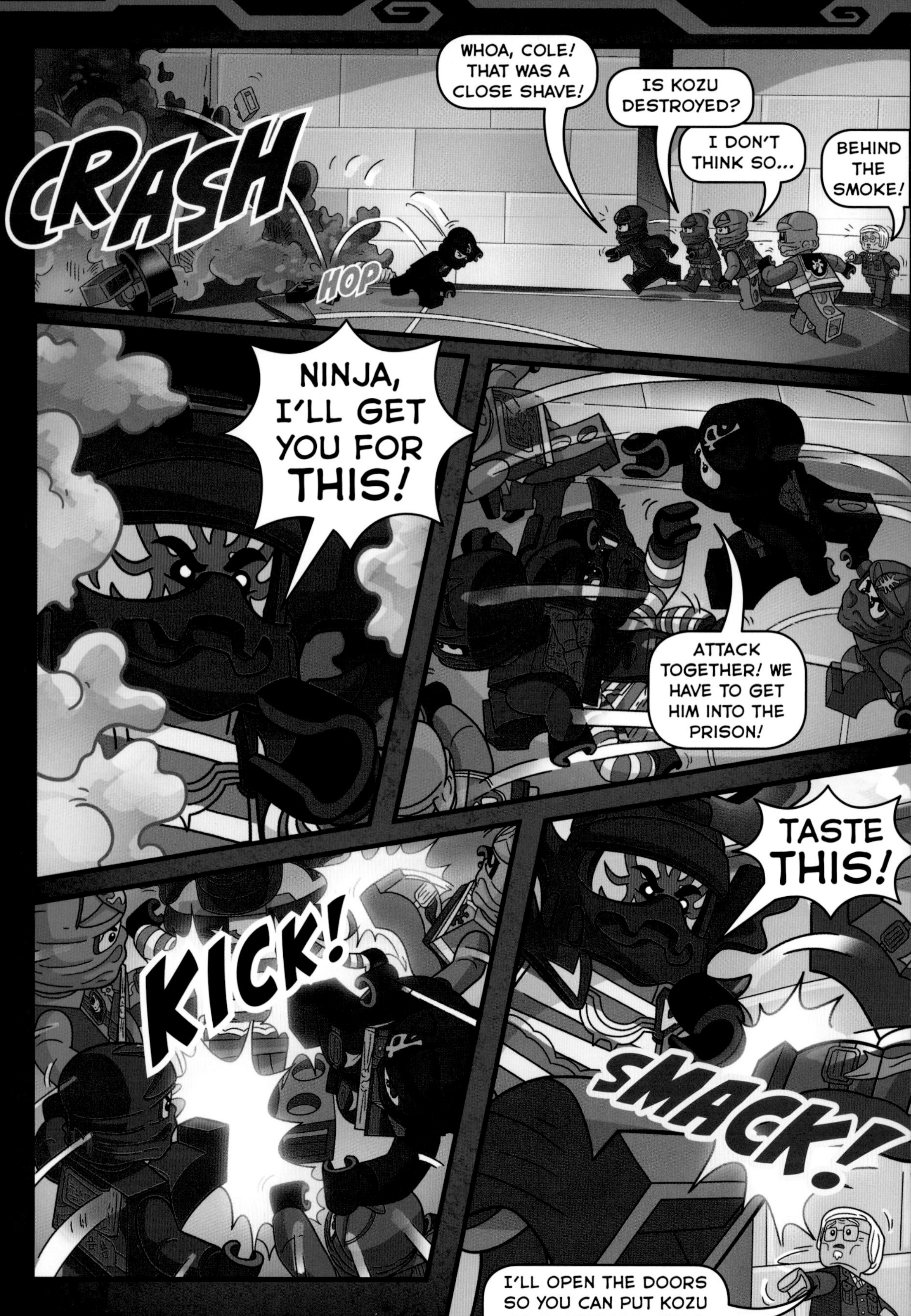
CRASH
WHOA, COLE! THAT WAS A CLOSE SHAVE!
IS KOZU DESTROYED?
I DON'T THINK SO...
BEHIND THE SMOKE!
HOP
NINJA, I'LL GET YOU FOR THIS!
ATTACK TOGETHER! WE HAVE TO GET HIM INTO THE PRISON!
KICK!
TASTE THIS!
SMACK!
I'LL OPEN THE DOORS SO YOU CAN PUT KOZU BACK INTO HIS CELL!

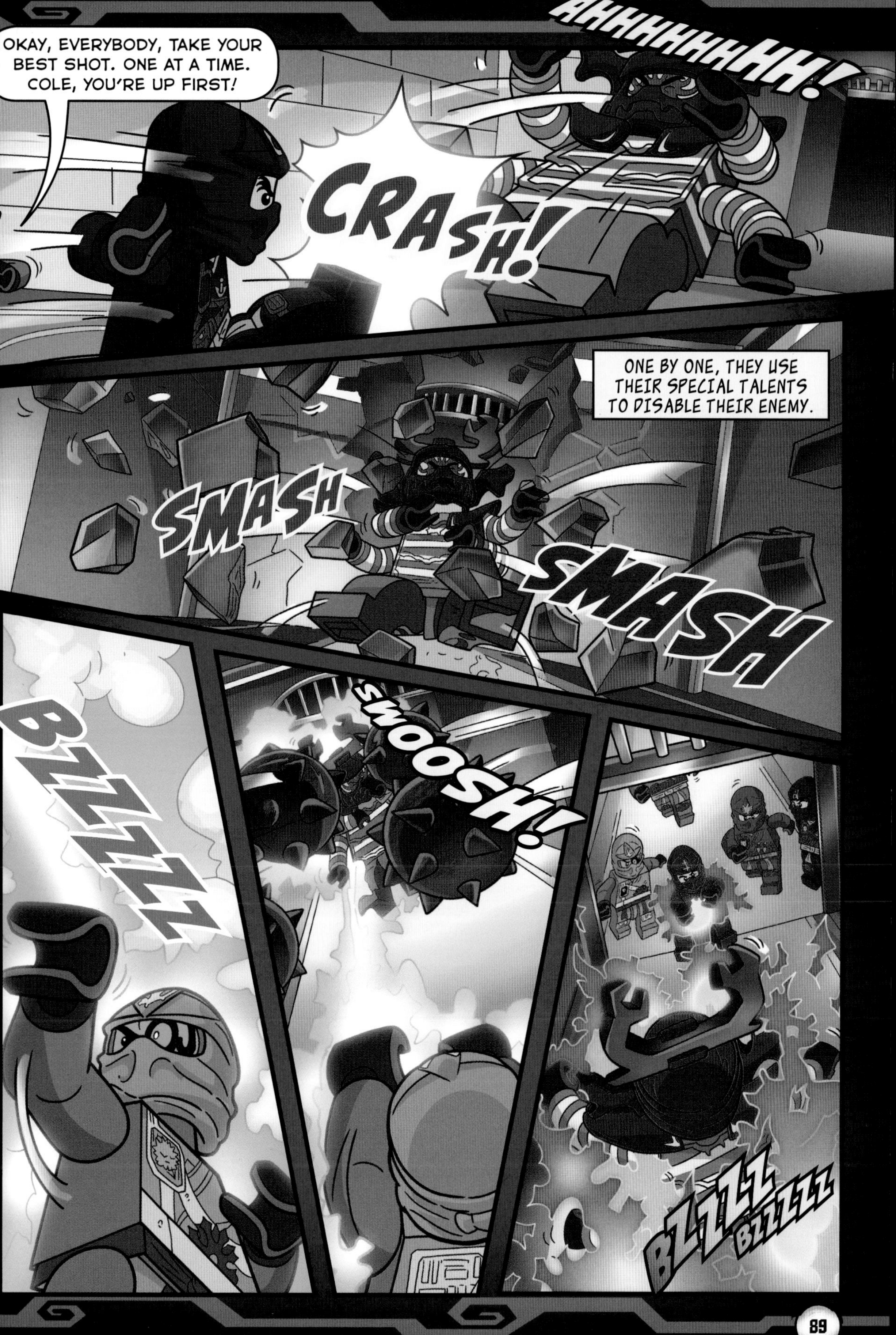
OKAY, EVERYBODY, TAKE YOUR BEST SHOT. ONE AT A TIME. COLE, YOU'RE UP FIRST!
AHHHHHHHHH!
CRASH!
ONE BY ONE, THEY USE THEIR SPECIAL TALENTS TO DISABLE THEIR ENEMY.
SMASH
SMASH
BZZZZ
SWOOSH!
BZZZZ
BZZZZZ

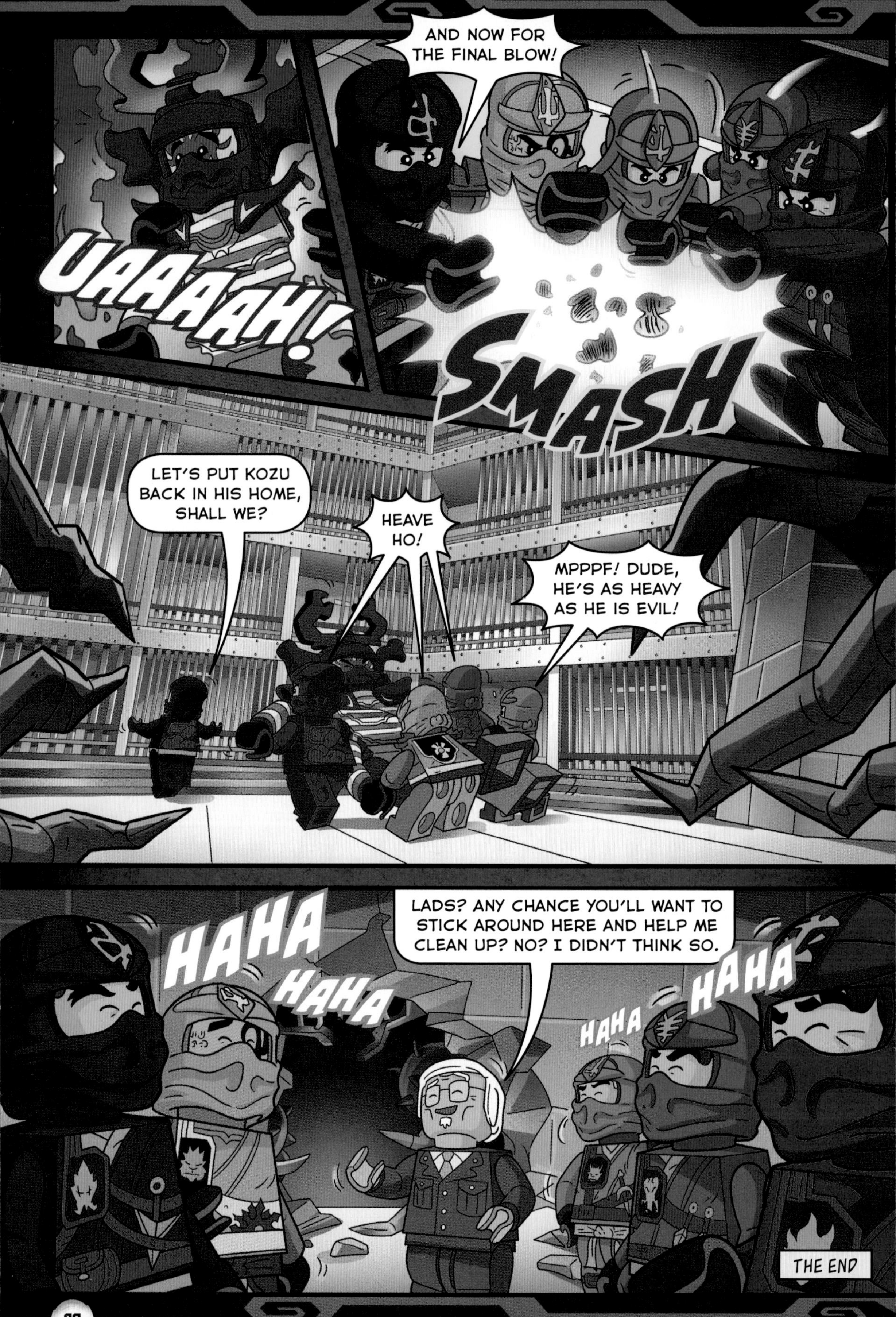

AND NOW FOR THE FINAL BLOW!
UAAAAAH!
SMASH
LET'S PUT KOZU BACK IN HIS HOME, SHALL WE?
HEAVE HO!
MPPPF! DUDE, HE'S AS HEAVY AS HE IS EVIL!
HAHA HAHA
LADS? ANY CHANCE YOU'LL WANT TO STICK AROUND HERE AND HELP ME CLEAN UP? NO? I DIDN'T THINK SO.
HAHA HAHA
THE END

NINJA IN DREAMLAND

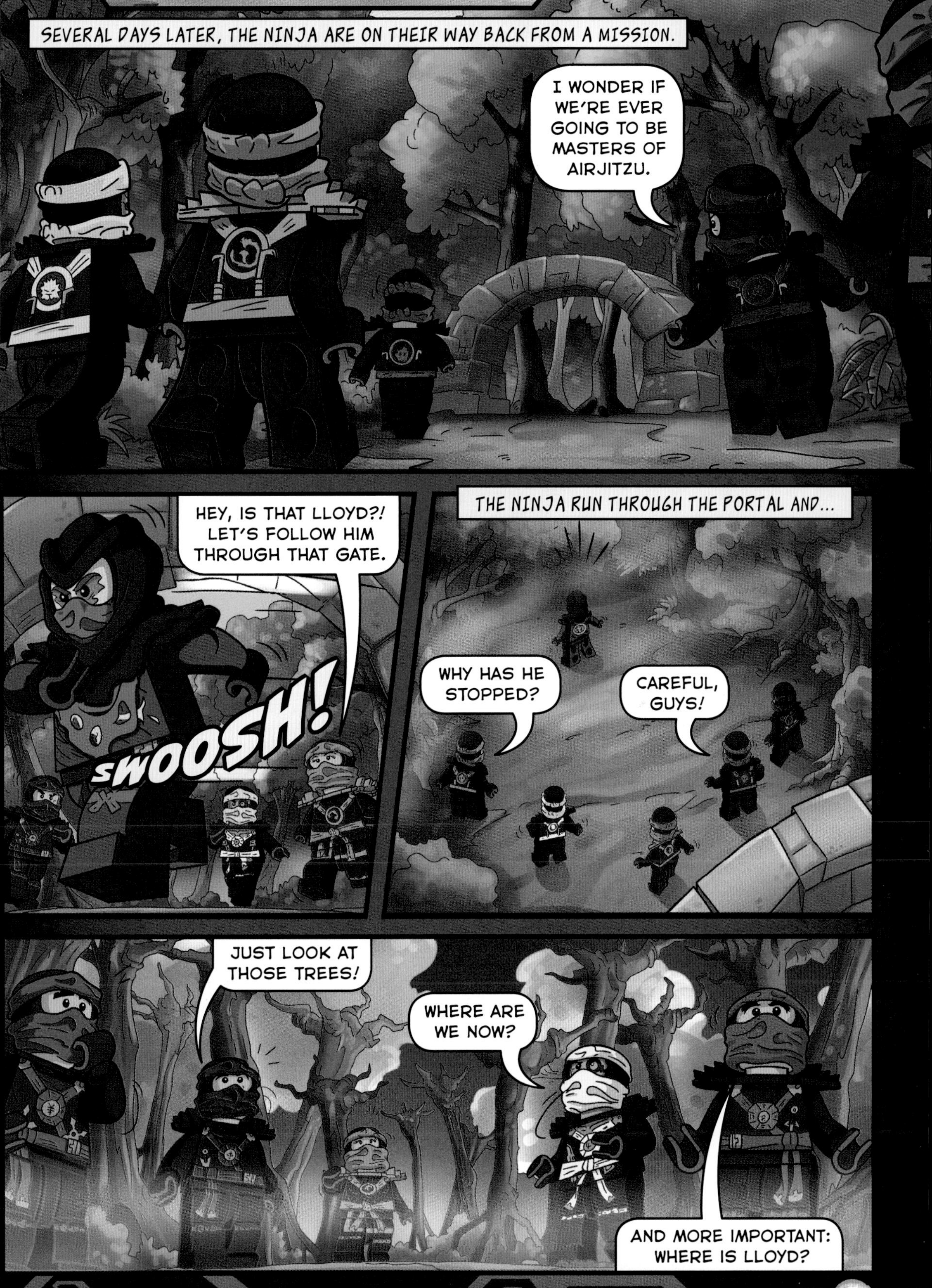

SEVERAL DAYS LATER, THE NINJA ARE ON THEIR WAY BACK FROM A MISSION.
I WONDER IF WE'RE EVER GOING TO BE MASTERS OF AIRJITZU.
HEY, IS THAT LLOYD?! LET'S FOLLOW HIM THROUGH THAT GATE.
SWOOSH!
THE NINJA RUN THROUGH THE PORTAL AND...
WHY HAS HE STOPPED?
CAREFUL, GUYS!
JUST LOOK AT THOSE TREES!
WHERE ARE WE NOW?
AND MORE IMPORTANT: WHERE IS LLOYD?

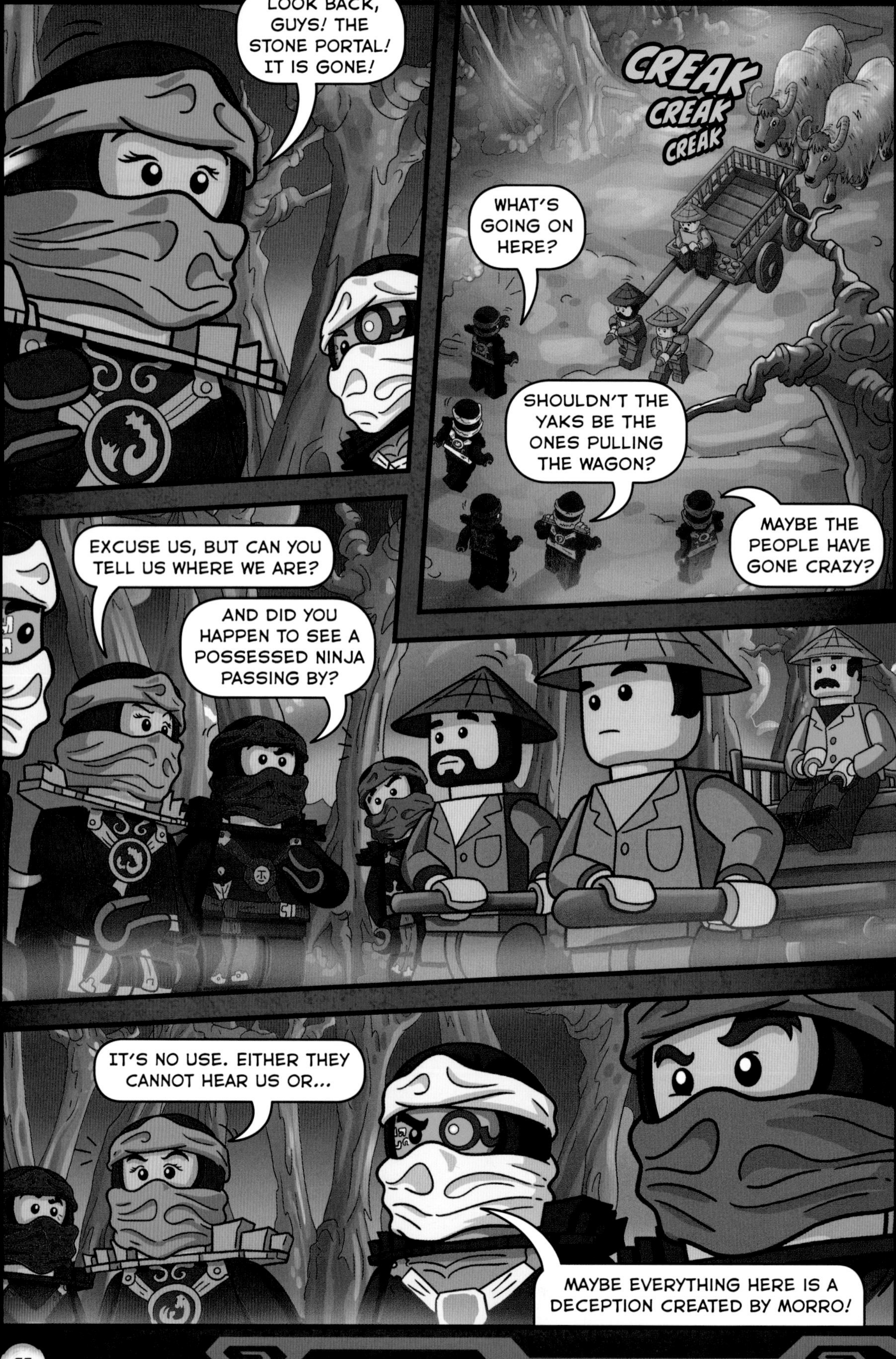
LOOK BACK, GUYS! THE STONE PORTAL! IT IS GONE!
CREAK
CREAK
CREAK
WHAT'S GOING ON HERE?
SHOULDN'T THE YAKS BE THE ONES PULLING THE WAGON?
MAYBE THE PEOPLE HAVE GONE CRAZY?
EXCUSE US, BUT CAN YOU TELL US WHERE WE ARE?
AND DID YOU HAPPEN TO SEE A POSSESSED NINJA PASSING BY?
IT'S NO USE. EITHER THEY CANNOT HEAR US OR...
MAYBE EVERYTHING HERE IS A DECEPTION CREATED BY MORRO!

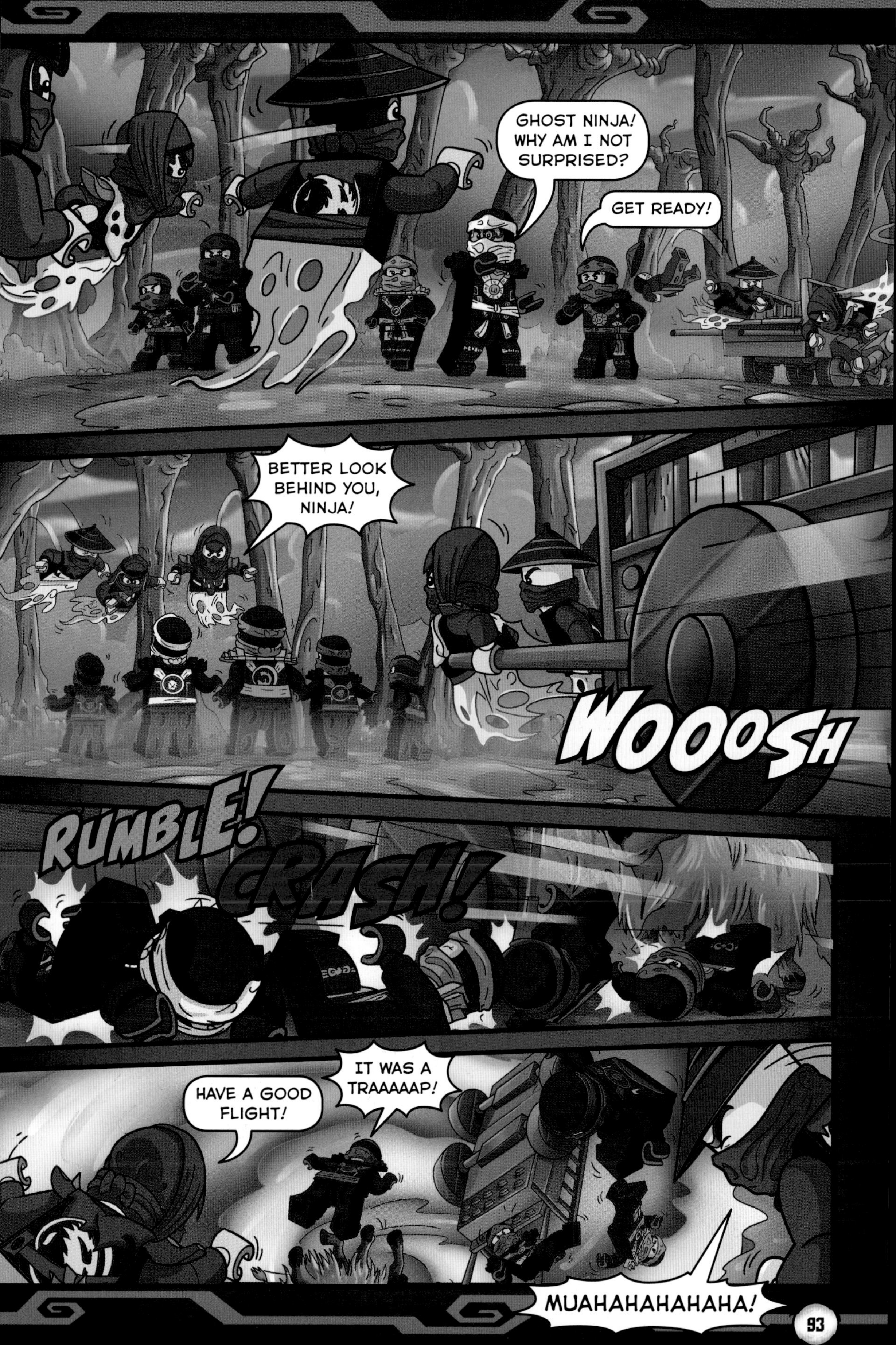

GHOST NINJA! WHY AM I NOT SURPRISED?
GET READY!
BETTER LOOK BEHIND YOU, NINJA!
WOOOSH
RUMBLE!
CRASH!
HAVE A GOOD FLIGHT!
IT WAS A TRAAAAAP!
MUAHAHAHAHAHA!

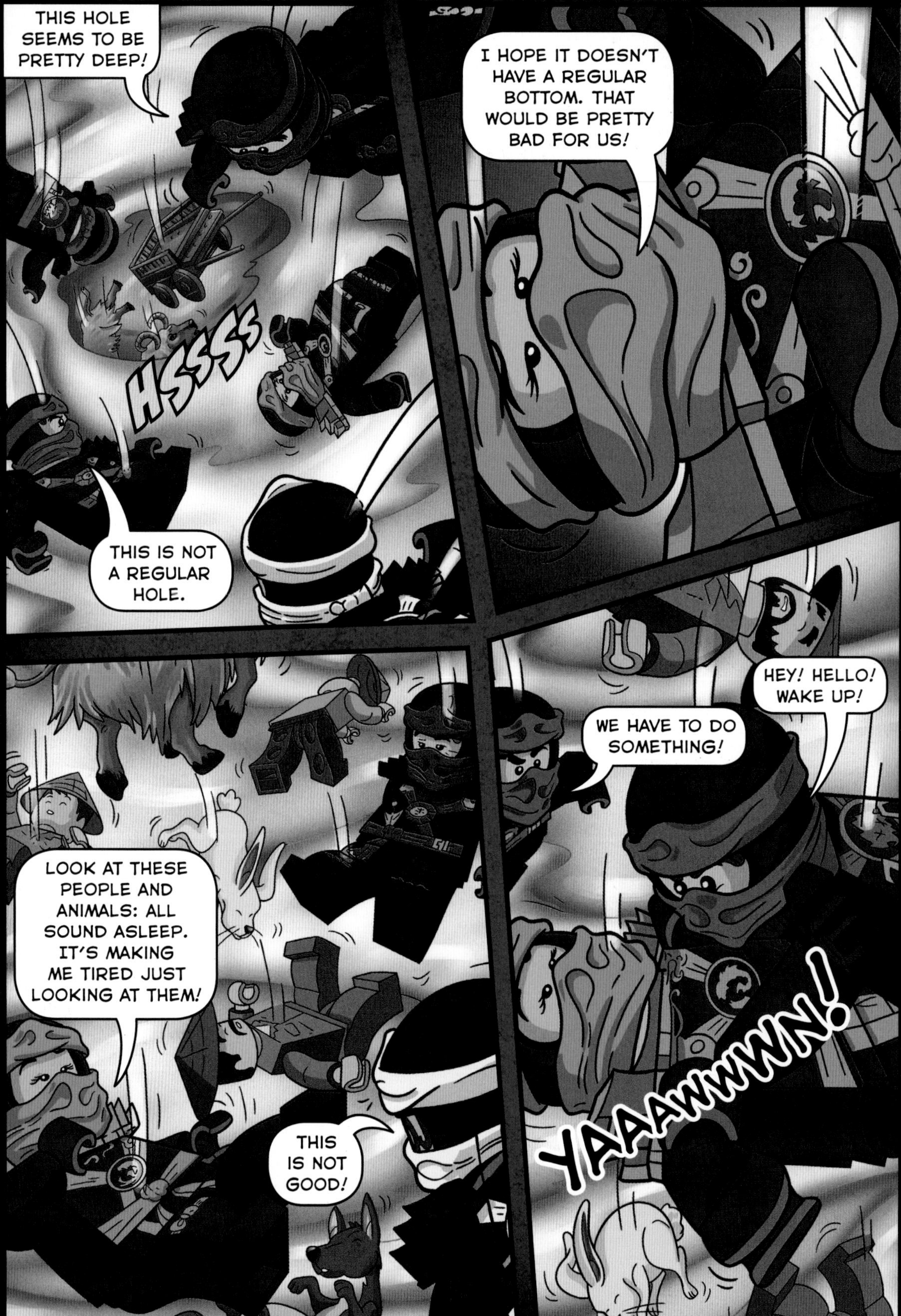
THIS HOLE SEEMS TO BE PRETTY DEEP!
HSSSSS
THIS IS NOT A REGULAR HOLE.
I HOPE IT DOESN'T HAVE A REGULAR BOTTOM. THAT WOULD BE PRETTY BAD FOR US!
LOOK AT THESE PEOPLE AND ANIMALS: ALL SOUND ASLEEP. IT'S MAKING ME TIRED JUST LOOKING AT THEM!
THIS IS NOT GOOD!
WE HAVE TO DO SOMETHING!
HEY! HELLO! WAKE UP!
YAAAWWWN!

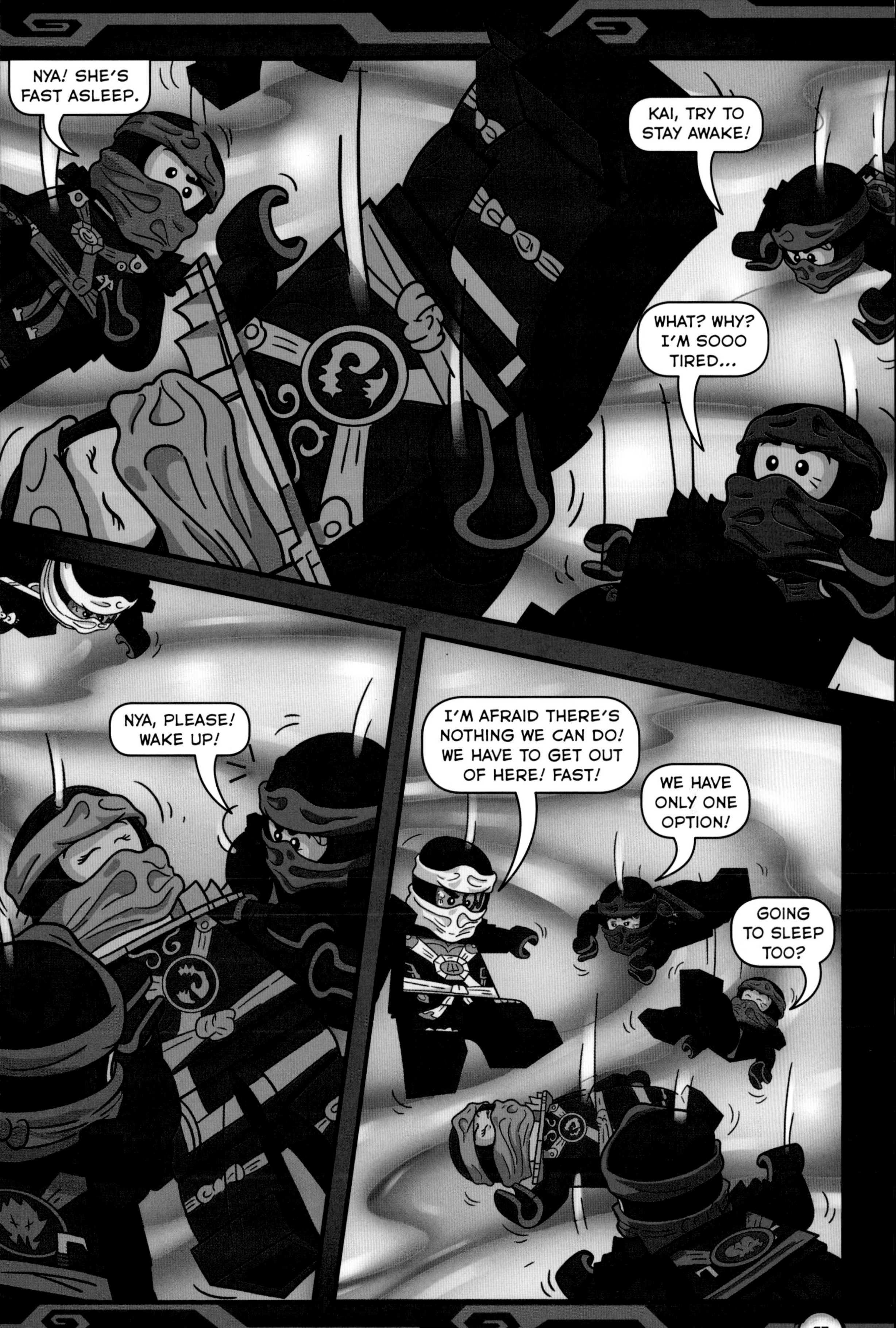
NYA! SHE'S FAST ASLEEP.
KAI, TRY TO STAY AWAKE!
WHAT? WHY? I'M SOOO TIRED...
NYA, PLEASE! WAKE UP!
I'M AFRAID THERE'S NOTHING WE CAN DO! WE HAVE TO GET OUT OF HERE! FAST!
WE HAVE ONLY ONE OPTION!
GOING TO SLEEP TOO?

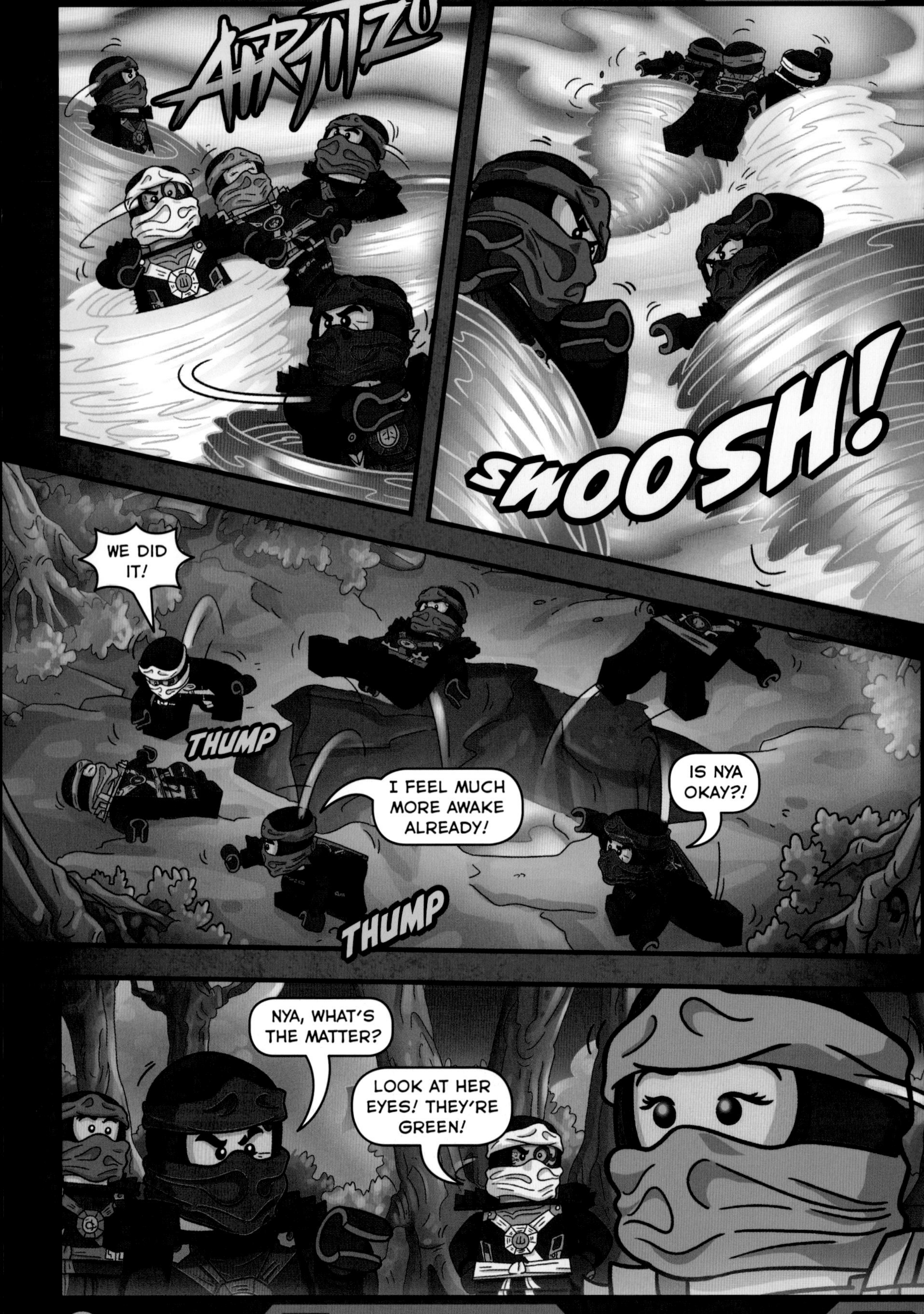
AIRJITZU
SWOOSH!
WE DID IT!
THUMP
I FEEL MUCH MORE AWAKE ALREADY!
IS NYA OKAY?!
THUMP
NYA, WHAT'S THE MATTER?
LOOK AT HER EYES! THEY'RE GREEN!

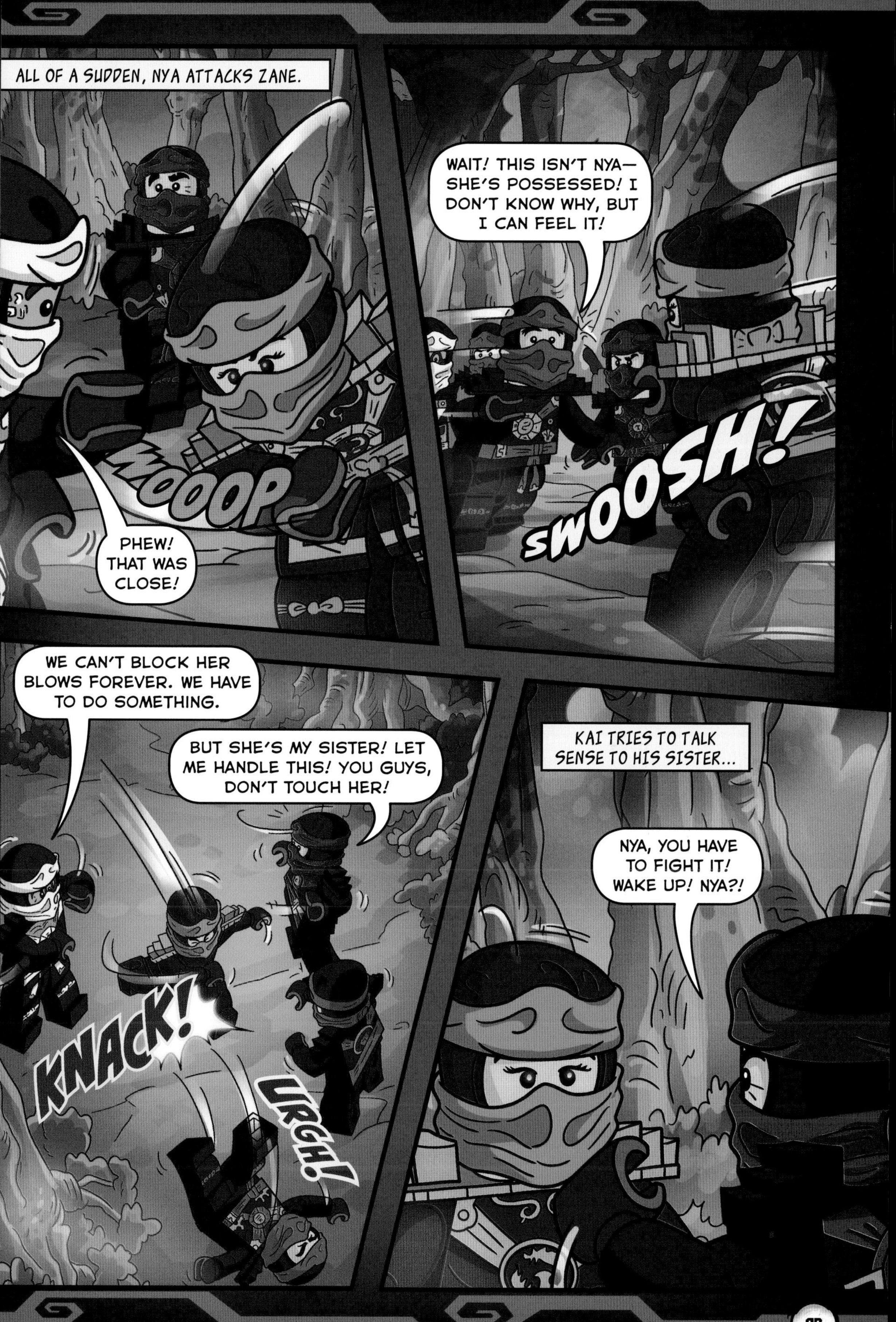

ALL OF A SUDDEN, NYA ATTACKS ZANE.
WOOOP
PHEW! THAT WAS CLOSE!
WAIT! THIS ISN'T NYA— SHE'S POSSESSED! I DON'T KNOW WHY, BUT I CAN FEEL IT!
SWOOSH!
WE CAN'T BLOCK HER BLOWS FOREVER. WE HAVE TO DO SOMETHING.
BUT SHE'S MY SISTER! LET ME HANDLE THIS! YOU GUYS, DON'T TOUCH HER!
KNACK!
URGH!
KAI TRIES TO TALK SENSE TO HIS SISTER...
NYA, YOU HAVE TO FIGHT IT! WAKE UP! NYA?!

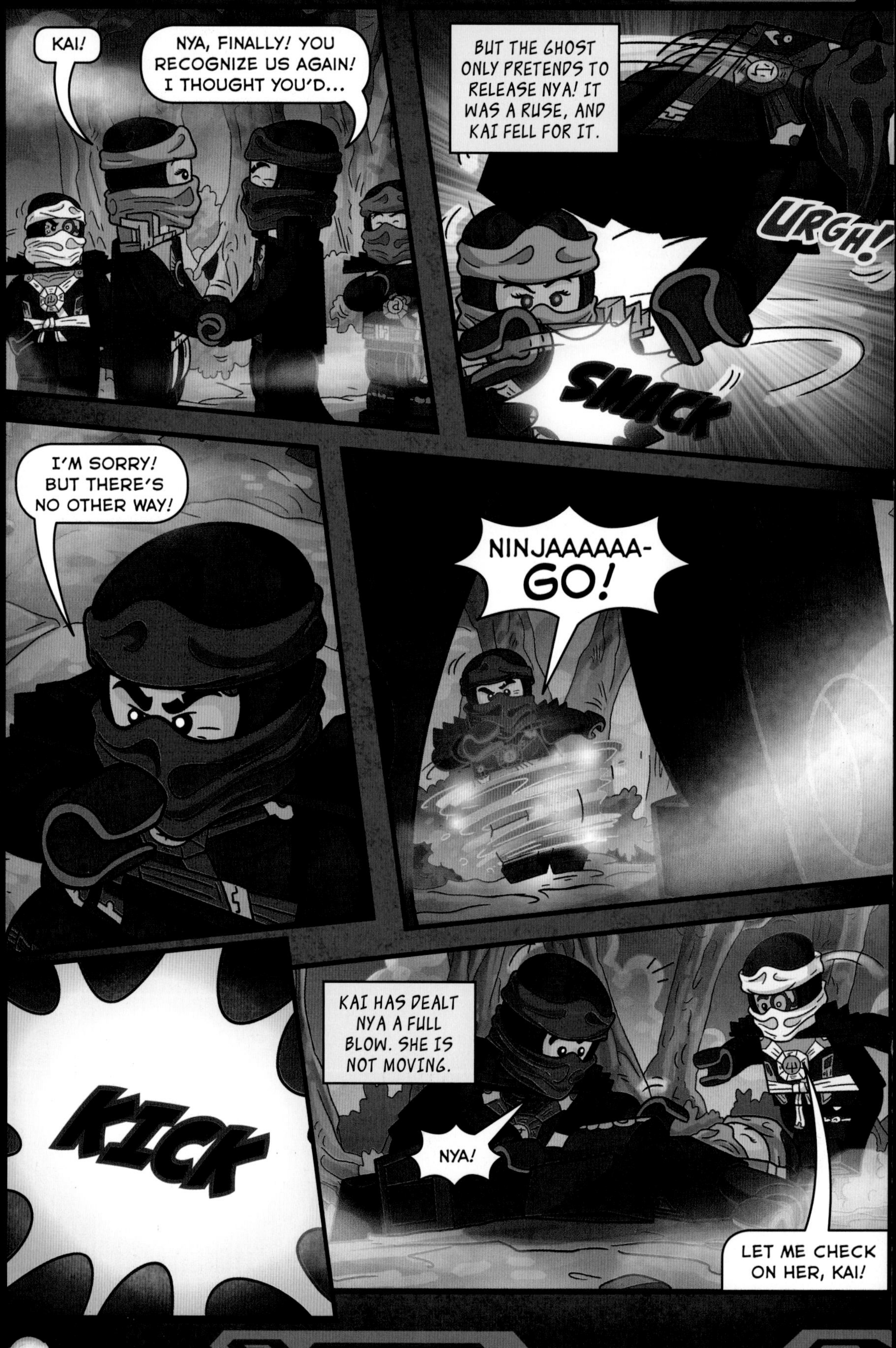
KAI!
NYA, FINALLY! YOU RECOGNIZE US AGAIN! I THOUGHT YOU'D...
BUT THE GHOST ONLY PRETENDS TO RELEASE NYA! IT WAS A RUSE, AND KAI FELL FOR IT.
URGH!
SMACK
I'M SORRY! BUT THERE'S NO OTHER WAY!
NINJAAAAAA-GO!
KICK
KAI HAS DEALT NYA A FULL BLOW. SHE IS NOT MOVING.
NYA!
LET ME CHECK ON HER, KAI!

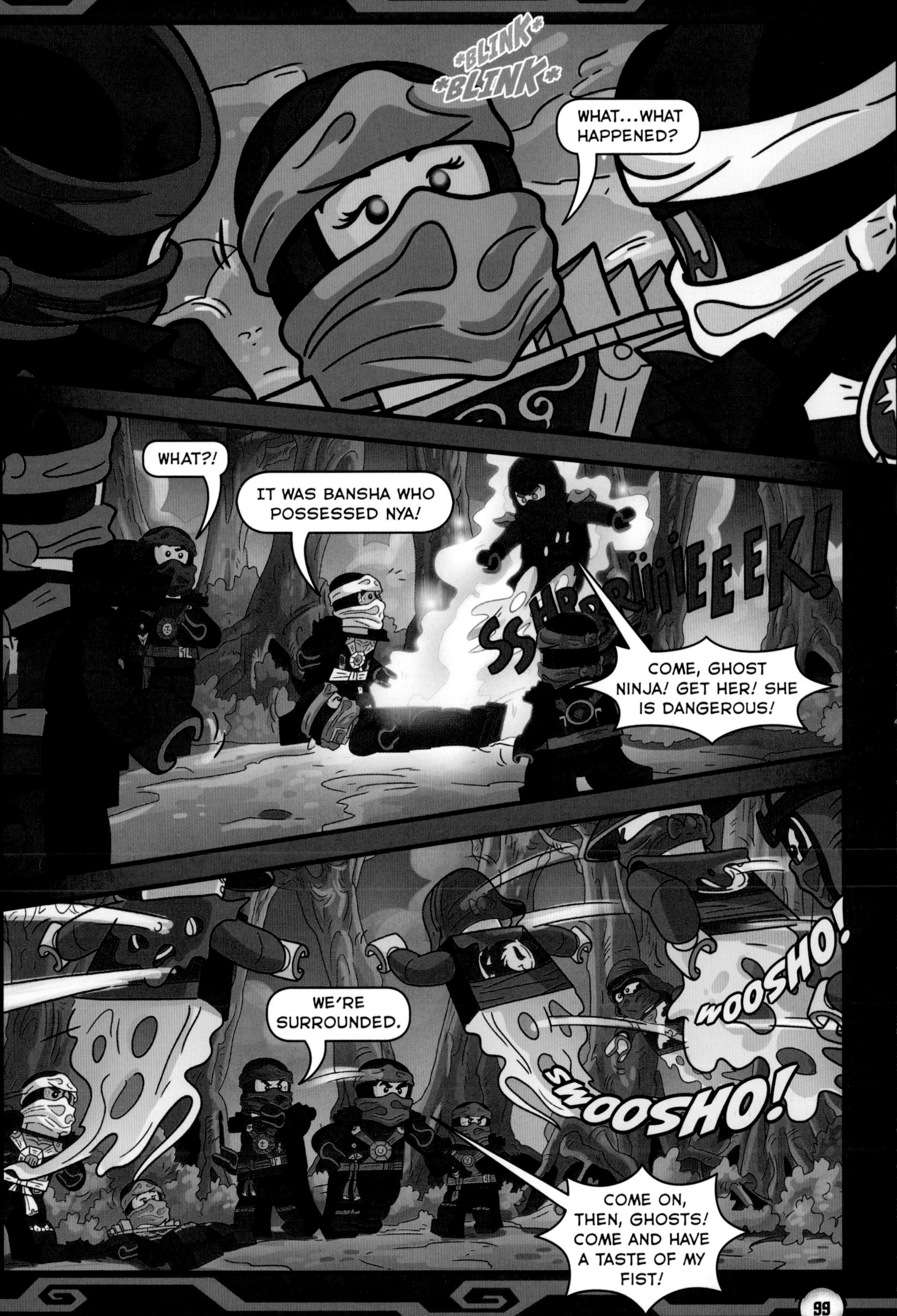
BLINK
BLINK
WHAT...WHAT HAPPENED?
WHAT?!
IT WAS BANSHA WHO POSSESSED NYA!
SSHRRRIIIIEEEEK!
COME, GHOST NINJA! GET HER! SHE IS DANGEROUS!
WE'RE SURROUNDED.
WOOSHO!
SWOOSHO!
COME ON, THEN, GHOSTS! COME AND HAVE A TASTE OF MY FIST!

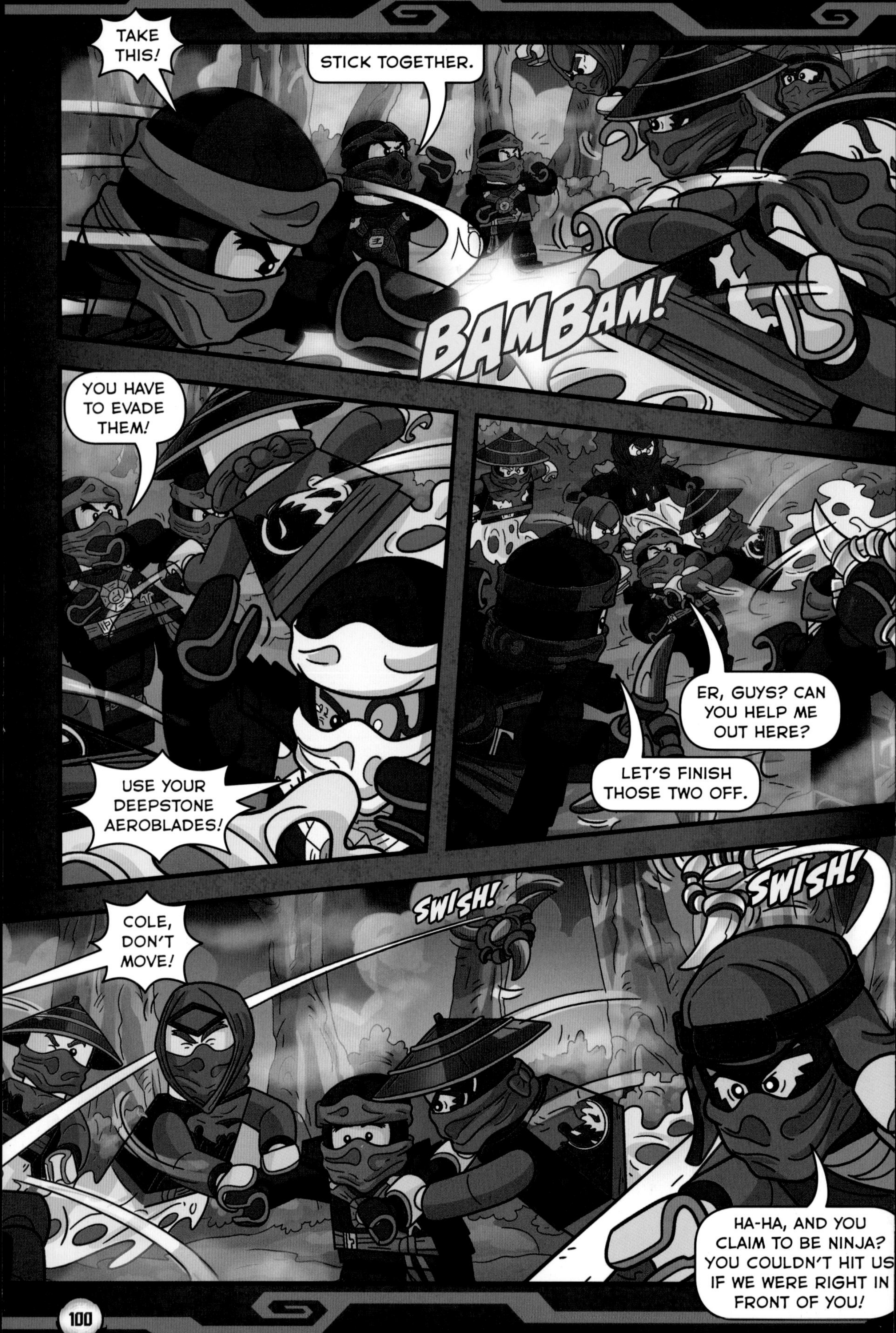
TAKE THIS!
STICK TOGETHER.
BAMBAM!
YOU HAVE TO EVADE THEM!
USE YOUR DEEPSTONE AEROBLADES!
ER, GUYS? CAN YOU HELP ME OUT HERE?
LET'S FINISH THOSE TWO OFF.
SWISH!
SWISH!
COLE, DON'T MOVE!
HA-HA, AND YOU CLAIM TO BE NINJA? YOU COULDN'T HIT US IF WE WERE RIGHT IN FRONT OF YOU!

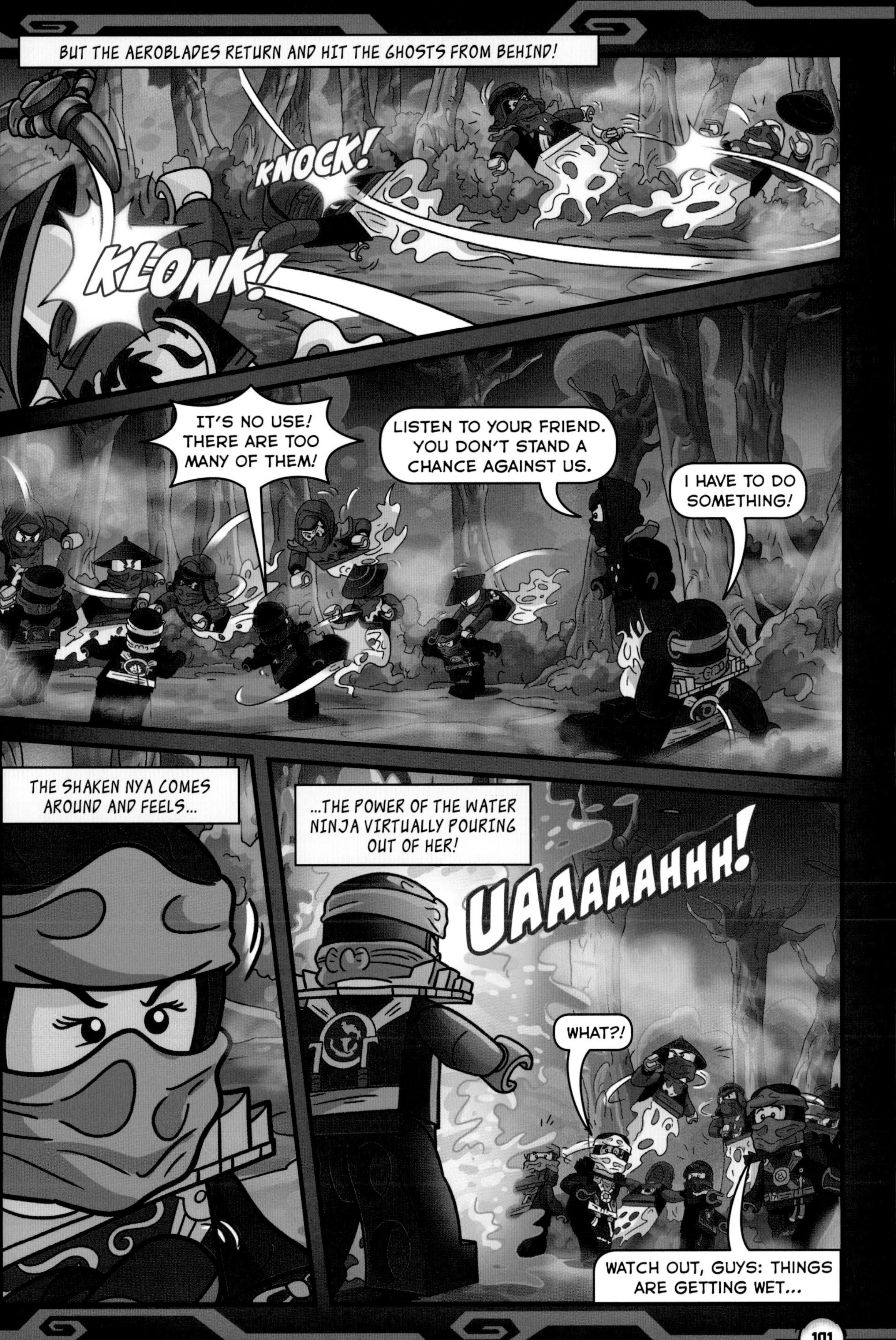

BUT THE AEROBLADES RETURN AND HIT THE GHOSTS FROM BEHIND!
KNOCK!
KLONK!
IT'S NO USE! THERE ARE TOO MANY OF THEM!
LISTEN TO YOUR FRIEND. YOU DON'T STAND A CHANCE AGAINST US.
I HAVE TO DO SOMETHING!
THE SHAKEN NYA COMES AROUND AND FEELS...
...THE POWER OF THE WATER NINJA VIRTUALLY POURING OUT OF HER!
UAAAAAHHH!
WHAT?!
WATCH OUT, GUYS: THINGS ARE GETTING WET...

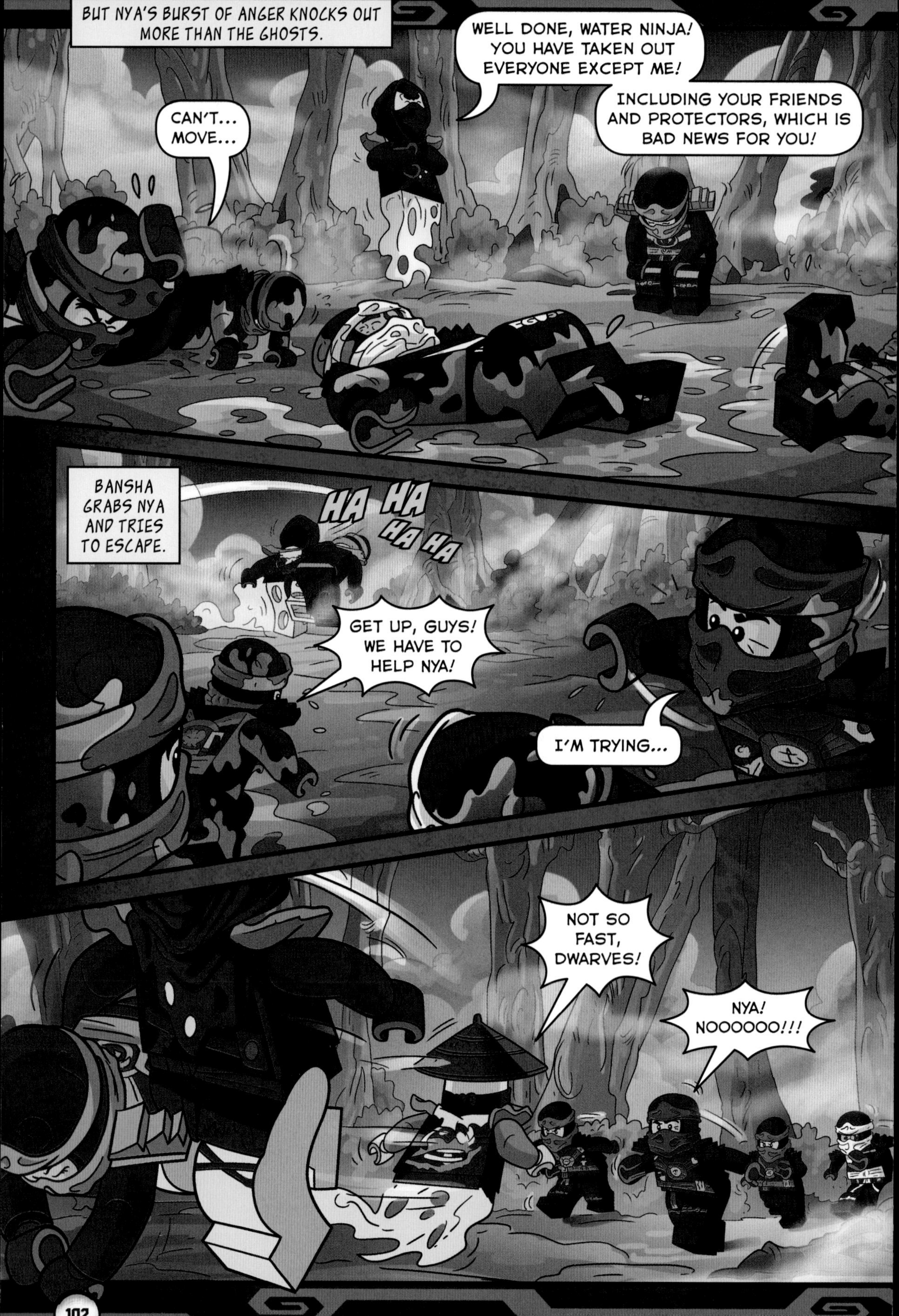
BUT NYA'S BURST OF ANGER KNOCKS OUT MORE THAN THE GHOSTS.
CAN'T... MOVE...
WELL DONE, WATER NINJA! YOU HAVE TAKEN OUT EVERYONE EXCEPT ME!
INCLUDING YOUR FRIENDS AND PROTECTORS, WHICH IS BAD NEWS FOR YOU!
BANSHA GRABS NYA AND TRIES TO ESCAPE.
HA HA HA HA
GET UP, GUYS! WE HAVE TO HELP NYA!
I'M TRYING...
NOT SO FAST, DWARVES!
NYA! NOOOOOO!!!

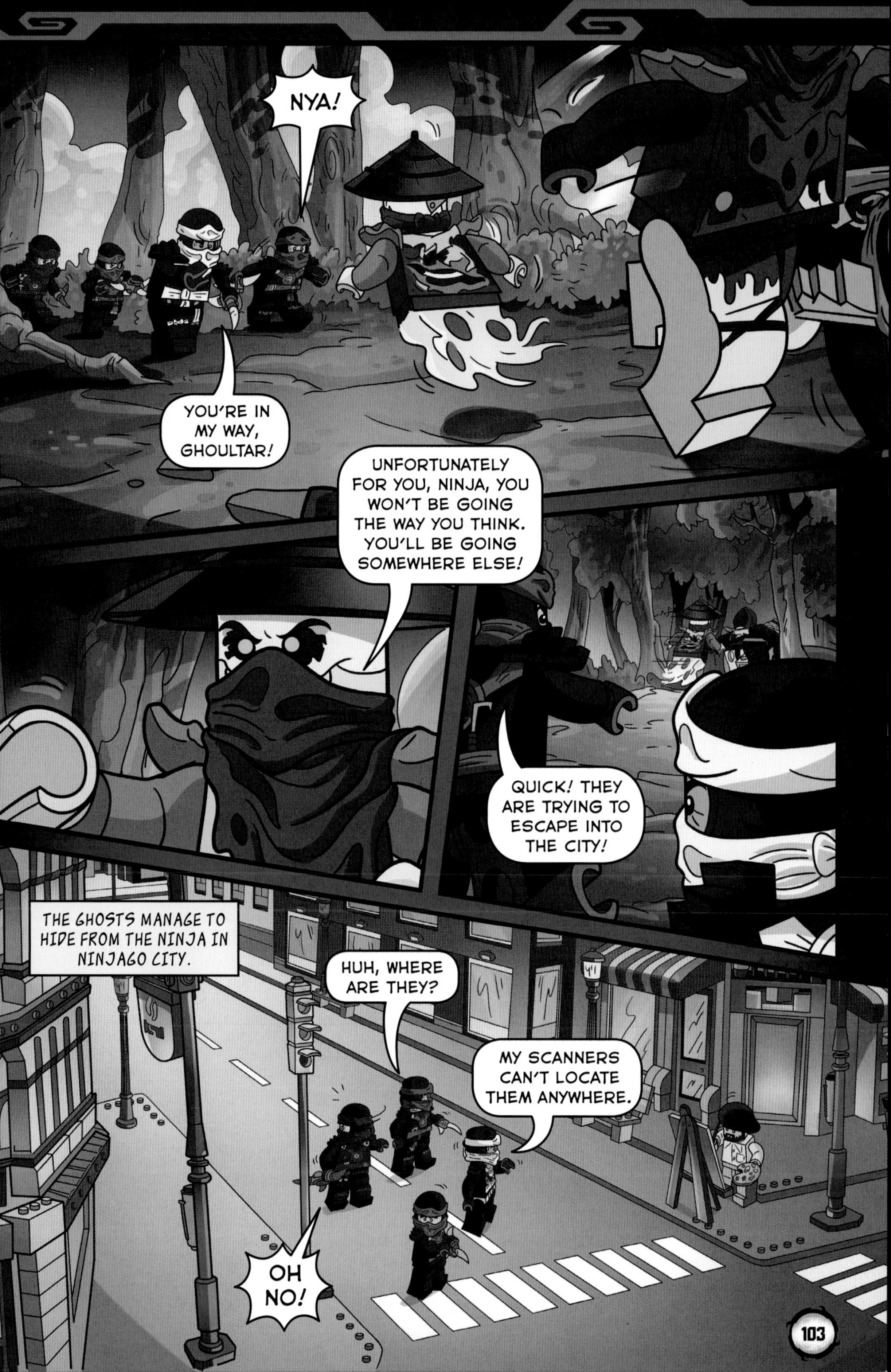

NYA!
YOU'RE IN MY WAY, GHOULTAR!
UNFORTUNATELY FOR YOU, NINJA, YOU WON'T BE GOING THE WAY YOU THINK. YOU'LL BE GOING SOMEWHERE ELSE!
QUICK! THEY ARE TRYING TO ESCAPE INTO THE CITY!
THE GHOSTS MANAGE TO HIDE FROM THE NINJA IN NINJAGO CITY.
HUH, WHERE ARE THEY?
MY SCANNERS CAN'T LOCATE THEM ANYWHERE.
OH NO!

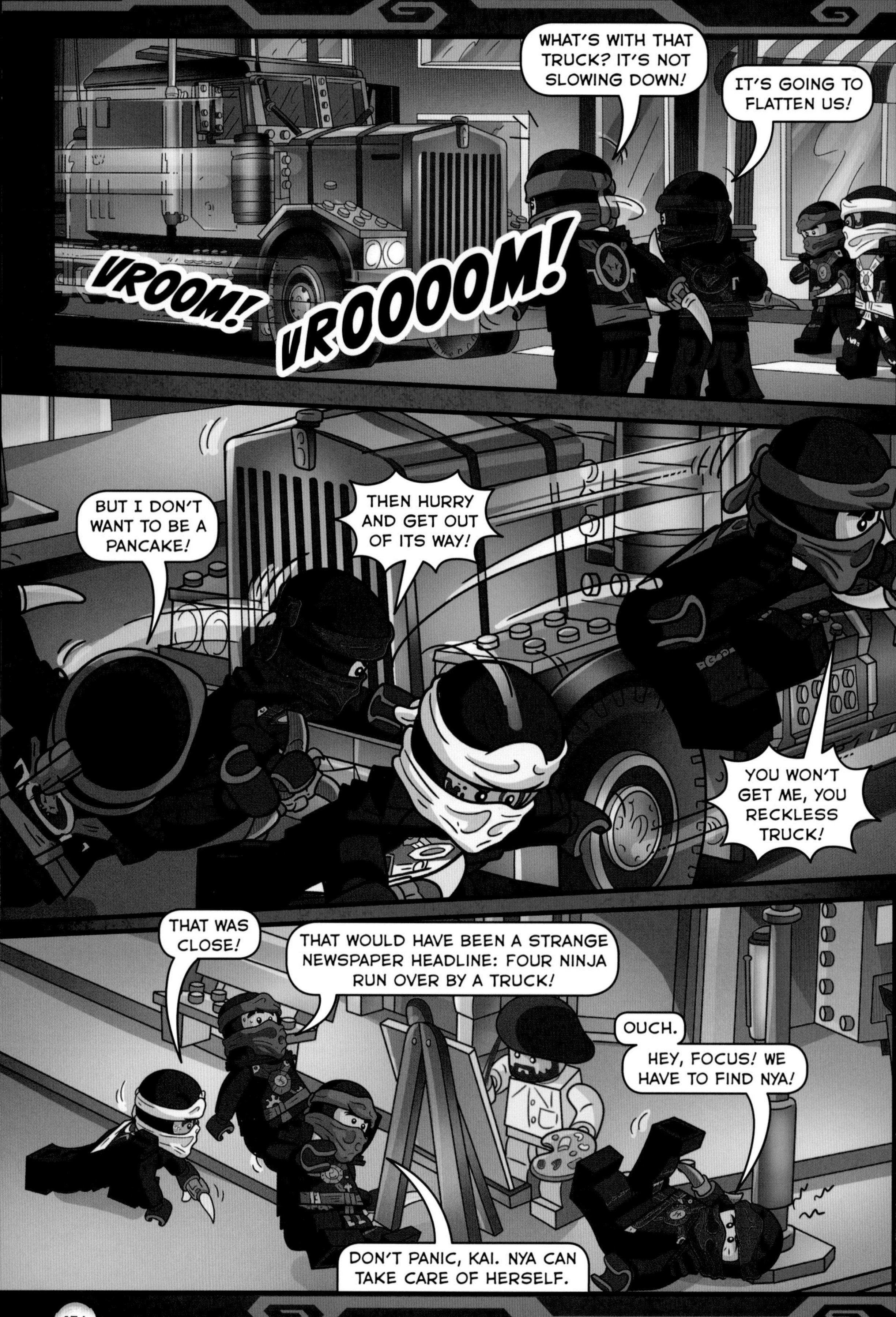
WHAT'S WITH THAT TRUCK? IT'S NOT SLOWING DOWN!
IT'S GOING TO FLATTEN US!
VROOM!
VROOOOM!
BUT I DON'T WANT TO BE A PANCAKE!
THEN HURRY AND GET OUT OF ITS WAY!
YOU WON'T GET ME, YOU RECKLESS TRUCK!
THAT WAS CLOSE!
THAT WOULD HAVE BEEN A STRANGE NEWSPAPER HEADLINE: FOUR NINJA RUN OVER BY A TRUCK!
OUCH.
HEY, FOCUS! WE HAVE TO FIND NYA!
DON'T PANIC, KAI. NYA CAN TAKE CARE OF HERSELF.

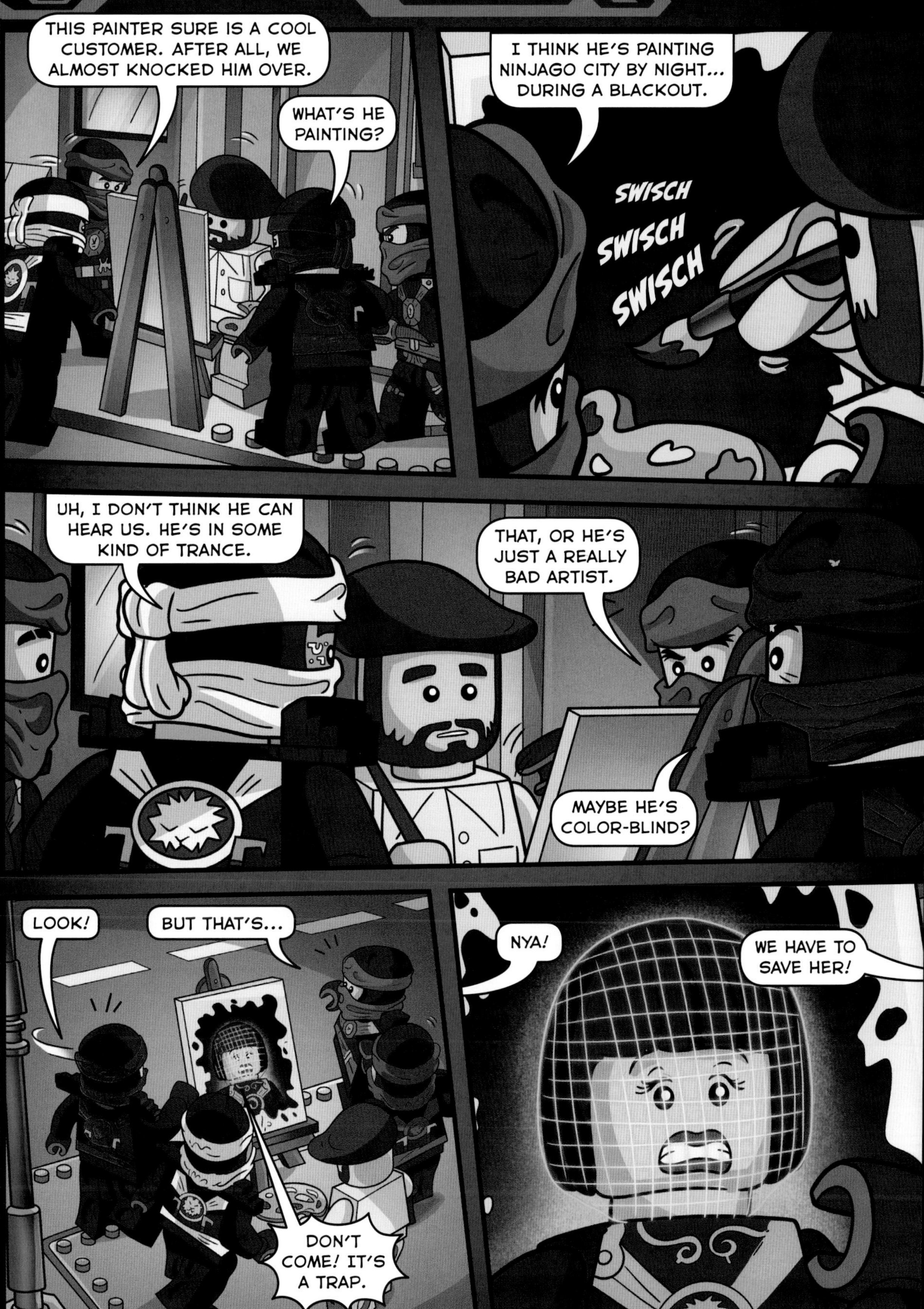
THIS PAINTER SURE IS A COOL CUSTOMER. AFTER ALL, WE ALMOST KNOCKED HIM OVER.
WHAT'S HE PAINTING?
I THINK HE'S PAINTING NINJAGO CITY BY NIGHT... DURING A BLACKOUT.
SWISCH
SWISCH
SWISCH
UH, I DON'T THINK HE CAN HEAR US. HE'S IN SOME KIND OF TRANCE.
THAT, OR HE'S JUST A REALLY BAD ARTIST.
MAYBE HE'S COLOR-BLIND?
LOOK!
BUT THAT'S...
DON'T COME! IT'S A TRAP.
NYA!
WE HAVE TO SAVE HER!

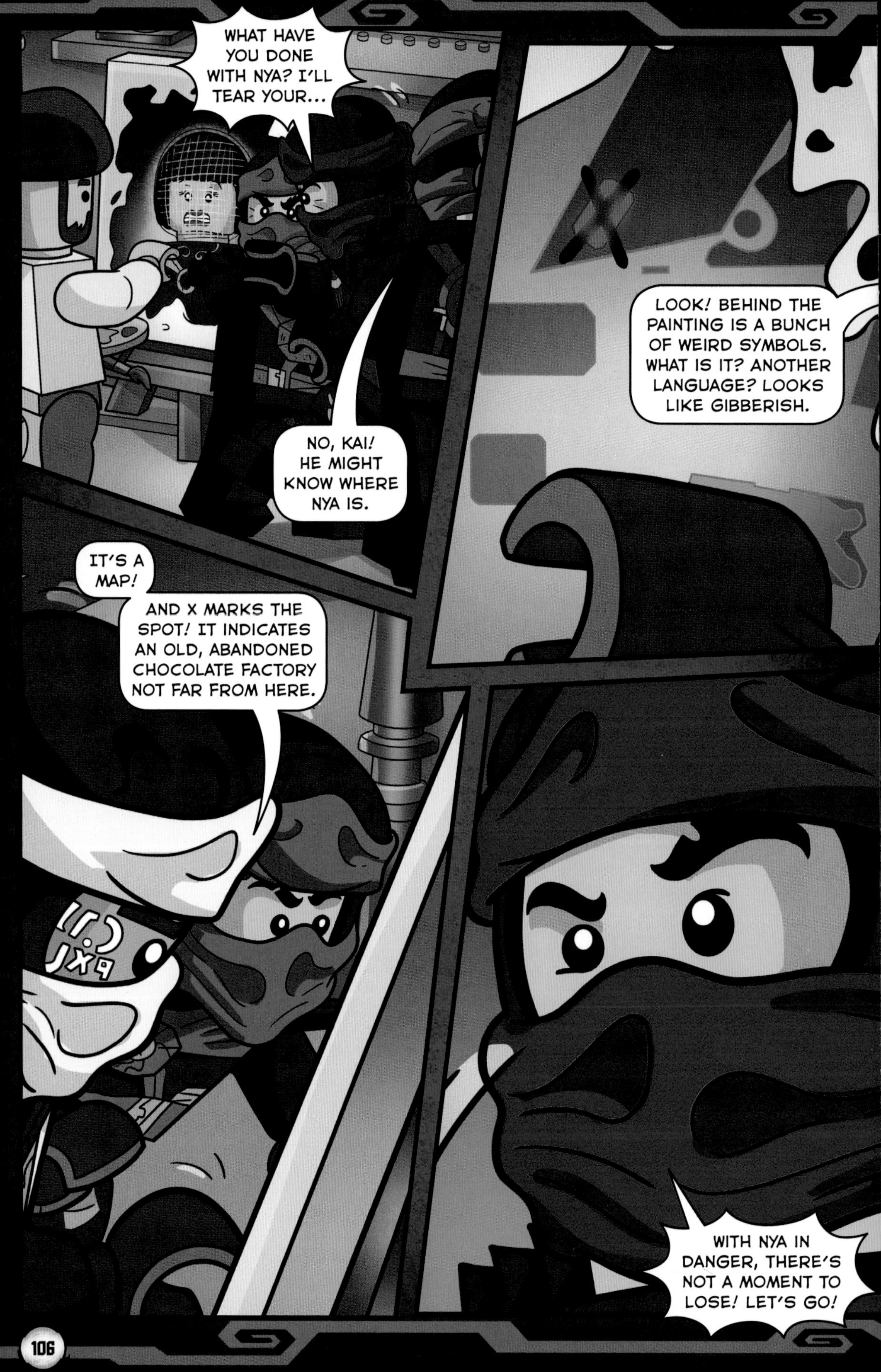
WHAT HAVE YOU DONE WITH NYA? I'LL TEAR YOUR...
NO, KAI! HE MIGHT KNOW WHERE NYA IS.
LOOK! BEHIND THE PAINTING IS A BUNCH OF WEIRD SYMBOLS. WHAT IS IT? ANOTHER LANGUAGE? LOOKS LIKE GIBBERISH.
IT'S A MAP!
AND X MARKS THE SPOT! IT INDICATES AN OLD, ABANDONED CHOCOLATE FACTORY NOT FAR FROM HERE.
WITH NYA IN DANGER, THERE'S NOT A MOMENT TO LOSE! LET'S GO!

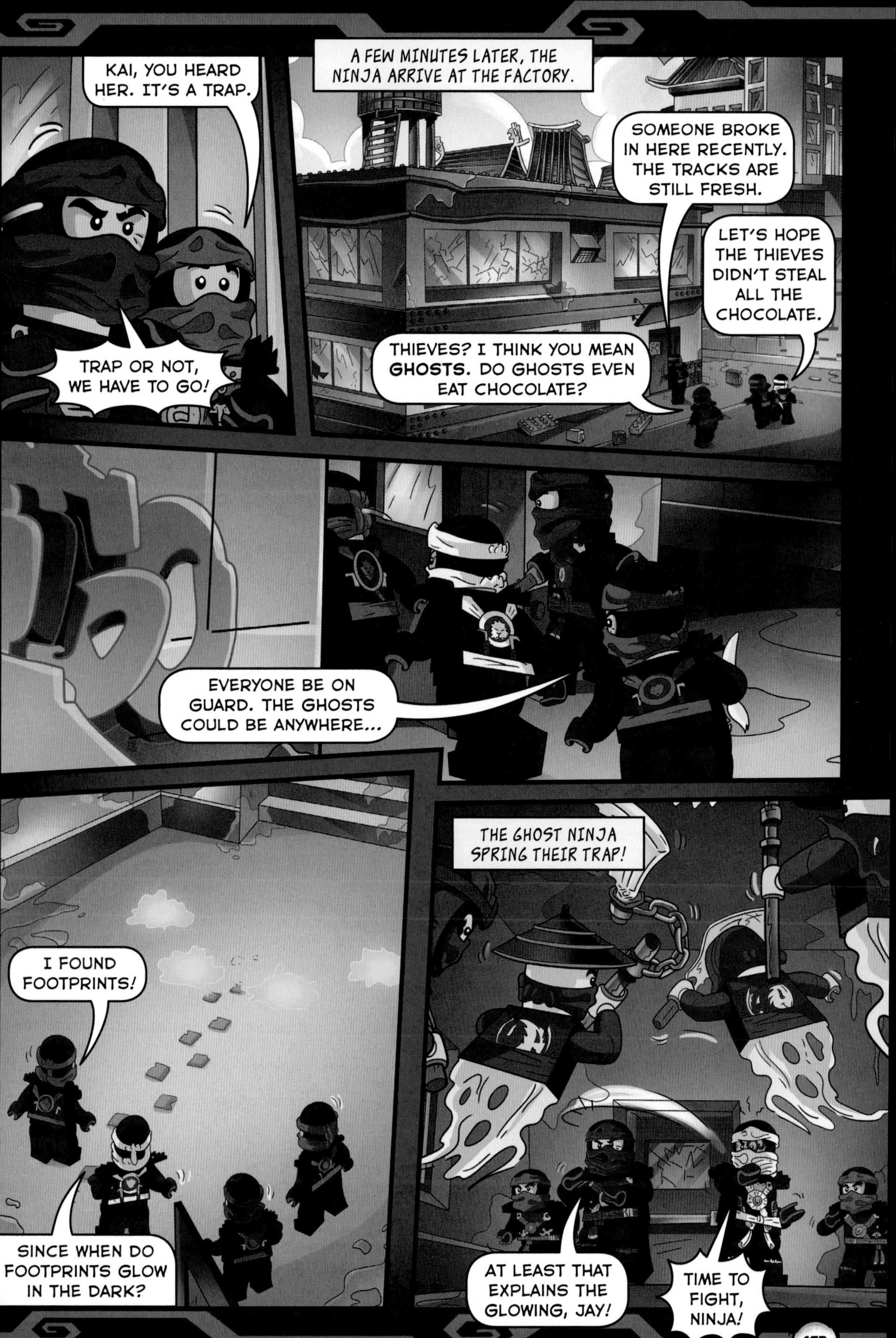
KAI, YOU HEARD HER. IT'S A TRAP.
TRAP OR NOT, WE HAVE TO GO!
A FEW MINUTES LATER, THE NINJA ARRIVE AT THE FACTORY.
SOMEONE BROKE IN HERE RECENTLY. THE TRACKS ARE STILL FRESH.
LET'S HOPE THE THIEVES DIDN'T STEAL ALL THE CHOCOLATE.
THIEVES? I THINK YOU MEAN GHOSTS. DO GHOSTS EVEN EAT CHOCOLATE?
EVERYONE BE ON GUARD. THE GHOSTS COULD BE ANYWHERE...
I FOUND FOOTPRINTS!
SINCE WHEN DO FOOTPRINTS GLOW IN THE DARK?
THE GHOST NINJA SPRING THEIR TRAP!
AT LEAST THAT EXPLAINS THE GLOWING, JAY!
TIME TO FIGHT, NINJA!

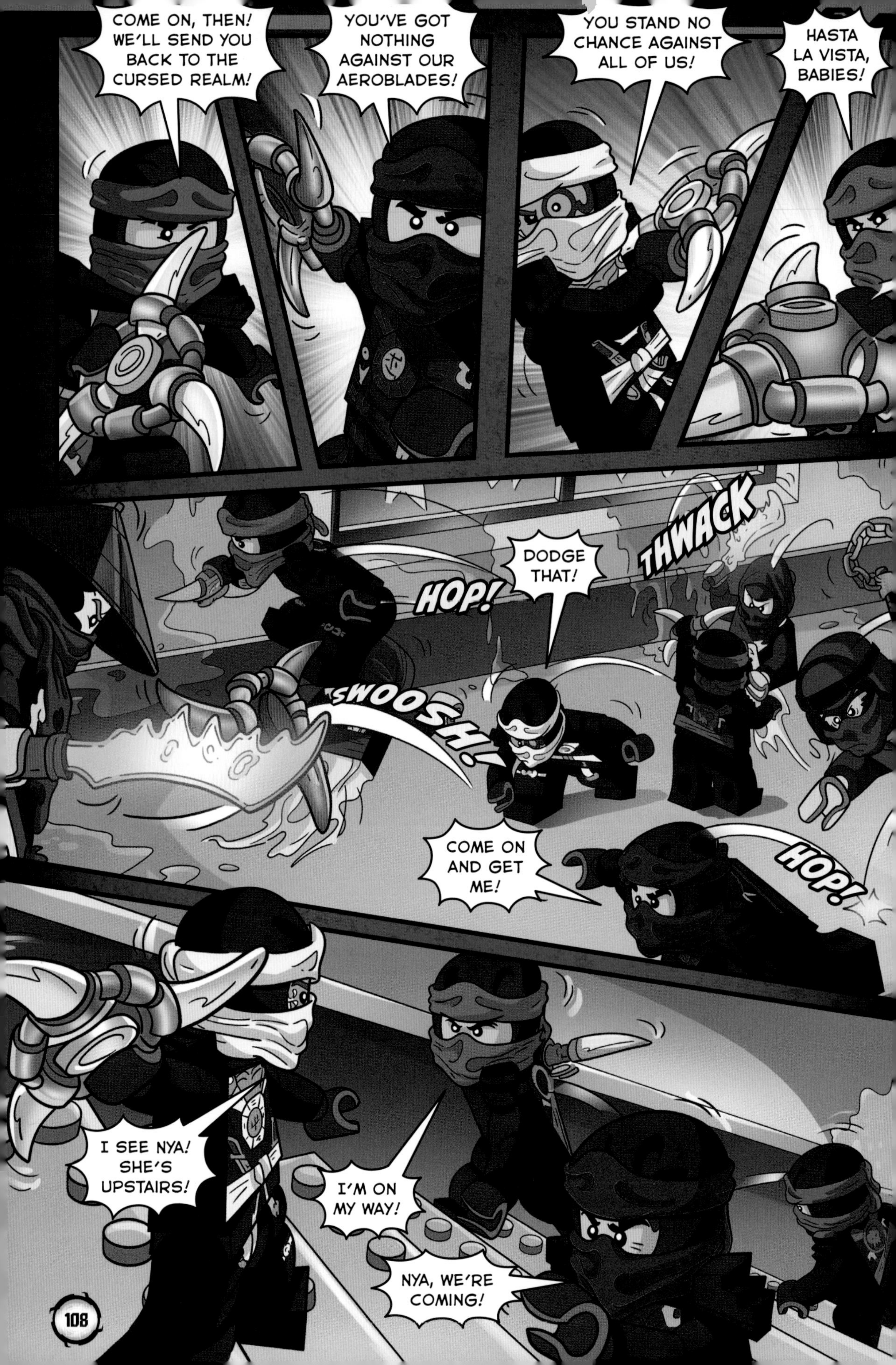
COME ON, THEN! WE'LL SEND YOU BACK TO THE CURSED REALM!
YOU'VE GOT NOTHING AGAINST OUR AEROBLADES!
YOU STAND NO CHANCE AGAINST ALL OF US!
HASTA LA VISTA, BABIES!
THWACK
DODGE THAT!
HOP!
SWOOSH!
COME ON AND GET ME!
HOP!
I SEE NYA! SHE'S UPSTAIRS!
I'M ON MY WAY!
NYA, WE'RE COMING!

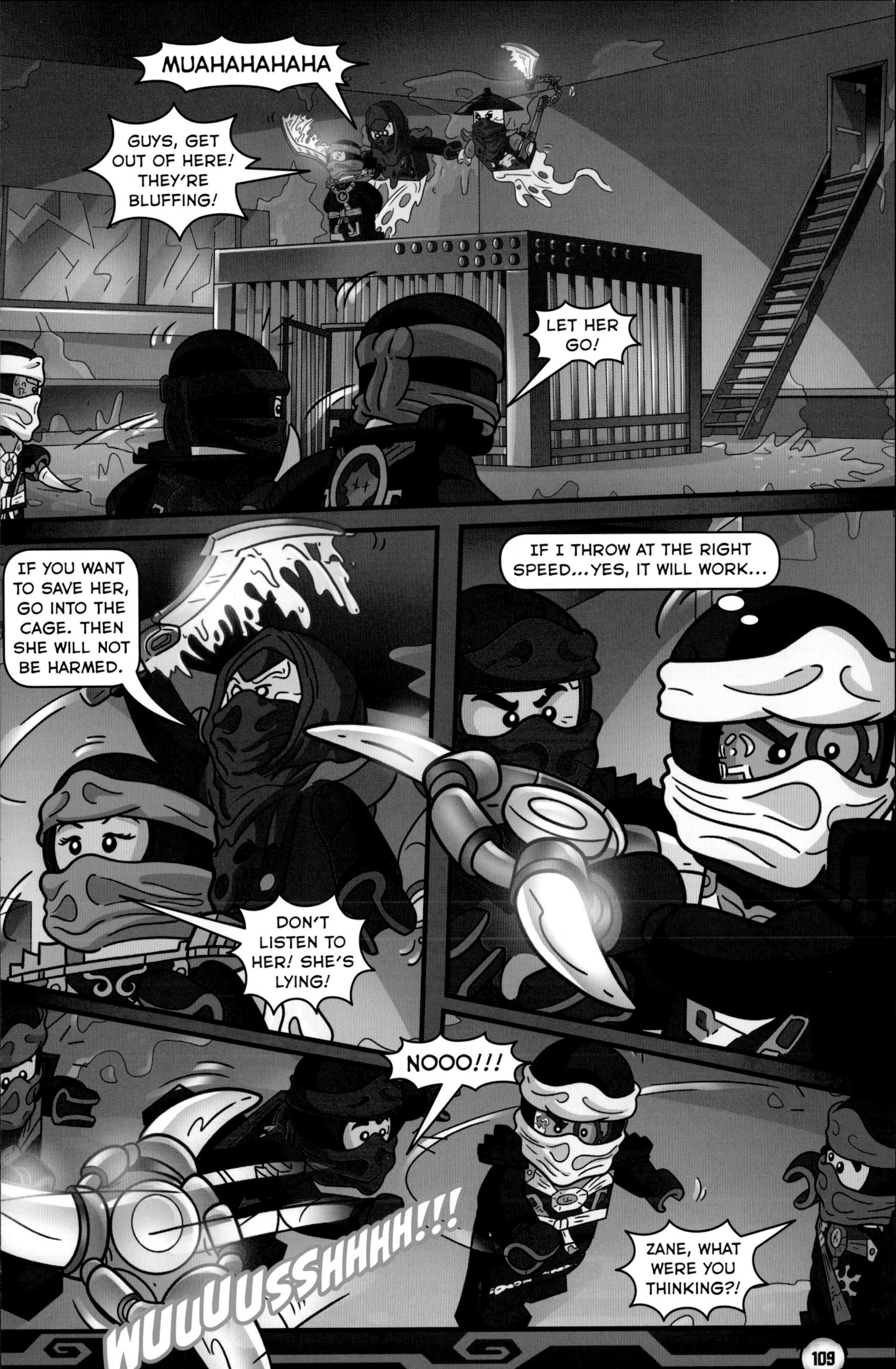

MUAHAHAHAHA
GUYS, GET OUT OF HERE! THEY'RE BLUFFING!
LET HER GO!
IF YOU WANT TO SAVE HER, GO INTO THE CAGE. THEN SHE WILL NOT BE HARMED.
DON'T LISTEN TO HER! SHE'S LYING!
IF I THROW AT THE RIGHT SPEED...YES, IT WILL WORK...
NOOO!!!
WUUUUSSHHHH!!!
ZANE, WHAT WERE YOU THINKING?!

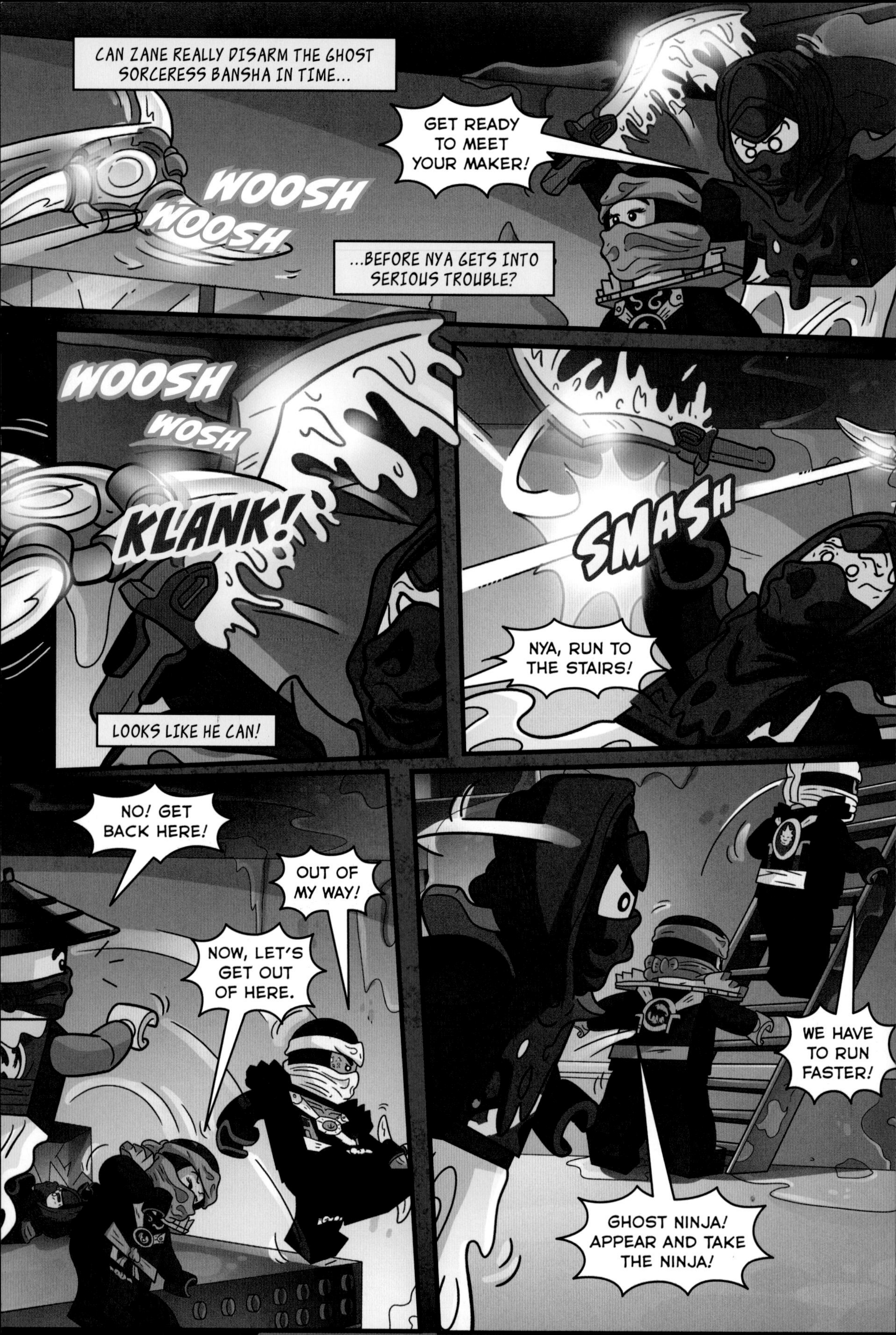
CAN ZANE REALLY DISARM THE GHOST SORCERESS BANSHA IN TIME...
GET READY TO MEET YOUR MAKER!
WOOSH
WOOSH
...BEFORE NYA GETS INTO SERIOUS TROUBLE?
WOOSH
WOSH
KLANK!
LOOKS LIKE HE CAN!
SMASH
NYA, RUN TO THE STAIRS!
NO! GET BACK HERE!
OUT OF MY WAY!
NOW, LET'S GET OUT OF HERE.
WE HAVE TO RUN FASTER!
GHOST NINJA! APPEAR AND TAKE THE NINJA!

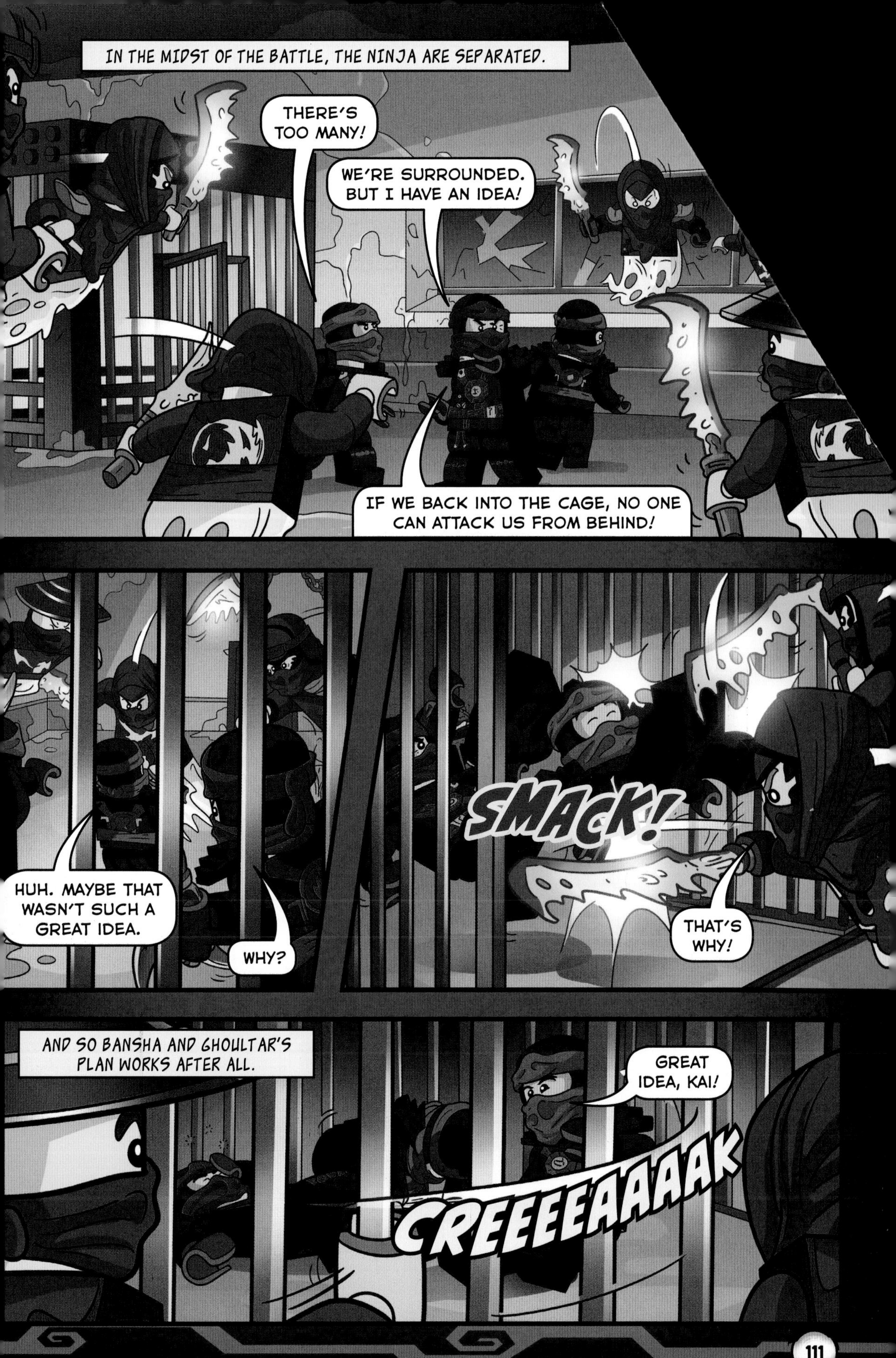
IN THE MIDST OF THE BATTLE, THE NINJA ARE SEPARATED.
THERE'S TOO MANY!
WE'RE SURROUNDED. BUT I HAVE AN IDEA!
IF WE BACK INTO THE CAGE, NO ONE CAN ATTACK US FROM BEHIND!
HUH. MAYBE THAT WASN'T SUCH A GREAT IDEA.
WHY?
SMACK!
THAT'S WHY!
AND SO BANSHA AND GHOULTAR'S PLAN WORKS AFTER ALL.
GREAT IDEA, KAI!
CREEEEAAAAK

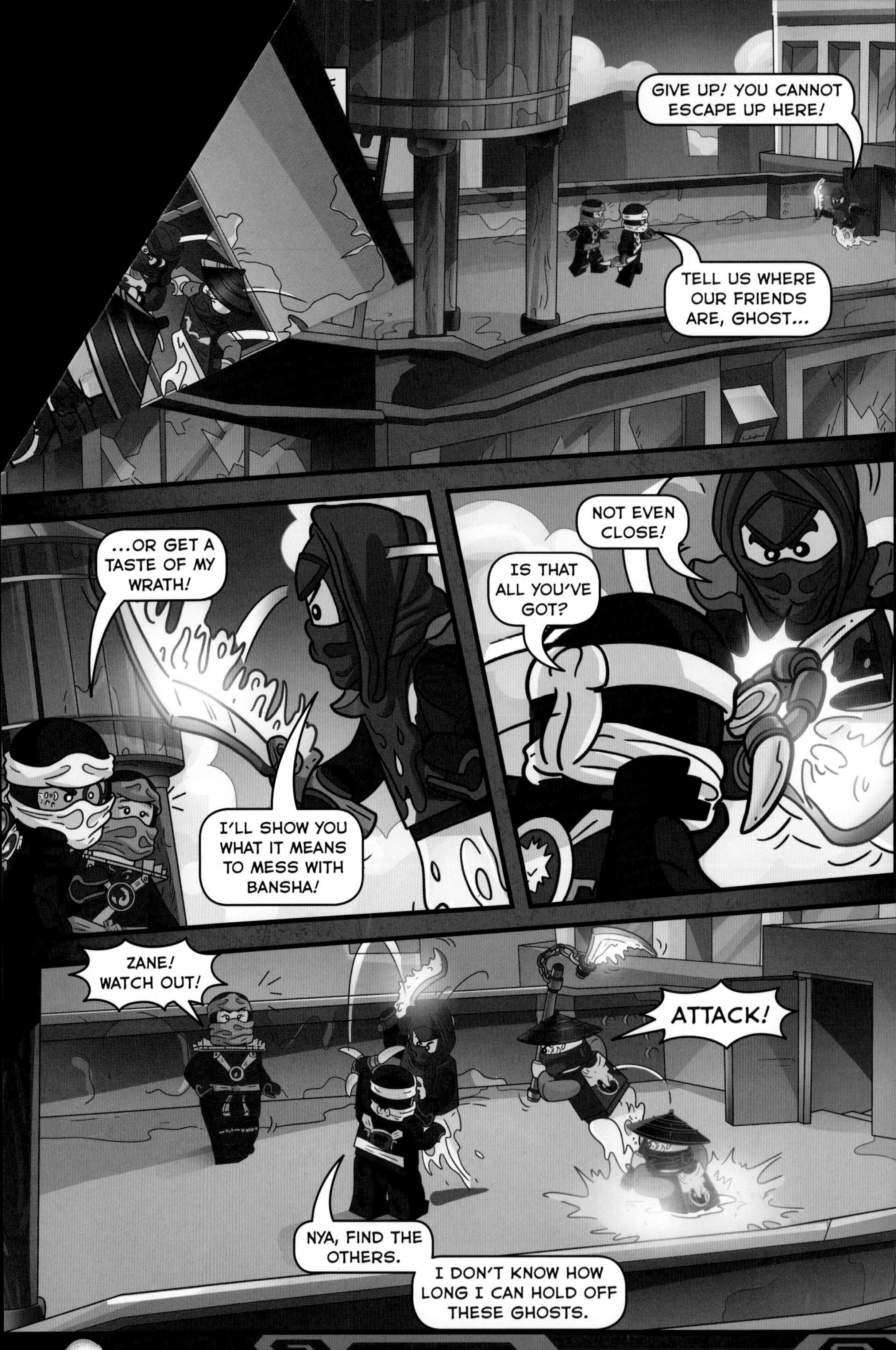
GIVE UP! YOU CANNOT ESCAPE UP HERE!
TELL US WHERE OUR FRIENDS ARE, GHOST...
...OR GET A TASTE OF MY WRATH!
I'LL SHOW YOU WHAT IT MEANS TO MESS WITH BANSHA!
NOT EVEN CLOSE!
IS THAT ALL YOU'VE GOT?
ZANE! WATCH OUT!
ATTACK!
NYA, FIND THE OTHERS.
I DON'T KNOW HOW LONG I CAN HOLD OFF THESE GHOSTS.

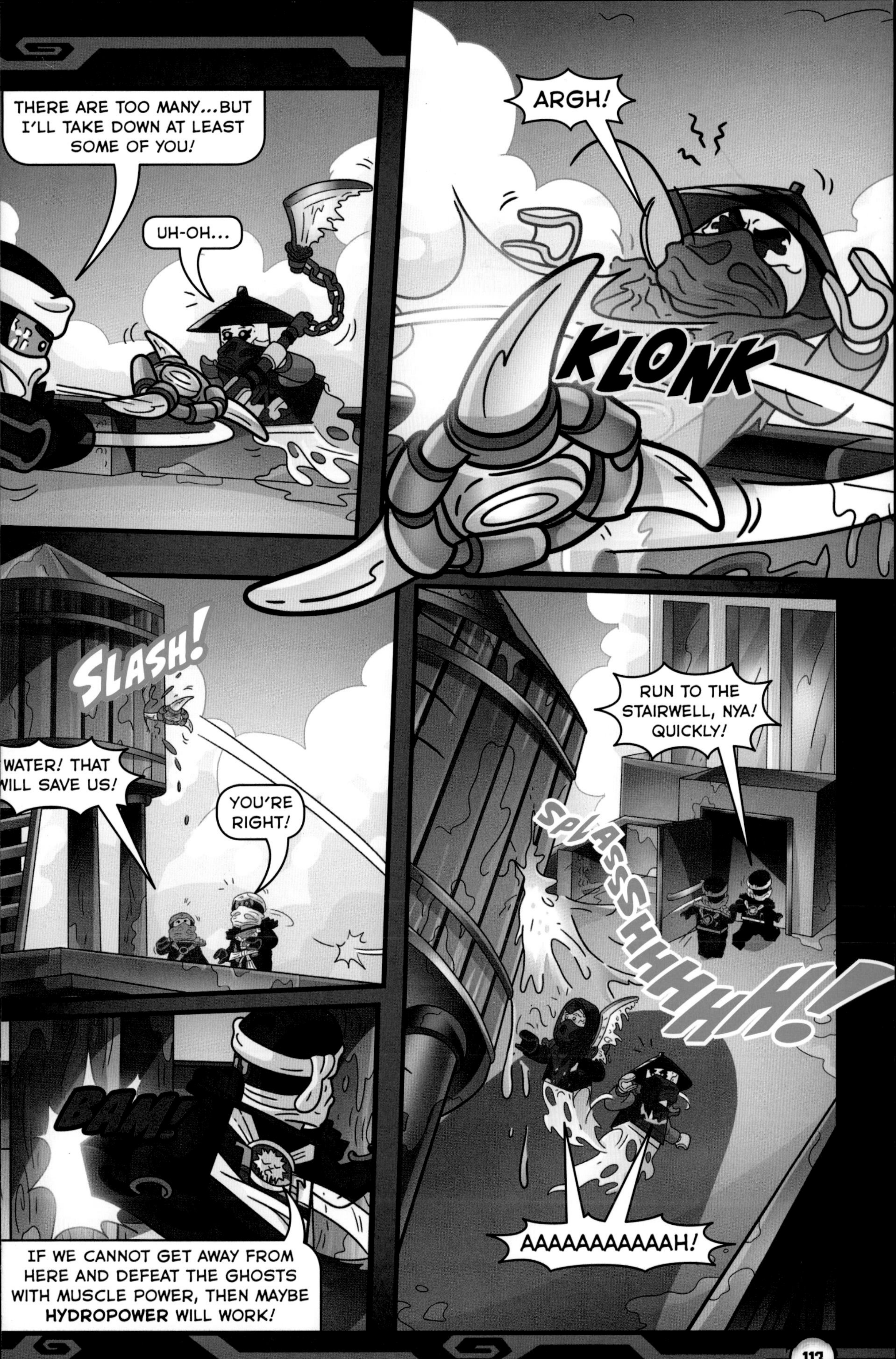

THERE ARE TOO MANY...BUT I'LL TAKE DOWN AT LEAST SOME OF YOU!
UH-OH...
ARGH!
KLONK
SLASH!
WATER! THAT WILL SAVE US!
YOU'RE RIGHT!
BAM!
IF WE CANNOT GET AWAY FROM HERE AND DEFEAT THE GHOSTS WITH MUSCLE POWER, THEN MAYBE **HYDROPOWER** WILL WORK!
RUN TO THE STAIRWELL, NYA! QUICKLY!
SPLASSSHHHHHH!
AAAAAAAAAAAH!

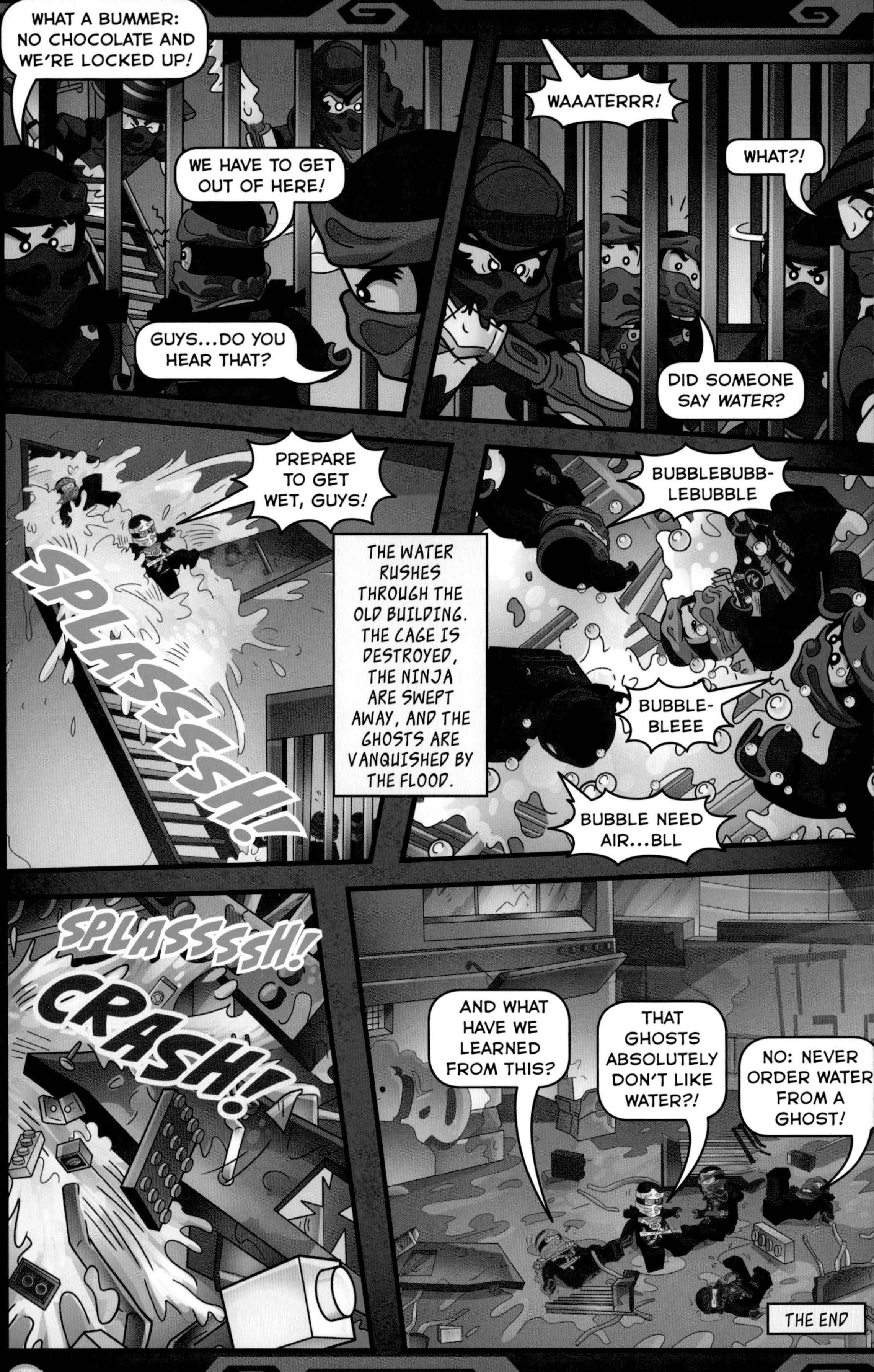
WHAT A BUMMER: NO CHOCOLATE AND WE'RE LOCKED UP!
WE HAVE TO GET OUT OF HERE!
GUYS...DO YOU HEAR THAT?
WAAATERRR!
WHAT?!
DID SOMEONE SAY WATER?
PREPARE TO GET WET, GUYS!
SPLASSSSH!
THE WATER RUSHES THROUGH THE OLD BUILDING. THE CAGE IS DESTROYED, THE NINJA ARE SWEPT AWAY, AND THE GHOSTS ARE VANQUISHED BY THE FLOOD.
BUBBLEBUBB-LEBUBBLE
BUBBLE-BLEEE
BUBBLE NEED AIR...BLL
SPLASSSSH!
CRASH!
AND WHAT HAVE WE LEARNED FROM THIS?
THAT GHOSTS ABSOLUTELY DON'T LIKE WATER?!
NO: NEVER ORDER WATER FROM A GHOST!
THE END

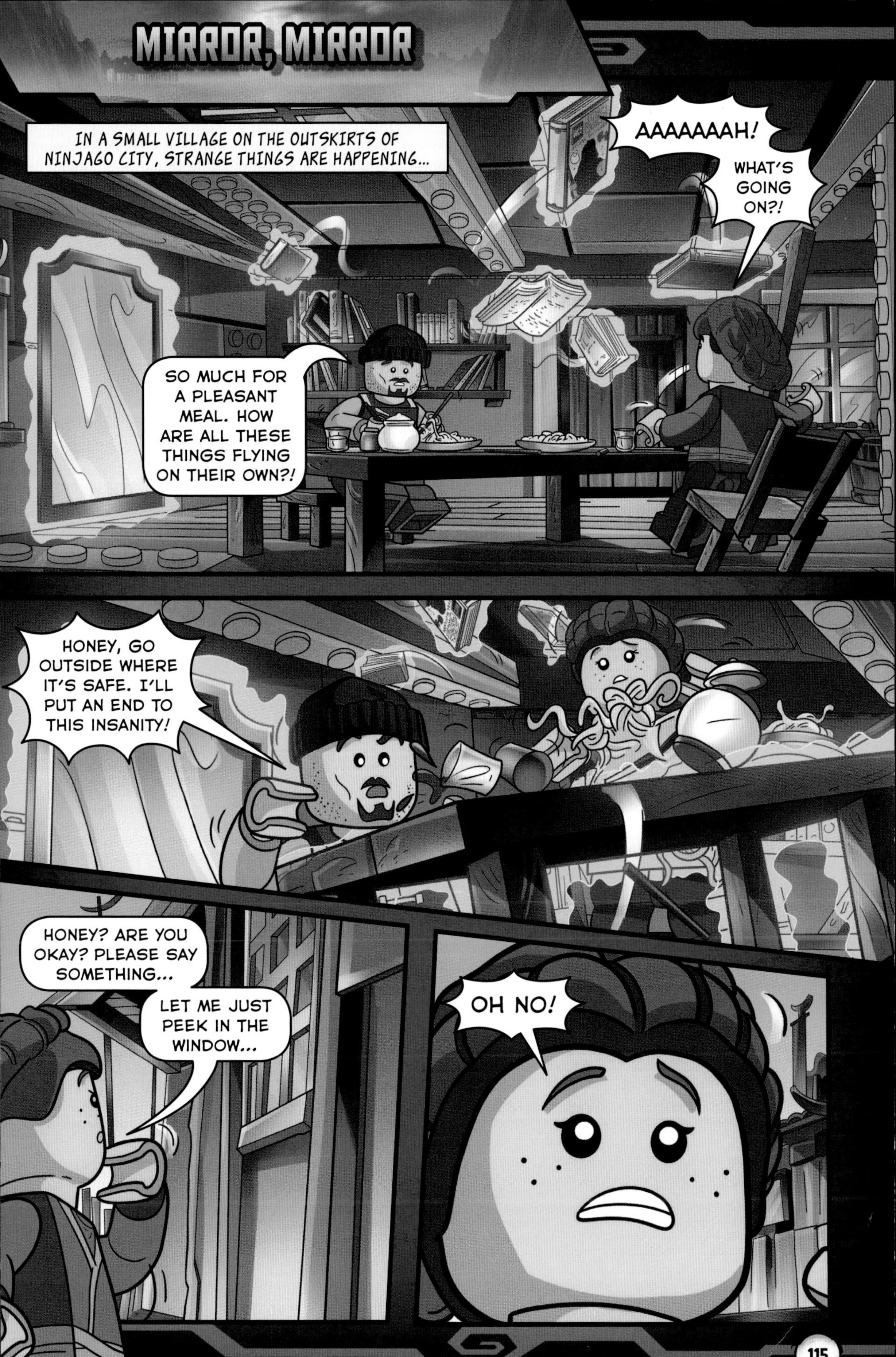
MIRROR, MIRROR
IN A SMALL VILLAGE ON THE OUTSKIRTS OF NINJAGO CITY, STRANGE THINGS ARE HAPPENING...
AAAAAAAH!
WHAT'S GOING ON?!
SO MUCH FOR A PLEASANT MEAL. HOW ARE ALL THESE THINGS FLYING ON THEIR OWN?!
HONEY, GO OUTSIDE WHERE IT'S SAFE. I'LL PUT AN END TO THIS INSANITY!
HONEY? ARE YOU OKAY? PLEASE SAY SOMETHING...
LET ME JUST PEEK IN THE WINDOW...
OH NO!

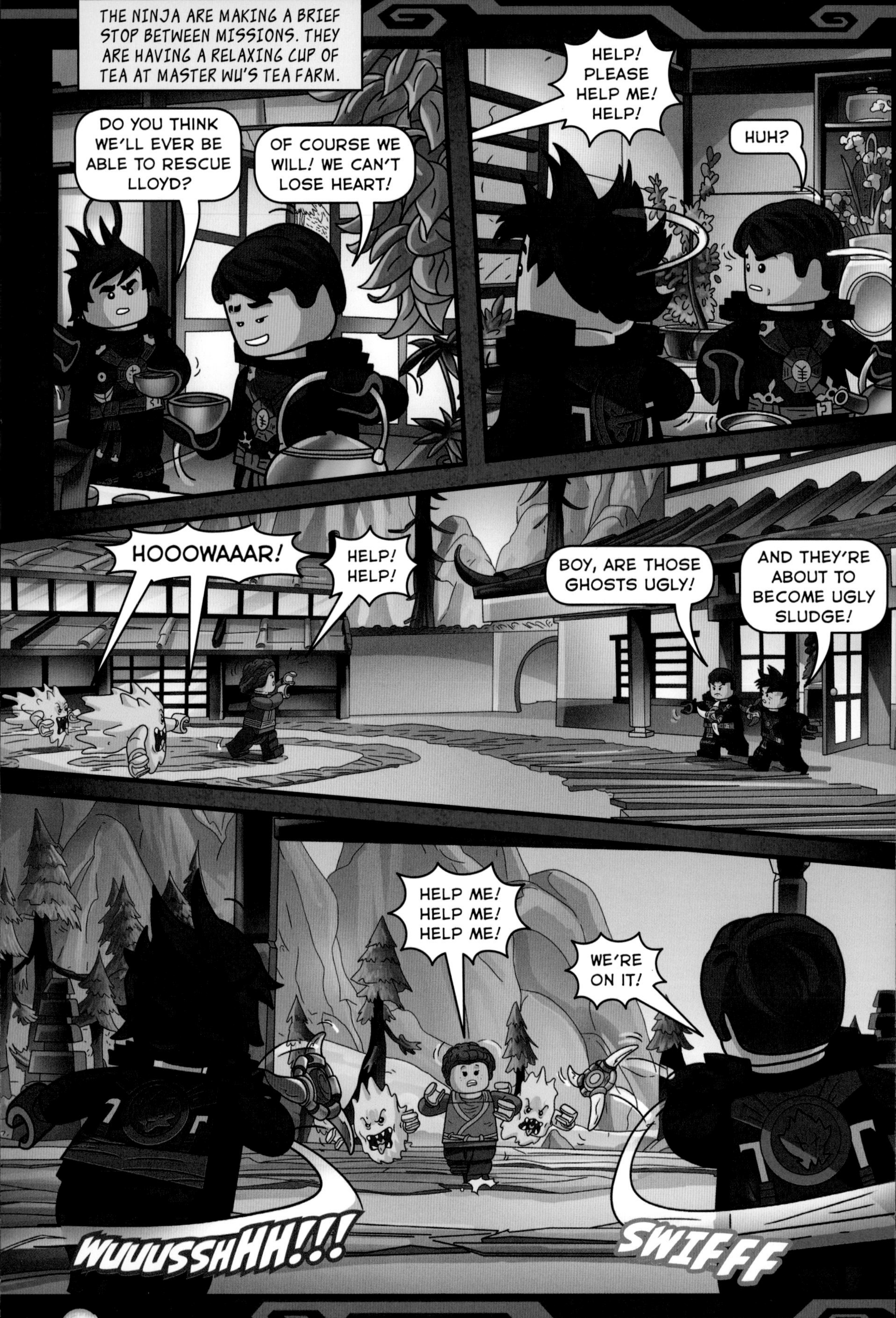
THE NINJA ARE MAKING A BRIEF STOP BETWEEN MISSIONS. THEY ARE HAVING A RELAXING CUP OF TEA AT MASTER WU'S TEA FARM.
DO YOU THINK WE'LL EVER BE ABLE TO RESCUE LLOYD?
OF COURSE WE WILL! WE CAN'T LOSE HEART!
HELP! PLEASE HELP ME! HELP!
HUH?
HOOOWAAAR!
HELP! HELP!
BOY, ARE THOSE GHOSTS UGLY!
AND THEY'RE ABOUT TO BECOME UGLY SLUDGE!
HELP ME! HELP ME! HELP ME!
WE'RE ON IT!
WUUUSSHHH!!!
SWIFFF

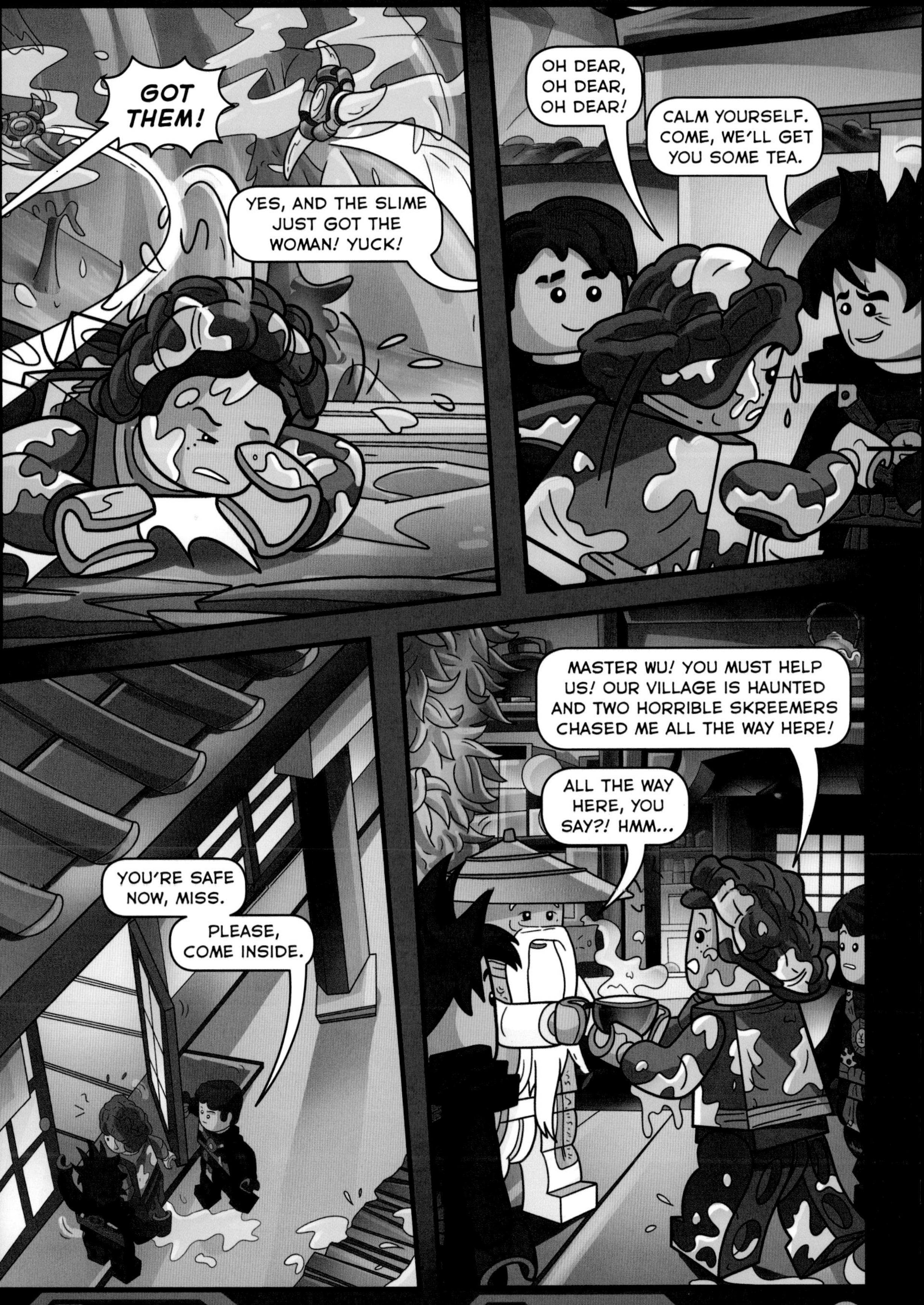
GOT THEM!
YES, AND THE SLIME JUST GOT THE WOMAN! YUCK!
OH DEAR, OH DEAR, OH DEAR!
CALM YOURSELF. COME, WE'LL GET YOU SOME TEA.
YOU'RE SAFE NOW, MISS.
PLEASE, COME INSIDE.
MASTER WU! YOU MUST HELP US! OUR VILLAGE IS HAUNTED AND TWO HORRIBLE SKREEMERS CHASED ME ALL THE WAY HERE!
ALL THE WAY HERE, YOU SAY?! HMM...

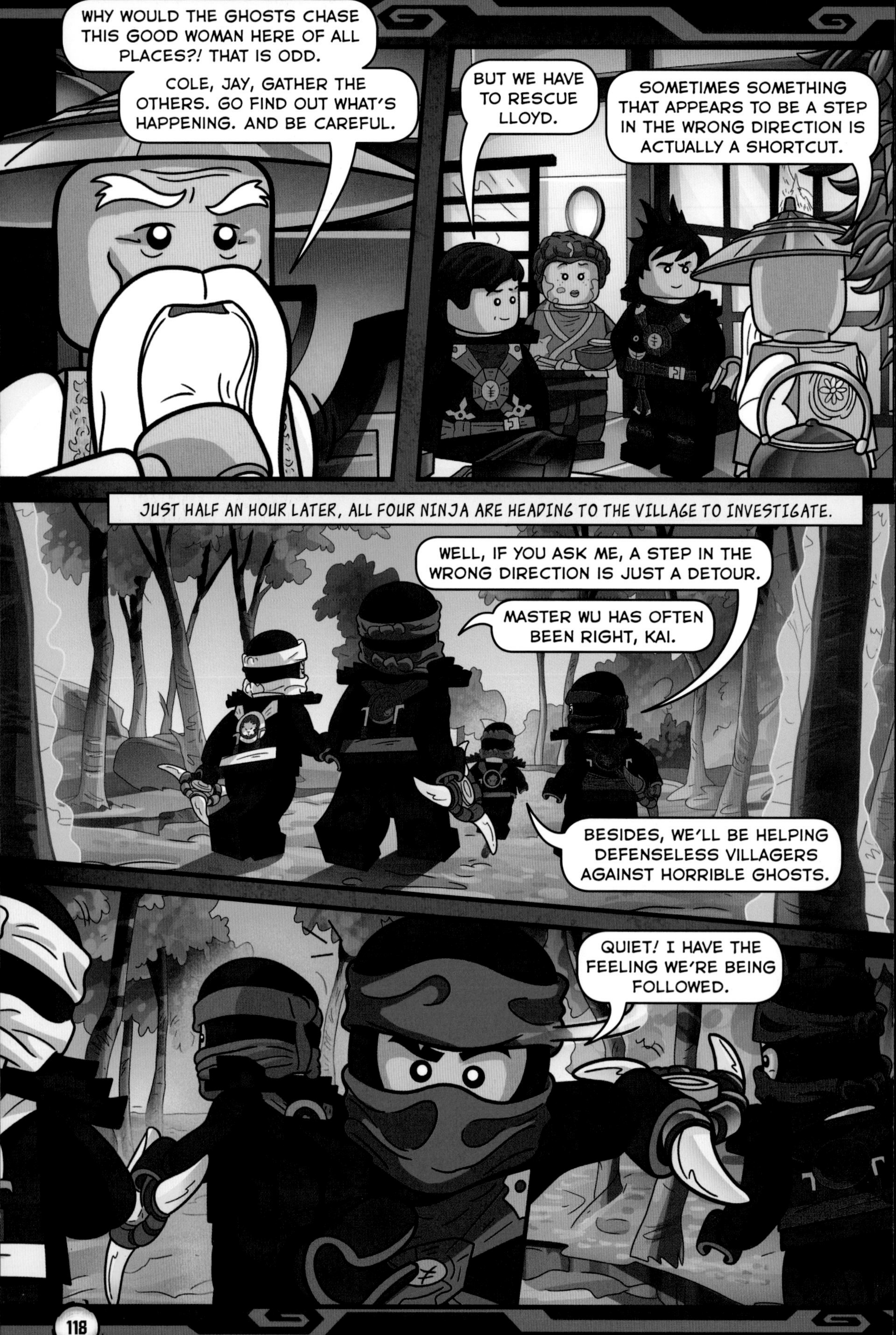
WHY WOULD THE GHOSTS CHASE THIS GOOD WOMAN HERE OF ALL PLACES?! THAT IS ODD.
COLE, JAY, GATHER THE OTHERS. GO FIND OUT WHAT'S HAPPENING. AND BE CAREFUL.
BUT WE HAVE TO RESCUE LLOYD.
SOMETIMES SOMETHING THAT APPEARS TO BE A STEP IN THE WRONG DIRECTION IS ACTUALLY A SHORTCUT.
JUST HALF AN HOUR LATER, ALL FOUR NINJA ARE HEADING TO THE VILLAGE TO INVESTIGATE.
WELL, IF YOU ASK ME, A STEP IN THE WRONG DIRECTION IS JUST A DETOUR.
MASTER WU HAS OFTEN BEEN RIGHT, KAI.
BESIDES, WE'LL BE HELPING DEFENSELESS VILLAGERS AGAINST HORRIBLE GHOSTS.
QUIET! I HAVE THE FEELING WE'RE BEING FOLLOWED.

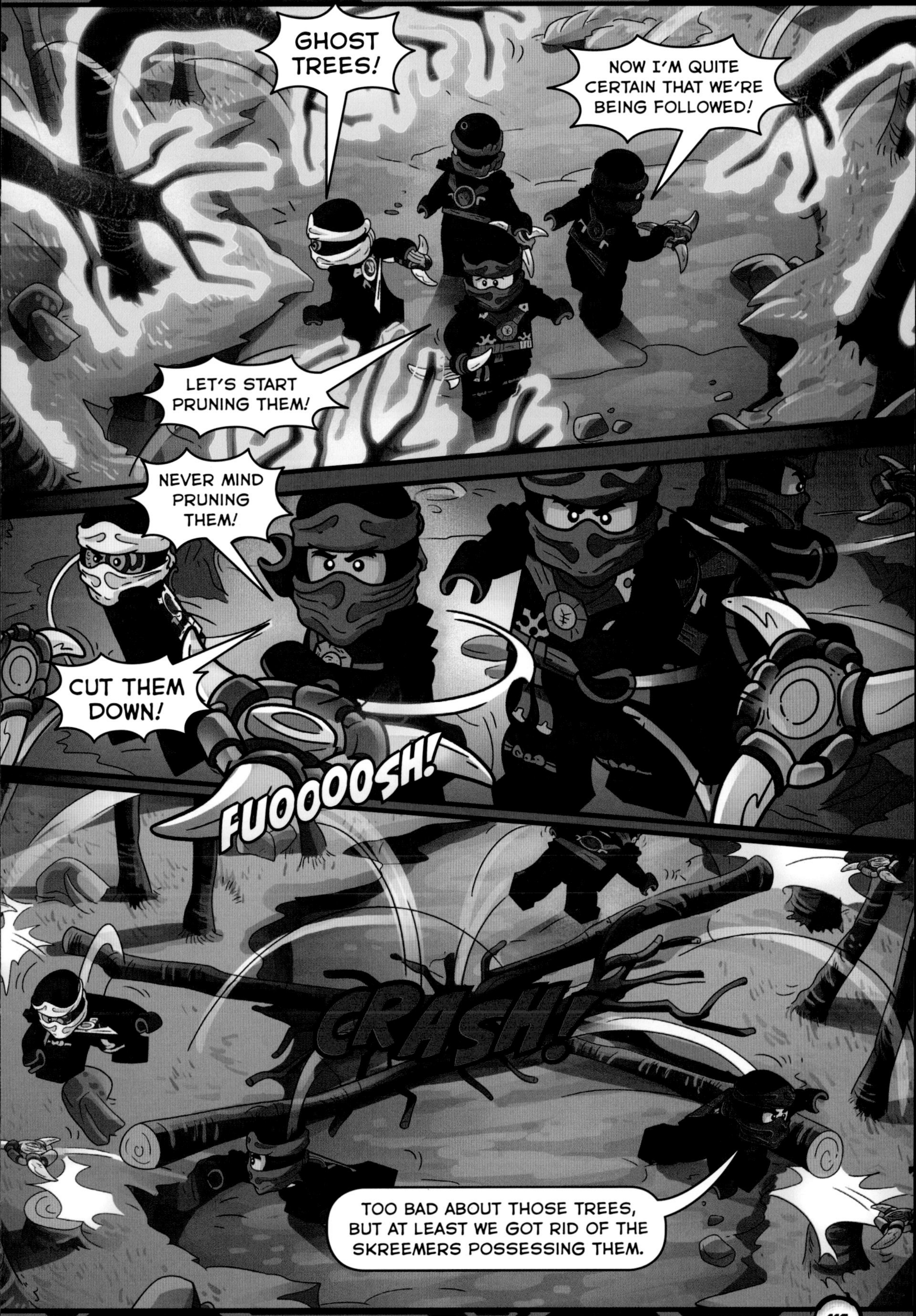
GHOST TREES!
NOW I'M QUITE CERTAIN THAT WE'RE BEING FOLLOWED!
LET'S START PRUNING THEM!
NEVER MIND PRUNING THEM!
CUT THEM DOWN!
FUOOOOSH!
CRASH!
TOO BAD ABOUT THOSE TREES, BUT AT LEAST WE GOT RID OF THE SKREEMERS POSSESSING THEM.

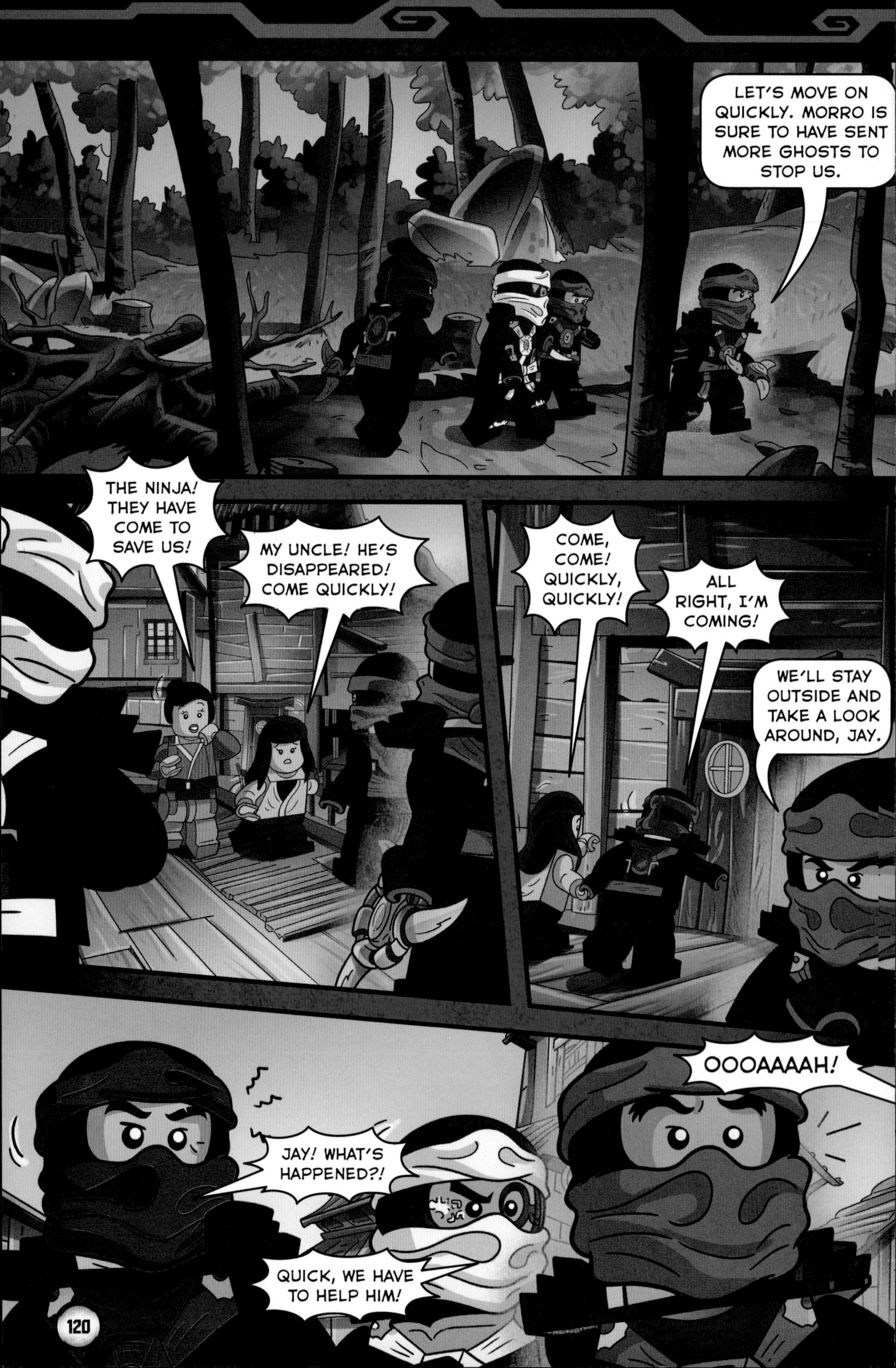
LET'S MOVE ON QUICKLY. MORRO IS SURE TO HAVE SENT MORE GHOSTS TO STOP US.
THE NINJA! THEY HAVE COME TO SAVE US!
MY UNCLE! HE'S DISAPPEARED! COME QUICKLY!
COME, COME! QUICKLY, QUICKLY!
ALL RIGHT, I'M COMING!
WE'LL STAY OUTSIDE AND TAKE A LOOK AROUND, JAY.
OOOAAAAH!
JAY! WHAT'S HAPPENED?!
QUICK, WE HAVE TO HELP HIM!

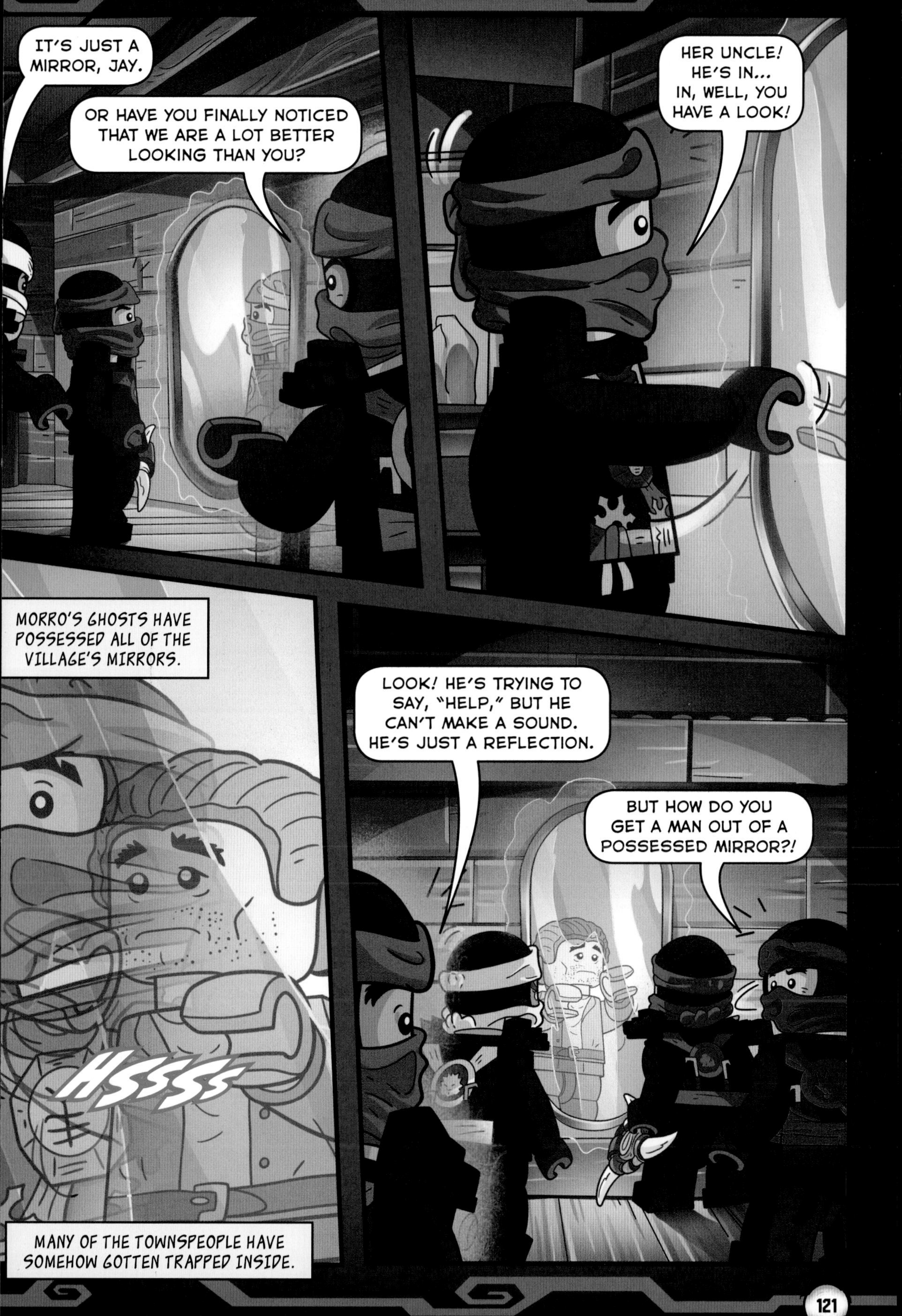
IT'S JUST A MIRROR, JAY.
OR HAVE YOU FINALLY NOTICED THAT WE ARE A LOT BETTER LOOKING THAN YOU?
HER UNCLE! HE'S IN... IN, WELL, YOU HAVE A LOOK!
MORRO'S GHOSTS HAVE POSSESSED ALL OF THE VILLAGE'S MIRRORS.
HSSSS
MANY OF THE TOWNSPEOPLE HAVE SOMEHOW GOTTEN TRAPPED INSIDE.
LOOK! HE'S TRYING TO SAY, "HELP," BUT HE CAN'T MAKE A SOUND. HE'S JUST A REFLECTION.
BUT HOW DO YOU GET A MAN OUT OF A POSSESSED MIRROR?!

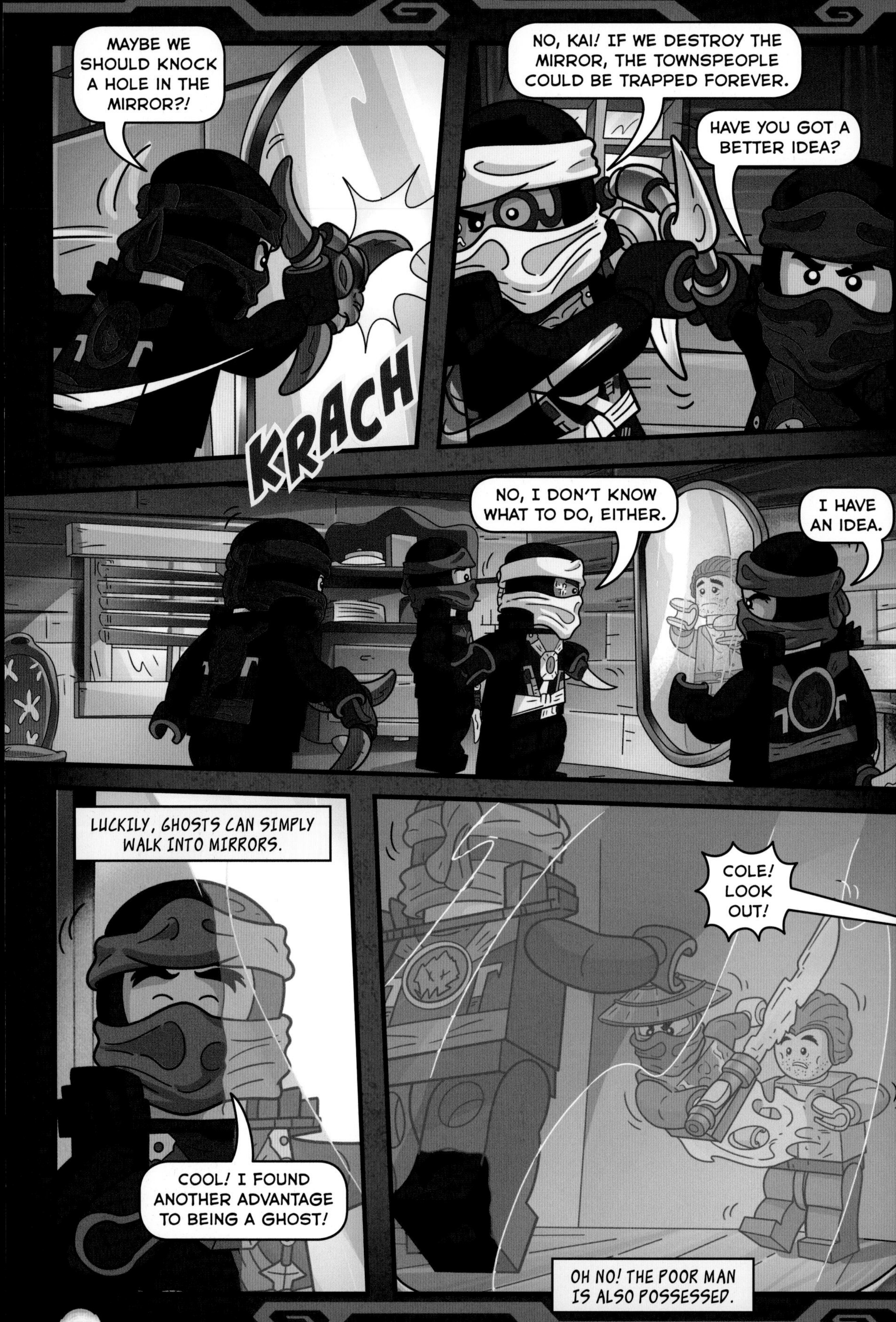
MAYBE WE SHOULD KNOCK A HOLE IN THE MIRROR?!
KRACH
NO, KAI! IF WE DESTROY THE MIRROR, THE TOWNSPEOPLE COULD BE TRAPPED FOREVER.
HAVE YOU GOT A BETTER IDEA?
NO, I DON'T KNOW WHAT TO DO, EITHER.
I HAVE AN IDEA.
LUCKILY, GHOSTS CAN SIMPLY WALK INTO MIRRORS.
COOL! I FOUND ANOTHER ADVANTAGE TO BEING A GHOST!
COLE! LOOK OUT!
OH NO! THE POOR MAN IS ALSO POSSESSED.

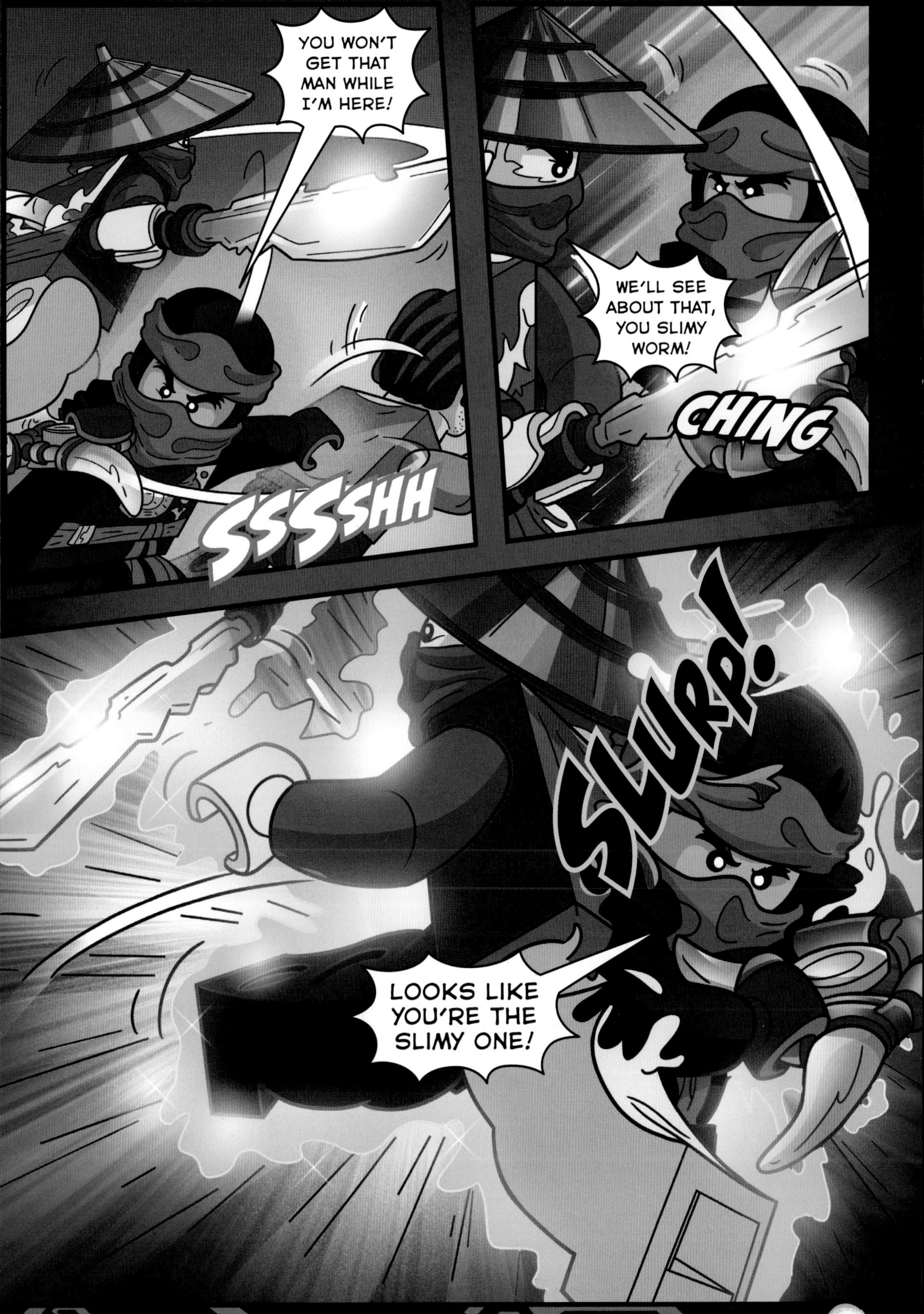
YOU WON'T GET THAT MAN WHILE I'M HERE!
SSSSHH
WE'LL SEE ABOUT THAT, YOU SLIMY WORM!
CHING
SLURP!
LOOKS LIKE YOU'RE THE SLIMY ONE!

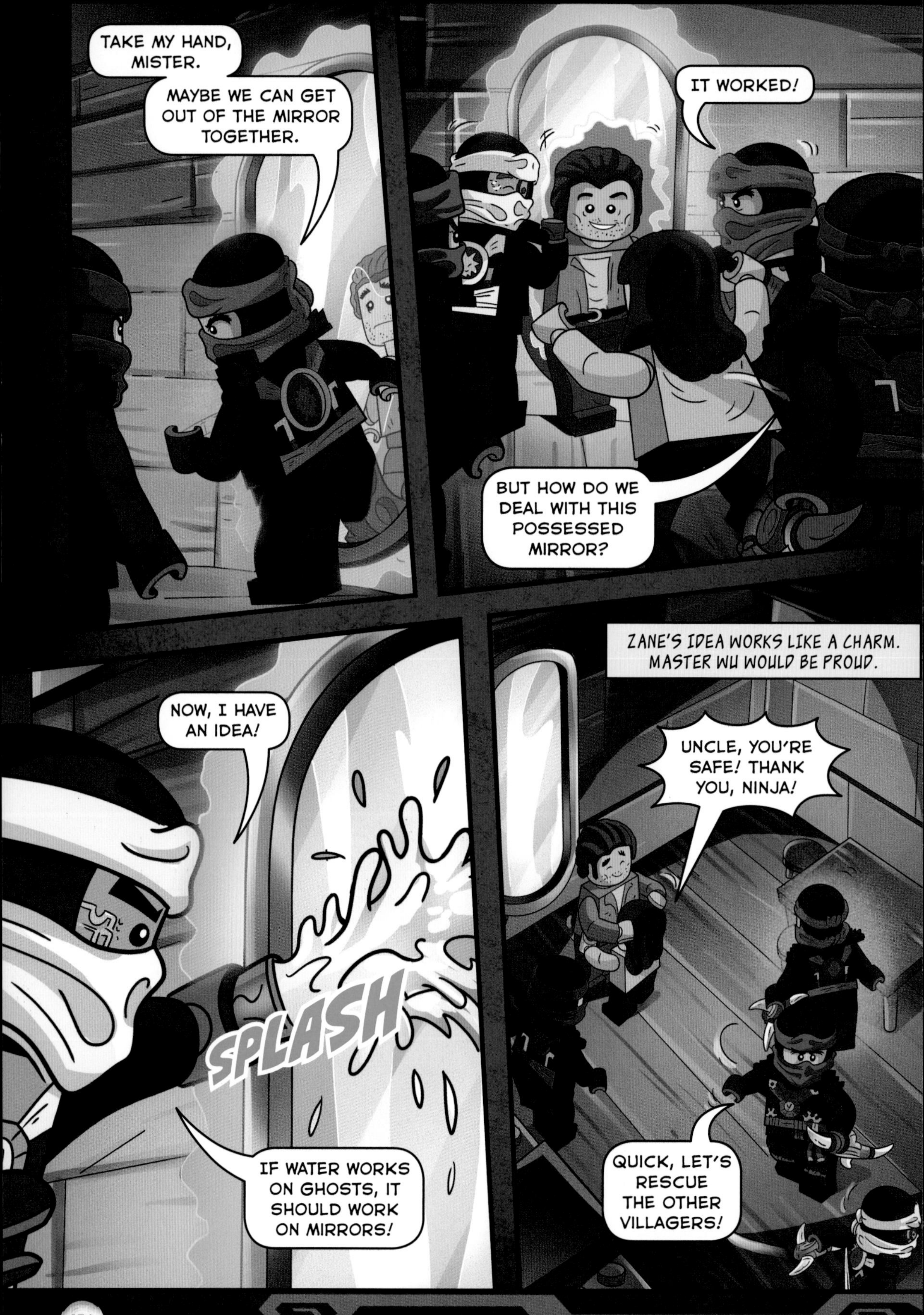
TAKE MY HAND, MISTER.
MAYBE WE CAN GET OUT OF THE MIRROR TOGETHER.
IT WORKED!
BUT HOW DO WE DEAL WITH THIS POSSESSED MIRROR?
NOW, I HAVE AN IDEA!
SPLASH
IF WATER WORKS ON GHOSTS, IT SHOULD WORK ON MIRRORS!
ZANE'S IDEA WORKS LIKE A CHARM. MASTER WU WOULD BE PROUD.
UNCLE, YOU'RE SAFE! THANK YOU, NINJA!
QUICK, LET'S RESCUE THE OTHER VILLAGERS!

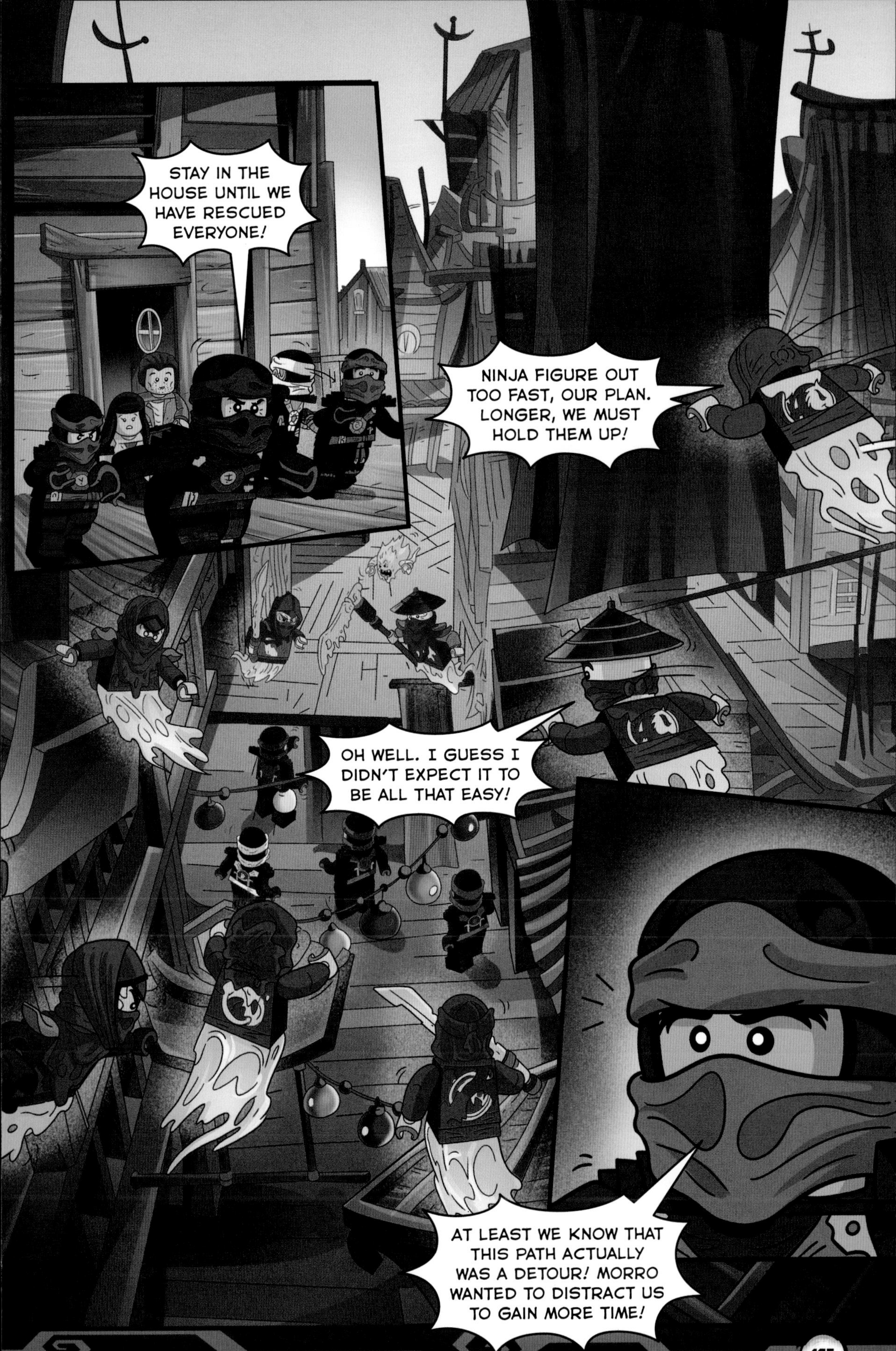
STAY IN THE HOUSE UNTIL WE HAVE RESCUED EVERYONE!
NINJA FIGURE OUT TOO FAST, OUR PLAN. LONGER, WE MUST HOLD THEM UP!
OH WELL. I GUESS I DIDN'T EXPECT IT TO BE ALL THAT EASY!
AT LEAST WE KNOW THAT THIS PATH ACTUALLY WAS A DETOUR! MORRO WANTED TO DISTRACT US TO GAIN MORE TIME!

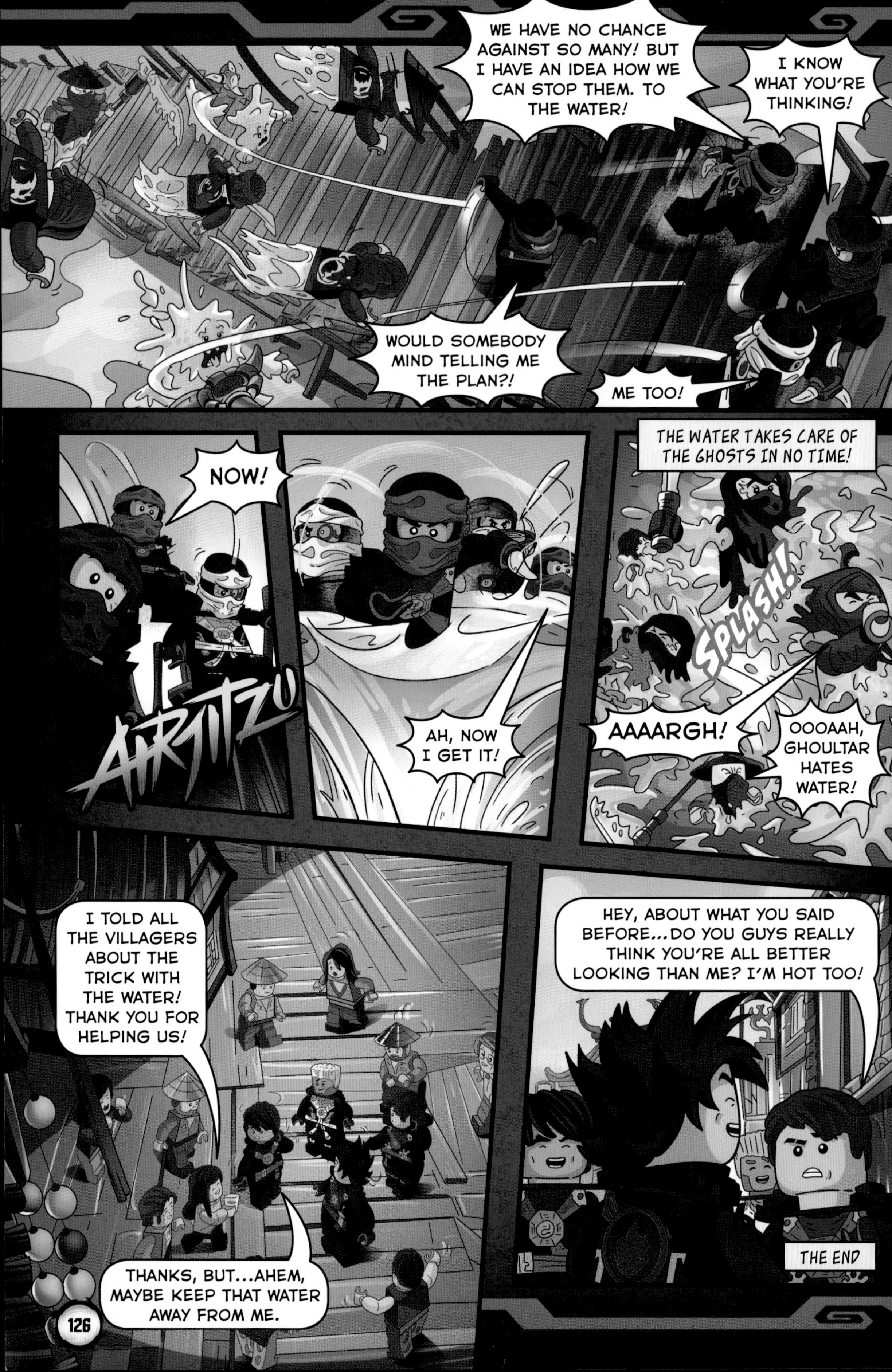

WE HAVE NO CHANCE AGAINST SO MANY! BUT I HAVE AN IDEA HOW WE CAN STOP THEM. TO THE WATER!
I KNOW WHAT YOU'RE THINKING!
WOULD SOMEBODY MIND TELLING ME THE PLAN?!
ME TOO!
NOW!
AIRJITZU
AH, NOW I GET IT!
THE WATER TAKES CARE OF THE GHOSTS IN NO TIME!
SPLASH!
AAAARGH!
OOOAAH, GHOULTAR HATES WATER!
I TOLD ALL THE VILLAGERS ABOUT THE TRICK WITH THE WATER! THANK YOU FOR HELPING US!
THANKS, BUT...AHEM, MAYBE KEEP THAT WATER AWAY FROM ME.
HEY, ABOUT WHAT YOU SAID BEFORE...DO YOU GUYS REALLY THINK YOU'RE ALL BETTER LOOKING THAN ME? I'M HOT TOO!
THE END

THE LOST SCROLLS OF SPINJITZU

RONIN! HERO OR VILLAIN?

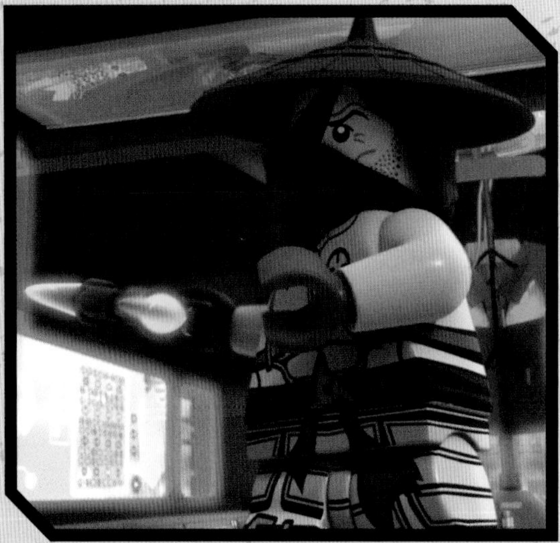

The only master Ronin serves is the almighty dollar. He's a thief who's known to have made a few bad bets—including selling his soul to the Soul Archer. When his path intersects with the ninja, Ronin has a chance to make things right and be a hero for once. But what's in it for him?

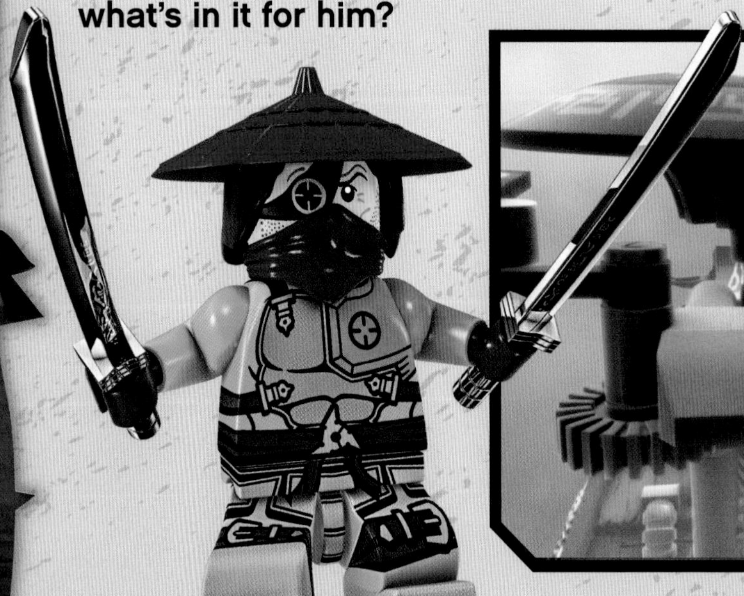

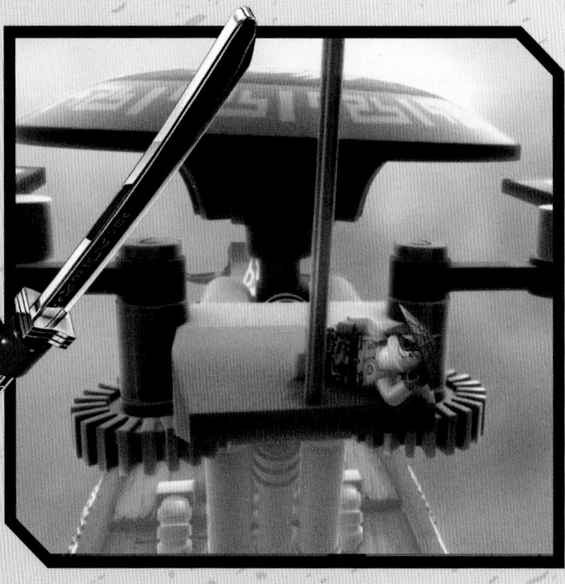

MORRO, MASTER OF WIND

Morro was Master Wu's first pupil. Long ago, after seeing his command of the wind, Wu trained him to be the Green Ninja. But there was a darkness inside Morro and a thirst to be the best, like no other. This worried Wu, and when the  Golden Weapons didn't react in the Green Ninja ceremony, Wu tried to convince Morro to give up...but he wouldn't.

Wanting to prove Wu wrong, Morro went out in search of the Lost Tomb of the First Spinjitzu Master but never came back. Little did Wu realize, Morro was banished to the Cursed Realm, where he patiently waited to get a second chance to become the Green Ninja, and when Lord Garmadon opened the door while defeating Master Chen, Morro finally got his wish.

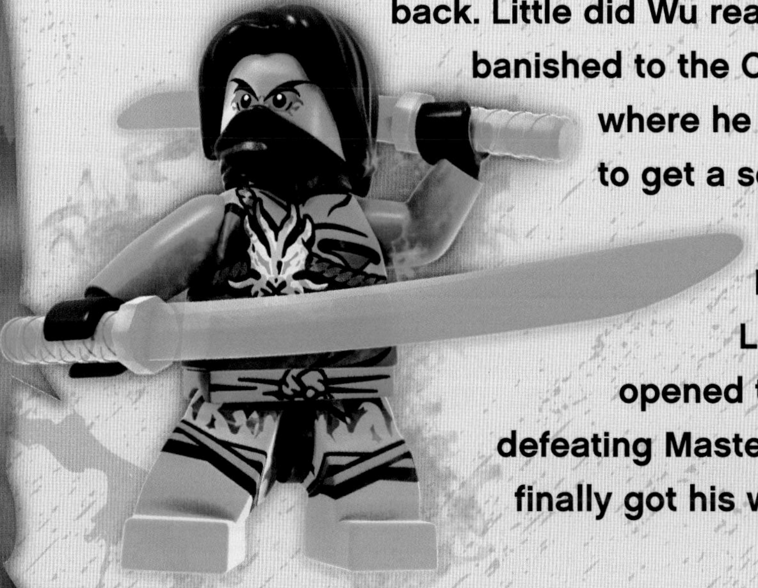

THE PREEMINENT

The Preeminent isn't just the ruler of the Cursed Realm, she IS the Cursed Realm. All encompassing, she has a primordial thirst to curse all that she touches. That means  she won't be satisfied with just Ninjago—she won't stop until she has devoured all sixteen realms.

SOUL ARCHER

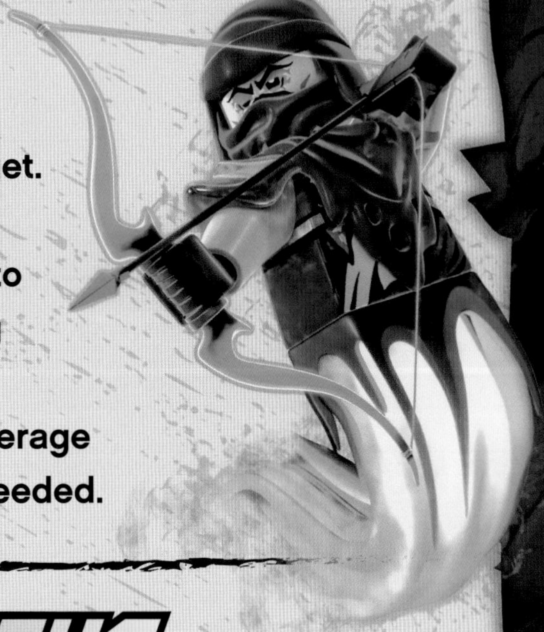

Soul Archer never misses. With his supernatural bow and arrows, he always finds his target. This Ghost Archer is Morro's right-hand man and a menace to the ninja. When he's not helping Morro, he's out there collecting souls and biding his time to leverage them to aid his evil will when needed.

BANSHA

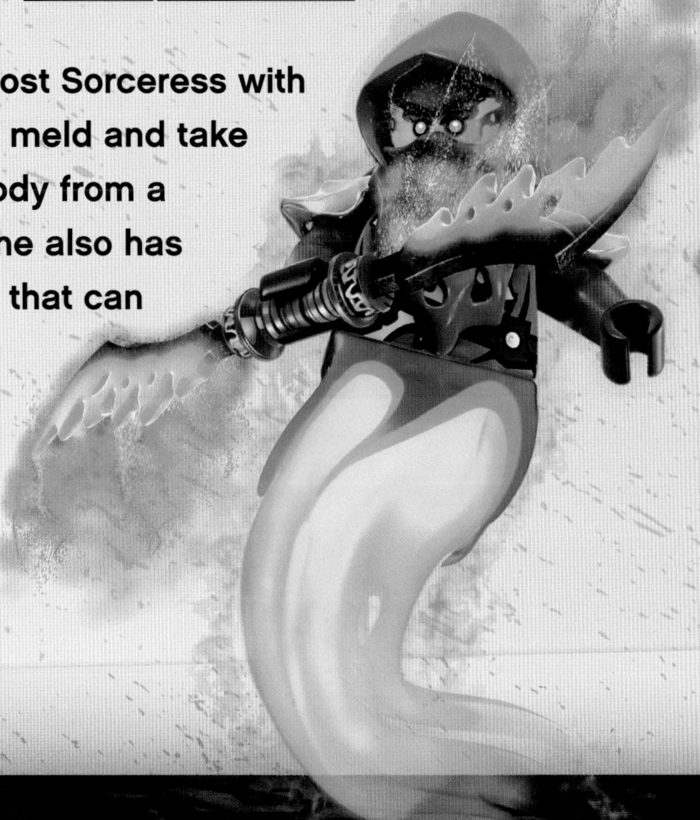

Bansha is a Ghost Sorceress with the power to mind meld and take over someone's body from a distant location. She also has a piercing scream that can shatter eardrums and cause catastrophic havoc.

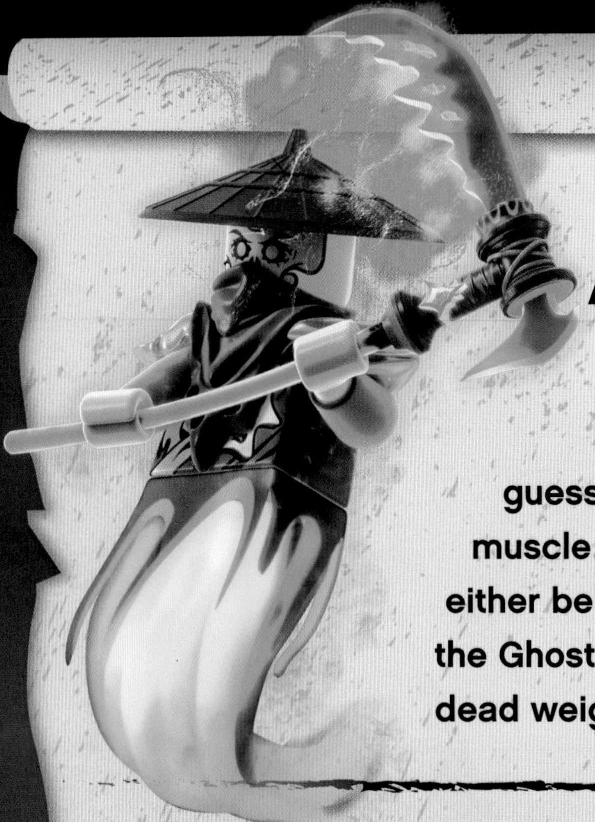

GHOULTAR

Dumb and strong, Ghoultar never second-guesses an order. As the ghost muscle of the group, Ghoultar can either be the strength needed to put the Ghost Generals over the top or the dead weight that will sink them.

WRAYTH

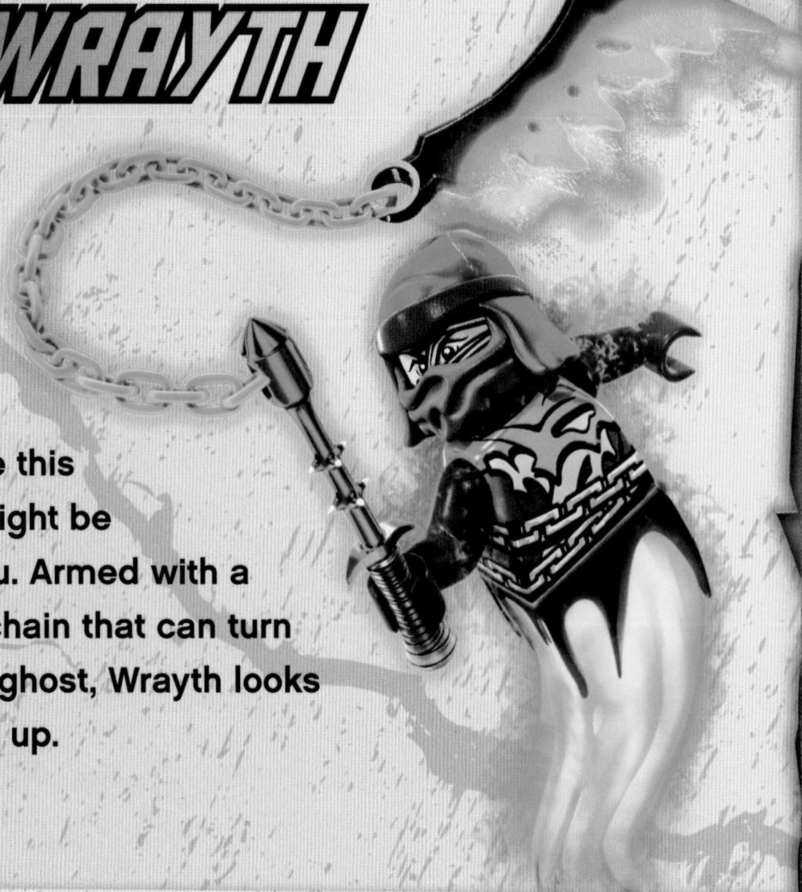

If you hear cackling and the rev of his ghost cycle, watch your back, because this Ghost Biker might be coming for you. Armed with a supernatural chain that can turn anyone into a ghost, Wrayth looks to tie the ninja up.

THE GHOST NINJA

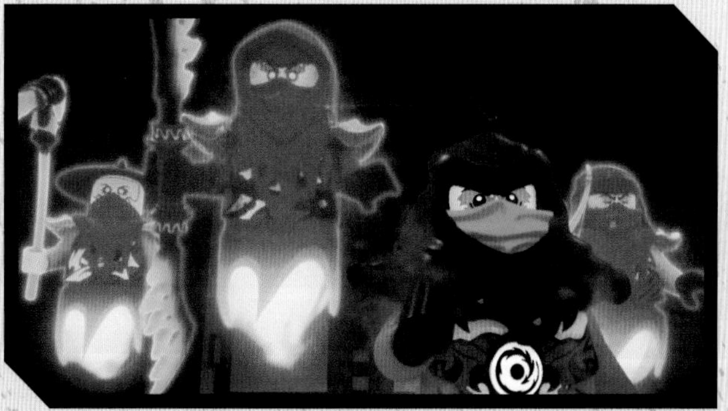

The ninja have battled their share of baddies, but these ghosts prove to be one of their biggest challenges yet. Not only can they possess nearly anyone and anything around, but the only way to stop one is with either water or weapons made of Deepstone.

DEEPSTONE AEROBLADES

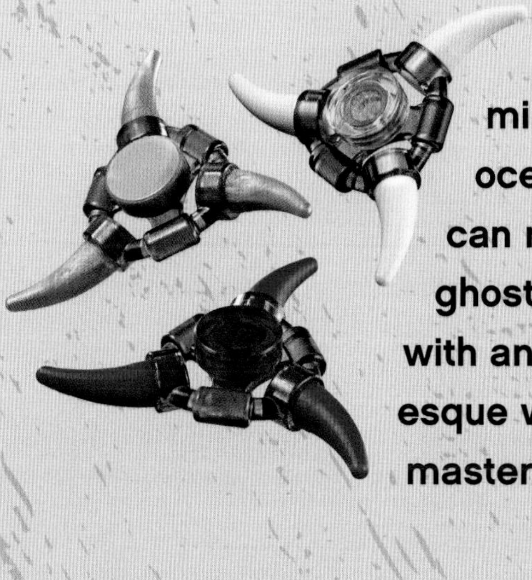

Deepstone is a rare mineral mined from the bottom of the ocean. Since it's the only solid that can make contact with an ethereal ghost, what better way to use it than with an Aeroblade—a boomerang-esque weapon that returns to its master...most of the time?

AIRJITZU

An ancient martial art created by Master Yang, Airjitzu allows a Spinjitzu Master to propel himself into the air and temporarily take flight. Or as Jay likes to call it—"Cyclondo!" It's a difficult art to master but integral to the ninja's mission.

THE REALM CRYSTAL

The Realm Crystal is so powerful, the First Spinjitzu Master kept it close to him at his hidden burial site because he didn't want it to fall into the wrong hands. The crystal has sixteen sides, and if exposed to light, it will open one of sixteen portals to other worlds. Morro is after the crystal because it is the only way for the Preeminent to cross over into Ninjago.

THE SWORD OF SANCTUARY

Though it looks like a normal sword, the Sword of Sanctuary foretells an opponent's next move within the reflection of its blade. Wielded properly, it's a devastating weapon that automatically gives the carrier the upper hand in battle, but it can also help guide its wielder through impossible traps and imminent danger.

THE ALLIED ARMOR OF AZURE

If ninja find themselves in a jam and in need of some help, they might want to wear this magical breastplate. If your opponent has it—look out, because at any moment he or she can conjure the aid of allies. When Morro steals it, he's able to usher a few ghost friends from the Cursed Realm.

STEEP WISDOM

Since Wu knows so much about teas, why not open a business? Much of the ninja's operations are run out of

Master Wu's tea farm—which is good, since they are struggling to find customers. When the ninja sell their shares to Ronin in exchange for some lifesaving help, Wu gets an unexpected business partner.

THE WAILING ALPS

The Wailing Alps are the tallest peaks in Ninjago and are named after the "wailing" wind gusts that could blow one clear off the mountain if not properly tied down.

They're cold, with unrelenting blizzards. As if these peaks weren't high enough, they are merely a stepping-stone to the Cloud Kingdom.

STIIX

If there's anything that smells worse than the coast, it's the dilapidated village of Stiix, which extends over it. In constant disrepair, Stiix is a rickety cesspool of fishmongers and

vagrants...which is why it's the perfect home for Ronin and his pawnshop. Eventually, Stiix becomes Morro's headquarters and the location of the Preeminent's arrival.

THE CLOUD KINGDOM

There's a kingdom in the clouds, and the denizens of this regal realm are doing more than just looking down on Ninjago—they are writing its destiny! It was they who decided Lloyd should be the Green Ninja, that Zane should be a Nindroid, and that Cole would be a ghost. But just because they have written the past, doesn't mean they always know the future.

(After all, those who live in the Cloud Kingdom may know a person's destiny, but they don't always know how those who live below will arrive at it.)

THE LOST TOMB OF THE FIRST SPINJITZU MASTER

It is a place of legend, thought never to have existed. But after finding an encoded message on Master Wu's staff, the ninja discover it's real. To actually get there is another 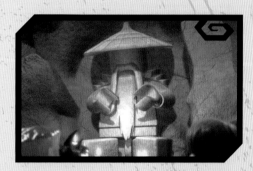 thing entirely. First they'll need to learn Airjitzu so they can get to the Cloud Kingdom. Then they must procure the Sword of Sanctuary to see past the deadly puzzle traps protecting the jewel of the burial site—the all-powerful Realm Crystal.

THE LIBRARY IN DOMU

In this awe-inspiring place, you can find any book written on anything...ever!

Managed by monks and students of history, this location will prove a valuable source of knowledge and history. What secrets does Ninjago's mysterious past hold? You can find the answers here if you dig deep enough in the seemingly infinite collection of books.

YANG'S HAUNTED TEMPLE

There were other masters in Ninjago, and not all of them as sweet as Wu. Master Yang was hard on his students, but he is responsible for creating Airjitzu—just the coolest thing since Spinjitzu. The problem is, Master Yang is no longer around, and now his spirit haunts his temple, an architectural relic from a bygone era of Ninjago.

CAN YOU DECODE THE SECRET MESSAGE?

A B C D E F G
H I J K L M N
O P Q R S T U
V W X Y Z

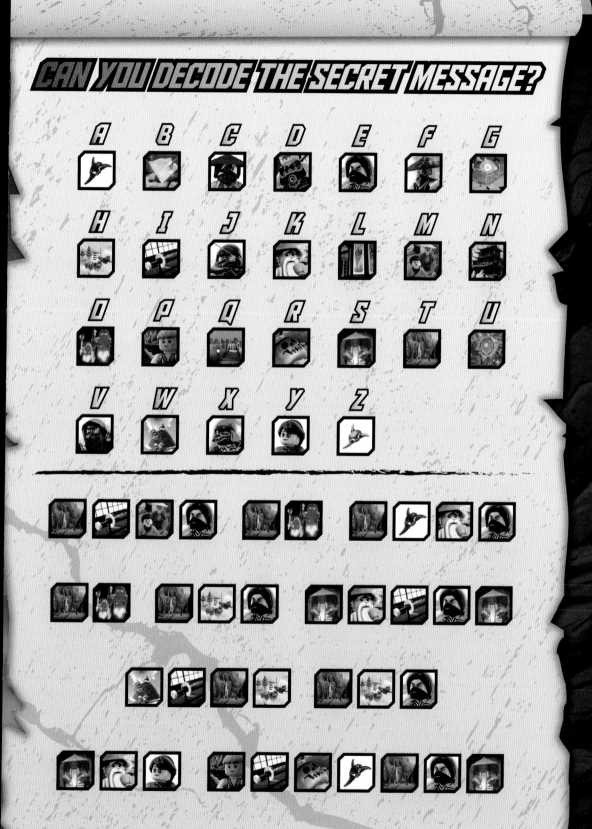

LEGO NINJAGO™ Masters of Spinjitzu

FROM GHOSTS TO PIRATES

Story and art by Blue Ocean Entertainment AG
Additional art by Caravan Studio

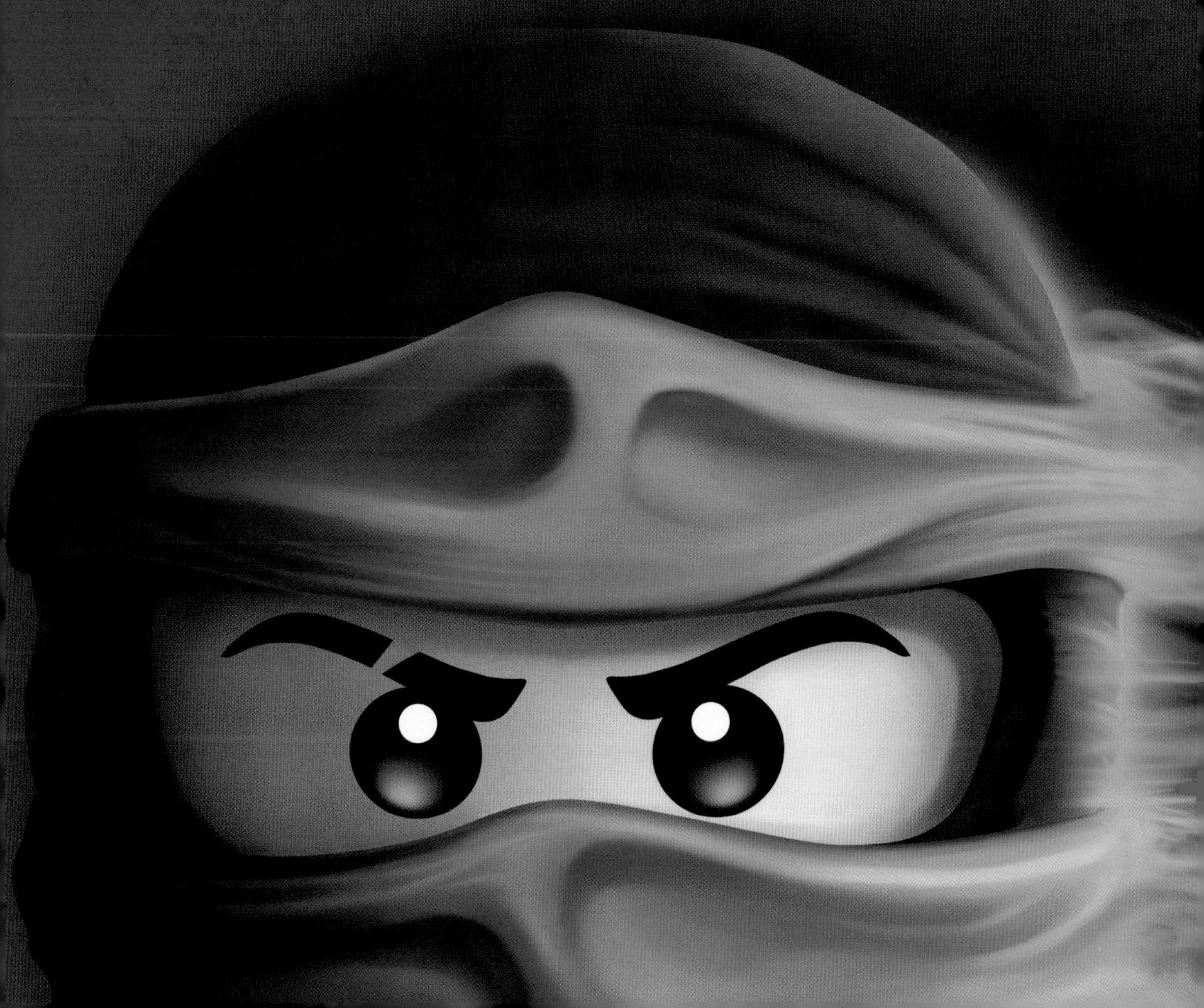

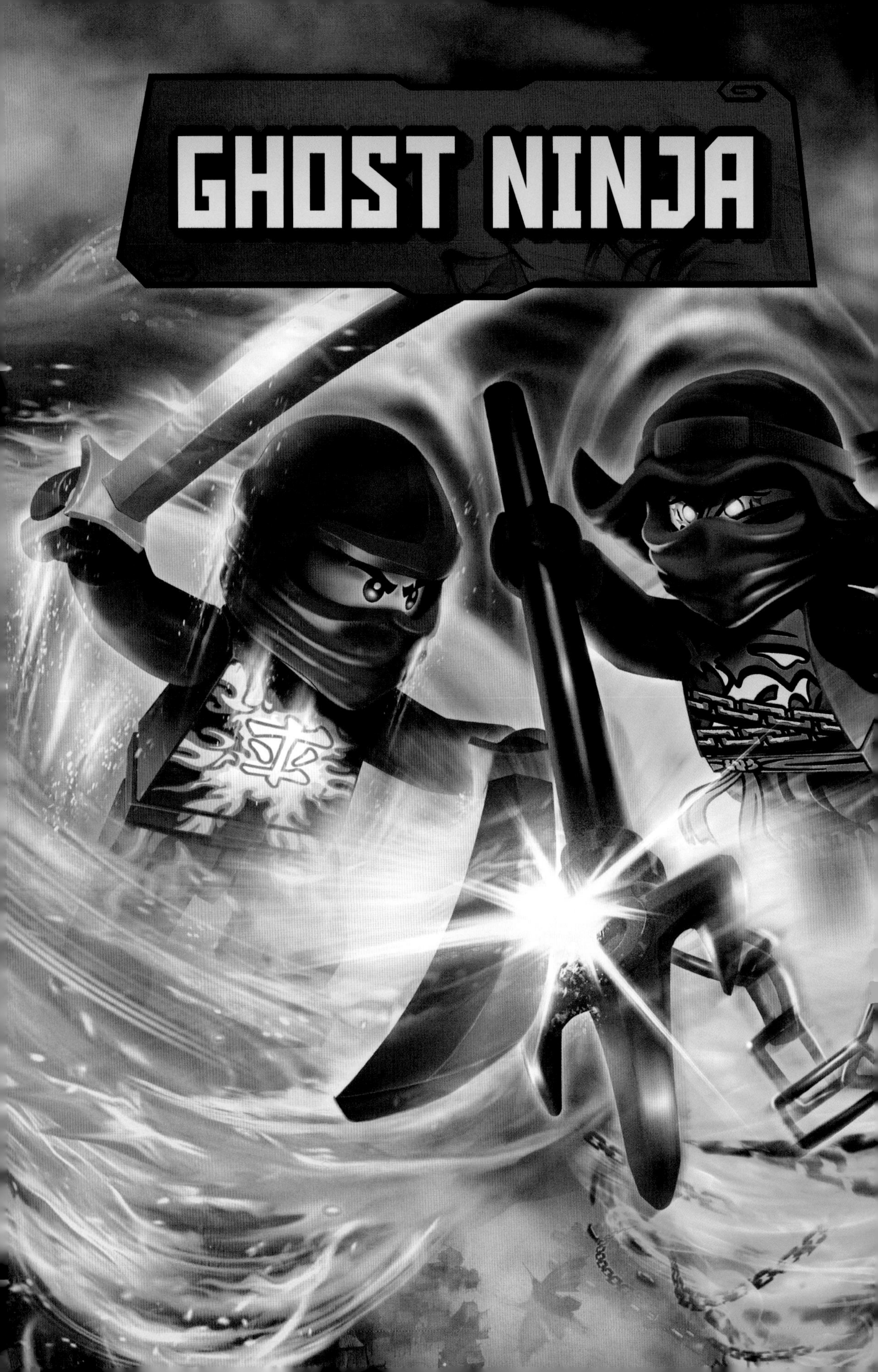
GHOST NINJA

It is a Season of Change...

Since defeating Master Chen and his army in the Tournament of Elements, the ninja have never been more united. Yet Lloyd mourns the loss of his father to the Cursed Realm and questions his path ahead. That's when a cold wind blows through Ninjago...

The cursed spirit of Morro—the Master of Wind, who also happens to be Master Wu's first pupil—has possessed Lloyd and seeks the Realm Crystal, and a way to help the evil Preeminent....

SCREAMING FUN AT THE AMUSEMENT PARK

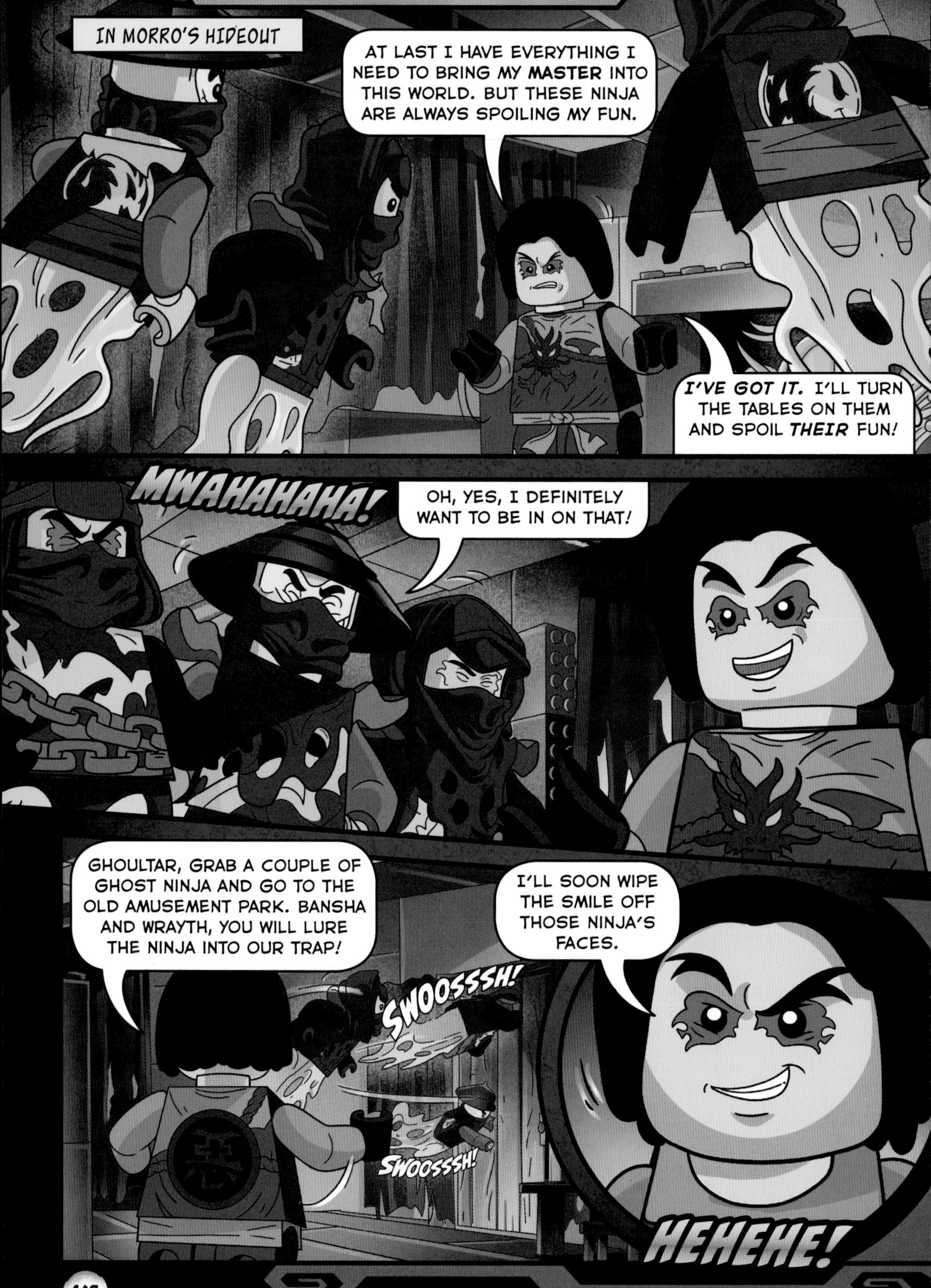

IN MORRO'S HIDEOUT
AT LAST I HAVE EVERYTHING I NEED TO BRING MY **MASTER** INTO THIS WORLD. BUT THESE NINJA ARE ALWAYS SPOILING MY FUN.
I'VE GOT IT. I'LL TURN THE TABLES ON THEM AND SPOIL ***THEIR*** FUN!
MWAHAHAHA!
OH, YES, I DEFINITELY WANT TO BE IN ON THAT!
GHOULTAR, GRAB A COUPLE OF GHOST NINJA AND GO TO THE OLD AMUSEMENT PARK. BANSHA AND WRAYTH, YOU WILL LURE THE NINJA INTO OUR TRAP!
SWOOSSSH!
SWOOSSSH!
I'LL SOON WIPE THE SMILE OFF THOSE NINJA'S FACES.
HEHEHE!

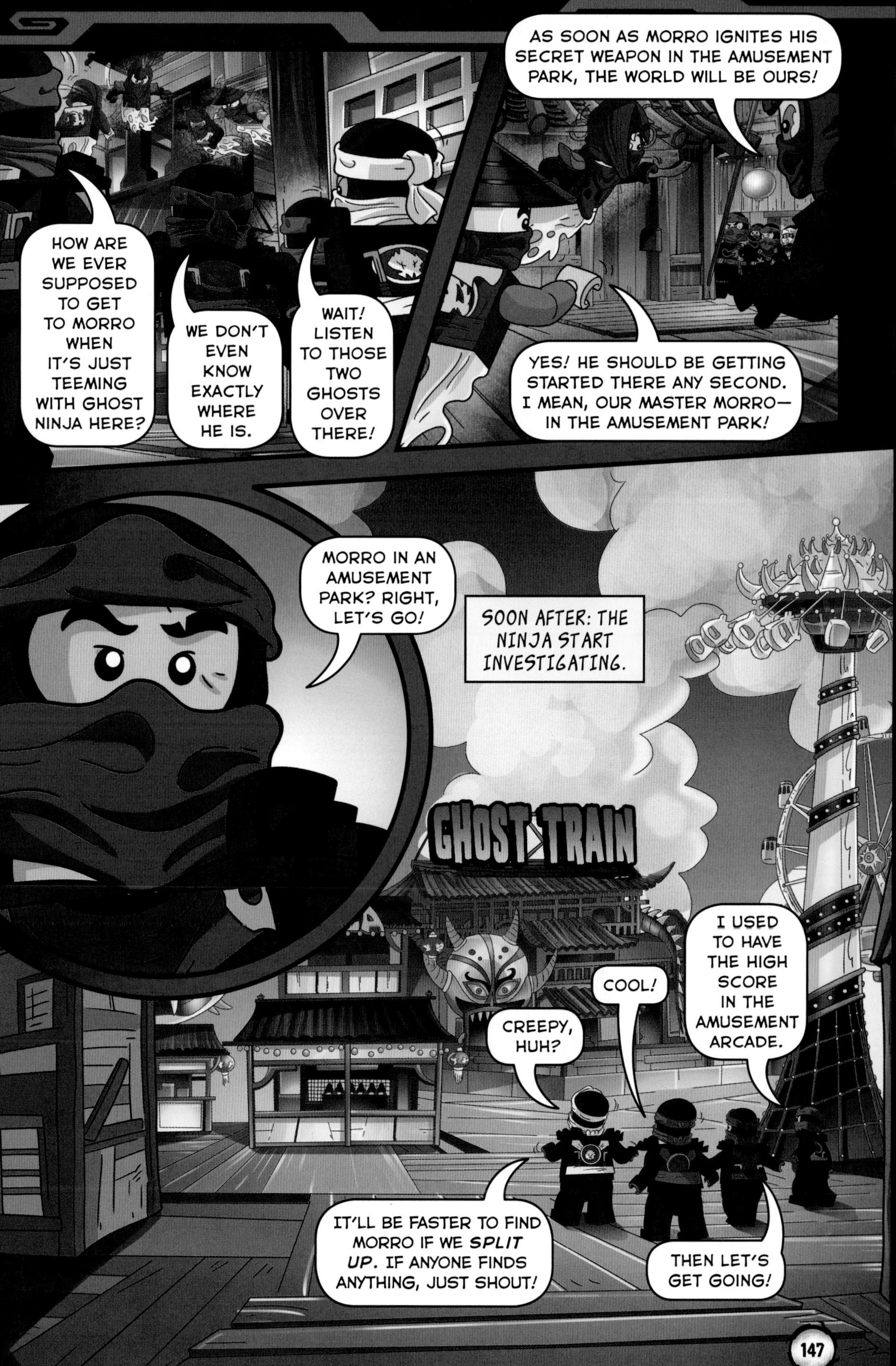
HOW ARE WE EVER SUPPOSED TO GET TO MORRO WHEN IT'S JUST TEEMING WITH GHOST NINJA HERE?
WE DON'T EVEN KNOW EXACTLY WHERE HE IS.
WAIT! LISTEN TO THOSE TWO GHOSTS OVER THERE!
AS SOON AS MORRO IGNITES HIS SECRET WEAPON IN THE AMUSEMENT PARK, THE WORLD WILL BE OURS!
YES! HE SHOULD BE GETTING STARTED THERE ANY SECOND. I MEAN, OUR MASTER MORRO— IN THE AMUSEMENT PARK!
MORRO IN AN AMUSEMENT PARK? RIGHT, LET'S GO!
SOON AFTER: THE NINJA START INVESTIGATING.
GHOST TRAIN
CREEPY, HUH?
COOL!
I USED TO HAVE THE HIGH SCORE IN THE AMUSEMENT ARCADE.
IT'LL BE FASTER TO FIND MORRO IF WE *SPLIT UP*. IF ANYONE FINDS ANYTHING, JUST SHOUT!
THEN LET'S GET GOING!

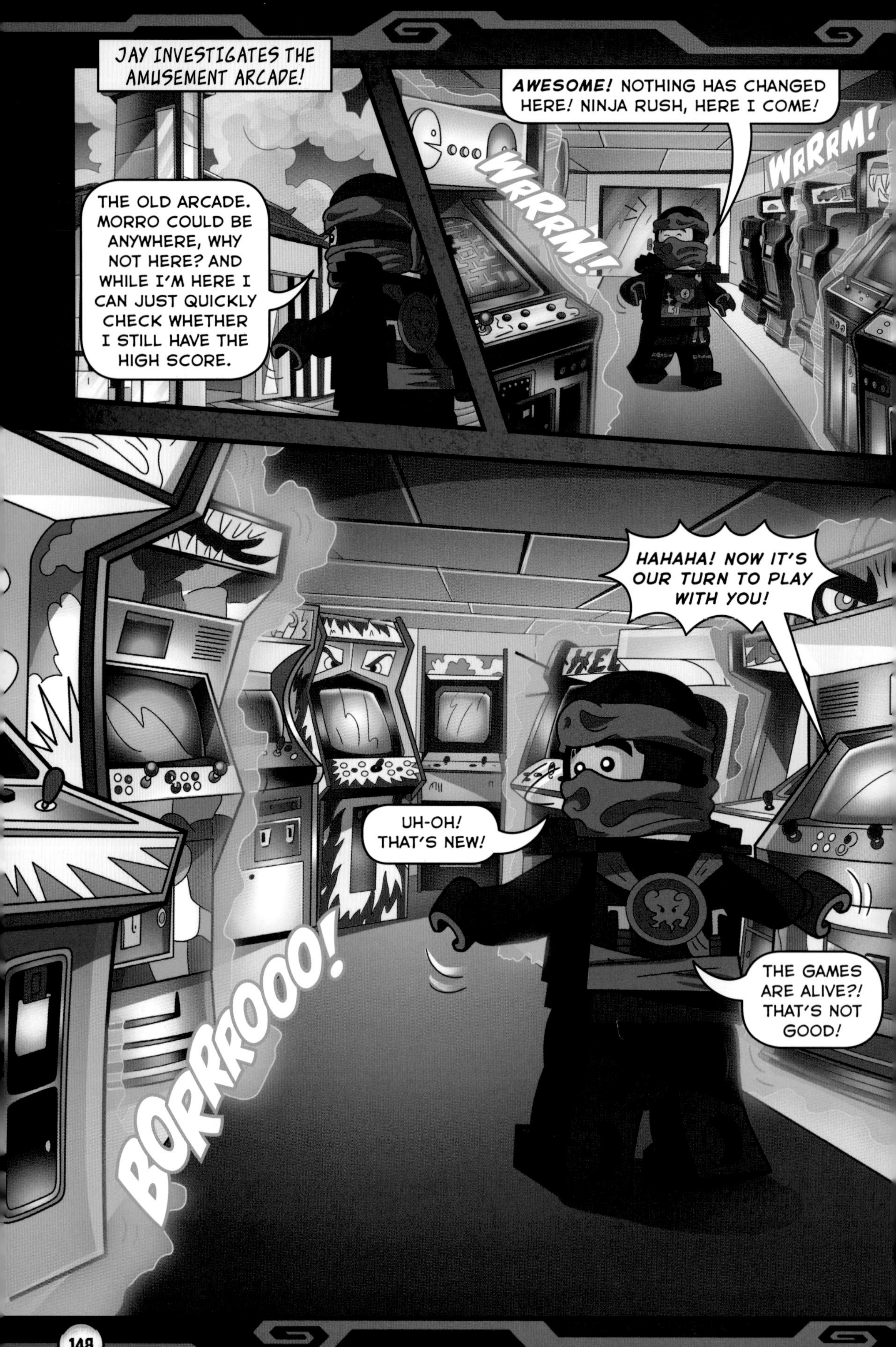
JAY INVESTIGATES THE AMUSEMENT ARCADE!
THE OLD ARCADE. MORRO COULD BE ANYWHERE, WHY NOT HERE? AND WHILE I'M HERE I CAN JUST QUICKLY CHECK WHETHER I STILL HAVE THE HIGH SCORE.
AWESOME! NOTHING HAS CHANGED HERE! NINJA RUSH, HERE I COME!
WRRRM!
WRRRM!
HAHAHA! NOW IT'S OUR TURN TO PLAY WITH YOU!
UH-OH! THAT'S NEW!
THE GAMES ARE ALIVE?! THAT'S NOT GOOD!
BORRROOO!

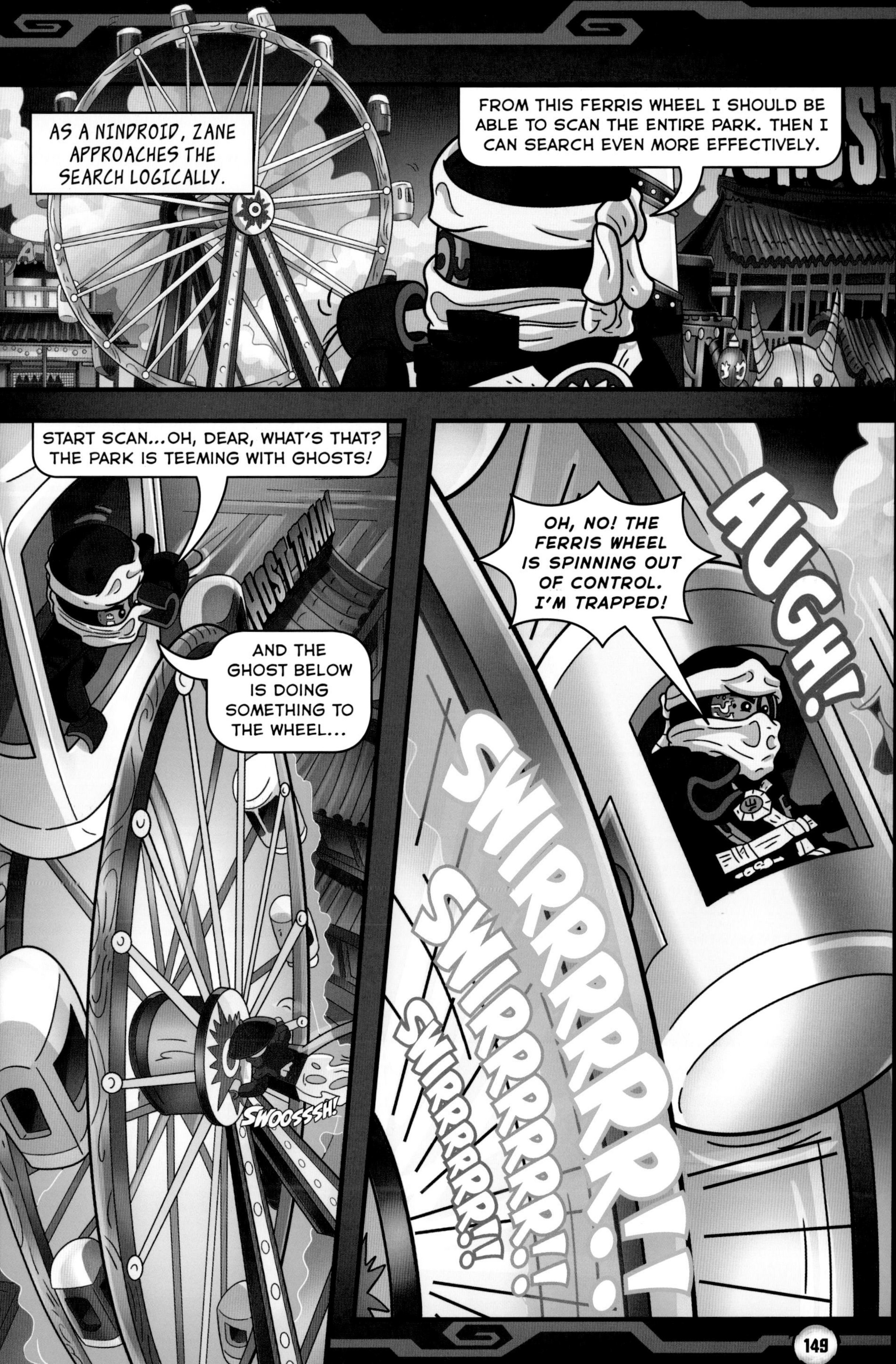
AS A NINDROID, ZANE APPROACHES THE SEARCH LOGICALLY.
FROM THIS FERRIS WHEEL I SHOULD BE ABLE TO SCAN THE ENTIRE PARK. THEN I CAN SEARCH EVEN MORE EFFECTIVELY.
START SCAN...OH, DEAR, WHAT'S THAT? THE PARK IS TEEMING WITH GHOSTS!
GHOST TRAIN
AND THE GHOST BELOW IS DOING SOMETHING TO THE WHEEL...
SWOOSSSH!
OH, NO! THE FERRIS WHEEL IS SPINNING OUT OF CONTROL. I'M TRAPPED!
AUGH!
SWIRRRRRR...!
SWIRRRRRR...!
SWIRRRRRR...!

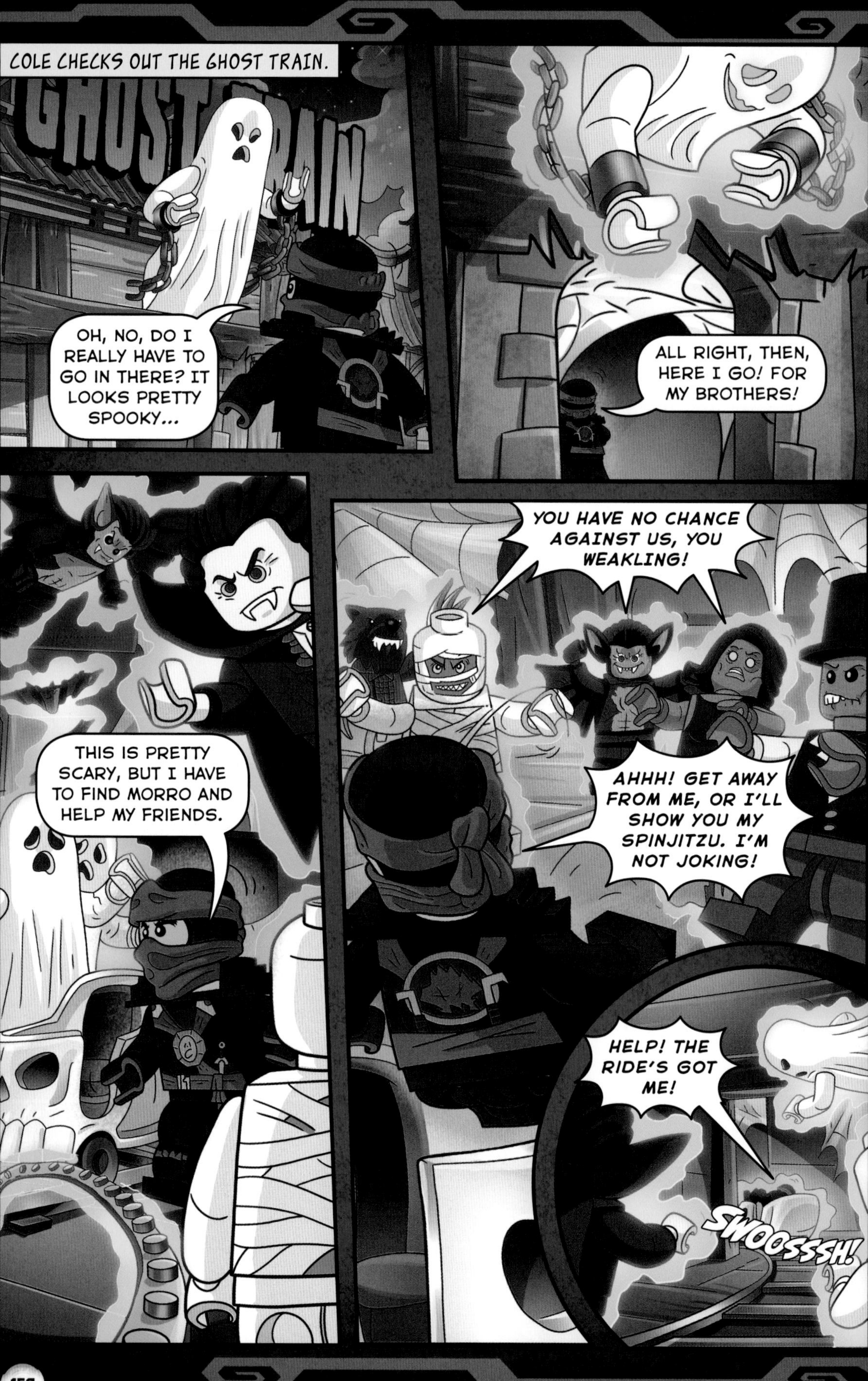
COLE CHECKS OUT THE GHOST TRAIN.
GHOST TRAIN
OH, NO, DO I REALLY HAVE TO GO IN THERE? IT LOOKS PRETTY SPOOKY...
ALL RIGHT, THEN, HERE I GO! FOR MY BROTHERS!
THIS IS PRETTY SCARY, BUT I HAVE TO FIND MORRO AND HELP MY FRIENDS.
YOU HAVE NO CHANCE AGAINST US, YOU WEAKLING!
AHHH! GET AWAY FROM ME, OR I'LL SHOW YOU MY SPINJITZU. I'M NOT JOKING!
HELP! THE RIDE'S GOT ME!
SWOOSSSH!

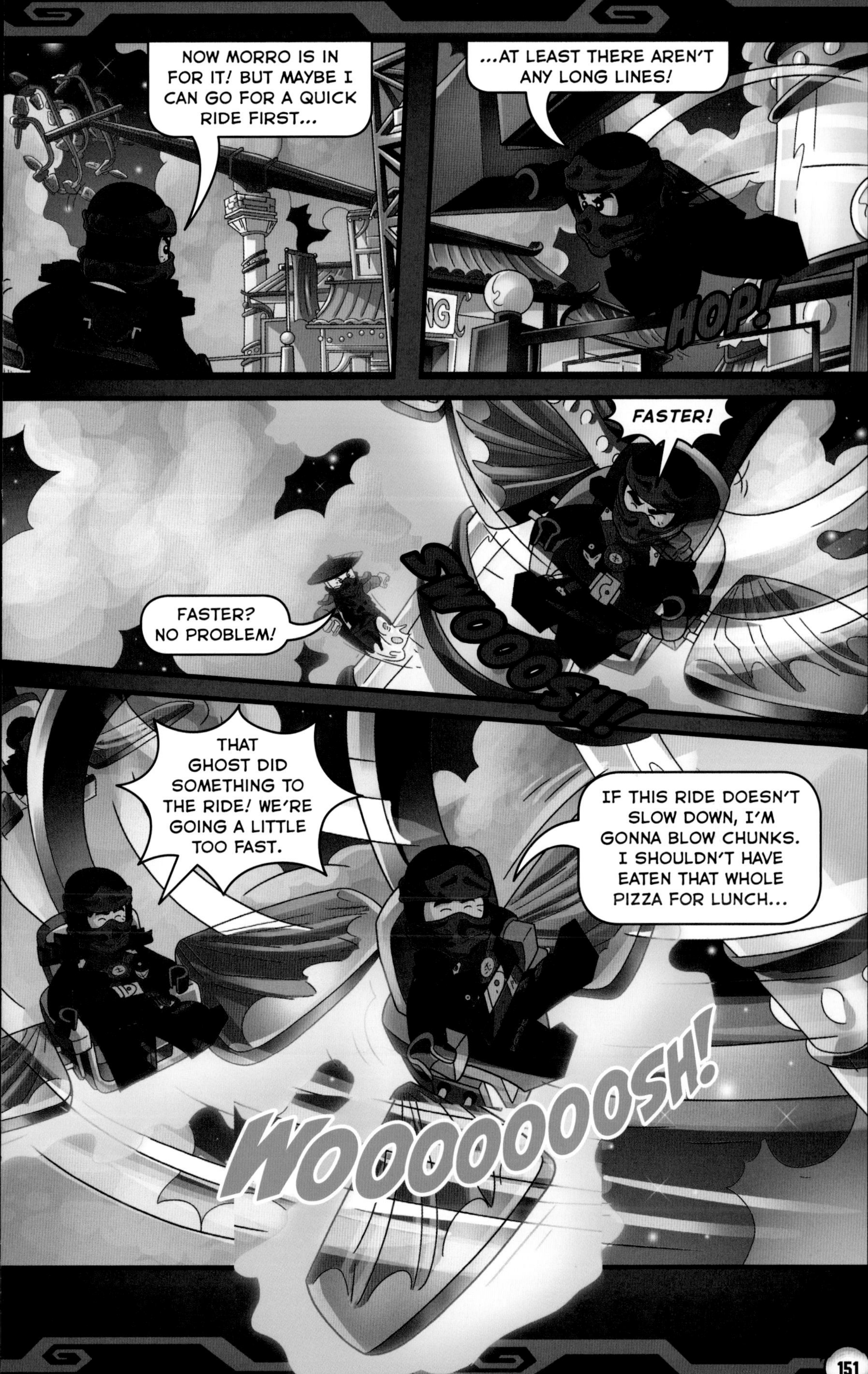

NOW MORRO IS IN FOR IT! BUT MAYBE I CAN GO FOR A QUICK RIDE FIRST...
...AT LEAST THERE AREN'T ANY LONG LINES!
HOP!
FASTER!
SWOOOOSH!
FASTER? NO PROBLEM!
THAT GHOST DID SOMETHING TO THE RIDE! WE'RE GOING A LITTLE TOO FAST.
IF THIS RIDE DOESN'T SLOW DOWN, I'M GONNA BLOW CHUNKS. I SHOULDN'T HAVE EATEN THAT WHOLE PIZZA FOR LUNCH...
WOOOOOOOSH!

ALL FOUR OF THE NINJA HAVE MANAGED TO GET THEMSELVES IN A BIND. MORRO'S GHOSTS HAVE TRAPPED THEM IN THE AMUSEMENT PARK. WILL THEY BE ABLE TO ESCAPE?!

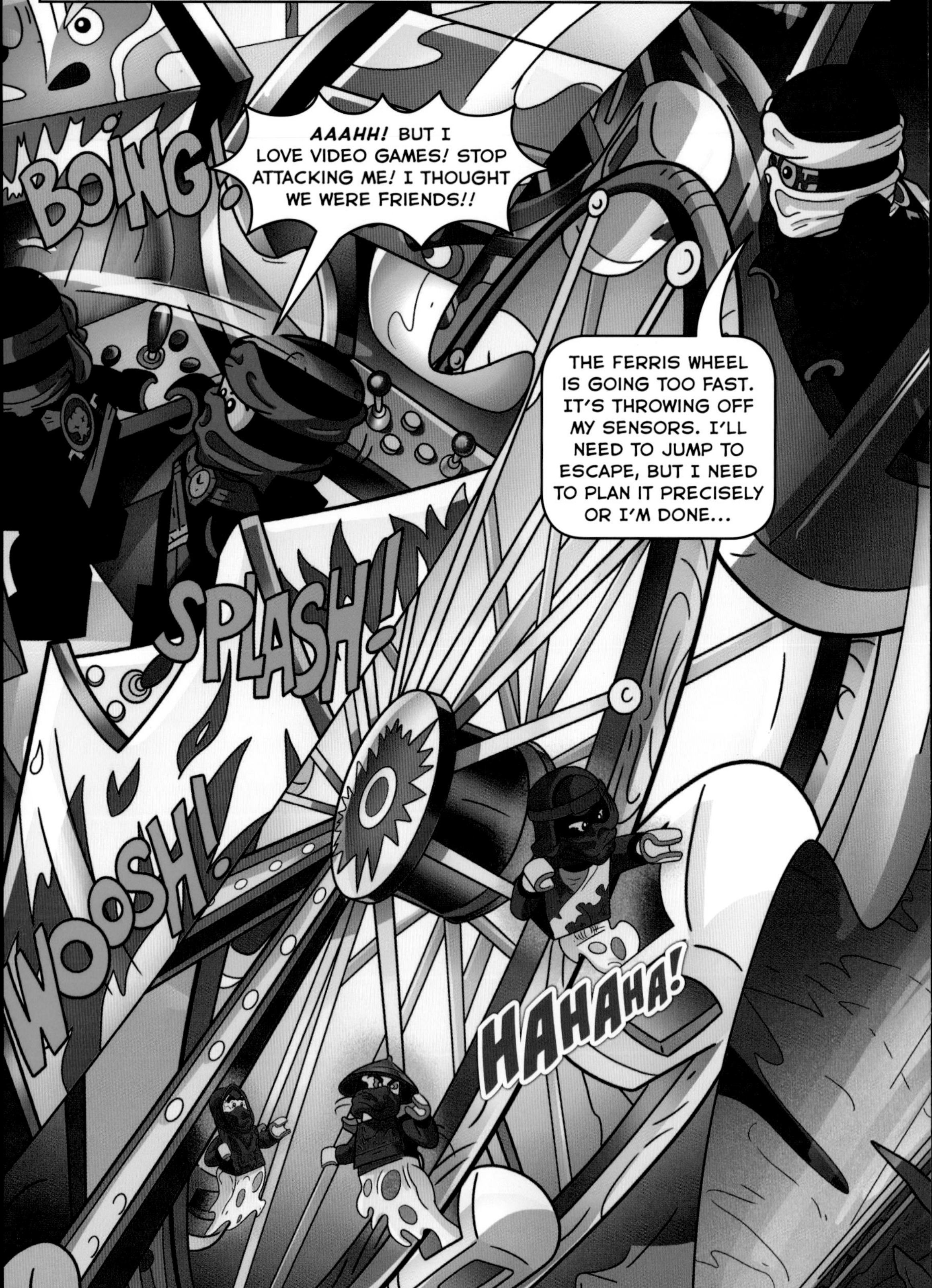
BOING!
AAAHH! BUT I LOVE VIDEO GAMES! STOP ATTACKING ME! I THOUGHT WE WERE FRIENDS!!
THE FERRIS WHEEL IS GOING TOO FAST. IT'S THROWING OFF MY SENSORS. I'LL NEED TO JUMP TO ESCAPE, BUT I NEED TO PLAN IT PRECISELY OR I'M DONE...
SPLASH!
WOOSH!
HAHAHA!

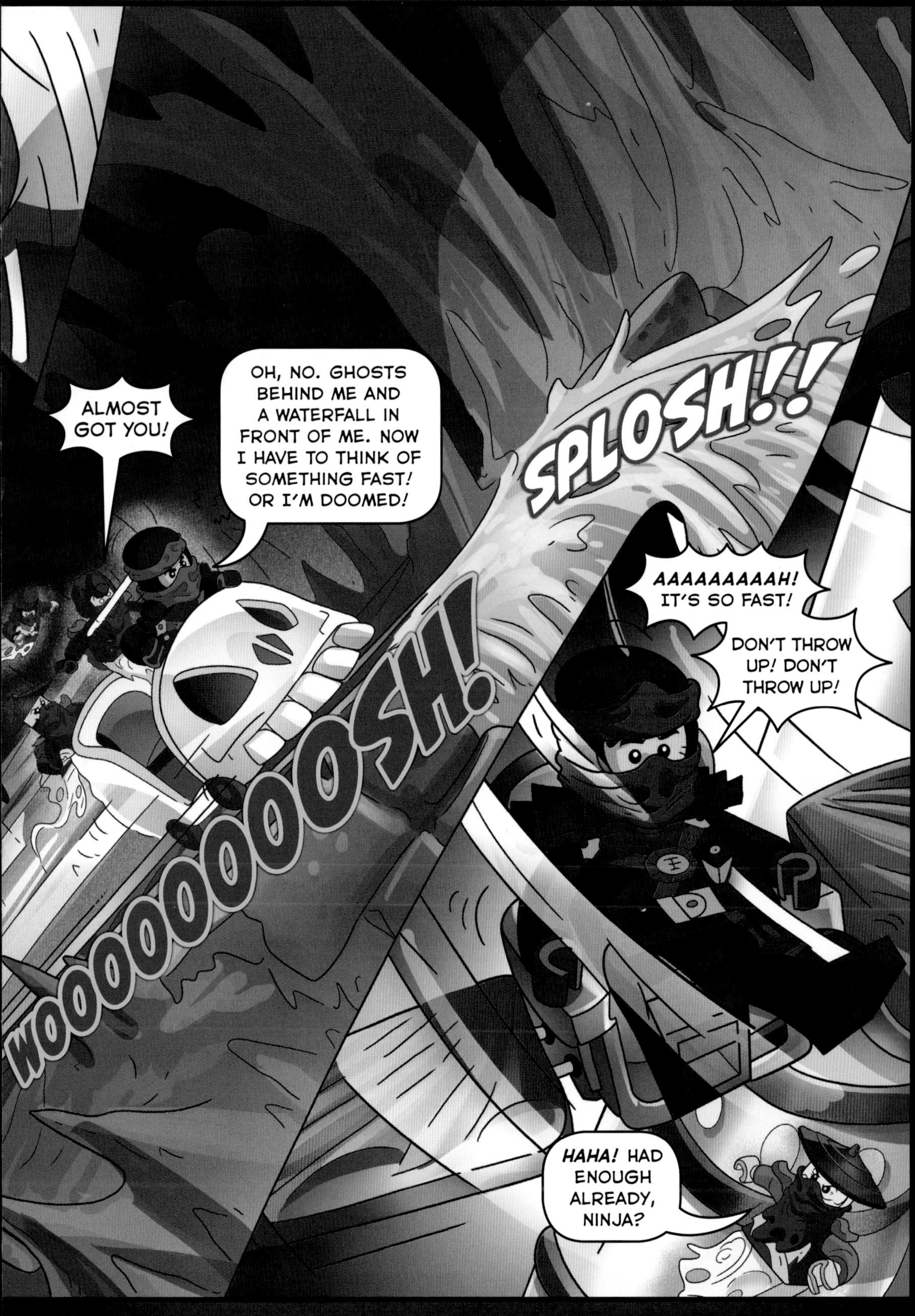
ALMOST GOT YOU!
OH, NO. GHOSTS BEHIND ME AND A WATERFALL IN FRONT OF ME. NOW I HAVE TO THINK OF SOMETHING FAST! OR I'M DOOMED!
SPLOSH!!!
WOOOOOOOOOSH!
AAAAAAAAAH! IT'S SO FAST!
DON'T THROW UP! DON'T THROW UP!
HAHA! HAD ENOUGH ALREADY, NINJA?

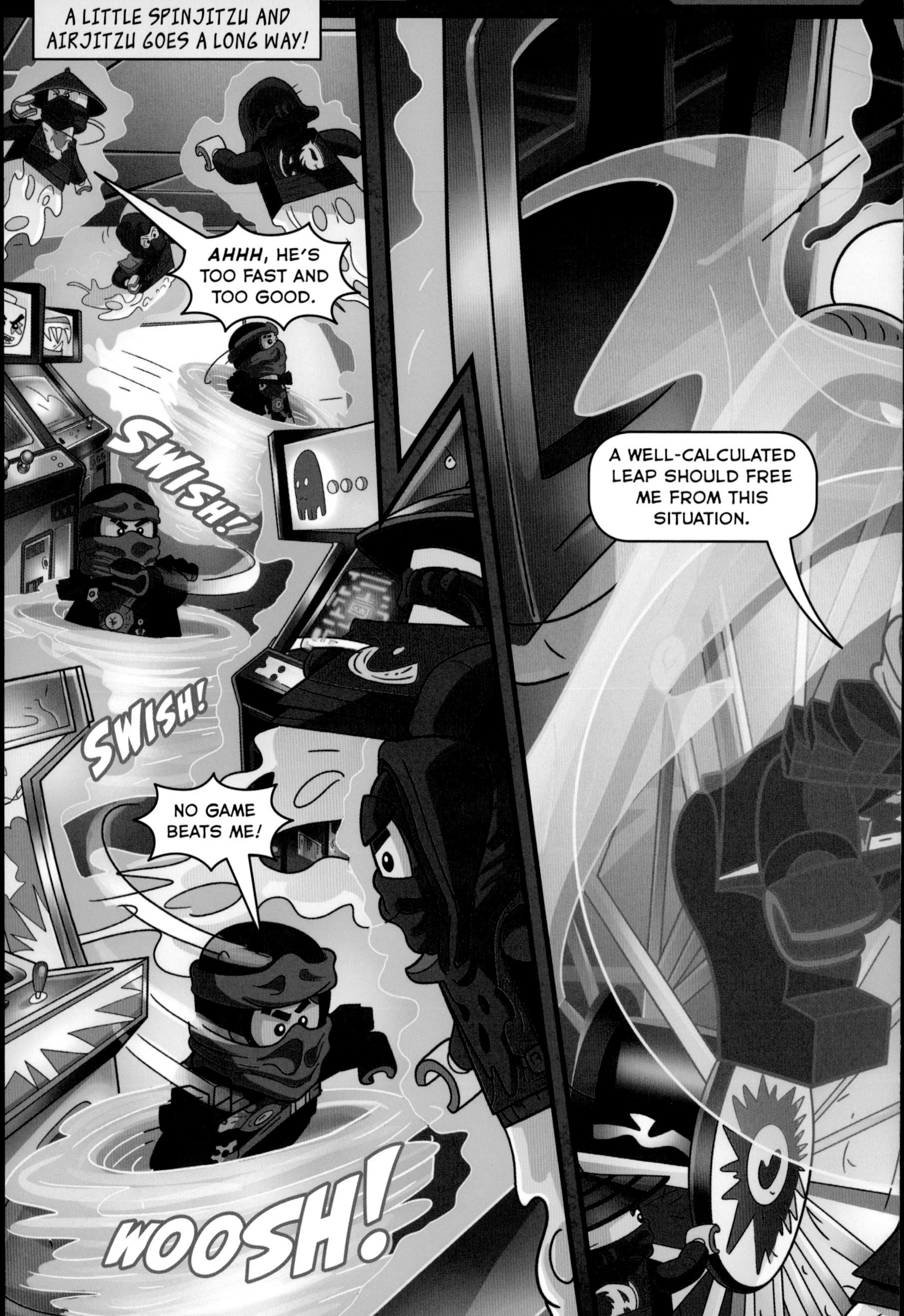
A LITTLE SPINJITZU AND AIRJITZU GOES A LONG WAY!
AHHH, HE'S TOO FAST AND TOO GOOD.
SWISH!
SWISH!
NO GAME BEATS ME!
WOOSH!
A WELL-CALCULATED LEAP SHOULD FREE ME FROM THIS SITUATION.

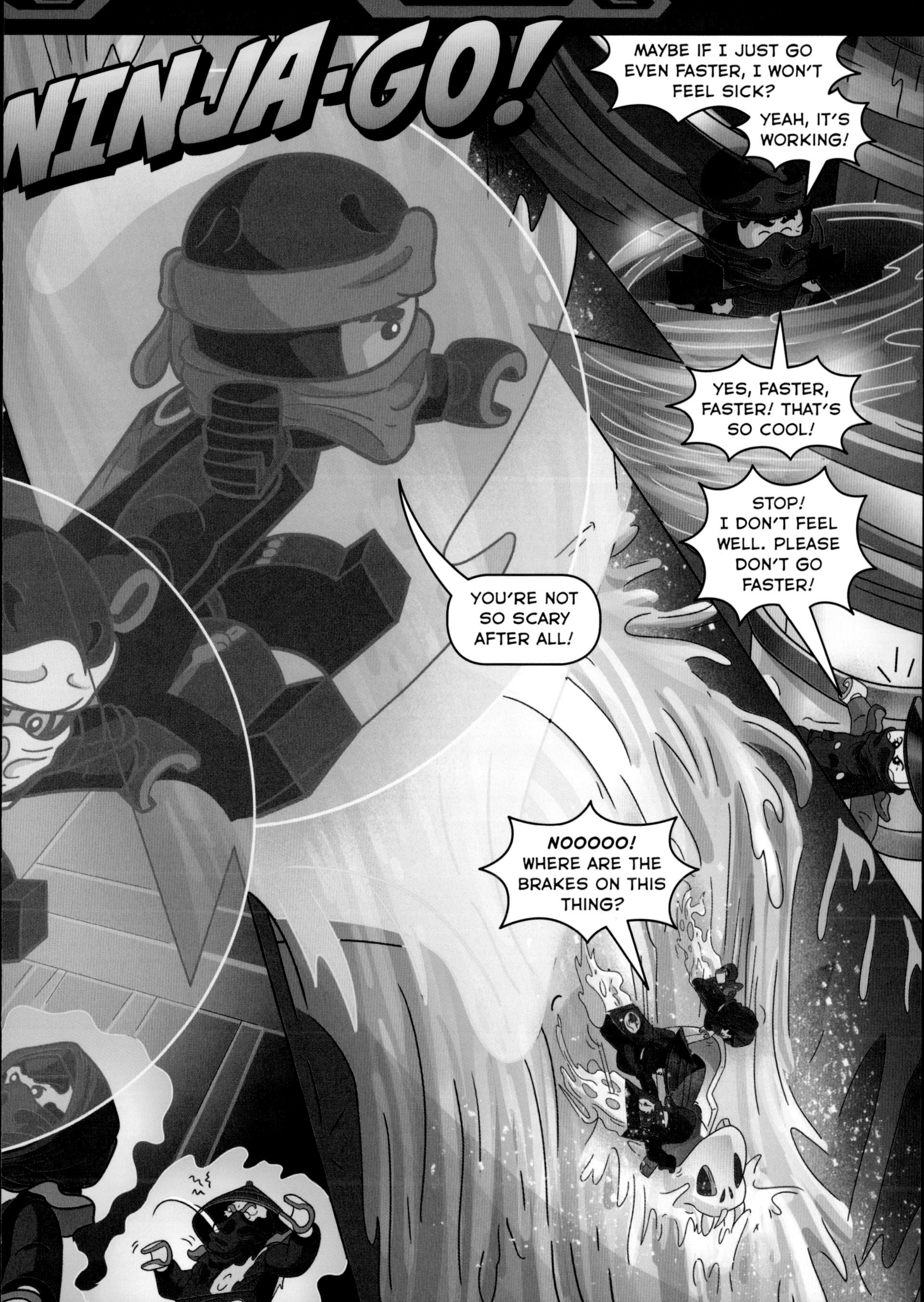
NINJA-GO!
MAYBE IF I JUST GO EVEN FASTER, I WON'T FEEL SICK?
YEAH, IT'S WORKING!
YES, FASTER, FASTER! THAT'S SO COOL!
STOP! I DON'T FEEL WELL. PLEASE DON'T GO FASTER!
YOU'RE NOT SO SCARY AFTER ALL!
NOOOOO! WHERE ARE THE BRAKES ON THIS THING?

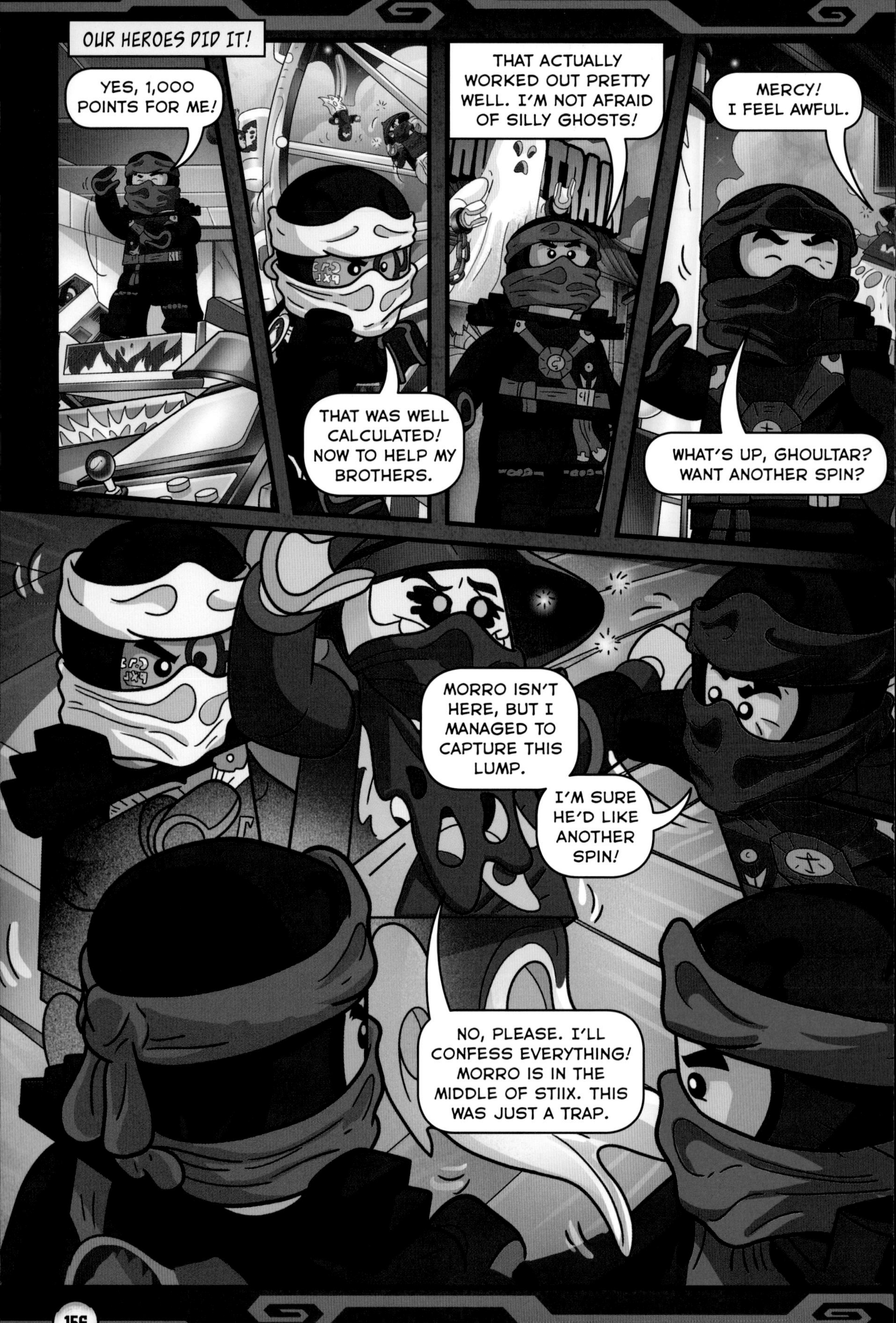
OUR HEROES DID IT!
YES, 1,000 POINTS FOR ME!
THAT WAS WELL CALCULATED! NOW TO HELP MY BROTHERS.
THAT ACTUALLY WORKED OUT PRETTY WELL. I'M NOT AFRAID OF SILLY GHOSTS!
MERCY! I FEEL AWFUL.
WHAT'S UP, GHOULTAR? WANT ANOTHER SPIN?
MORRO ISN'T HERE, BUT I MANAGED TO CAPTURE THIS LUMP.
I'M SURE HE'D LIKE ANOTHER SPIN!
NO, PLEASE. I'LL CONFESS EVERYTHING! MORRO IS IN THE MIDDLE OF STIIX. THIS WAS JUST A TRAP.

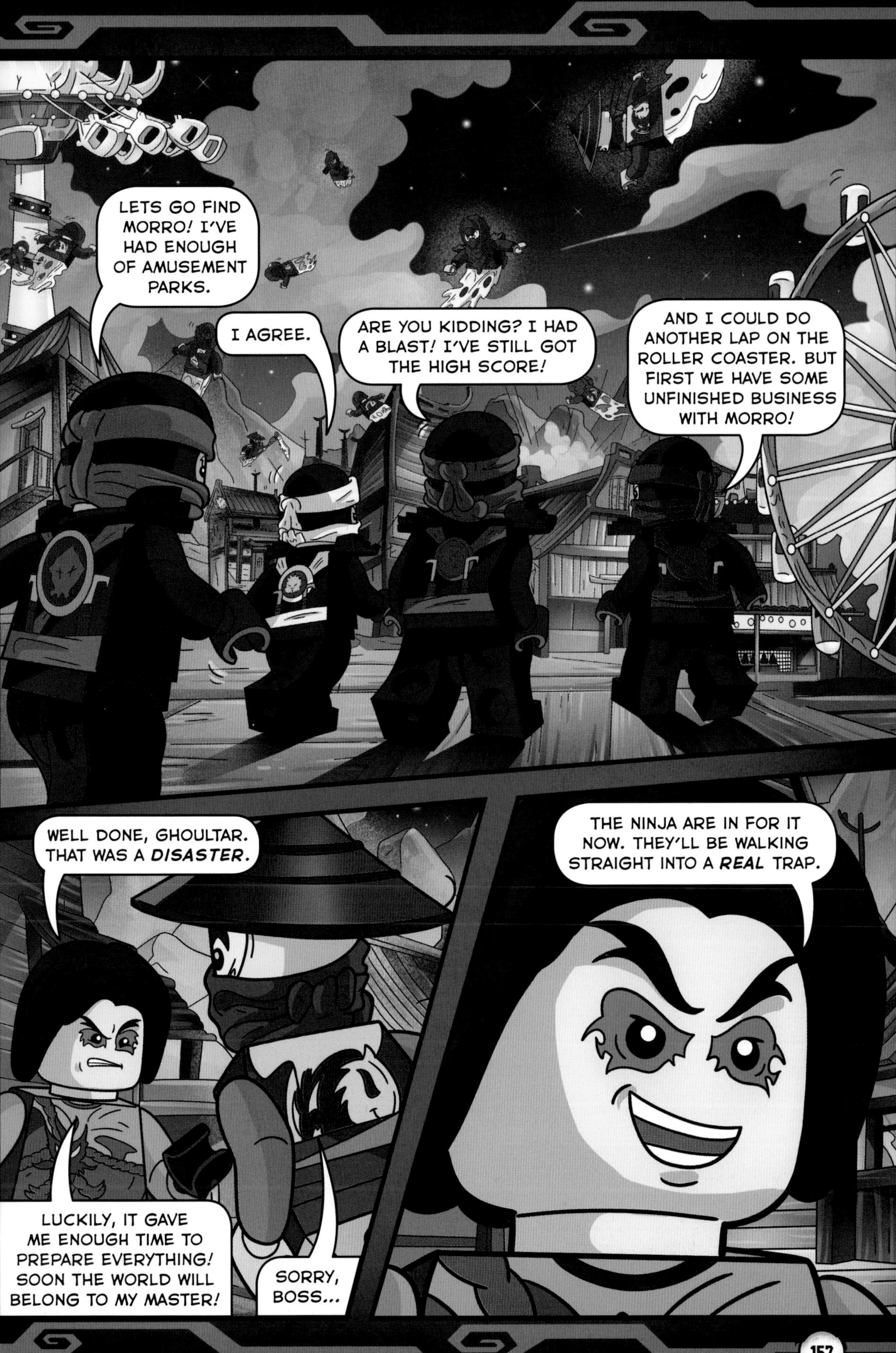
LETS GO FIND MORRO! I'VE HAD ENOUGH OF AMUSEMENT PARKS.
I AGREE.
ARE YOU KIDDING? I HAD A BLAST! I'VE STILL GOT THE HIGH SCORE!
AND I COULD DO ANOTHER LAP ON THE ROLLER COASTER. BUT FIRST WE HAVE SOME UNFINISHED BUSINESS WITH MORRO!
WELL DONE, GHOULTAR. THAT WAS A *DISASTER*.
LUCKILY, IT GAVE ME ENOUGH TIME TO PREPARE EVERYTHING! SOON THE WORLD WILL BELONG TO MY MASTER!
SORRY, BOSS...
THE NINJA ARE IN FOR IT NOW. THEY'LL BE WALKING STRAIGHT INTO A *REAL* TRAP.

THE GRAND FINALE!

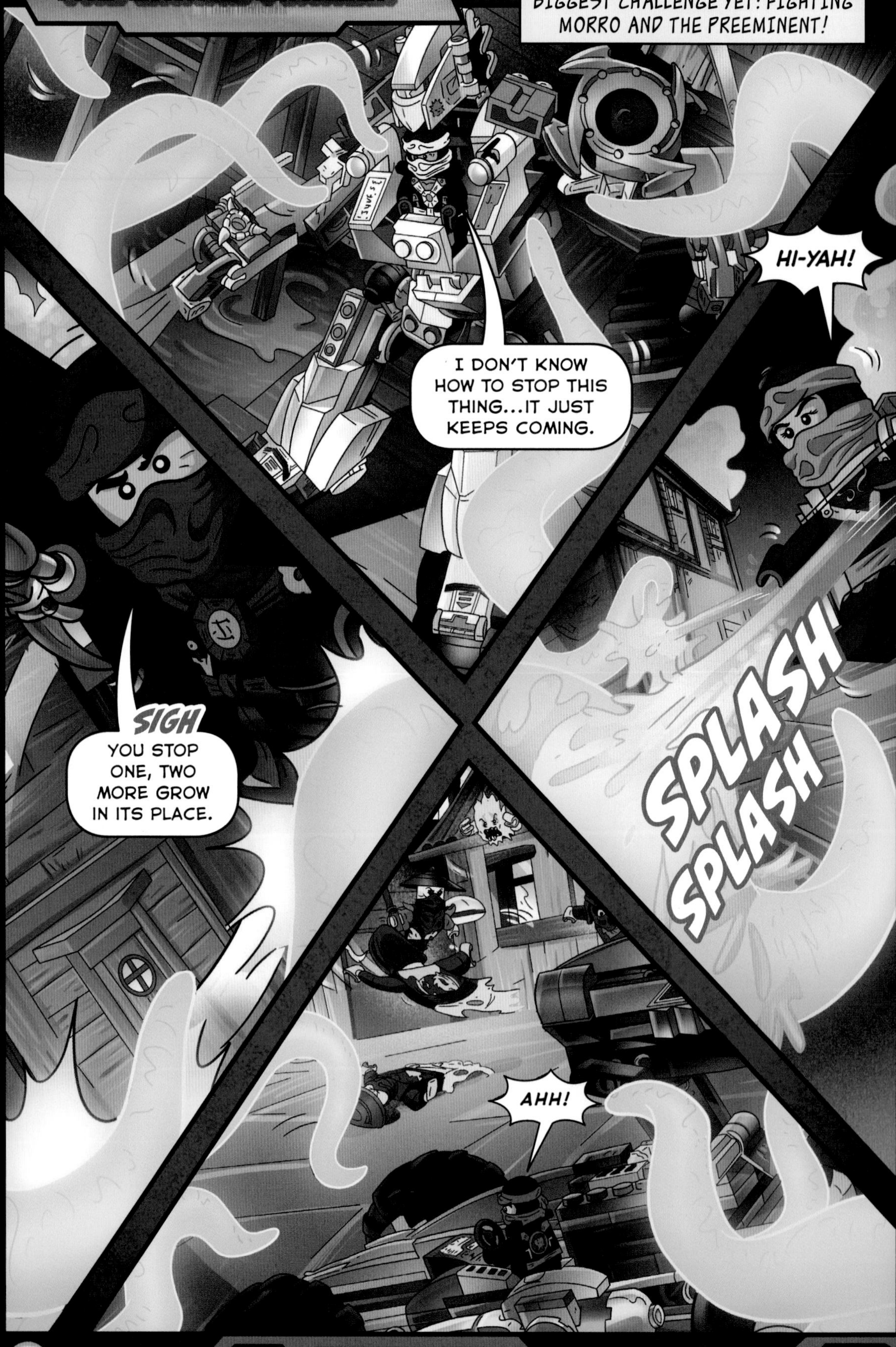
THE NINJA ARE FACING THEIR BIGGEST CHALLENGE YET: FIGHTING MORRO AND THE PREEMINENT!
I DON'T KNOW HOW TO STOP THIS THING...IT JUST KEEPS COMING.
HI-YAH!
SIGH
YOU STOP ONE, TWO MORE GROW IN ITS PLACE.
SPLASH
SPLASH
AHH!

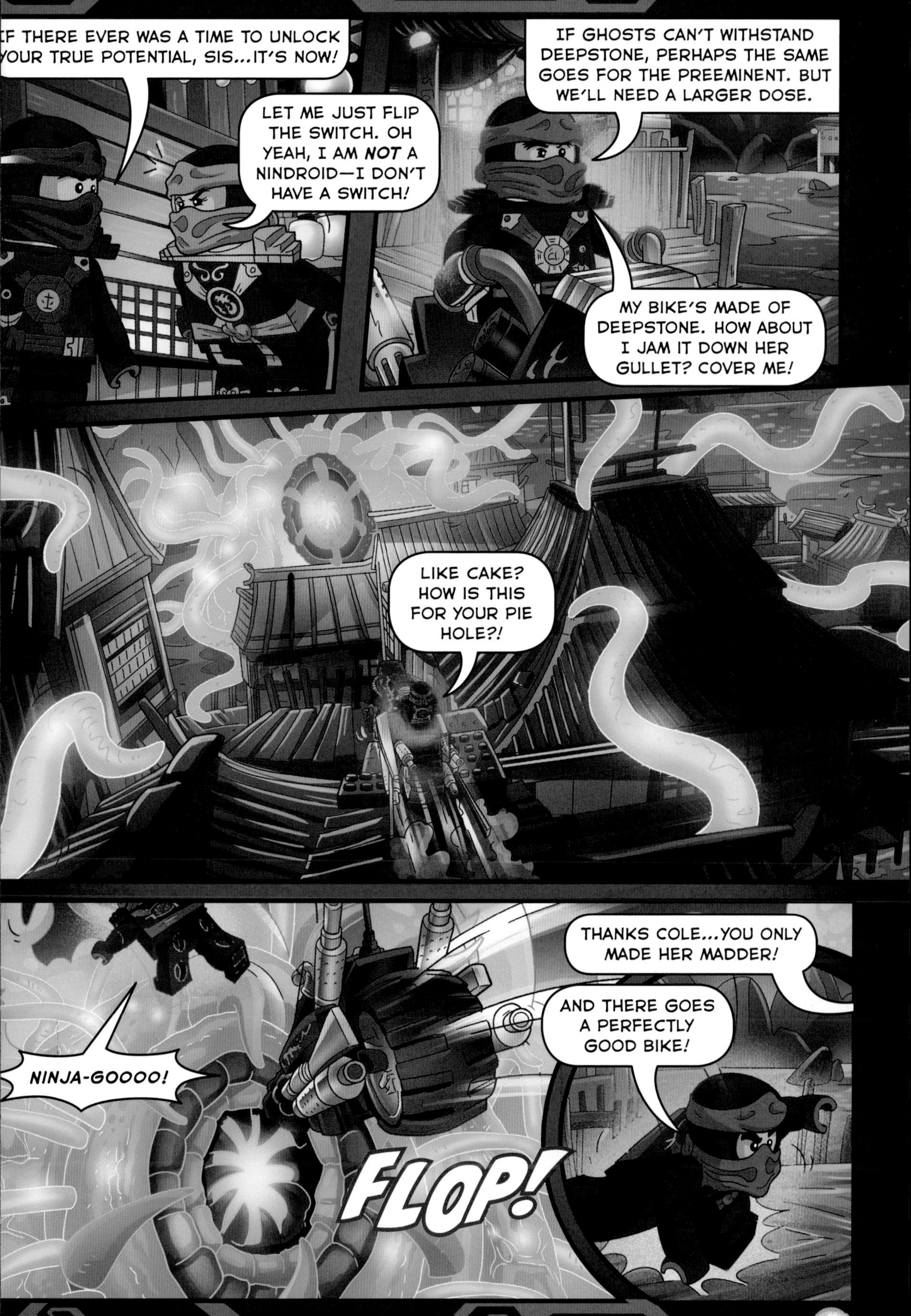
IF THERE EVER WAS A TIME TO UNLOCK YOUR TRUE POTENTIAL, SIS...IT'S NOW!
LET ME JUST FLIP THE SWITCH. OH YEAH, I AM *NOT* A NINDROID—I DON'T HAVE A SWITCH!
IF GHOSTS CAN'T WITHSTAND DEEPSTONE, PERHAPS THE SAME GOES FOR THE PREEMINENT. BUT WE'LL NEED A LARGER DOSE.
MY BIKE'S MADE OF DEEPSTONE. HOW ABOUT I JAM IT DOWN HER GULLET? COVER ME!
LIKE CAKE? HOW IS THIS FOR YOUR PIE HOLE?!
NINJA-GOOOO!
THANKS COLE...YOU ONLY MADE HER MADDER!
AND THERE GOES A PERFECTLY GOOD BIKE!
FLOP!

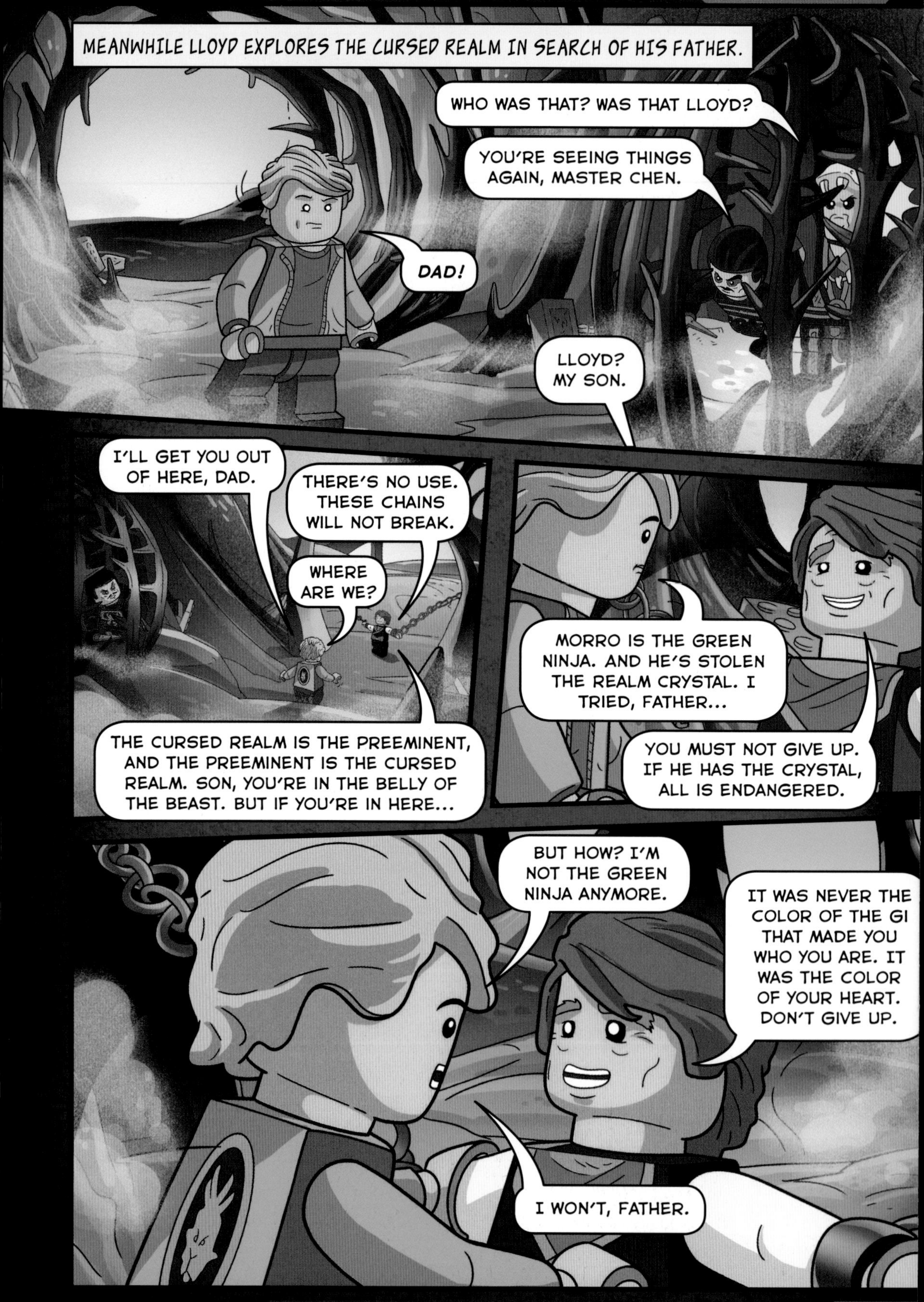
MEANWHILE LLOYD EXPLORES THE CURSED REALM IN SEARCH OF HIS FATHER.
WHO WAS THAT? WAS THAT LLOYD?
YOU'RE SEEING THINGS AGAIN, MASTER CHEN.
DAD!
LLOYD? MY SON.
I'LL GET YOU OUT OF HERE, DAD.
THERE'S NO USE. THESE CHAINS WILL NOT BREAK.
WHERE ARE WE?
THE CURSED REALM IS THE PREEMINENT, AND THE PREEMINENT IS THE CURSED REALM. SON, YOU'RE IN THE BELLY OF THE BEAST. BUT IF YOU'RE IN HERE...
MORRO IS THE GREEN NINJA. AND HE'S STOLEN THE REALM CRYSTAL. I TRIED, FATHER...
YOU MUST NOT GIVE UP. IF HE HAS THE CRYSTAL, ALL IS ENDANGERED.
BUT HOW? I'M NOT THE GREEN NINJA ANYMORE.
IT WAS NEVER THE COLOR OF THE GI THAT MADE YOU WHO YOU ARE. IT WAS THE COLOR OF YOUR HEART. DON'T GIVE UP.
I WON'T, FATHER.

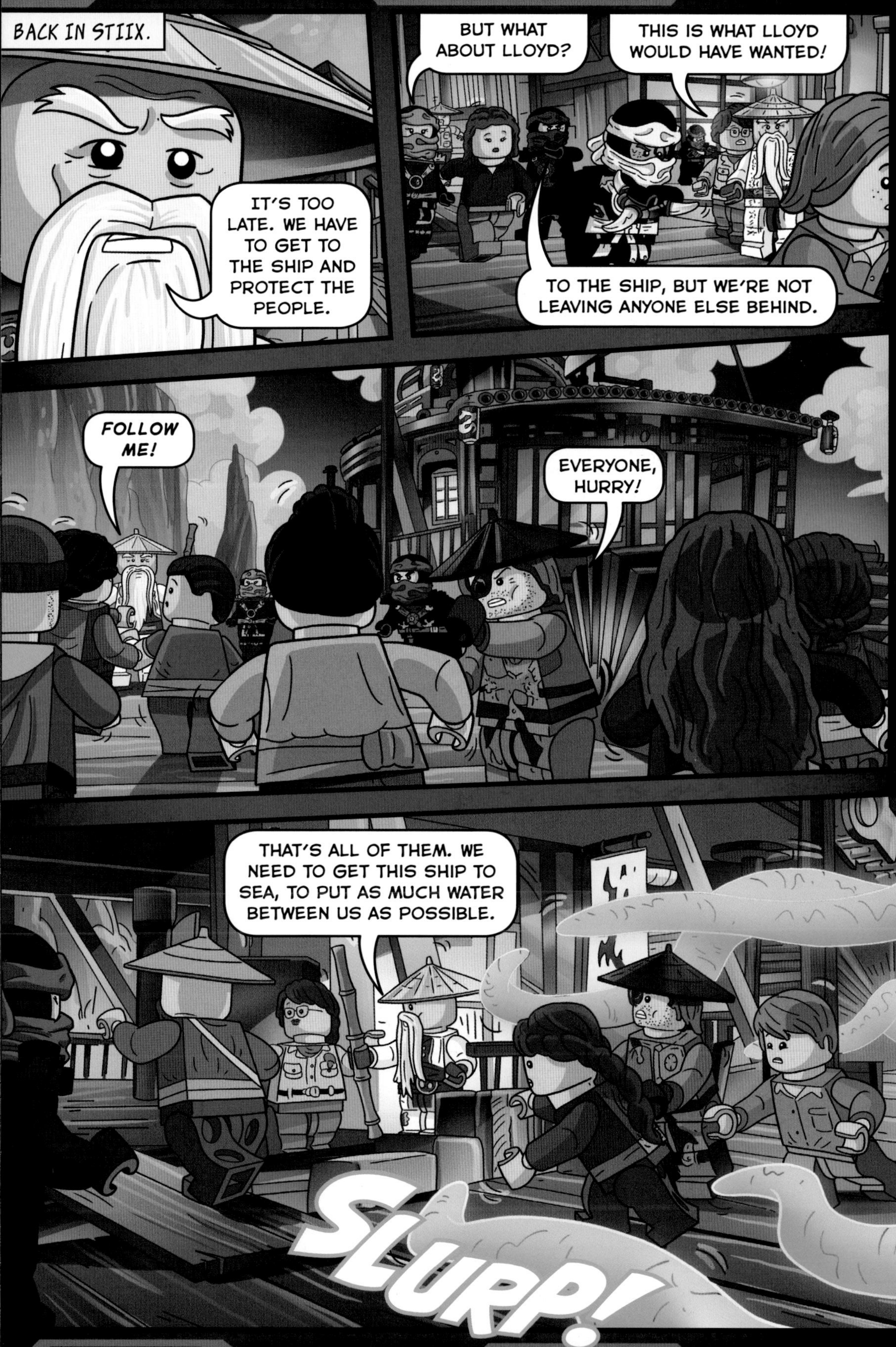
BACK IN STIIX.
IT'S TOO LATE. WE HAVE TO GET TO THE SHIP AND PROTECT THE PEOPLE.
BUT WHAT ABOUT LLOYD?
THIS IS WHAT LLOYD WOULD HAVE WANTED!
TO THE SHIP, BUT WE'RE NOT LEAVING ANYONE ELSE BEHIND.
FOLLOW ME!
EVERYONE, HURRY!
THAT'S ALL OF THEM. WE NEED TO GET THIS SHIP TO SEA, TO PUT AS MUCH WATER BETWEEN US AS POSSIBLE.
SLURP!

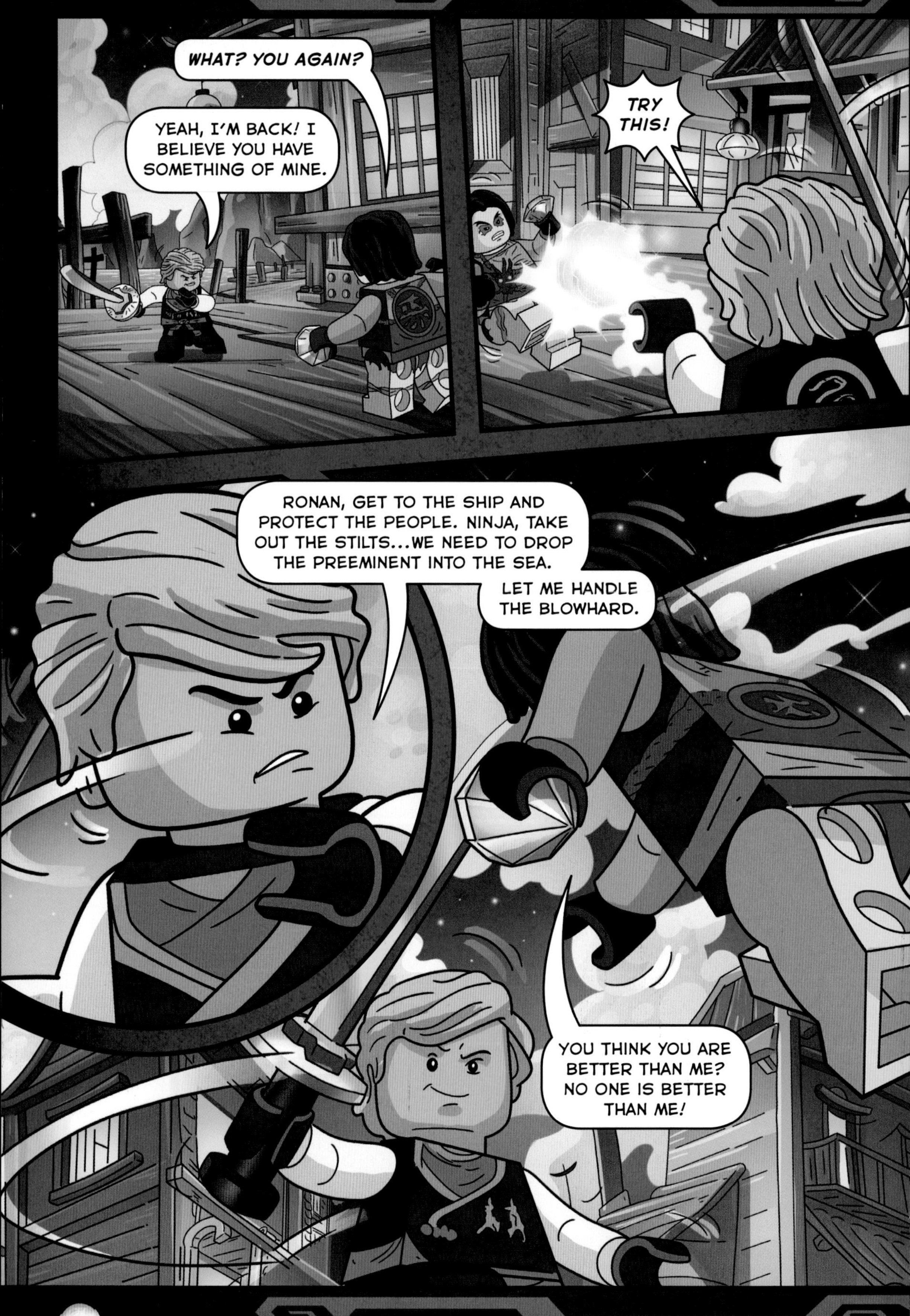
WHAT? YOU AGAIN?
YEAH, I'M BACK! I BELIEVE YOU HAVE SOMETHING OF MINE.
TRY THIS!
RONAN, GET TO THE SHIP AND PROTECT THE PEOPLE. NINJA, TAKE OUT THE STILTS...WE NEED TO DROP THE PREEMINENT INTO THE SEA.
LET ME HANDLE THE BLOWHARD.
YOU THINK YOU ARE BETTER THAN ME? NO ONE IS BETTER THAN ME!

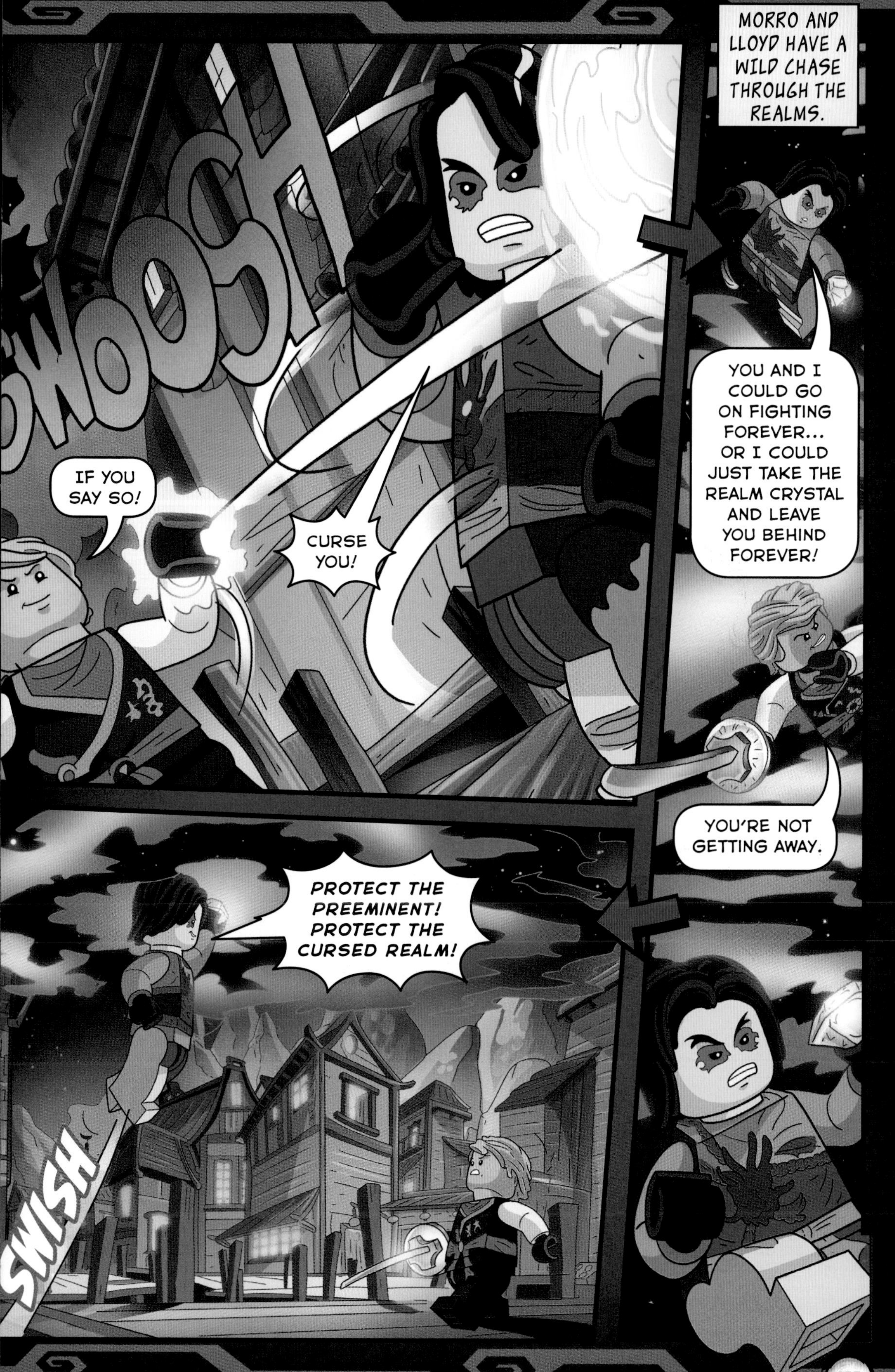

MORRO AND LLOYD HAVE A WILD CHASE THROUGH THE REALMS.
WHOOSH
IF YOU SAY SO!
CURSE YOU!
YOU AND I COULD GO ON FIGHTING FOREVER... OR I COULD JUST TAKE THE REALM CRYSTAL AND LEAVE YOU BEHIND FOREVER!
YOU'RE NOT GETTING AWAY.
PROTECT THE PREEMINENT! PROTECT THE CURSED REALM!
SWISH

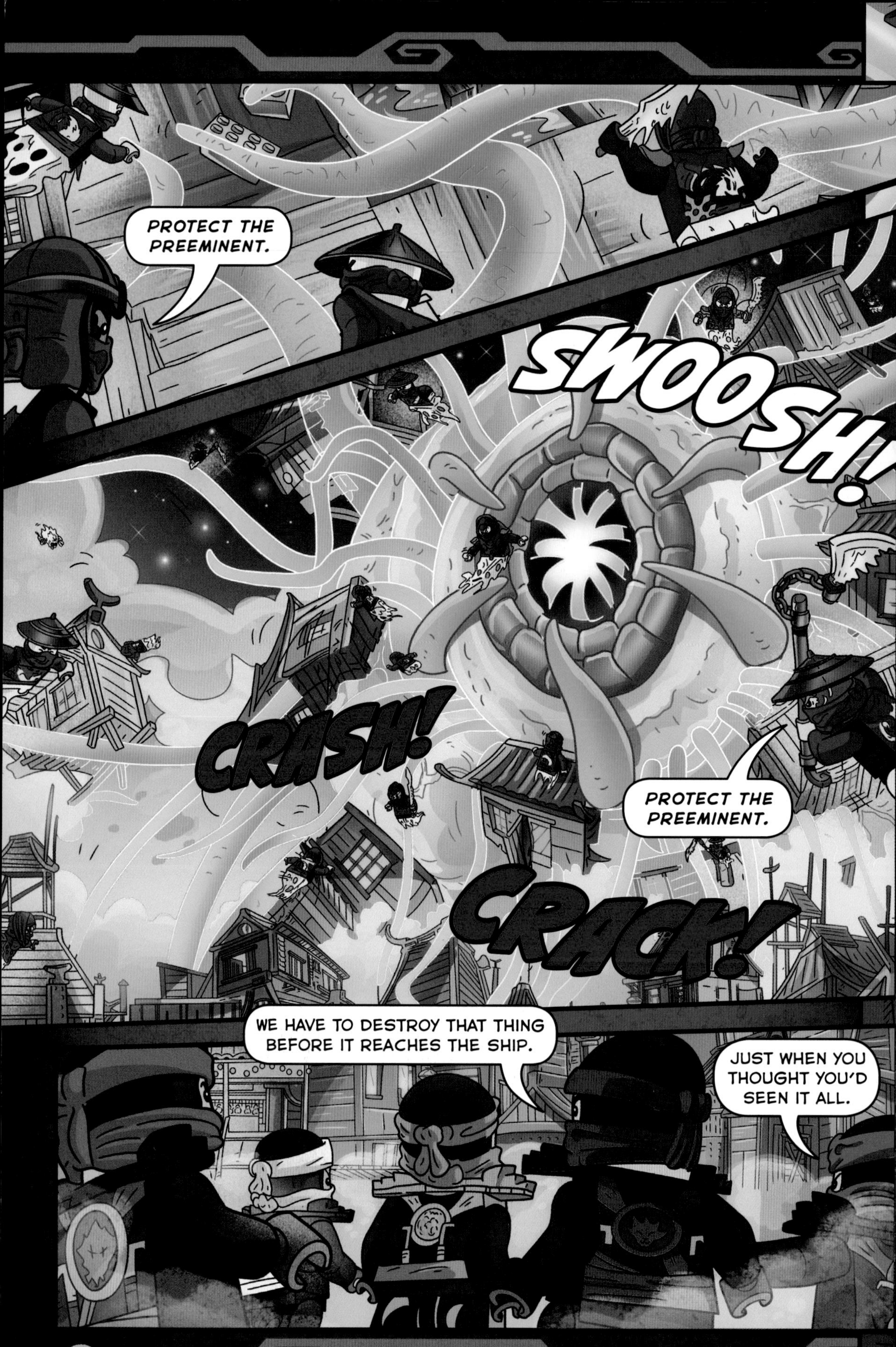
PROTECT THE PREEMINENT.
SWOOSH!
CRASH!
PROTECT THE PREEMINENT.
CRACK!
WE HAVE TO DESTROY THAT THING BEFORE IT REACHES THE SHIP.
JUST WHEN YOU THOUGHT YOU'D SEEN IT ALL.

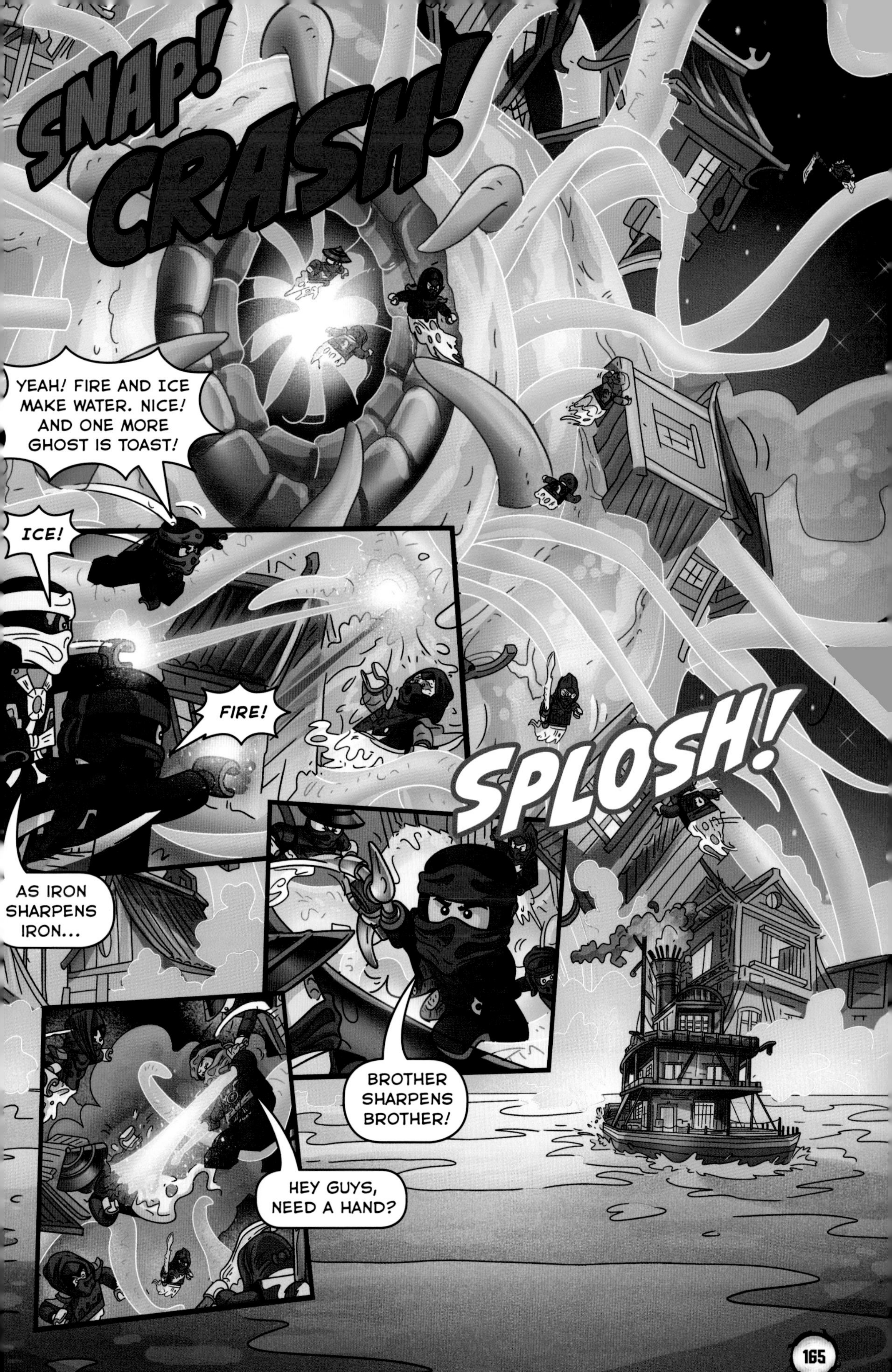
SNAP!
CRASH!
YEAH! FIRE AND ICE MAKE WATER. NICE! AND ONE MORE GHOST IS TOAST!
ICE!
FIRE!
SPLOSH!
AS IRON SHARPENS IRON...
BROTHER SHARPENS BROTHER!
HEY GUYS, NEED A HAND?

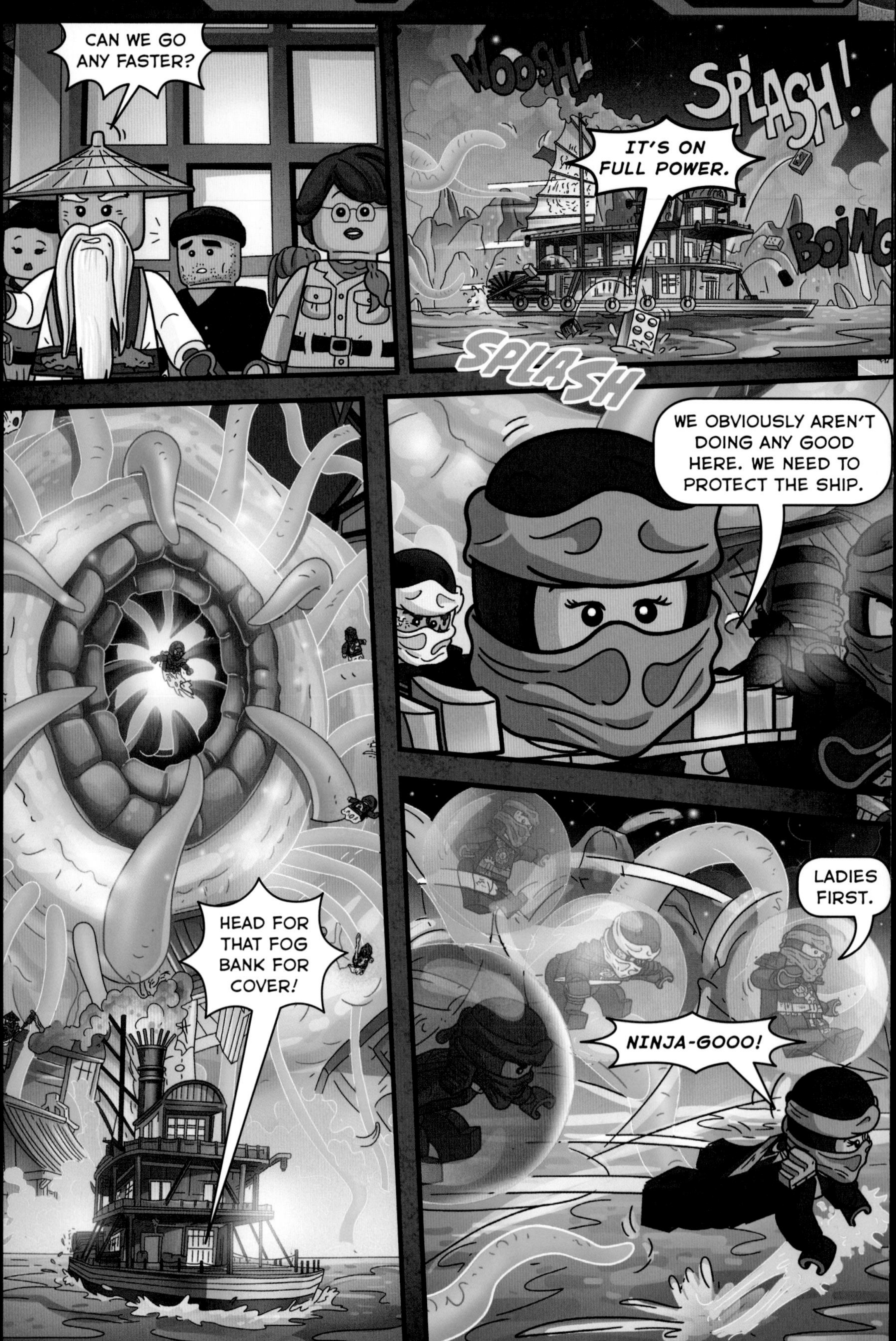
CAN WE GO ANY FASTER?
WOOSH!
SPLASH!
IT'S ON FULL POWER.
BOING
SPLASH
WE OBVIOUSLY AREN'T DOING ANY GOOD HERE. WE NEED TO PROTECT THE SHIP.
HEAD FOR THAT FOG BANK FOR COVER!
LADIES FIRST.
NINJA-GOOO!

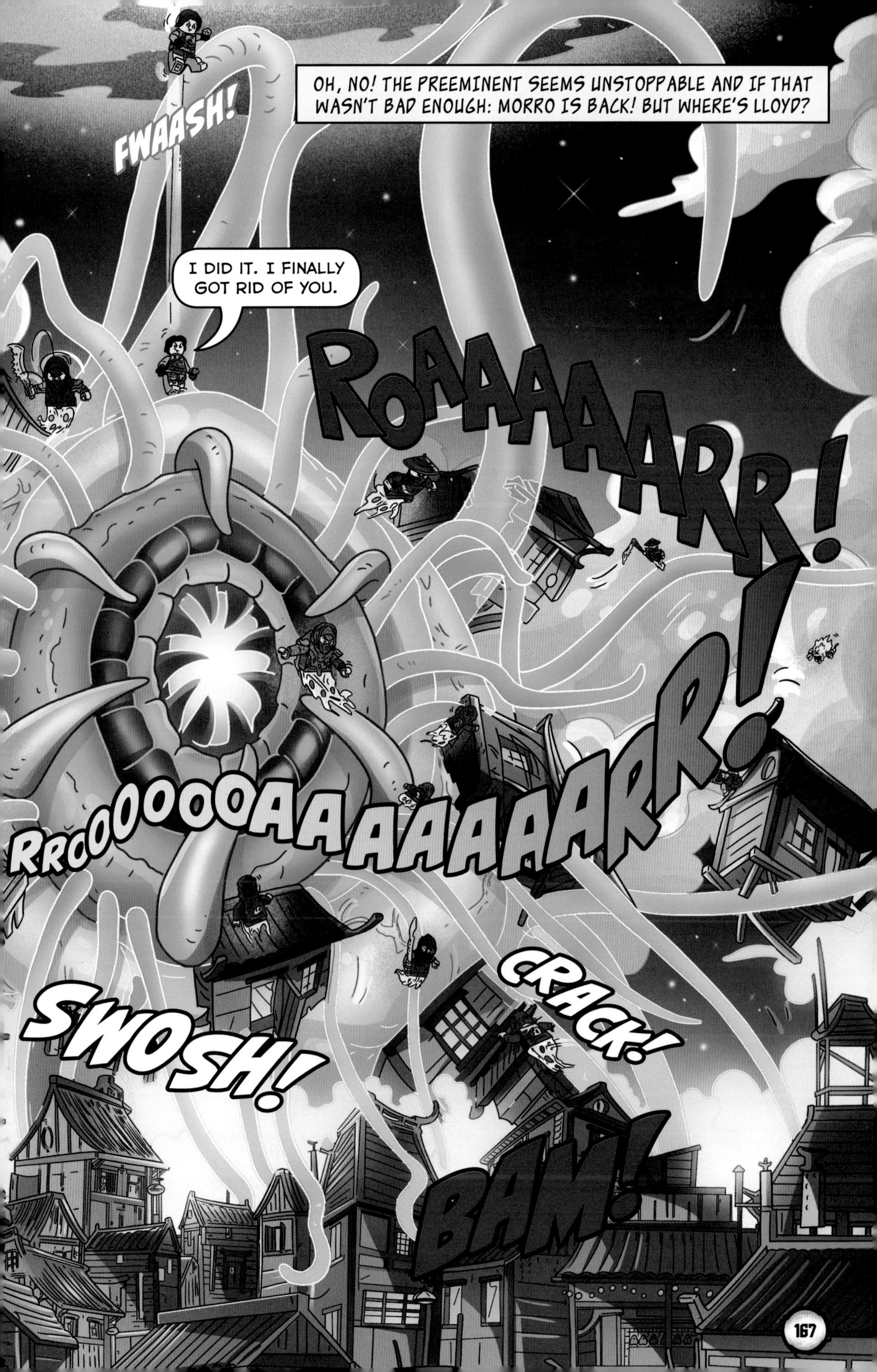
OH, NO! THE PREEMINENT SEEMS UNSTOPPABLE AND IF THAT WASN'T BAD ENOUGH: MORRO IS BACK! BUT WHERE'S LLOYD?
FWAASH!
I DID IT. I FINALLY GOT RID OF YOU.
ROAAAAAARR!
RROOOOOOAAAAAAARR!
SWOSH!
CRACK!
BAM!

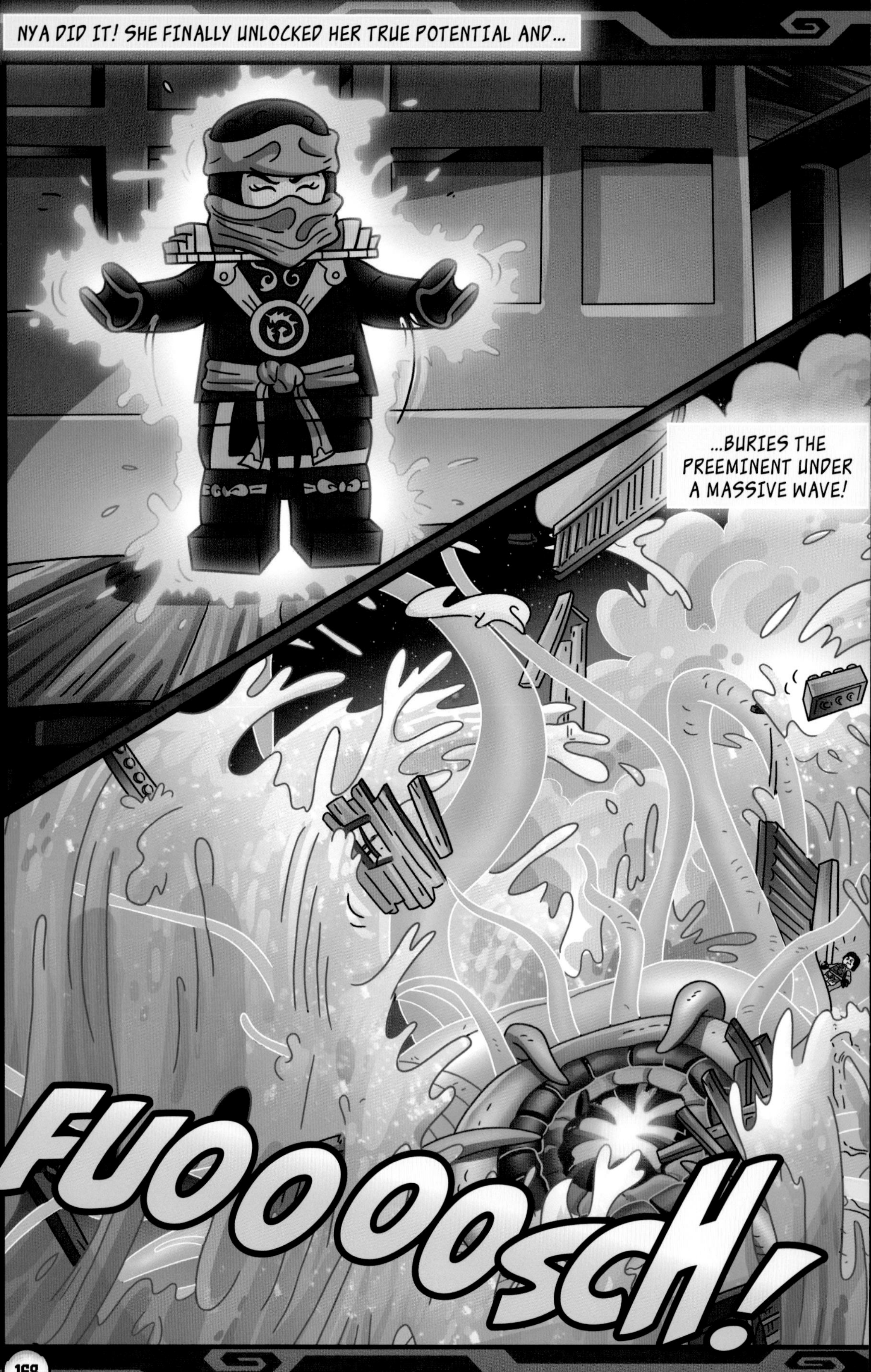
NYA DID IT! SHE FINALLY UNLOCKED HER TRUE POTENTIAL AND...
...BURIES THE PREEMINENT UNDER A MASSIVE WAVE!
FUOOOOOSCH!

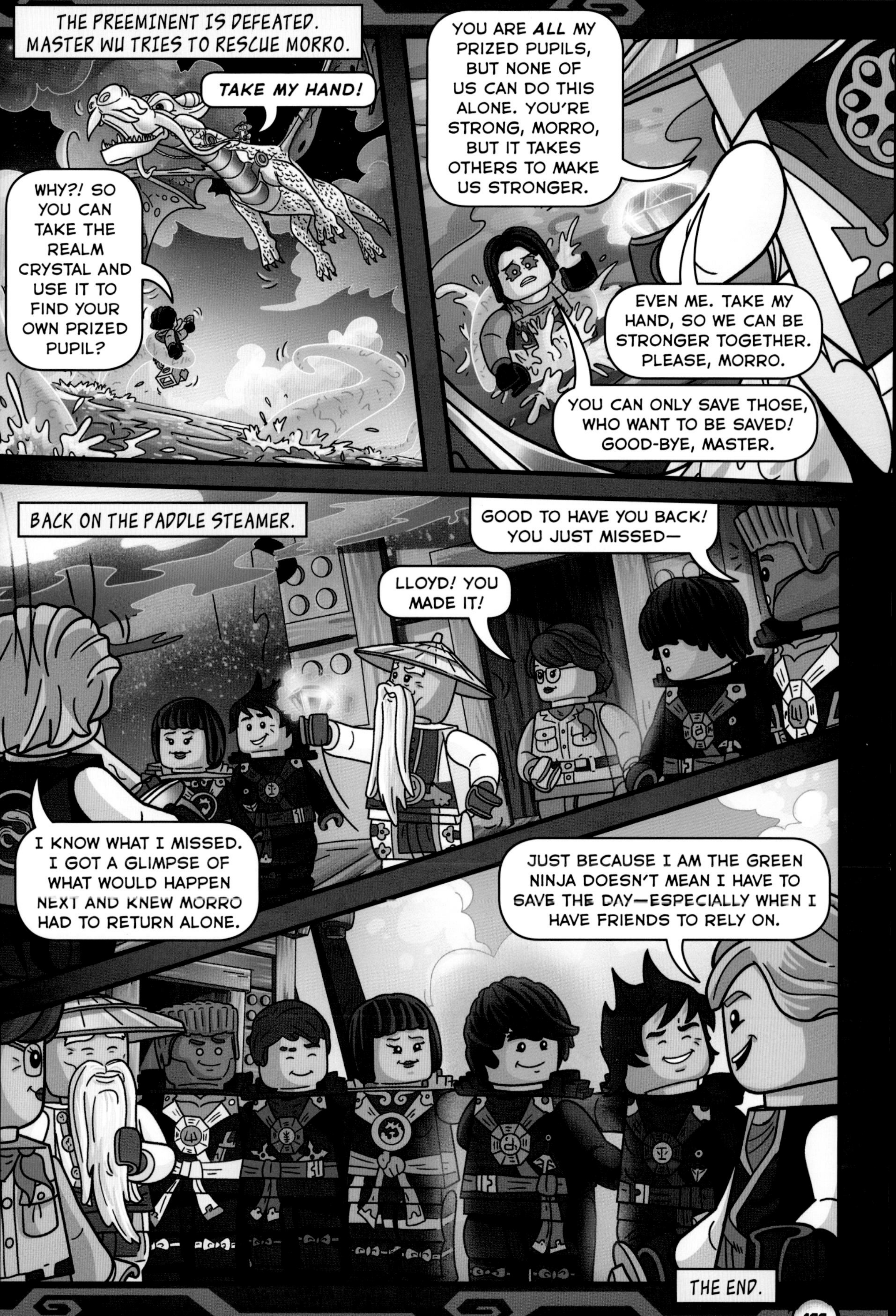
THE PREEMINENT IS DEFEATED. MASTER WU TRIES TO RESCUE MORRO.
TAKE MY HAND!
WHY?! SO YOU CAN TAKE THE REALM CRYSTAL AND USE IT TO FIND YOUR OWN PRIZED PUPIL?
YOU ARE ALL MY PRIZED PUPILS, BUT NONE OF US CAN DO THIS ALONE. YOU'RE STRONG, MORRO, BUT IT TAKES OTHERS TO MAKE US STRONGER.
EVEN ME. TAKE MY HAND, SO WE CAN BE STRONGER TOGETHER. PLEASE, MORRO.
YOU CAN ONLY SAVE THOSE, WHO WANT TO BE SAVED! GOOD-BYE, MASTER.
BACK ON THE PADDLE STEAMER.
GOOD TO HAVE YOU BACK! YOU JUST MISSED—
LLOYD! YOU MADE IT!
I KNOW WHAT I MISSED. I GOT A GLIMPSE OF WHAT WOULD HAPPEN NEXT AND KNEW MORRO HAD TO RETURN ALONE.
JUST BECAUSE I AM THE GREEN NINJA DOESN'T MEAN I HAVE TO SAVE THE DAY—ESPECIALLY WHEN I HAVE FRIENDS TO RELY ON.
THE END.

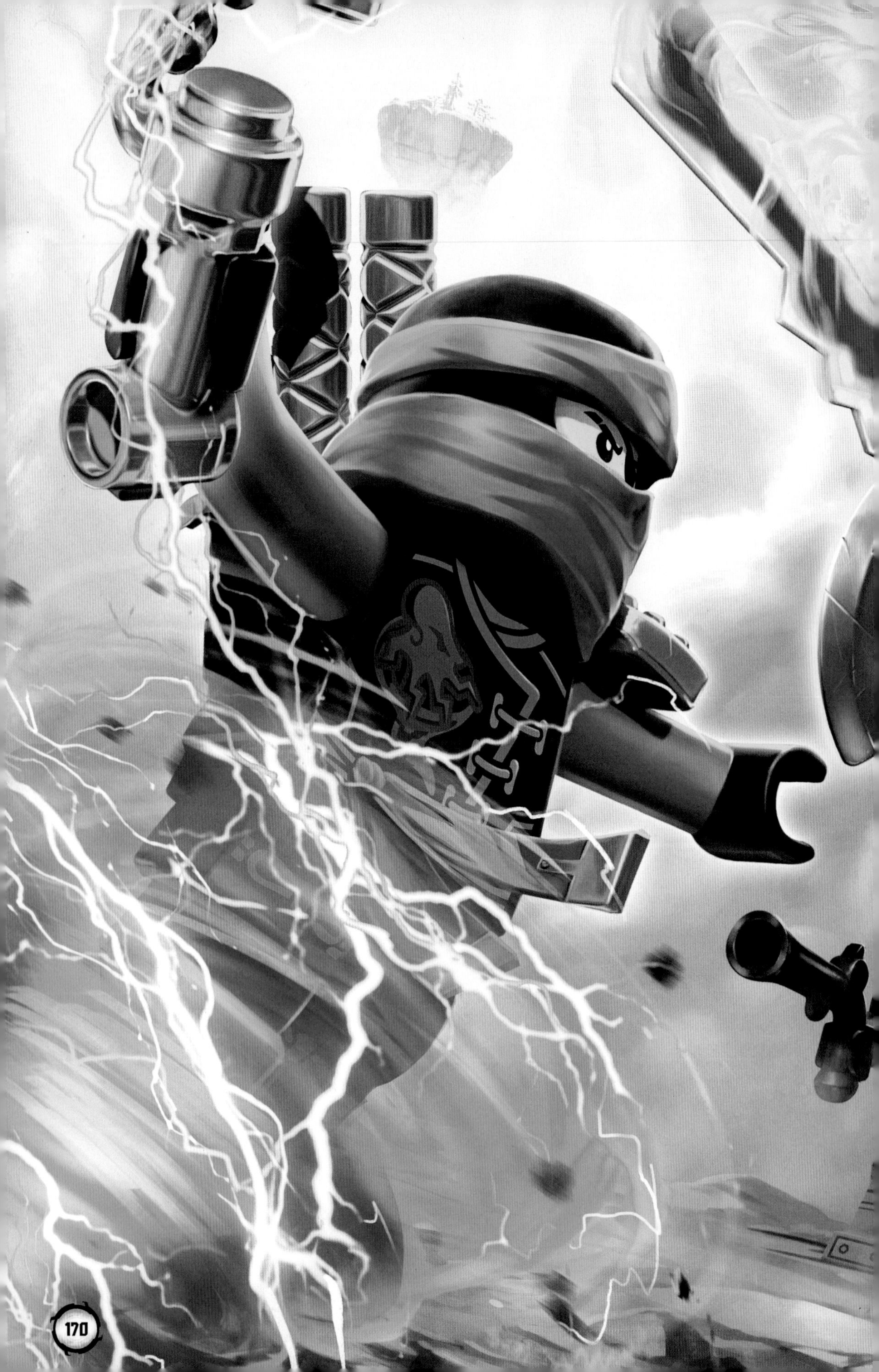

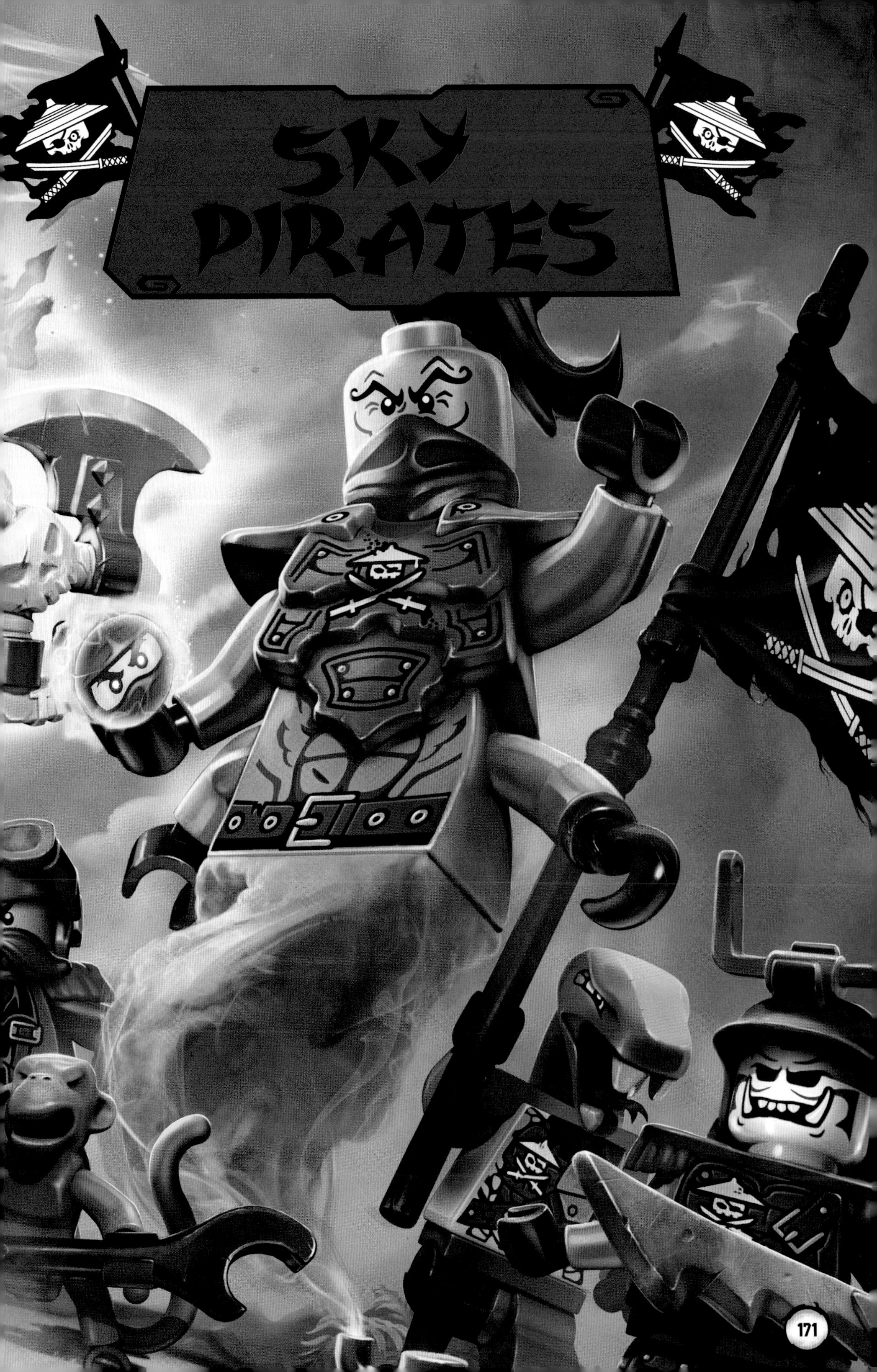
SKY PIRATES

NINJAGO NEWS

+++ breaking news +++ a new threat f

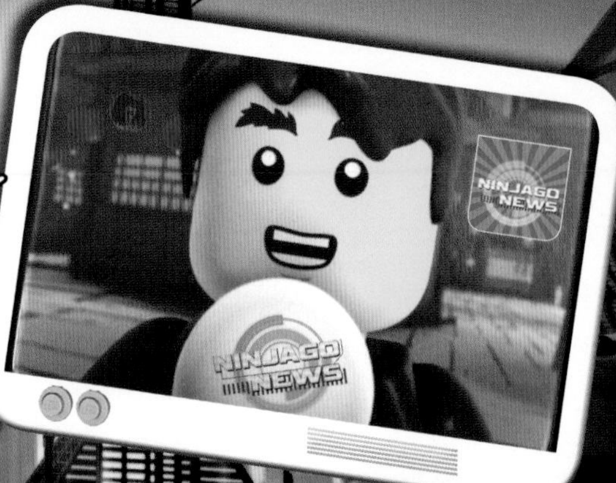
NINJAGO NEWS
NINJAGO NEWS

AFTER OUR BRAVE NINJA DEFEATED THE EVIL MORRO, THE NEXT MENACE IS ALREADY LYING IN WAIT FOR THEM: SKY PIRATES! WILL THE NINJA BE ABLE TO SAVE THE WORLD YET AGAIN?

TOP NEWS

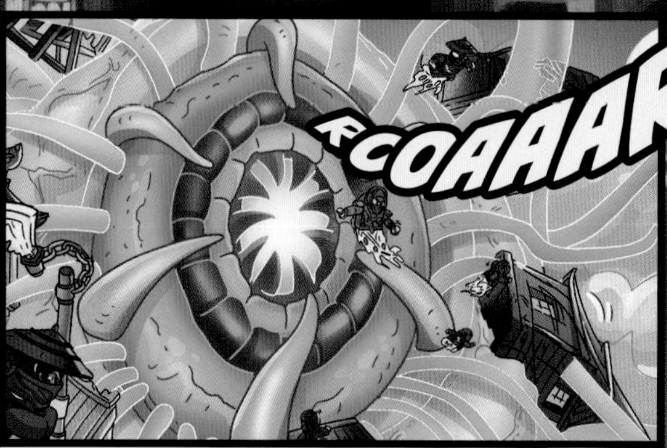
RCOAAAR!

Oh, no, Morro and the Preeminent are attacking!

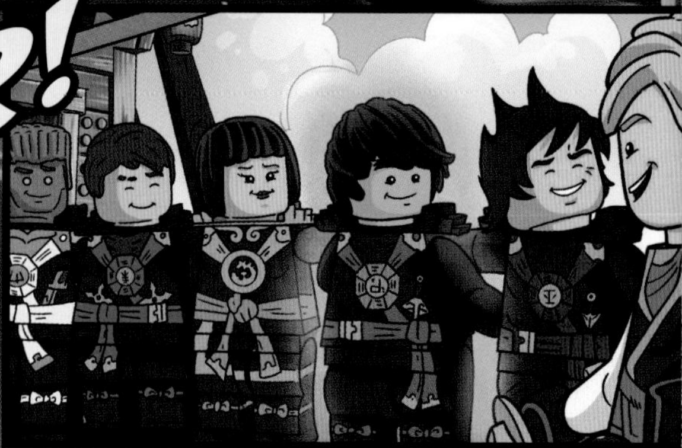

This cool team can handle anything!

NO MORE EVIL GHOSTS!

At last, it's over! The brave ninja have proven their skills as ghost hunters and defeated the mean Morro and his evil master. As a Master-in-Training, Lloyd learned that he can rely on his friends. Nya unlocked her full potential and defeated the ghosts with a huge wave. The only one who is still allowed to be ghostly is Cole!

A NEW MISSION!

No time to recover! The ninja may be the stars of Ninjago City, but they cannot afford to rest on their laurels. Reports have been reaching us of raids by evil pirates in sinister flying machines. Our heroes are preparing to defend Ninjago! Or are they? **Find out next.**

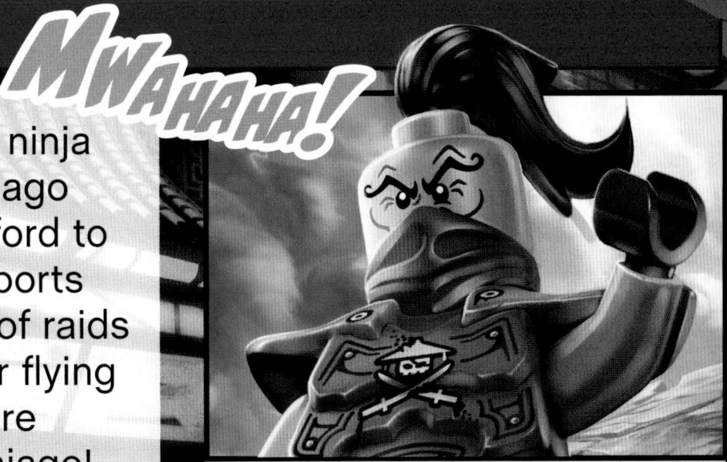
MWAHAHA!

Nadakhan is the new villain!

THE PIRATE'S STORY

Led by the nasty Djinn Nadakhan, the pirates want to take over Ninjago City! Apparently, the Sky Pirates come from a realm called Djinjago and have only one goal: to destroy our world! If you see these dastardly airborne villains, make sure to keep a safe distance. They can't be trusted—they're pirates!

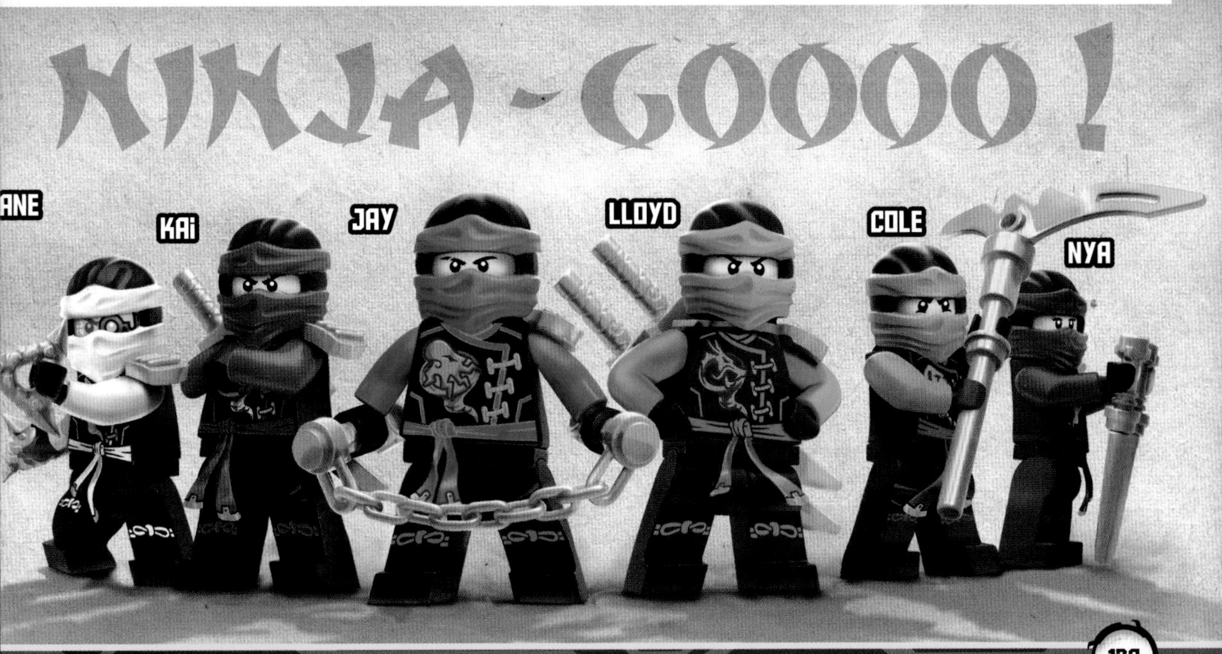
NINJA-GOOOO!
ANE
KAi
JAY
LLOYD
COLE
NYA

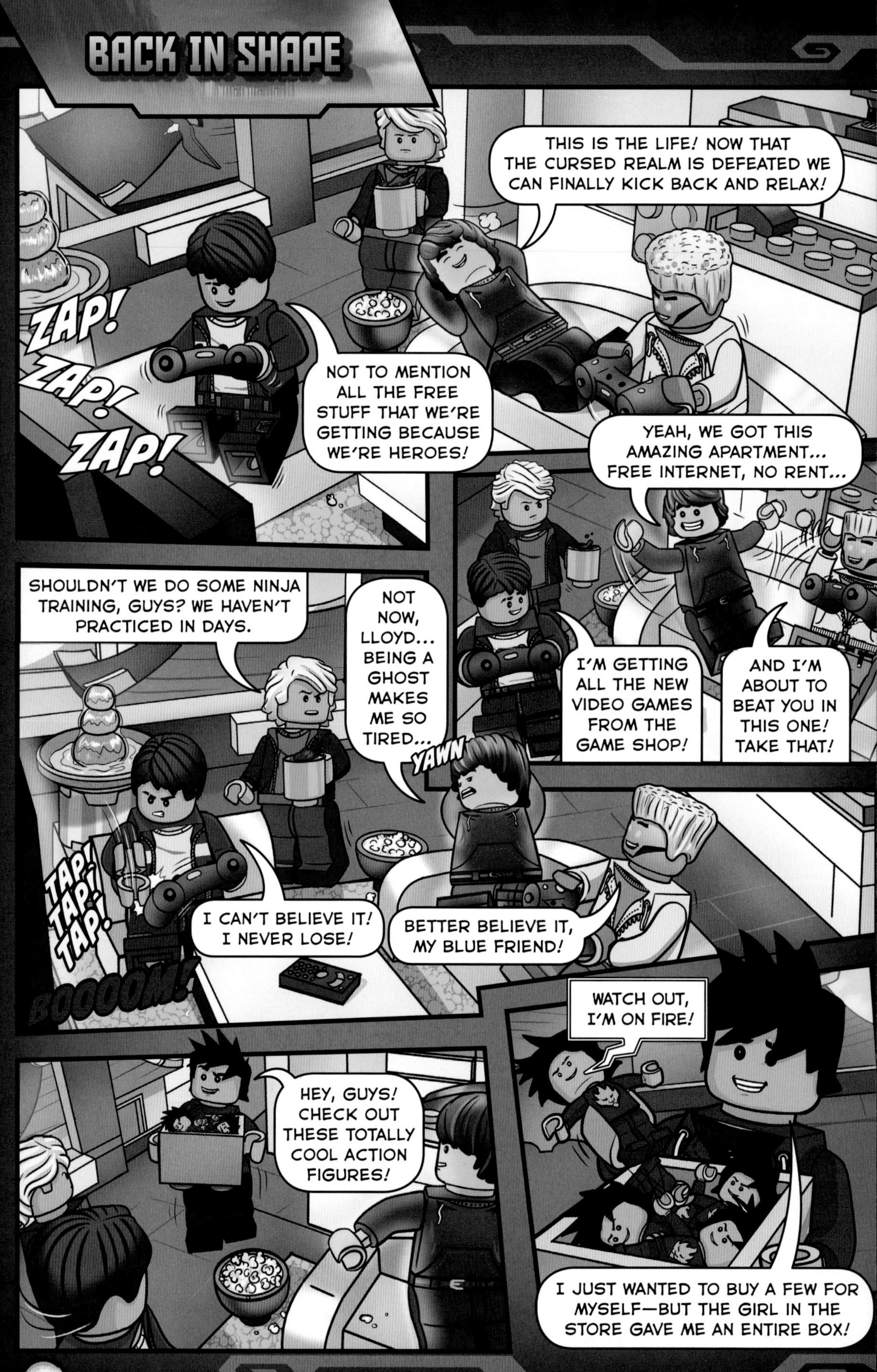
BACK IN SHAPE
THIS IS THE LIFE! NOW THAT THE CURSED REALM IS DEFEATED WE CAN FINALLY KICK BACK AND RELAX!
ZAP! ZAP! ZAP!
NOT TO MENTION ALL THE FREE STUFF THAT WE'RE GETTING BECAUSE WE'RE HEROES!
YEAH, WE GOT THIS AMAZING APARTMENT... FREE INTERNET, NO RENT...
I'M GETTING ALL THE NEW VIDEO GAMES FROM THE GAME SHOP!
AND I'M ABOUT TO BEAT YOU IN THIS ONE! TAKE THAT!
SHOULDN'T WE DO SOME NINJA TRAINING, GUYS? WE HAVEN'T PRACTICED IN DAYS.
NOT NOW, LLOYD... BEING A GHOST MAKES ME SO TIRED...
YAWN
TAP! TAP! TAP!
BOOOOOM!
I CAN'T BELIEVE IT! I NEVER LOSE!
BETTER BELIEVE IT, MY BLUE FRIEND!
HEY, GUYS! CHECK OUT THESE TOTALLY COOL ACTION FIGURES!
WATCH OUT, I'M ON FIRE!
I JUST WANTED TO BUY A FEW FOR MYSELF—BUT THE GIRL IN THE STORE GAVE ME AN ENTIRE BOX!

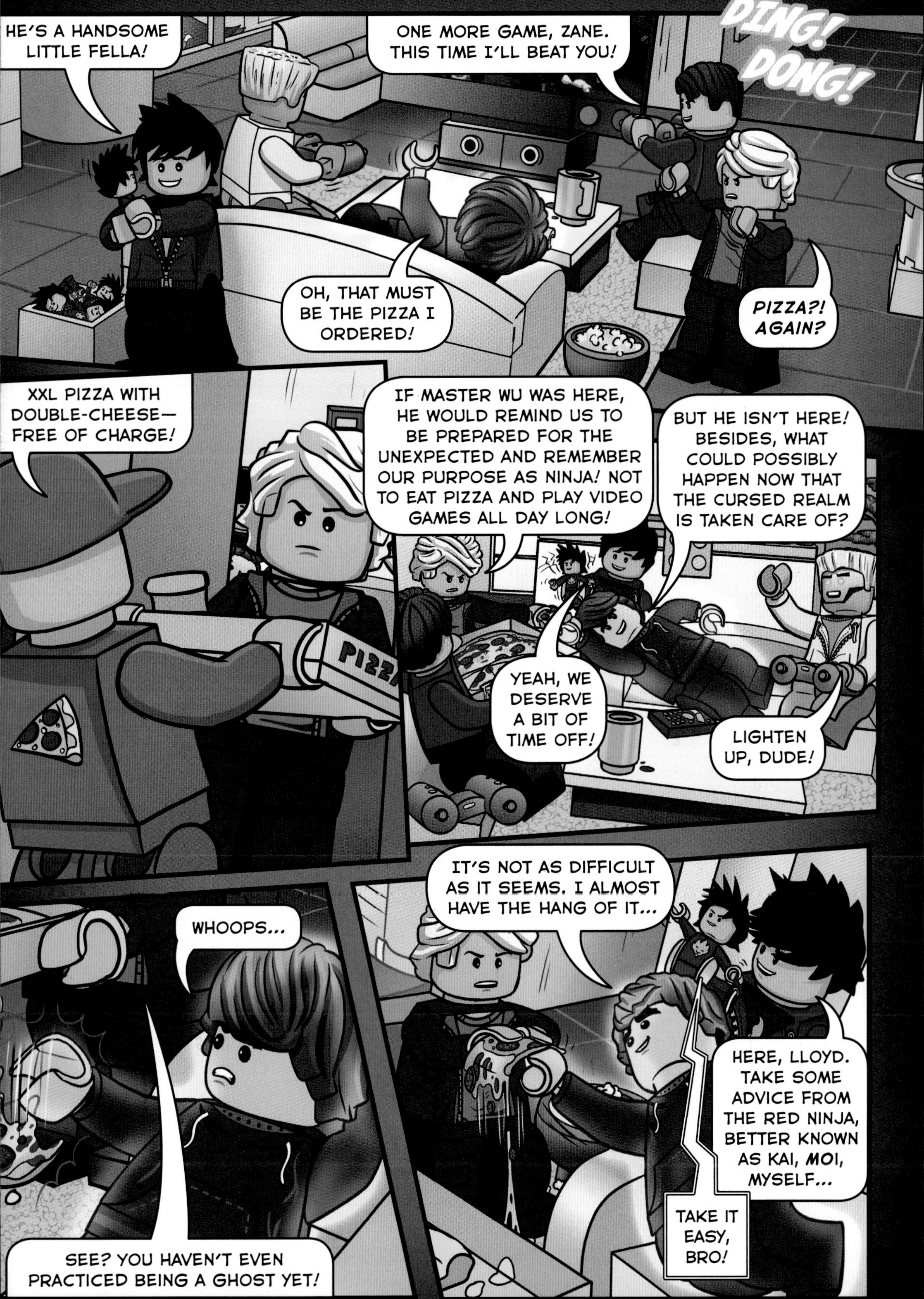
HE'S A HANDSOME LITTLE FELLA!
ONE MORE GAME, ZANE. THIS TIME I'LL BEAT YOU!
DING! DONG!
OH, THAT MUST BE THE PIZZA I ORDERED!
PIZZA?! AGAIN?
XXL PIZZA WITH DOUBLE-CHEESE— FREE OF CHARGE!
PIZZA
IF MASTER WU WAS HERE, HE WOULD REMIND US TO BE PREPARED FOR THE UNEXPECTED AND REMEMBER OUR PURPOSE AS NINJA! NOT TO EAT PIZZA AND PLAY VIDEO GAMES ALL DAY LONG!
BUT HE ISN'T HERE! BESIDES, WHAT COULD POSSIBLY HAPPEN NOW THAT THE CURSED REALM IS TAKEN CARE OF?
YEAH, WE DESERVE A BIT OF TIME OFF!
LIGHTEN UP, DUDE!
WHOOPS...
SEE? YOU HAVEN'T EVEN PRACTICED BEING A GHOST YET!
IT'S NOT AS DIFFICULT AS IT SEEMS. I ALMOST HAVE THE HANG OF IT...
HERE, LLOYD. TAKE SOME ADVICE FROM THE RED NINJA, BETTER KNOWN AS KAI, MOI, MYSELF...
TAKE IT EASY, BRO!

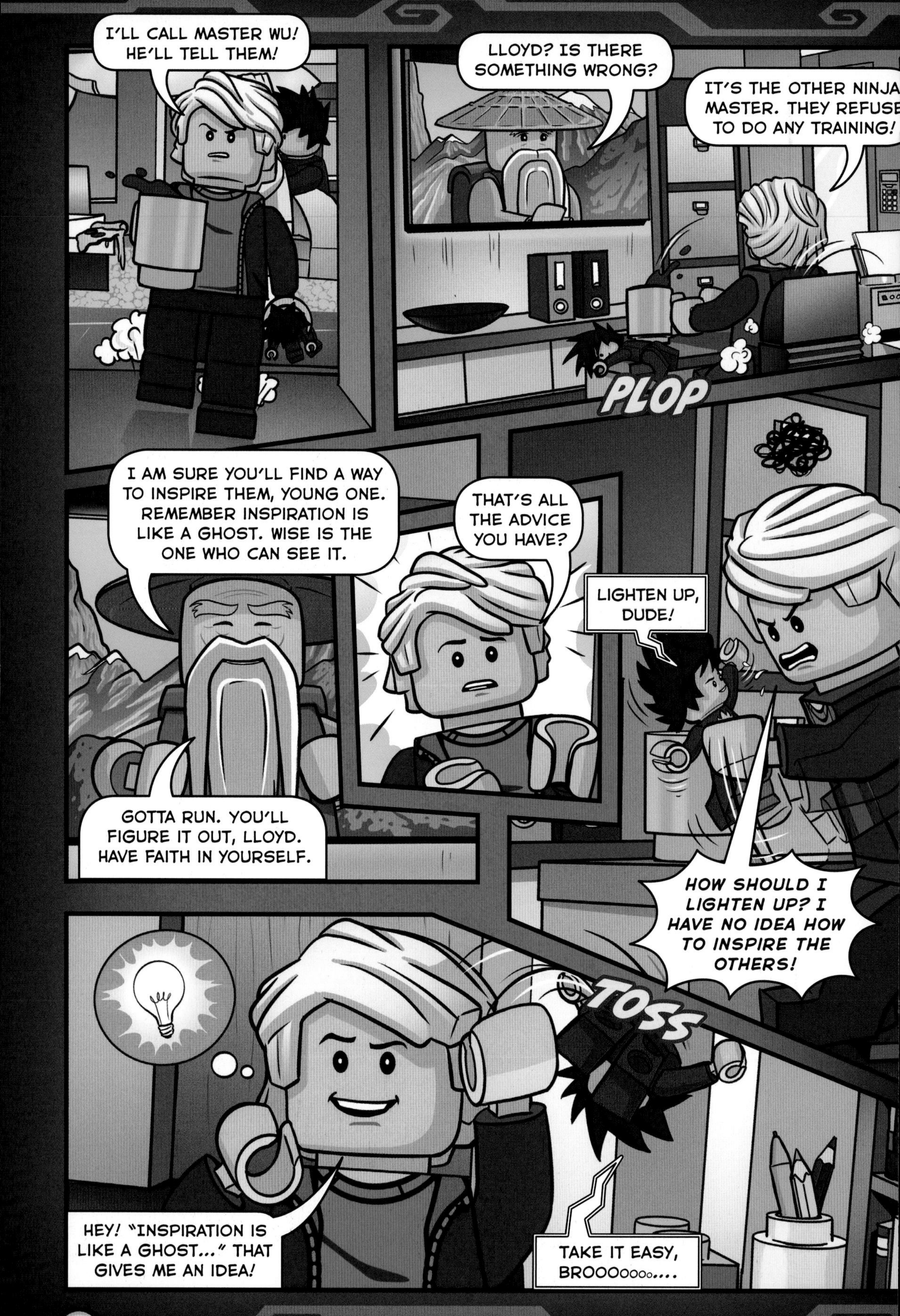
I'LL CALL MASTER WU! HE'LL TELL THEM!
LLOYD? IS THERE SOMETHING WRONG?
IT'S THE OTHER NINJA MASTER. THEY REFUSE TO DO ANY TRAINING!
PLOP
I AM SURE YOU'LL FIND A WAY TO INSPIRE THEM, YOUNG ONE. REMEMBER INSPIRATION IS LIKE A GHOST. WISE IS THE ONE WHO CAN SEE IT.
THAT'S ALL THE ADVICE YOU HAVE?
LIGHTEN UP, DUDE!
GOTTA RUN. YOU'LL FIGURE IT OUT, LLOYD. HAVE FAITH IN YOURSELF.
HOW SHOULD I LIGHTEN UP? I HAVE NO IDEA HOW TO INSPIRE THE OTHERS!
TOSS
HEY! "INSPIRATION IS LIKE A GHOST..." THAT GIVES ME AN IDEA!
TAKE IT EASY, BROOOoooo....

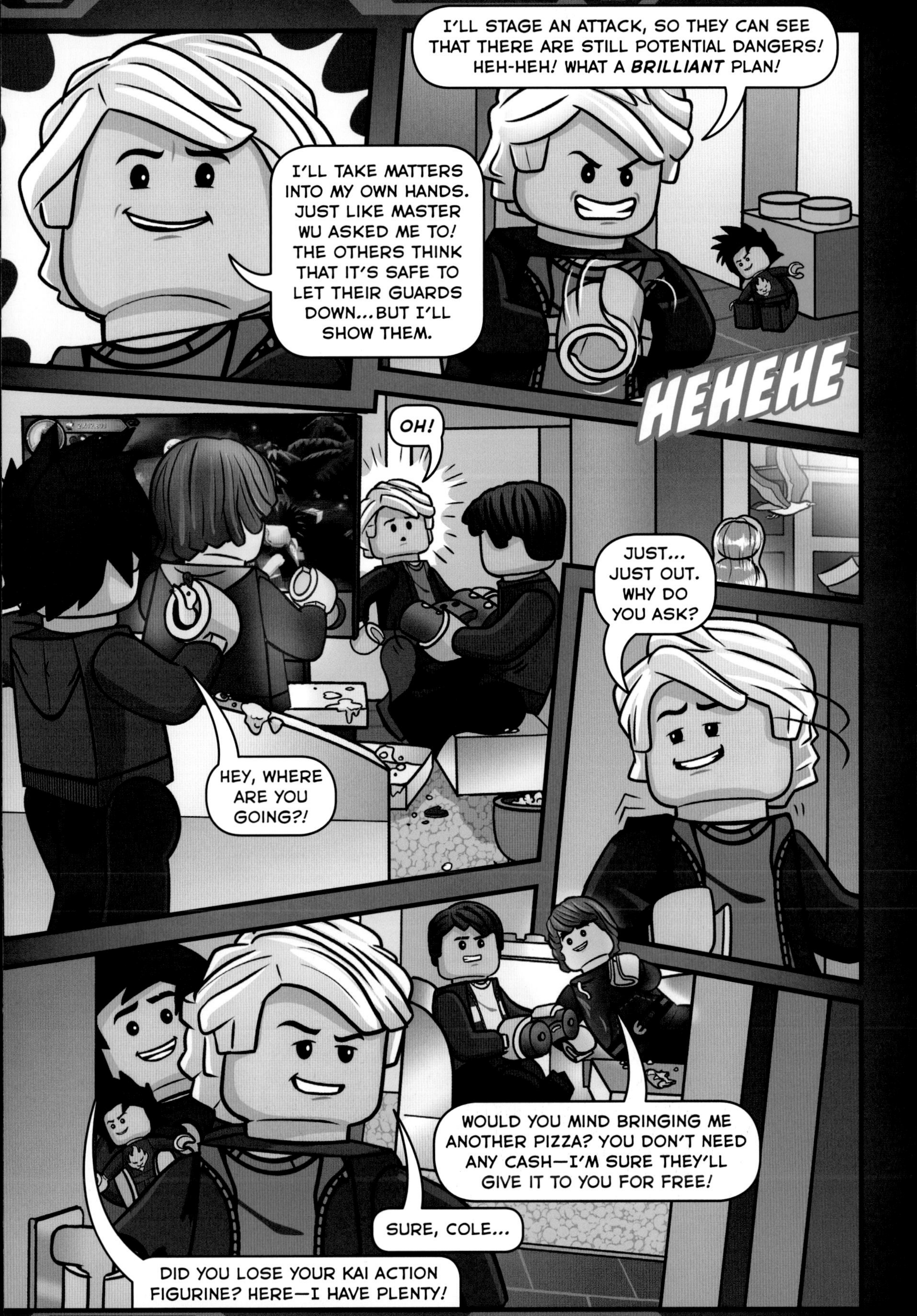
I'LL TAKE MATTERS INTO MY OWN HANDS. JUST LIKE MASTER WU ASKED ME TO! THE OTHERS THINK THAT IT'S SAFE TO LET THEIR GUARDS DOWN...BUT I'LL SHOW THEM.
I'LL STAGE AN ATTACK, SO THEY CAN SEE THAT THERE ARE STILL POTENTIAL DANGERS! HEH-HEH! WHAT A *BRILLIANT* PLAN!
HEHEHE
OH!
HEY, WHERE ARE YOU GOING?!
JUST... JUST OUT. WHY DO YOU ASK?
WOULD YOU MIND BRINGING ME ANOTHER PIZZA? YOU DON'T NEED ANY CASH—I'M SURE THEY'LL GIVE IT TO YOU FOR FREE!
SURE, COLE...
DID YOU LOSE YOUR KAI ACTION FIGURINE? HERE—I HAVE PLENTY!

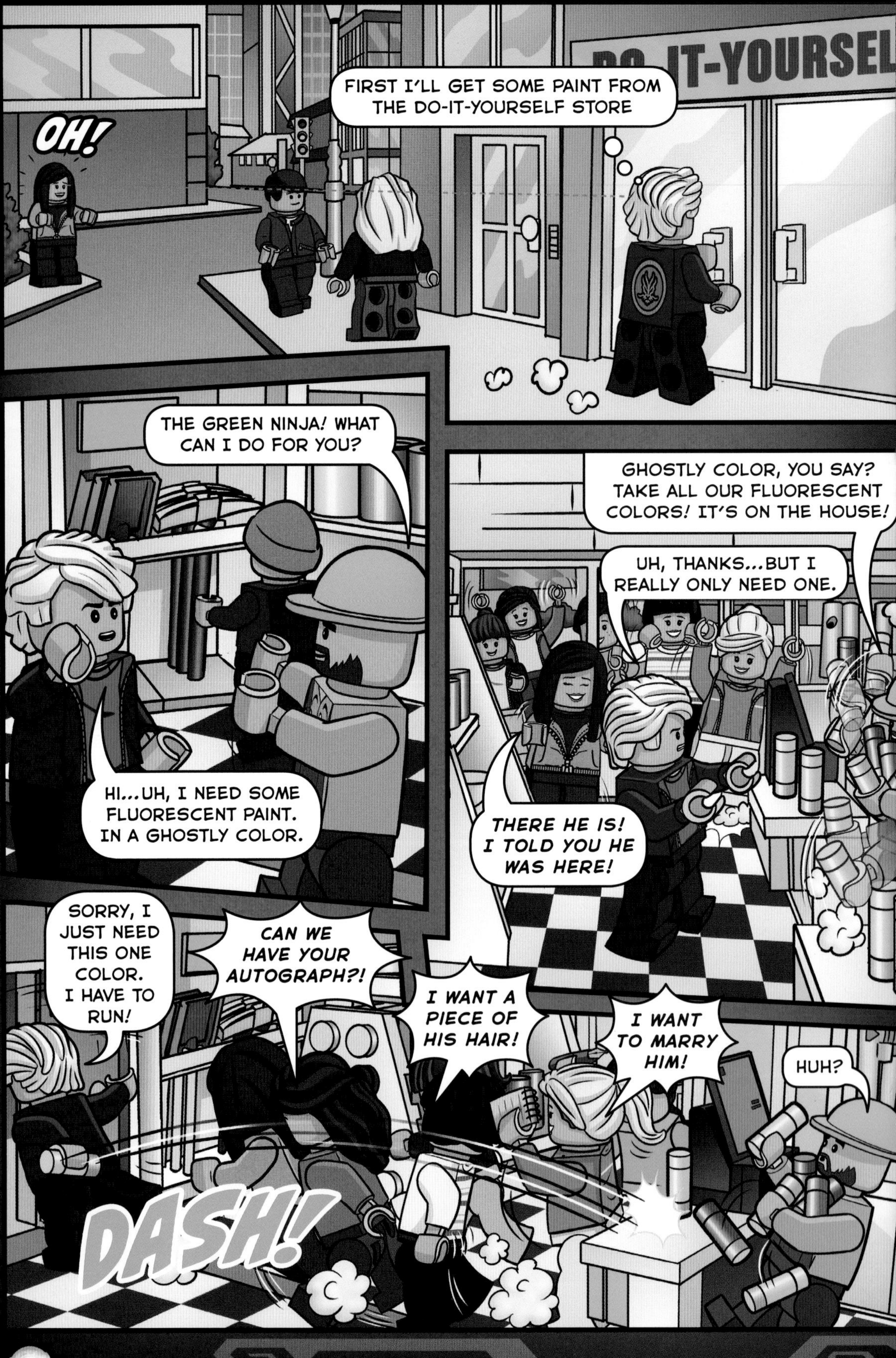
OH!
FIRST I'LL GET SOME PAINT FROM THE DO-IT-YOURSELF STORE
IT-YOURSEL
THE GREEN NINJA! WHAT CAN I DO FOR YOU?
HI...UH, I NEED SOME FLUORESCENT PAINT. IN A GHOSTLY COLOR.
GHOSTLY COLOR, YOU SAY? TAKE ALL OUR FLUORESCENT COLORS! IT'S ON THE HOUSE!
UH, THANKS...BUT I REALLY ONLY NEED ONE.
THERE HE IS! I TOLD YOU HE WAS HERE!
SORRY, I JUST NEED THIS ONE COLOR. I HAVE TO RUN!
CAN WE HAVE YOUR AUTOGRAPH?!
I WANT A PIECE OF HIS HAIR!
I WANT TO MARRY HIM!
HUH?
DASH!

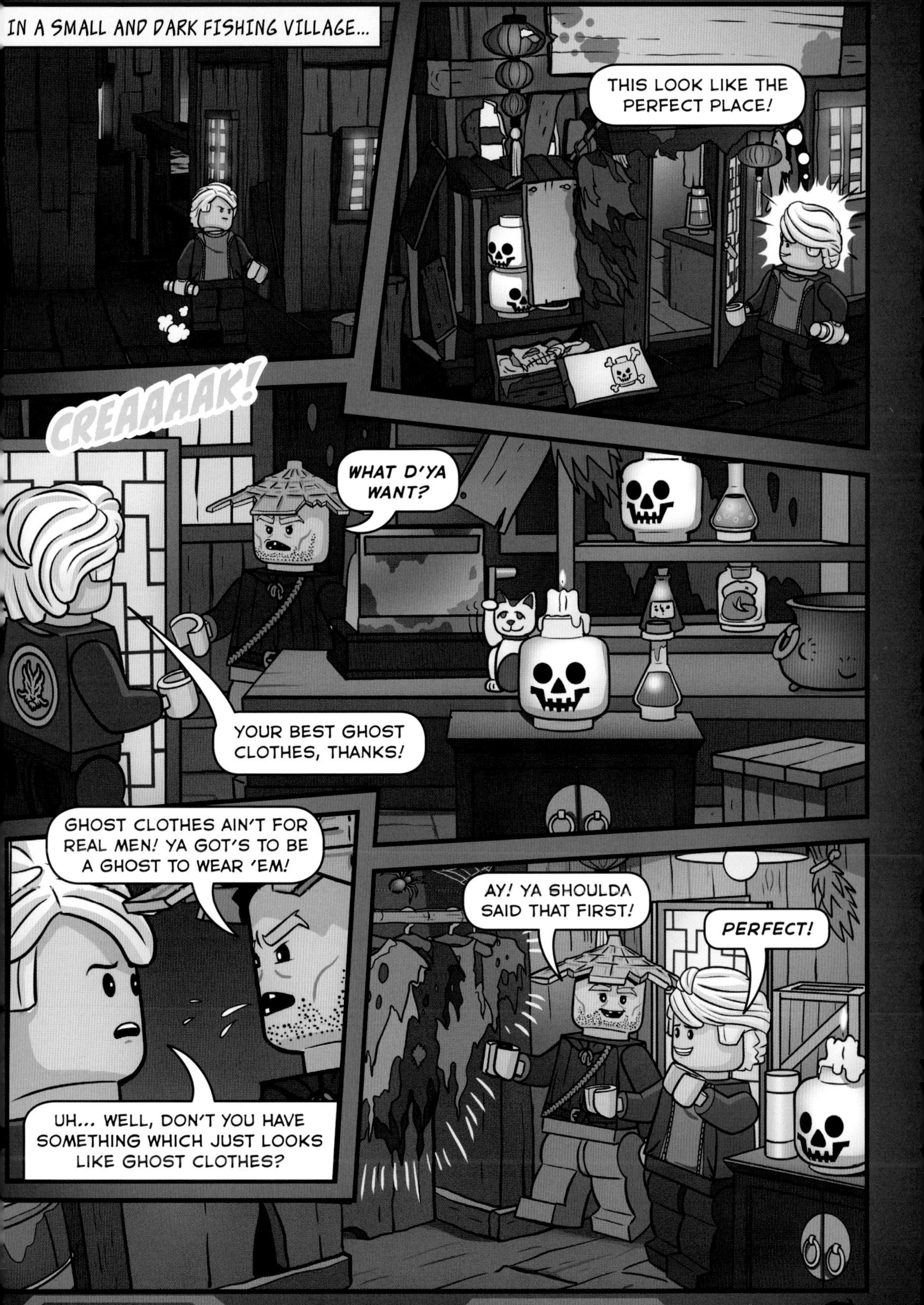
IN A SMALL AND DARK FISHING VILLAGE...
THIS LOOK LIKE THE PERFECT PLACE!
CREAAAAK!
WHAT D'YA WANT?
YOUR BEST GHOST CLOTHES, THANKS!
GHOST CLOTHES AIN'T FOR REAL MEN! YA GOT'S TO BE A GHOST TO WEAR 'EM!
UH... WELL, DON'T YOU HAVE SOMETHING WHICH JUST LOOKS LIKE GHOST CLOTHES?
AY! YA SHOULDA SAID THAT FIRST!
PERFECT!

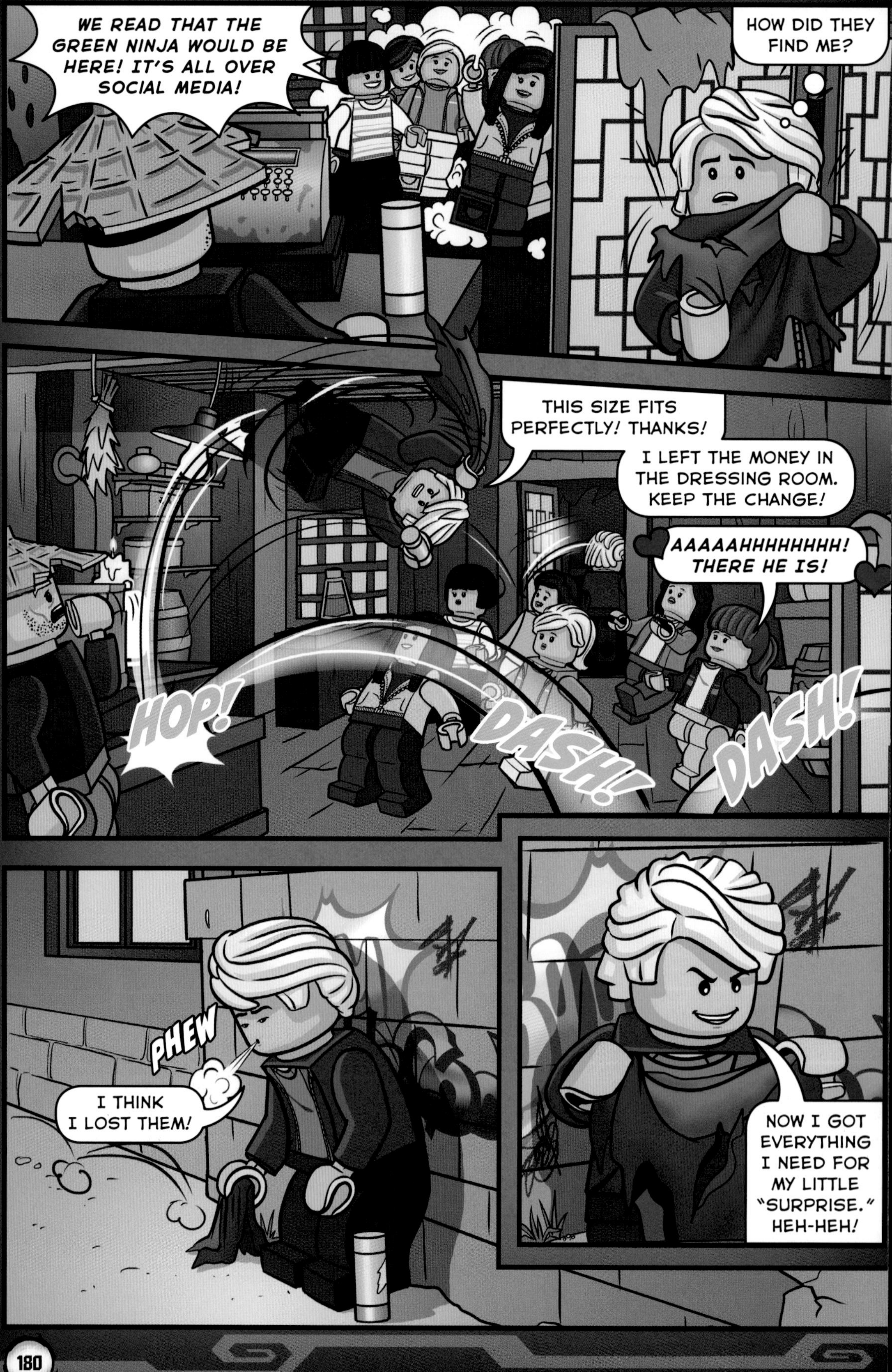
WE READ THAT THE GREEN NINJA WOULD BE HERE! IT'S ALL OVER SOCIAL MEDIA!
HOW DID THEY FIND ME?
THIS SIZE FITS PERFECTLY! THANKS!
I LEFT THE MONEY IN THE DRESSING ROOM. KEEP THE CHANGE!
AAAAAHHHHHHHH! THERE HE IS!
HOP!
DASH!
DASH!
PHEW
I THINK I LOST THEM!
NOW I GOT EVERYTHING I NEED FOR MY LITTLE "SURPRISE." HEH-HEH!

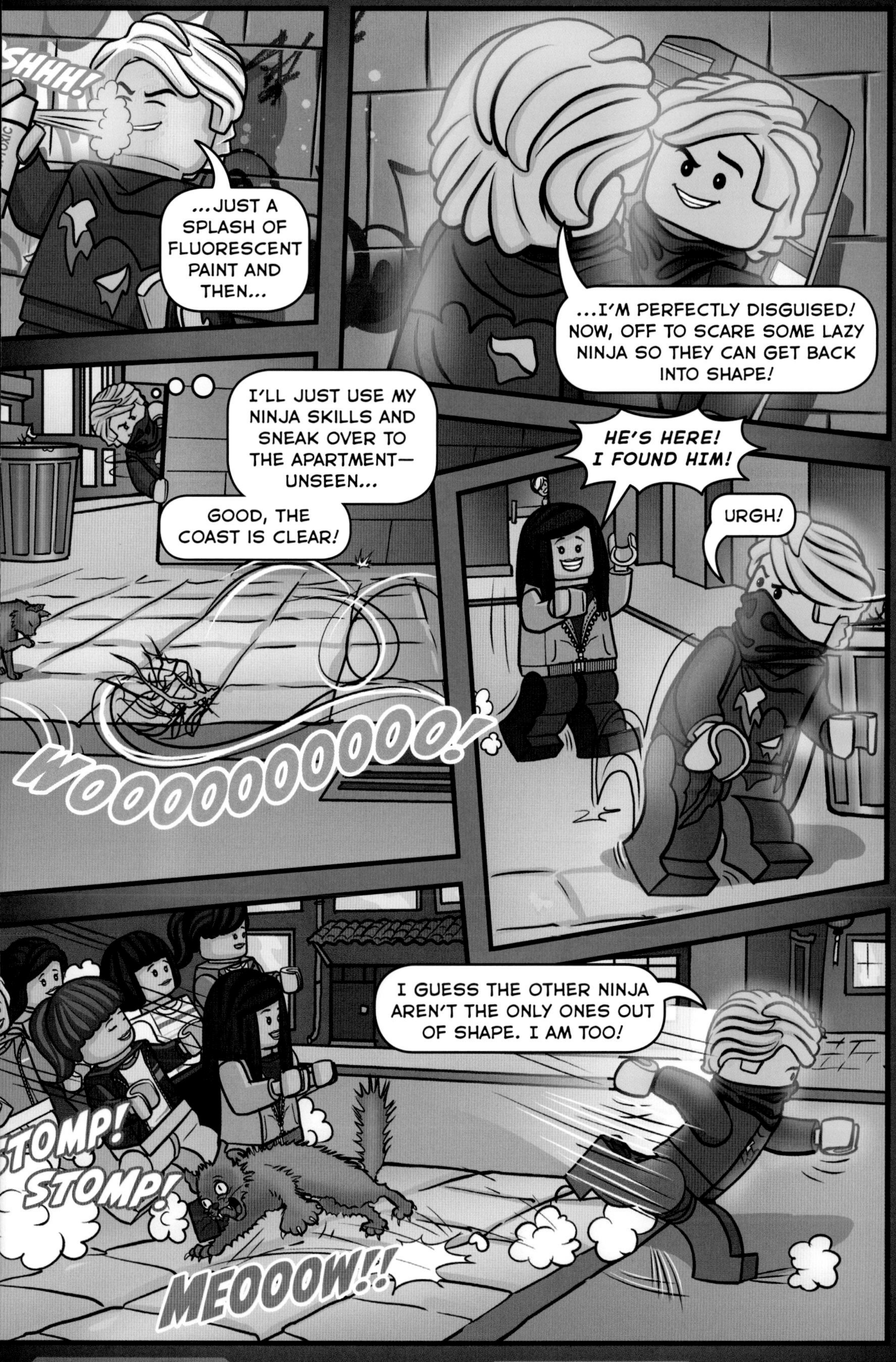
SHHH!
...JUST A SPLASH OF FLUORESCENT PAINT AND THEN...
...I'M PERFECTLY DISGUISED! NOW, OFF TO SCARE SOME LAZY NINJA SO THEY CAN GET BACK INTO SHAPE!
I'LL JUST USE MY NINJA SKILLS AND SNEAK OVER TO THE APARTMENT— UNSEEN...
GOOD, THE COAST IS CLEAR!
WOOOOOOOOOO!
HE'S HERE! I FOUND HIM!
URGH!
I GUESS THE OTHER NINJA AREN'T THE ONLY ONES OUT OF SHAPE. I AM TOO!
STOMP!
STOMP!
MEOOOW!!

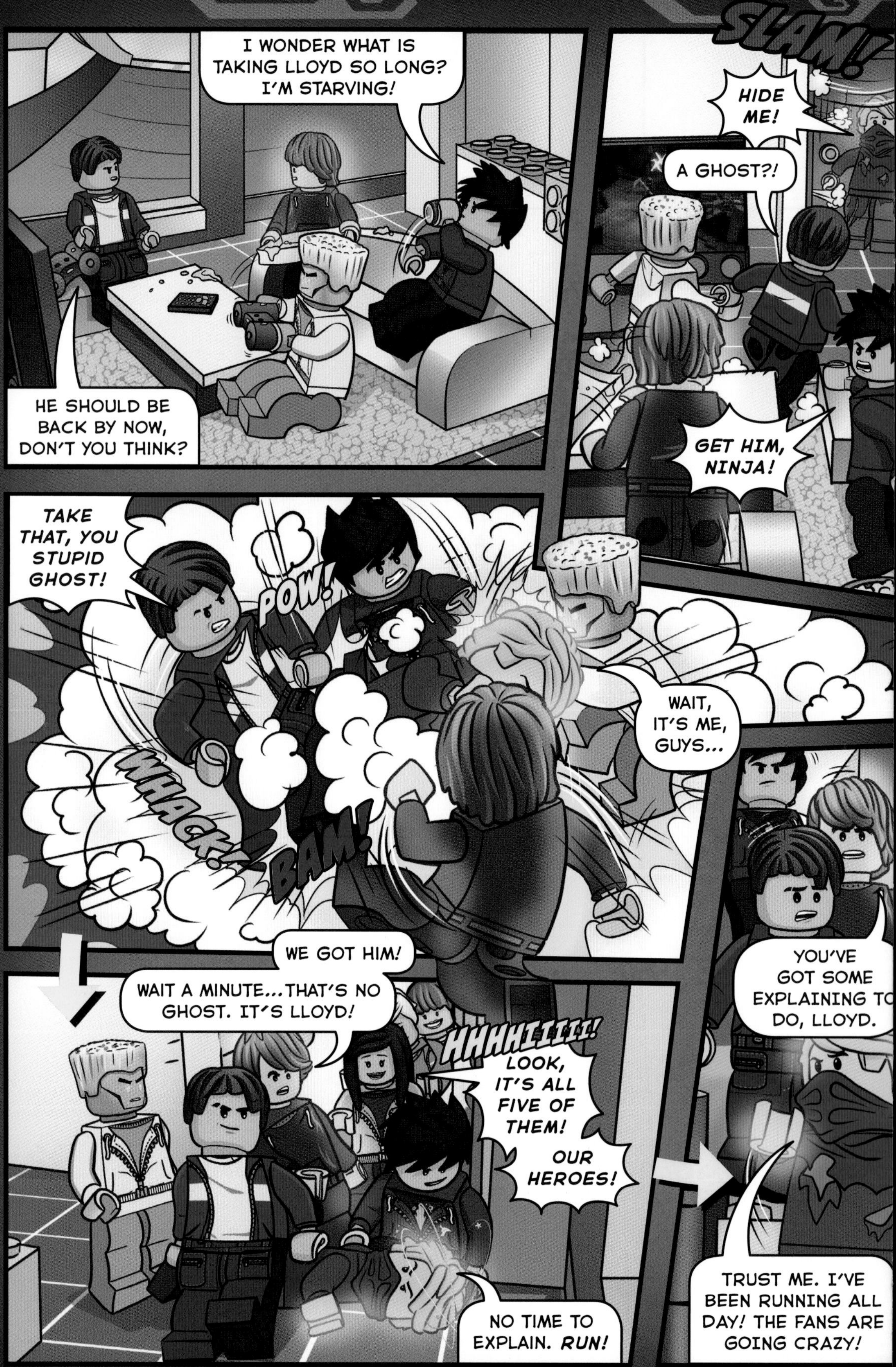
I WONDER WHAT IS TAKING LLOYD SO LONG? I'M STARVING!
HE SHOULD BE BACK BY NOW, DON'T YOU THINK?
SLAM!
HIDE ME!
A GHOST?!
GET HIM, NINJA!
TAKE THAT, YOU STUPID GHOST!
POW!
WHACK!
BAM!
WAIT, IT'S ME, GUYS...
YOU'VE GOT SOME EXPLAINING TO DO, LLOYD.
WE GOT HIM!
WAIT A MINUTE...THAT'S NO GHOST. IT'S LLOYD!
HHHHIIIII!
LOOK, IT'S ALL FIVE OF THEM!
OUR HEROES!
NO TIME TO EXPLAIN. RUN!
TRUST ME. I'VE BEEN RUNNING ALL DAY! THE FANS ARE GOING CRAZY!

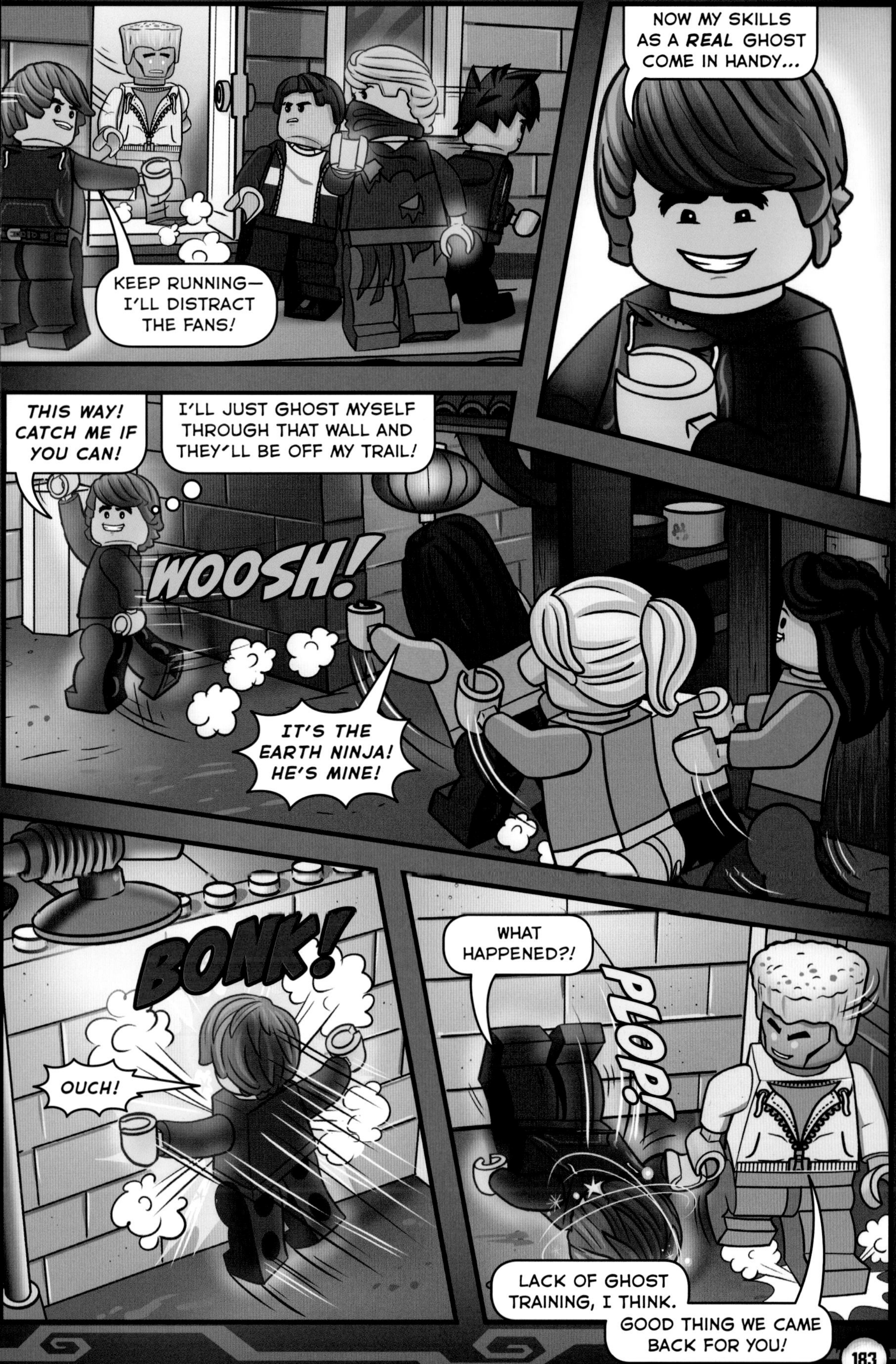
KEEP RUNNING—
I'LL DISTRACT
THE FANS!
NOW MY SKILLS
AS A *REAL* GHOST
COME IN HANDY...
THIS WAY!
CATCH ME IF
YOU CAN!
I'LL JUST GHOST MYSELF
THROUGH THAT WALL AND
THEY'LL BE OFF MY TRAIL!
WOOSH!
IT'S THE
EARTH NINJA!
HE'S MINE!
BONK!
OUCH!
WHAT
HAPPENED?!
PLOP!
LACK OF GHOST
TRAINING, I THINK.
GOOD THING WE CAME
BACK FOR YOU!

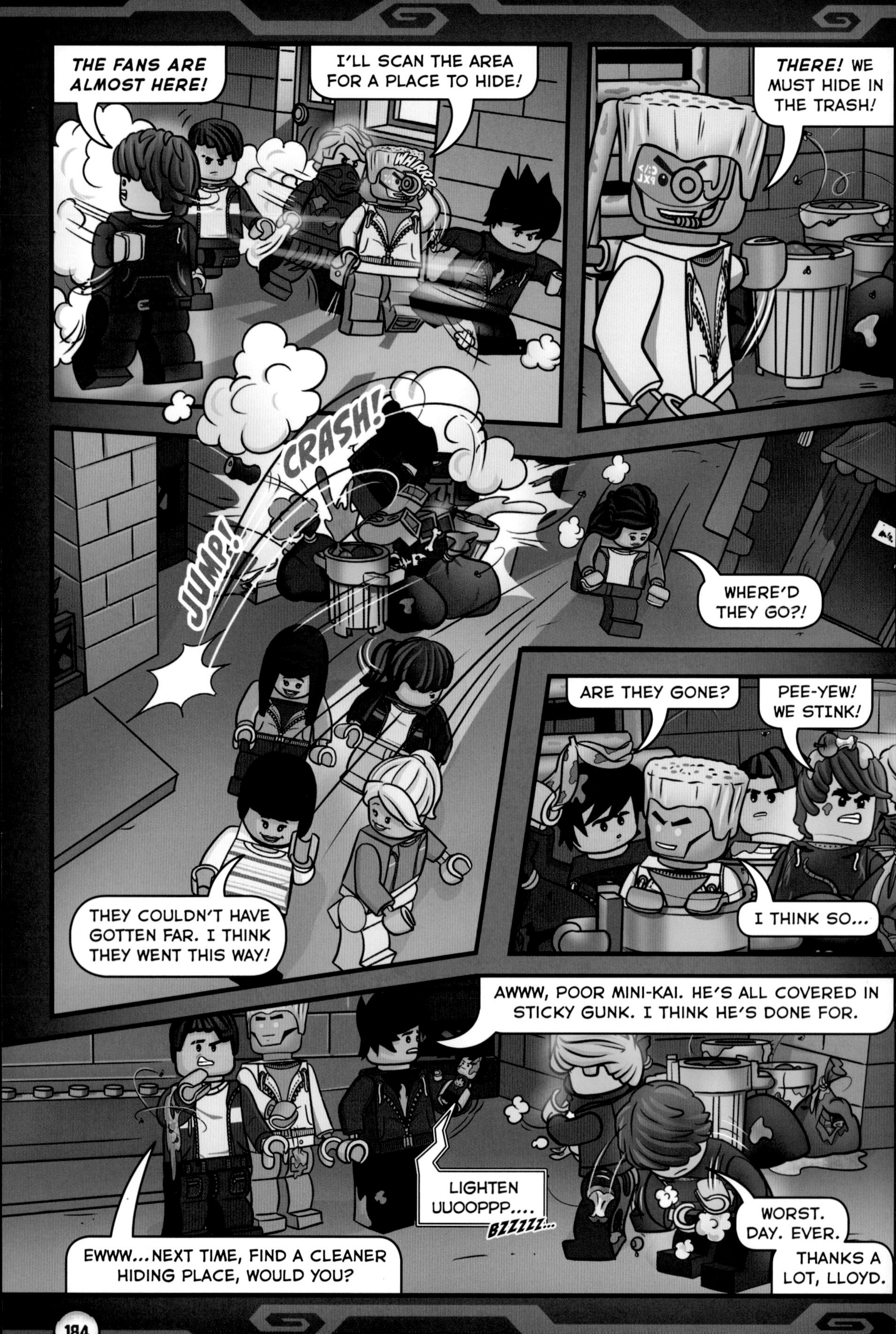
THE FANS ARE ALMOST HERE!
I'LL SCAN THE AREA FOR A PLACE TO HIDE!
WHIRRR
THERE! WE MUST HIDE IN THE TRASH!
JUMP!
CRASH!
WHERE'D THEY GO?!
THEY COULDN'T HAVE GOTTEN FAR. I THINK THEY WENT THIS WAY!
ARE THEY GONE?
PEE-YEW! WE STINK!
I THINK SO...
AWWW, POOR MINI-KAI. HE'S ALL COVERED IN STICKY GUNK. I THINK HE'S DONE FOR.
LIGHTEN UUOOPPP....
BZZZZZ...
EWWW...NEXT TIME, FIND A CLEANER HIDING PLACE, WOULD YOU?
WORST. DAY. EVER.
THANKS A LOT, LLOYD.

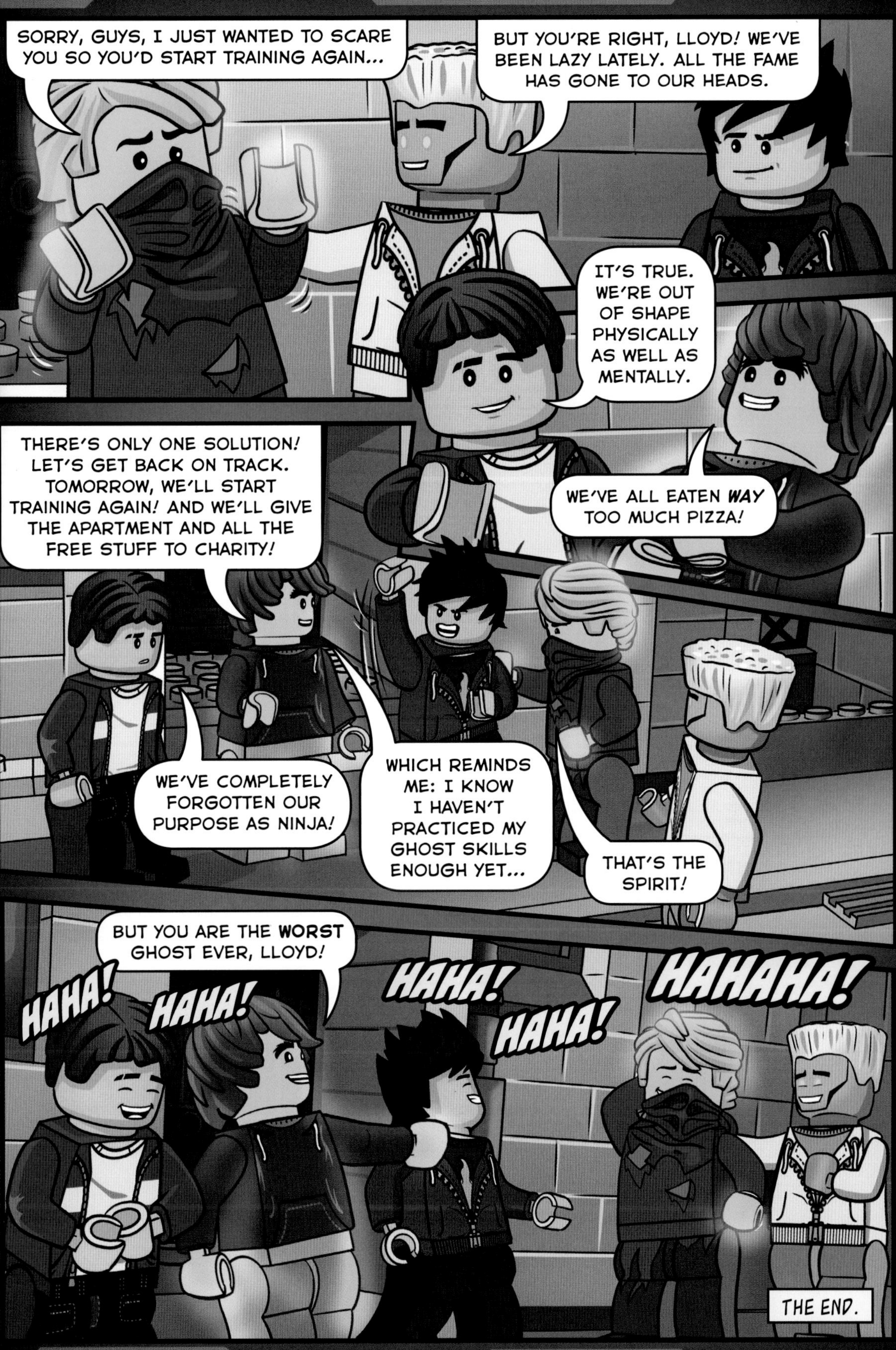
SORRY, GUYS, I JUST WANTED TO SCARE YOU SO YOU'D START TRAINING AGAIN...
BUT YOU'RE RIGHT, LLOYD! WE'VE BEEN LAZY LATELY. ALL THE FAME HAS GONE TO OUR HEADS.
IT'S TRUE. WE'RE OUT OF SHAPE PHYSICALLY AS WELL AS MENTALLY.
WE'VE ALL EATEN **WAY** TOO MUCH PIZZA!
THERE'S ONLY ONE SOLUTION! LET'S GET BACK ON TRACK. TOMORROW, WE'LL START TRAINING AGAIN! AND WE'LL GIVE THE APARTMENT AND ALL THE FREE STUFF TO CHARITY!
WE'VE COMPLETELY FORGOTTEN OUR PURPOSE AS NINJA!
WHICH REMINDS ME: I KNOW I HAVEN'T PRACTICED MY GHOST SKILLS ENOUGH YET...
THAT'S THE SPIRIT!
BUT YOU ARE THE **WORST** GHOST EVER, LLOYD!
HAHA!
HAHA!
HAHA!
HAHA!
HAHAHA!
THE END.

STUCK IN PRISON

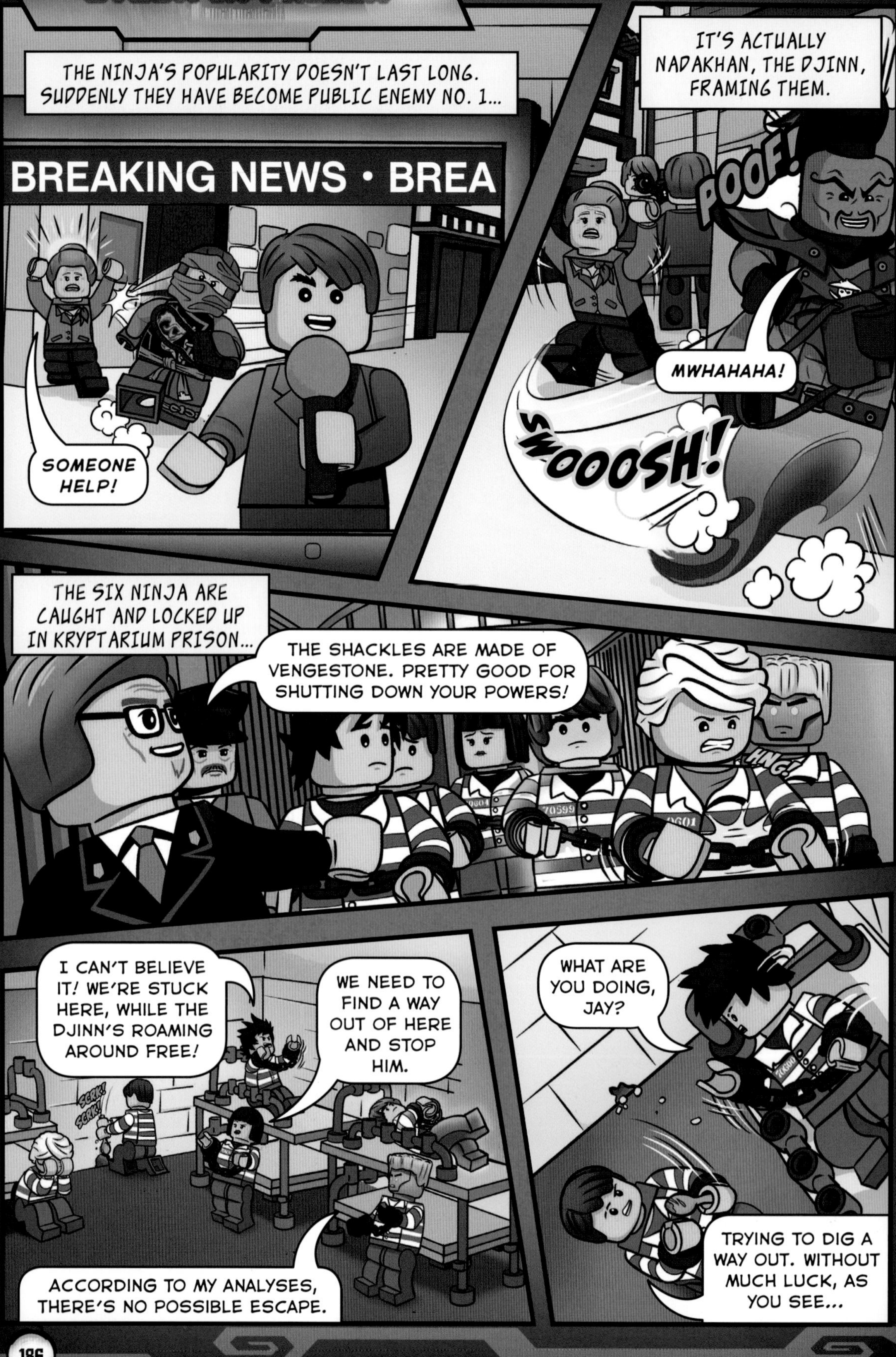

THE NINJA'S POPULARITY DOESN'T LAST LONG. SUDDENLY THEY HAVE BECOME PUBLIC ENEMY NO. 1...
BREAKING NEWS • BREA
SOMEONE HELP!
IT'S ACTUALLY NADAKHAN, THE DJINN, FRAMING THEM.
POOF!
MWHAHAHA!
SWOOOSH!
THE SIX NINJA ARE CAUGHT AND LOCKED UP IN KRYPTARIUM PRISON...
THE SHACKLES ARE MADE OF VENGESTONE. PRETTY GOOD FOR SHUTTING DOWN YOUR POWERS!
HNG!
I CAN'T BELIEVE IT! WE'RE STUCK HERE, WHILE THE DJINN'S ROAMING AROUND FREE!
WE NEED TO FIND A WAY OUT OF HERE AND STOP HIM.
SCRK! SCRK!
ACCORDING TO MY ANALYSES, THERE'S NO POSSIBLE ESCAPE.
WHAT ARE YOU DOING, JAY?
TRYING TO DIG A WAY OUT. WITHOUT MUCH LUCK, AS YOU SEE...

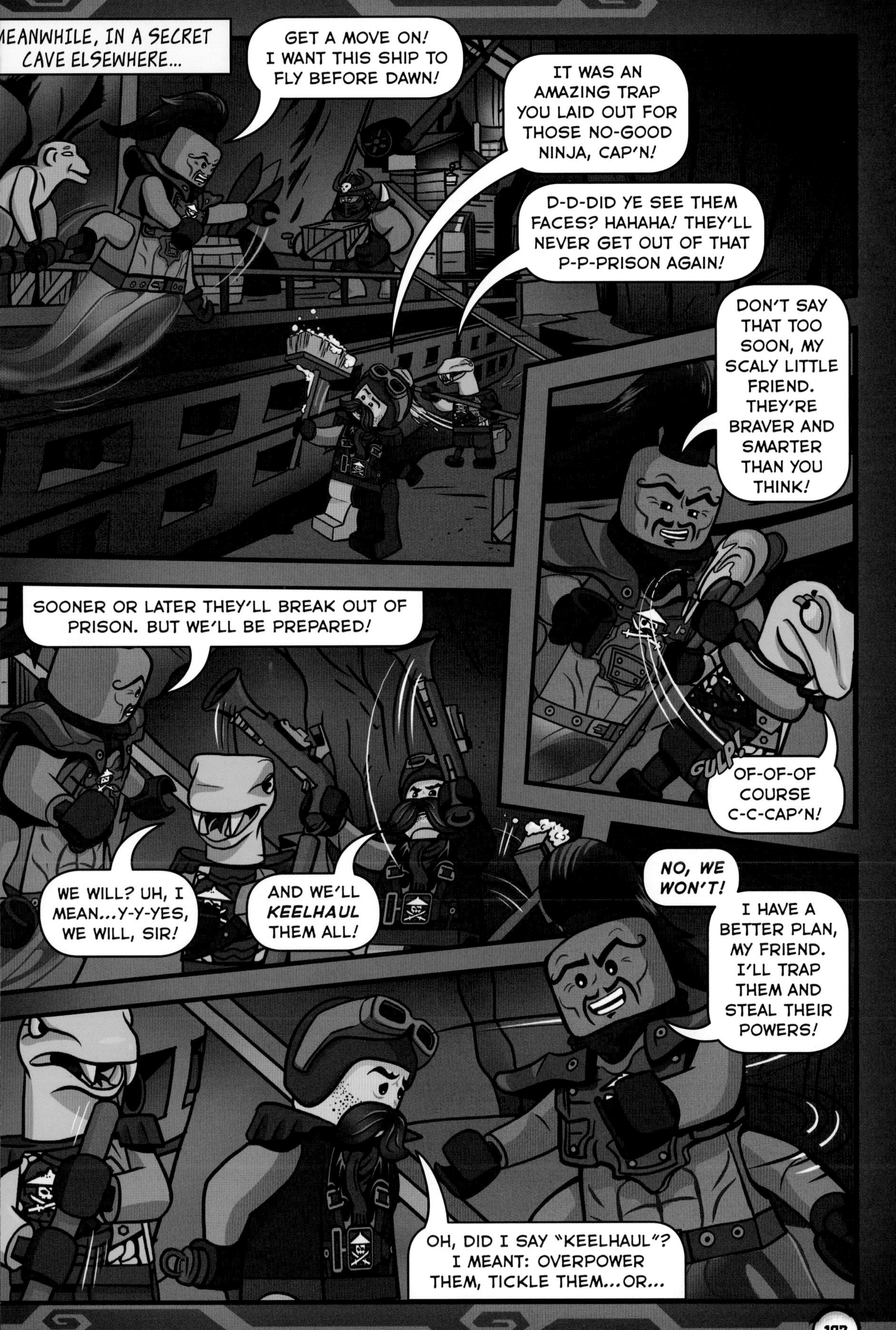
MEANWHILE, IN A SECRET CAVE ELSEWHERE...
GET A MOVE ON! I WANT THIS SHIP TO FLY BEFORE DAWN!
IT WAS AN AMAZING TRAP YOU LAID OUT FOR THOSE NO-GOOD NINJA, CAP'N!
D-D-DID YE SEE THEM FACES? HAHAHA! THEY'LL NEVER GET OUT OF THAT P-P-PRISON AGAIN!
DON'T SAY THAT TOO SOON, MY SCALY LITTLE FRIEND. THEY'RE BRAVER AND SMARTER THAN YOU THINK!
GULP!
OF-OF-OF COURSE C-C-CAP'N!
SOONER OR LATER THEY'LL BREAK OUT OF PRISON. BUT WE'LL BE PREPARED!
WE WILL? UH, I MEAN...Y-Y-YES, WE WILL, SIR!
AND WE'LL *KEELHAUL* THEM ALL!
NO, WE WON'T!
I HAVE A BETTER PLAN, MY FRIEND. I'LL TRAP THEM AND STEAL THEIR POWERS!
OH, DID I SAY "KEELHAUL"? I MEANT: OVERPOWER THEM, TICKLE THEM...OR...

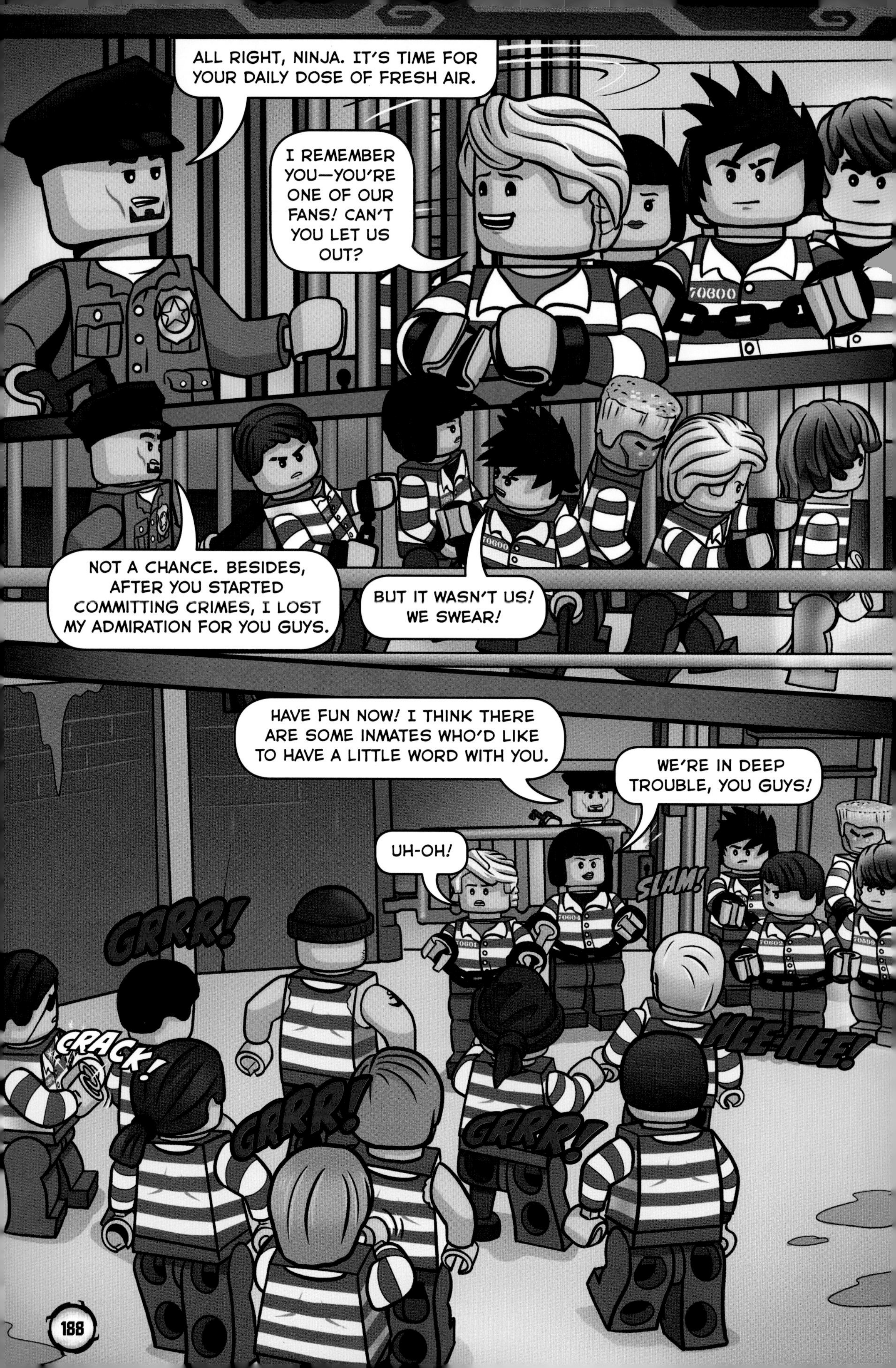
ALL RIGHT, NINJA. IT'S TIME FOR YOUR DAILY DOSE OF FRESH AIR.
I REMEMBER YOU—YOU'RE ONE OF OUR FANS! CAN'T YOU LET US OUT?
70600
NOT A CHANCE. BESIDES, AFTER YOU STARTED COMMITTING CRIMES, I LOST MY ADMIRATION FOR YOU GUYS.
BUT IT WASN'T US! WE SWEAR!
HAVE FUN NOW! I THINK THERE ARE SOME INMATES WHO'D LIKE TO HAVE A LITTLE WORD WITH YOU.
WE'RE IN DEEP TROUBLE, YOU GUYS!
UH-OH!
SLAM!
GRRR!
CRACK!
GRRR!
GRRR!
HEE-HEE!

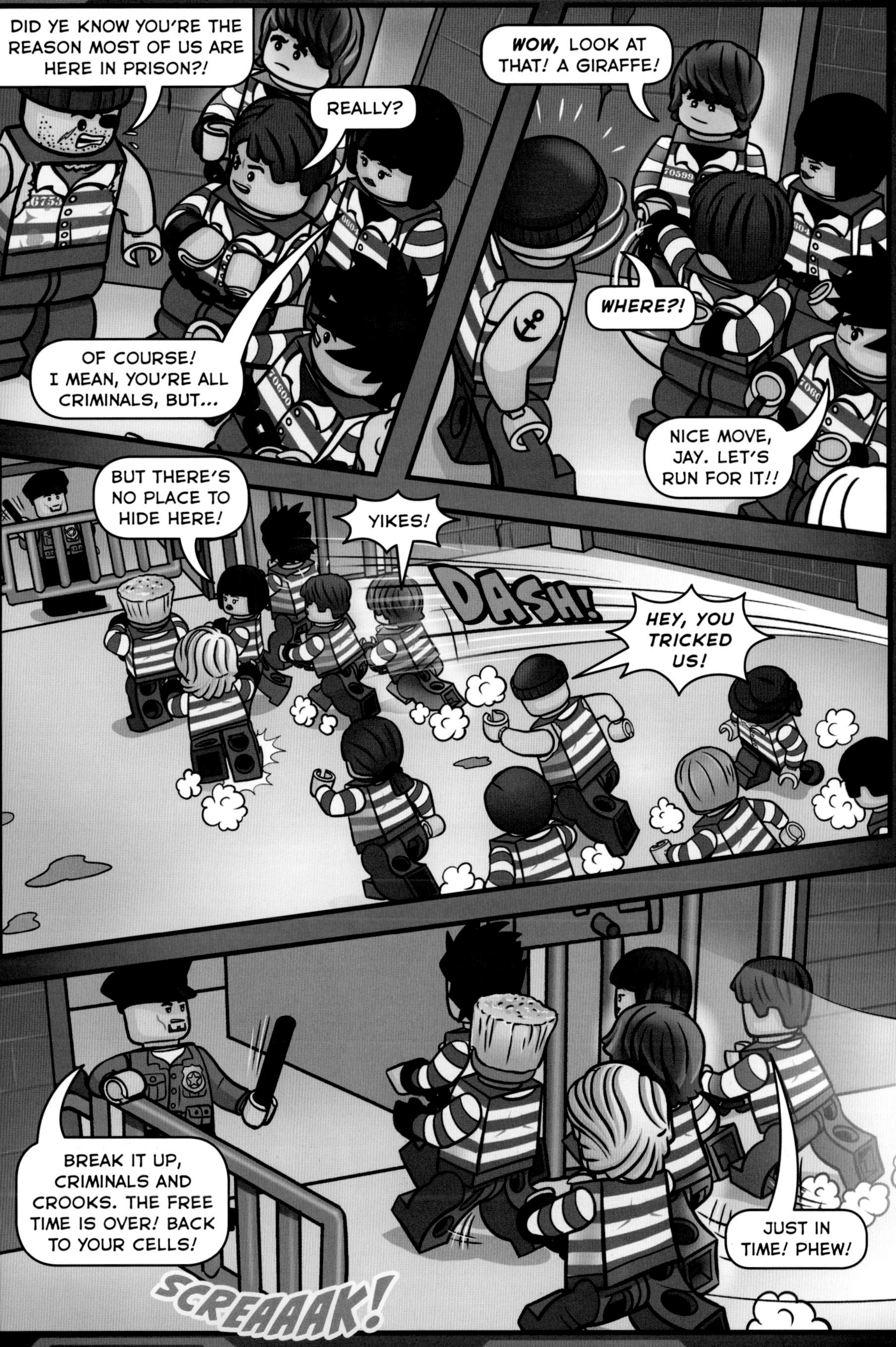
DID YE KNOW YOU'RE THE REASON MOST OF US ARE HERE IN PRISON?!
REALLY?
OF COURSE! I MEAN, YOU'RE ALL CRIMINALS, BUT...
WOW, LOOK AT THAT! A GIRAFFE!
WHERE?!
NICE MOVE, JAY. LET'S RUN FOR IT!!
BUT THERE'S NO PLACE TO HIDE HERE!
YIKES!
DASH!
HEY, YOU TRICKED US!
BREAK IT UP, CRIMINALS AND CROOKS. THE FREE TIME IS OVER! BACK TO YOUR CELLS!
JUST IN TIME! PHEW!
SCREAAAK!

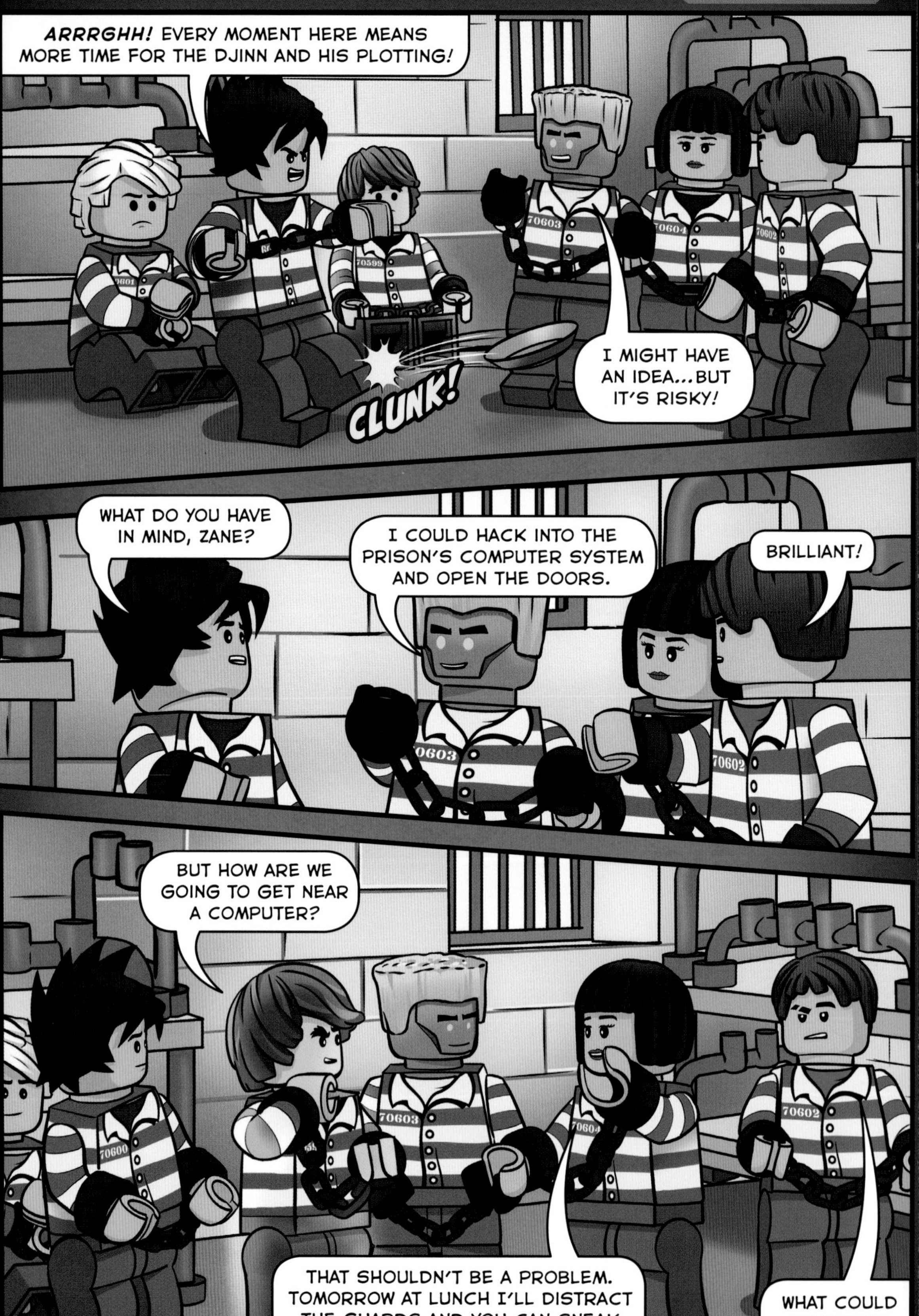
ARRRGHH! EVERY MOMENT HERE MEANS MORE TIME FOR THE DJINN AND HIS PLOTTING!
CLUNK!
I MIGHT HAVE AN IDEA...BUT IT'S RISKY!
WHAT DO YOU HAVE IN MIND, ZANE?
I COULD HACK INTO THE PRISON'S COMPUTER SYSTEM AND OPEN THE DOORS.
BRILLIANT!
BUT HOW ARE WE GOING TO GET NEAR A COMPUTER?
THAT SHOULDN'T BE A PROBLEM. TOMORROW AT LUNCH I'LL DISTRACT THE GUARDS AND YOU CAN SNEAK INTO THE COMPUTER ROOM.
WHAT COULD POSSIBLY GO WRONG?

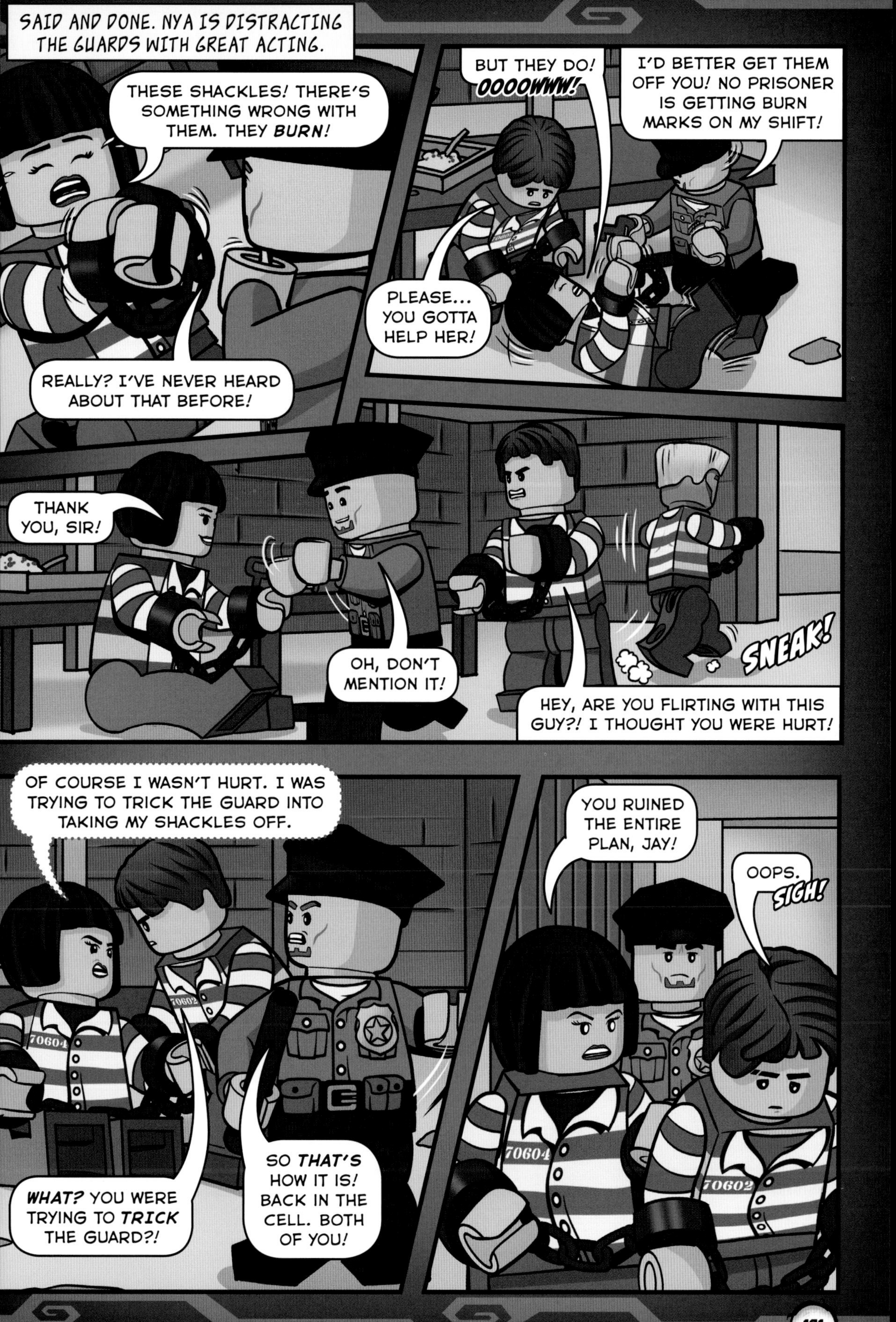
SAID AND DONE. NYA IS DISTRACTING THE GUARDS WITH GREAT ACTING.
THESE SHACKLES! THERE'S SOMETHING WRONG WITH THEM. THEY BURN!
REALLY? I'VE NEVER HEARD ABOUT THAT BEFORE!
BUT THEY DO! OOOOWWW!
I'D BETTER GET THEM OFF YOU! NO PRISONER IS GETTING BURN MARKS ON MY SHIFT!
PLEASE... YOU GOTTA HELP HER!
THANK YOU, SIR!
OH, DON'T MENTION IT!
SNEAK!
HEY, ARE YOU FLIRTING WITH THIS GUY?! I THOUGHT YOU WERE HURT!
OF COURSE I WASN'T HURT. I WAS TRYING TO TRICK THE GUARD INTO TAKING MY SHACKLES OFF.
WHAT? YOU WERE TRYING TO TRICK THE GUARD?!
SO THAT'S HOW IT IS! BACK IN THE CELL. BOTH OF YOU!
YOU RUINED THE ENTIRE PLAN, JAY!
OOPS. SIGH!

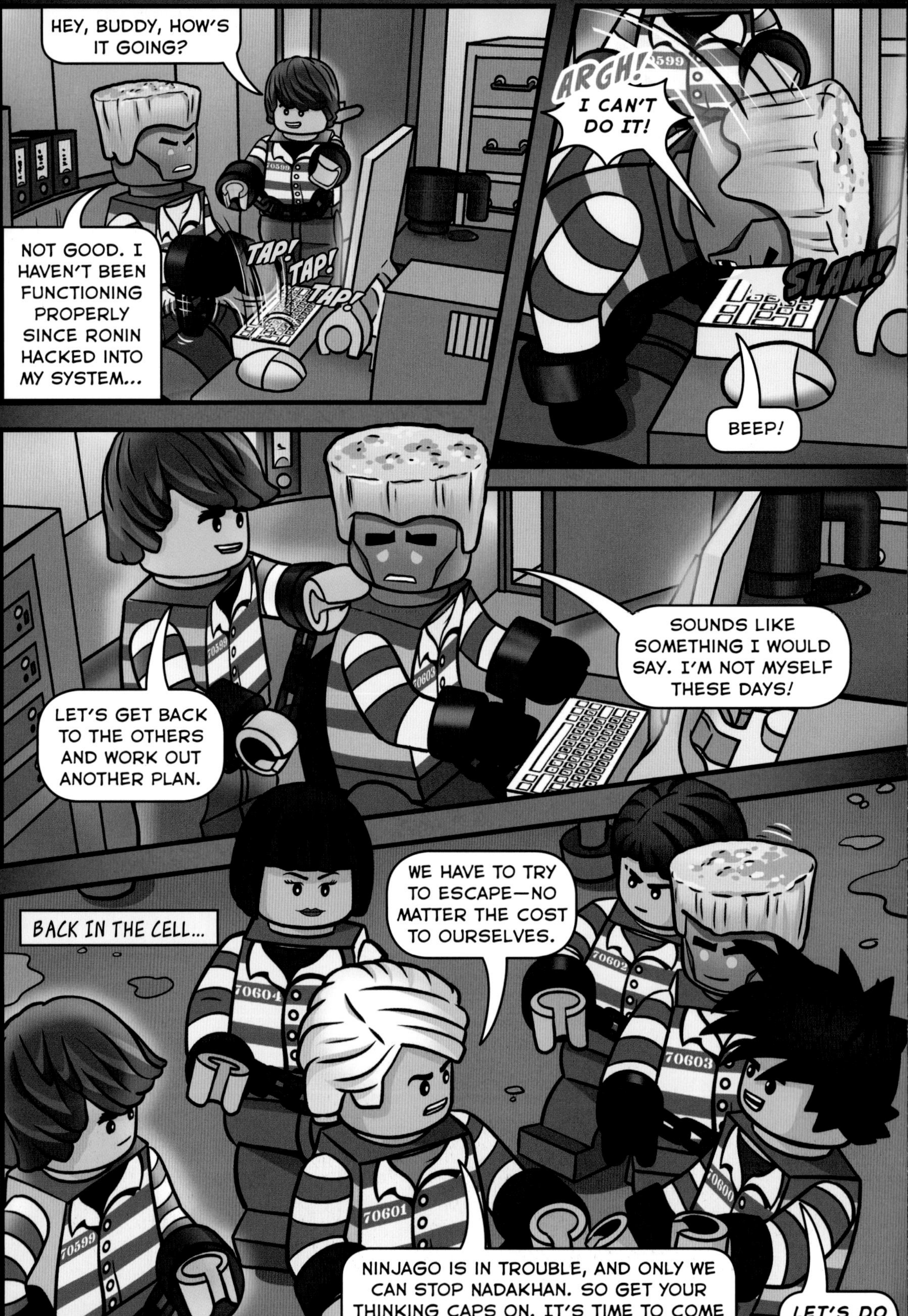

HEY, BUDDY, HOW'S IT GOING?
NOT GOOD. I HAVEN'T BEEN FUNCTIONING PROPERLY SINCE RONIN HACKED INTO MY SYSTEM...
TAP! TAP! TAP!
ARGH! I CAN'T DO IT!
SLAM!
BEEP!
SOUNDS LIKE SOMETHING I WOULD SAY. I'M NOT MYSELF THESE DAYS!
LET'S GET BACK TO THE OTHERS AND WORK OUT ANOTHER PLAN.
BACK IN THE CELL...
WE HAVE TO TRY TO ESCAPE—NO MATTER THE COST TO OURSELVES.
NINJAGO IS IN TROUBLE, AND ONLY WE CAN STOP NADAKHAN. SO GET YOUR THINKING CAPS ON. IT'S TIME TO COME UP WITH SOME ESCAPE PLANS!
LET'S DO THIS!

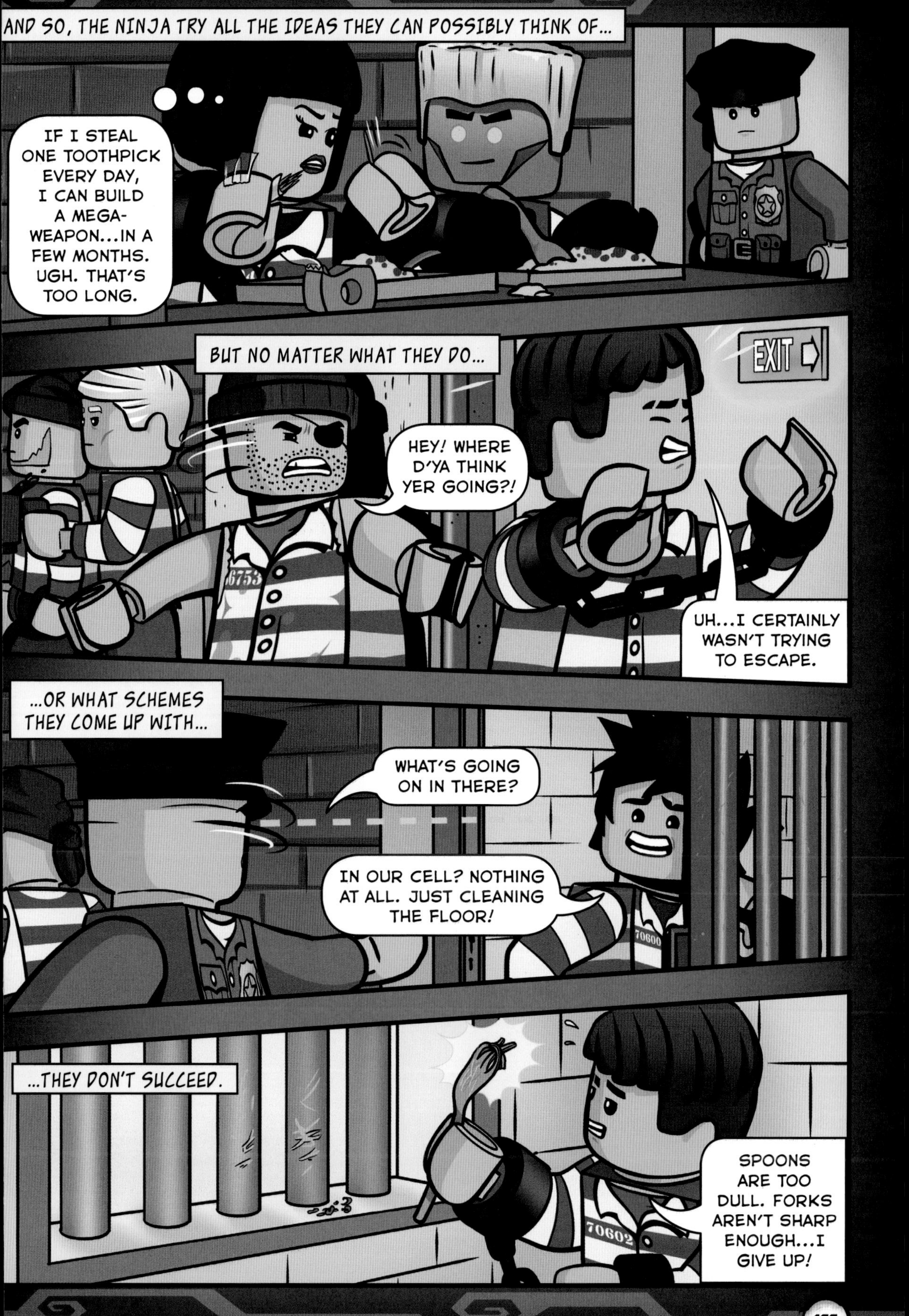
AND SO, THE NINJA TRY ALL THE IDEAS THEY CAN POSSIBLY THINK OF...
IF I STEAL ONE TOOTHPICK EVERY DAY, I CAN BUILD A MEGA-WEAPON...IN A FEW MONTHS. UGH. THAT'S TOO LONG.
BUT NO MATTER WHAT THEY DO...
EXIT
HEY! WHERE D'YA THINK YER GOING?!
UH...I CERTAINLY WASN'T TRYING TO ESCAPE.
...OR WHAT SCHEMES THEY COME UP WITH...
WHAT'S GOING ON IN THERE?
IN OUR CELL? NOTHING AT ALL. JUST CLEANING THE FLOOR!
...THEY DON'T SUCCEED.
SPOONS ARE TOO DULL. FORKS AREN'T SHARP ENOUGH...I GIVE UP!

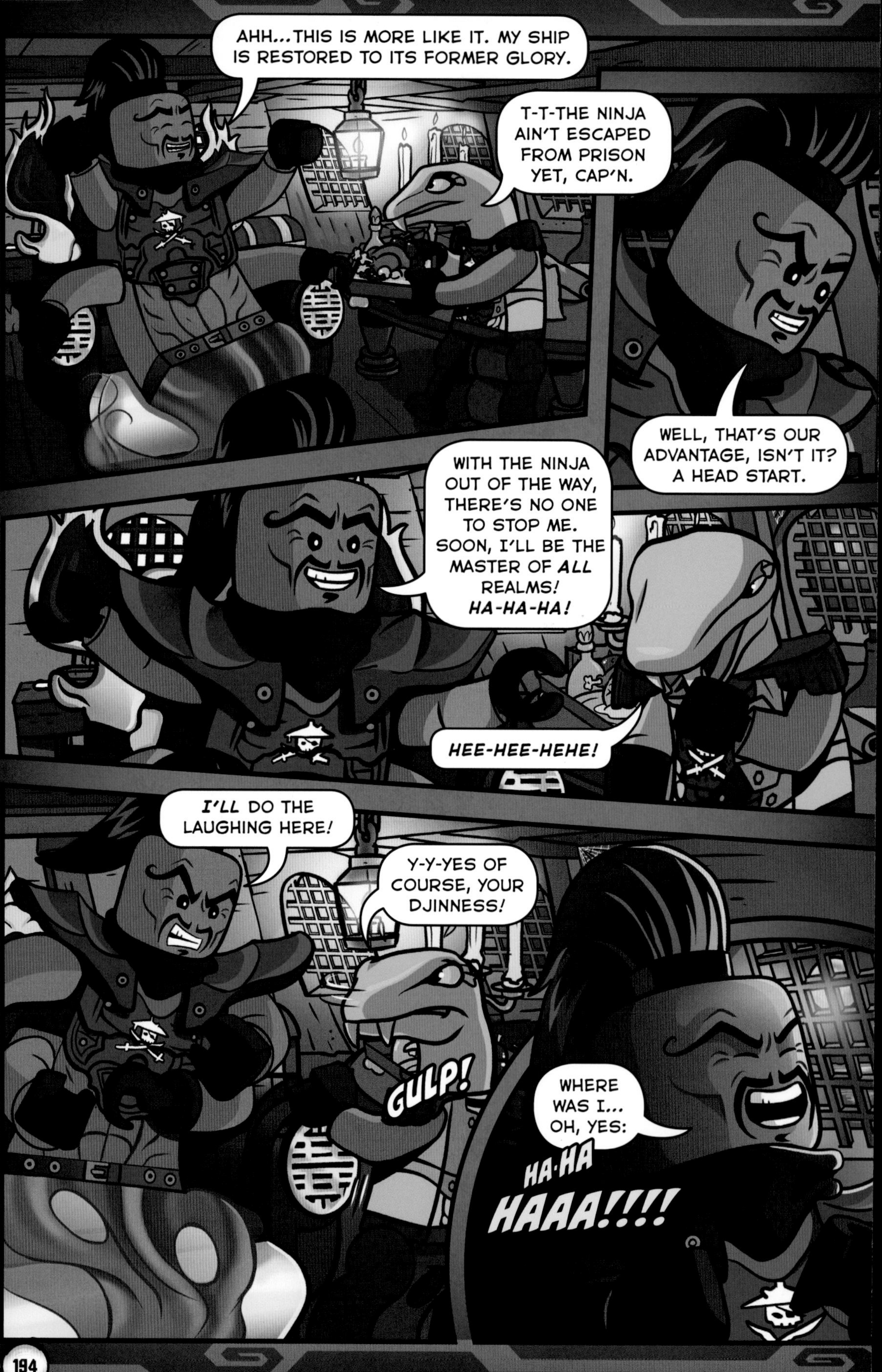
AHH...THIS IS MORE LIKE IT. MY SHIP IS RESTORED TO ITS FORMER GLORY.
T-T-THE NINJA AIN'T ESCAPED FROM PRISON YET, CAP'N.
WELL, THAT'S OUR ADVANTAGE, ISN'T IT? A HEAD START.
WITH THE NINJA OUT OF THE WAY, THERE'S NO ONE TO STOP ME. SOON, I'LL BE THE MASTER OF *ALL* REALMS! *HA-HA-HA!*
HEE-HEE-HEHE!
I'LL DO THE LAUGHING HERE!
Y-Y-YES OF COURSE, YOUR DJINNESS!
GULP!
WHERE WAS I... OH, YES:
HA-HA HAAA!!!!

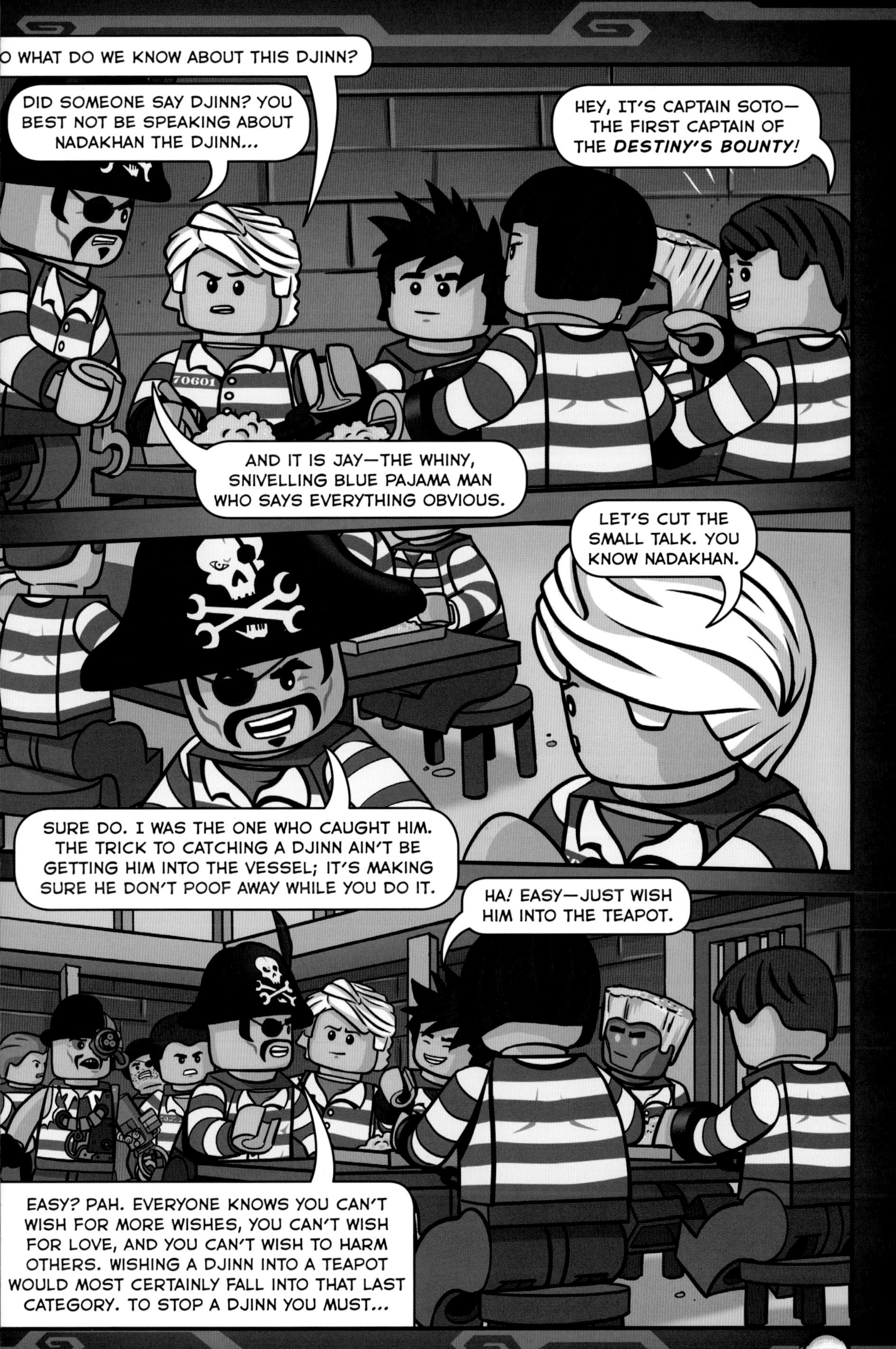
O WHAT DO WE KNOW ABOUT THIS DJINN?
DID SOMEONE SAY DJINN? YOU BEST NOT BE SPEAKING ABOUT NADAKHAN THE DJINN...
HEY, IT'S CAPTAIN SOTO—THE FIRST CAPTAIN OF THE *DESTINY'S BOUNTY!*
70601
AND IT IS JAY—THE WHINY, SNIVELLING BLUE PAJAMA MAN WHO SAYS EVERYTHING OBVIOUS.
LET'S CUT THE SMALL TALK. YOU KNOW NADAKHAN.
SURE DO. I WAS THE ONE WHO CAUGHT HIM. THE TRICK TO CATCHING A DJINN AIN'T BE GETTING HIM INTO THE VESSEL; IT'S MAKING SURE HE DON'T POOF AWAY WHILE YOU DO IT.
HA! EASY—JUST WISH HIM INTO THE TEAPOT.
EASY? PAH. EVERYONE KNOWS YOU CAN'T WISH FOR MORE WISHES, YOU CAN'T WISH FOR LOVE, AND YOU CAN'T WISH TO HARM OTHERS. WISHING A DJINN INTO A TEAPOT WOULD MOST CERTAINLY FALL INTO THAT LAST CATEGORY. TO STOP A DJINN YOU MUST...

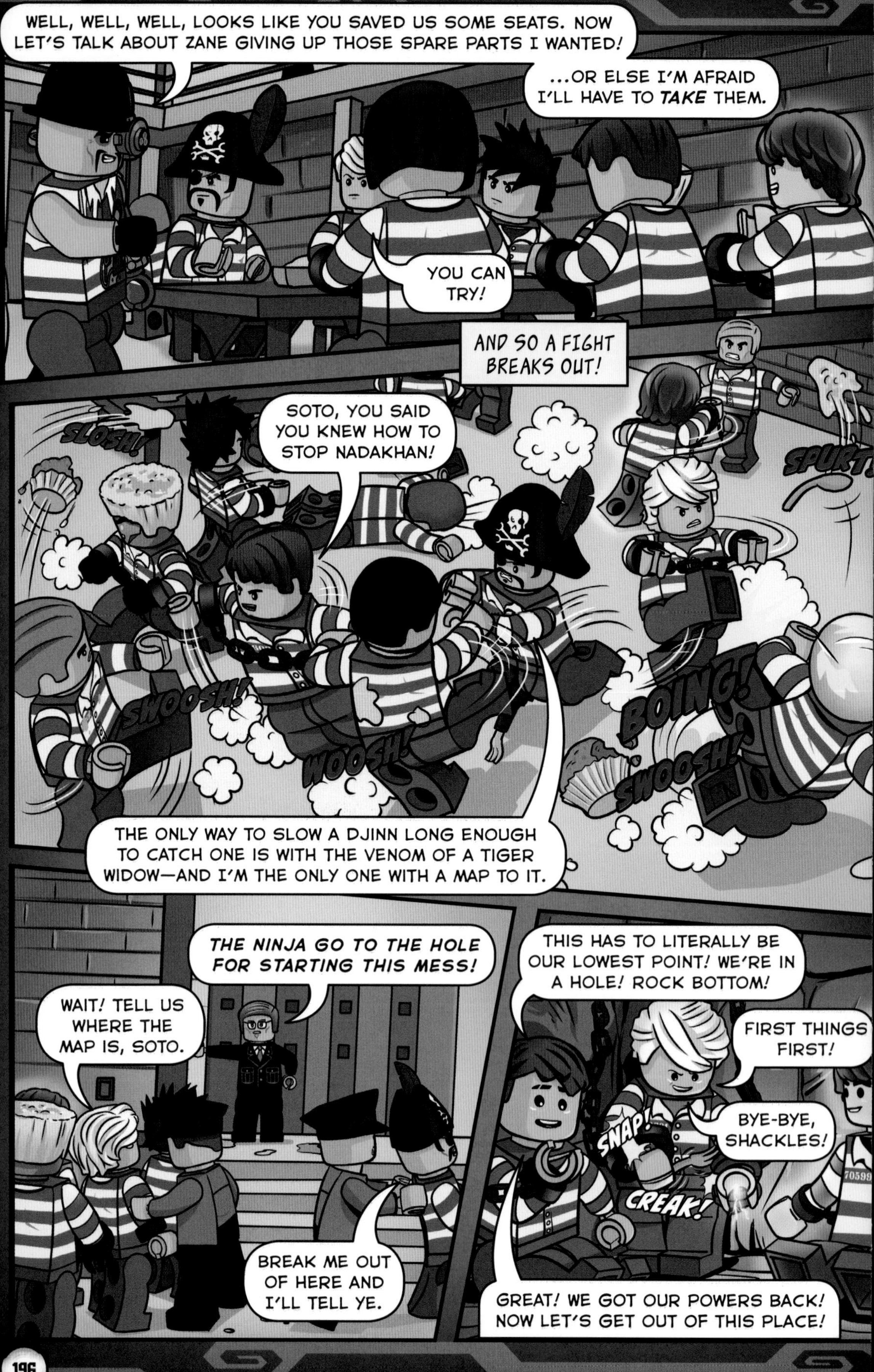
WELL, WELL, WELL, LOOKS LIKE YOU SAVED US SOME SEATS. NOW LET'S TALK ABOUT ZANE GIVING UP THOSE SPARE PARTS I WANTED!
...OR ELSE I'M AFRAID I'LL HAVE TO *TAKE* THEM.
YOU CAN TRY!
AND SO A FIGHT BREAKS OUT!
SOTO, YOU SAID YOU KNEW HOW TO STOP NADAKHAN!
SLOSH!
SPURT!
SWOOSH!
WOOSH!
BOING!
SWOOSH!
THE ONLY WAY TO SLOW A DJINN LONG ENOUGH TO CATCH ONE IS WITH THE VENOM OF A TIGER WIDOW—AND I'M THE ONLY ONE WITH A MAP TO IT.
THE NINJA GO TO THE HOLE FOR STARTING THIS MESS!
WAIT! TELL US WHERE THE MAP IS, SOTO.
BREAK ME OUT OF HERE AND I'LL TELL YE.
THIS HAS TO LITERALLY BE OUR LOWEST POINT! WE'RE IN A HOLE! ROCK BOTTOM!
FIRST THINGS FIRST!
SNAP!
BYE-BYE, SHACKLES!
CREAK!
GREAT! WE GOT OUR POWERS BACK! NOW LET'S GET OUT OF THIS PLACE!

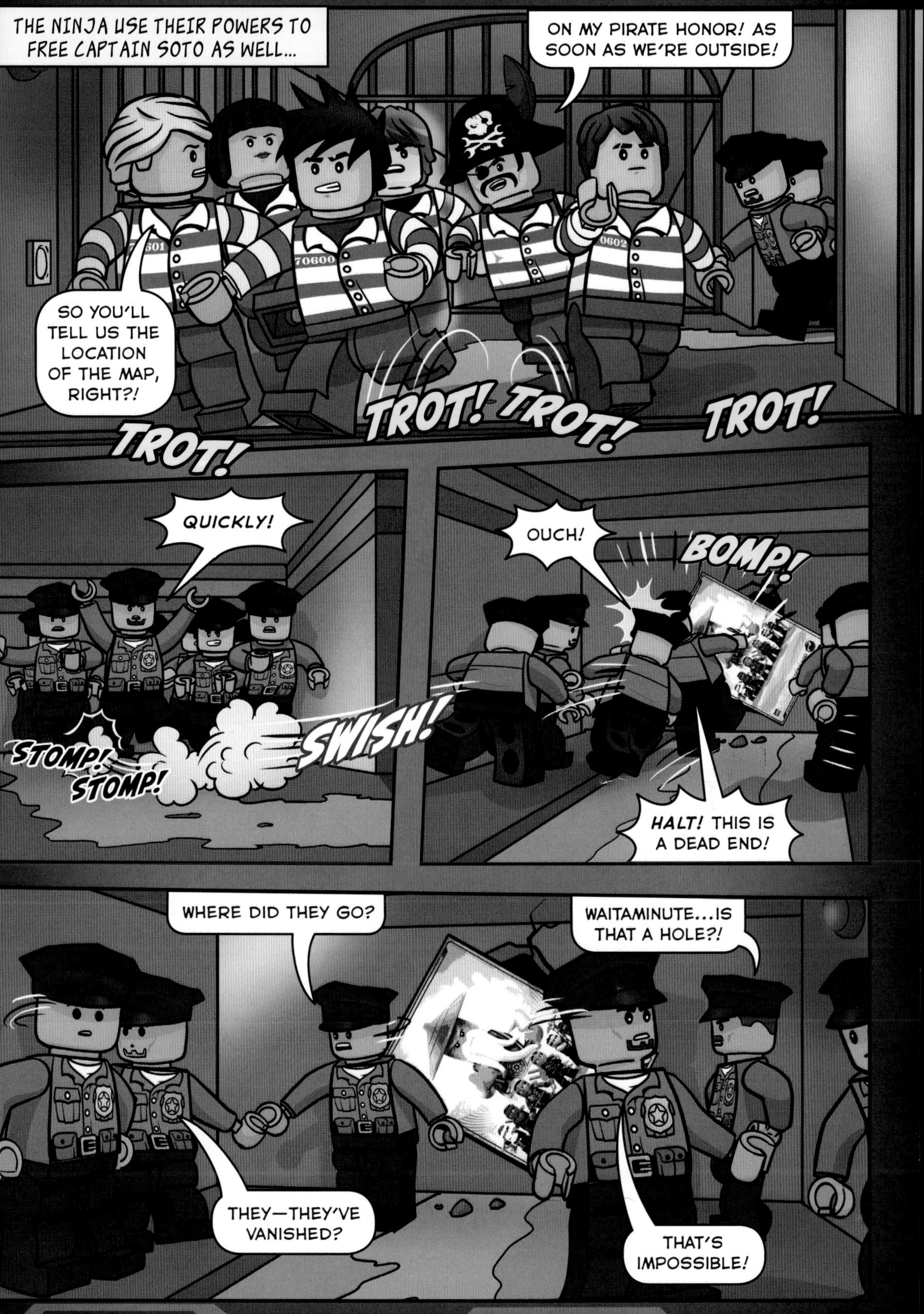
THE NINJA USE THEIR POWERS TO FREE CAPTAIN SOTO AS WELL...
ON MY PIRATE HONOR! AS SOON AS WE'RE OUTSIDE!
SO YOU'LL TELL US THE LOCATION OF THE MAP, RIGHT?!
TROT! TROT! TROT! TROT!
QUICKLY!
STOMP! STOMP!
SWISH!
OUCH!
BOMP!
HALT! THIS IS A DEAD END!
WHERE DID THEY GO?
WAITAMINUTE...IS THAT A HOLE?!
THEY—THEY'VE VANISHED?
THAT'S IMPOSSIBLE!

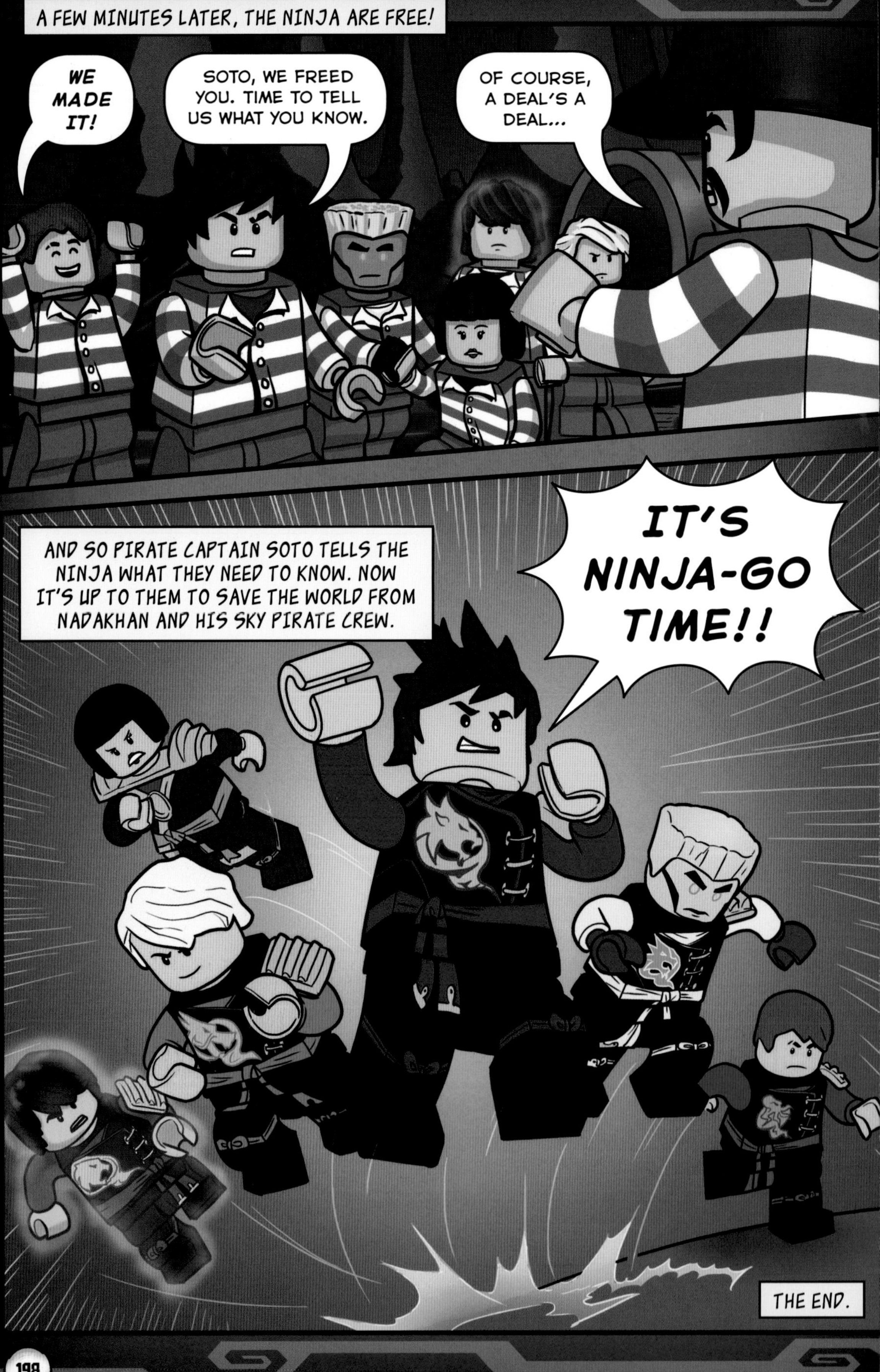
A FEW MINUTES LATER, THE NINJA ARE FREE!
WE MADE IT!
SOTO, WE FREED YOU. TIME TO TELL US WHAT YOU KNOW.
OF COURSE, A DEAL'S A DEAL...
AND SO PIRATE CAPTAIN SOTO TELLS THE NINJA WHAT THEY NEED TO KNOW. NOW IT'S UP TO THEM TO SAVE THE WORLD FROM NADAKHAN AND HIS SKY PIRATE CREW.
IT'S NINJA-GO TIME!!
THE END.

THE LOST SCROLLS OF SPINJITZU

Villains

THE SKY PIRATES

Long ago, during the era of the Stone Warriors, a group of pirates dominated the high seas. Led by their Djinn captain, Nadakhan, these fierce brigands raided coastal towns and merchant ships in their ship, the *Misfortune's Keep*. The sight of their vessel struck fear into the hearts of mariners everywhere.

Finally, the *Destiny's Bounty*, commanded by Captain Soto, tracked down the *Misfortune's Keep*. In the battle that followed, Soto succeeded in defeating Nadakhan. The Djinn was trapped in the Teapot of Tyrahn. And his pirate crew was marooned in assorted other realms. There, they remained for years.

Recently, Nadakhan was unwittingly let loose. Once he was free, he sought out his old band of pirates. They refit the *Misfortune's Keep* so she could fly, and the Djinn renamed his crew the Sky Pirates.

NADAKHAN

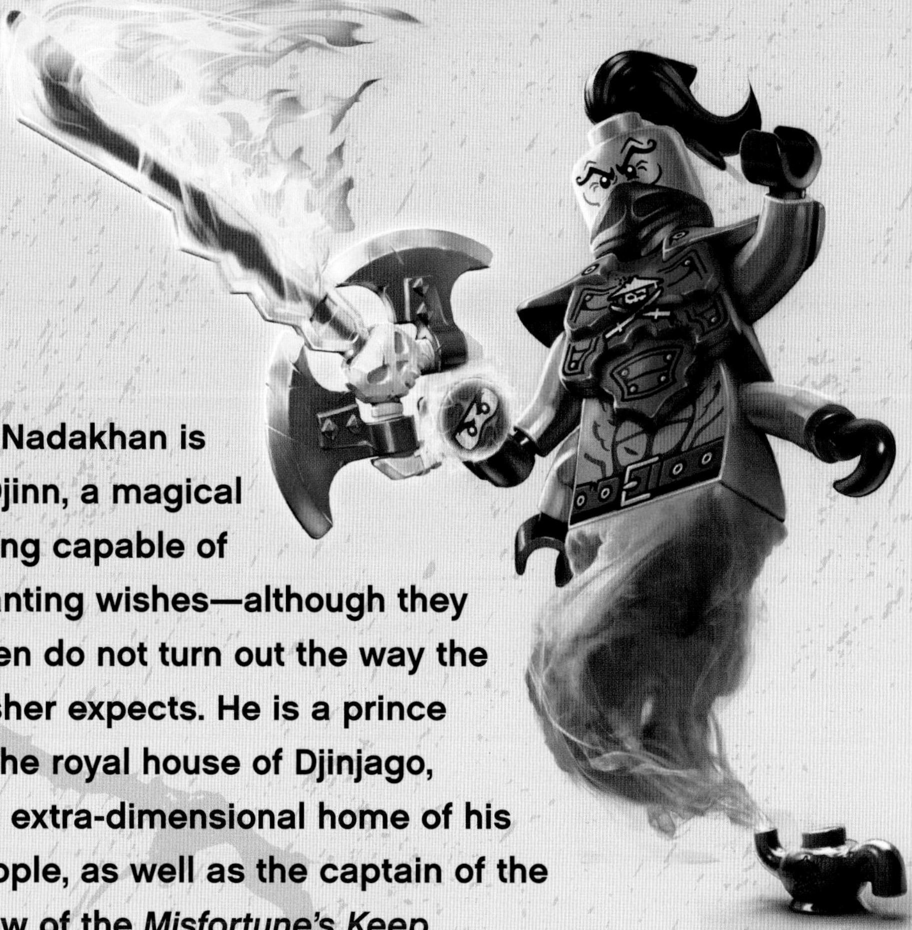

Nadakhan is a Djinn, a magical being capable of granting wishes—although they often do not turn out the way the wisher expects. He is a prince in the royal house of Djinjago, the extra-dimensional home of his people, as well as the captain of the crew of the *Misfortune's Keep*.

Long ago, he was captured by Captain Soto and trapped in the Teapot of Tyrahn. He remained there until being freed by a ghost named Clouse. Arrogant, manipulative, and cunning, Nadakhan vowed revenge on the ninja when he discovered they were accidentally responsible for the destruction of his home realm.

Armed with the Djinn Blade, he set out to capture the ninja, marry Nya (who looked exactly like his long-lost love), build a new version of Djinjago, and gain the power to grant himself unlimited wishes.

Nadakhan is capable of granting three wishes to an individual, although he twists the words of the wishes so they never turn out as expected. Instead, they're usually way, way worse. Those wishes cannot involve inflicting harm on another, acquiring the love of another, or requesting more wishes. If the first two wishes go badly, Nadakhan offers the opportunity to "wish it  all away," which results in the unfortunate wisher being trapped in the Djinn Blade. (And of course Nadakhan makes sure the first two wishes go badly.) Although  Nadakhan has the power to grant wishes to others, he is not able to grant his own.

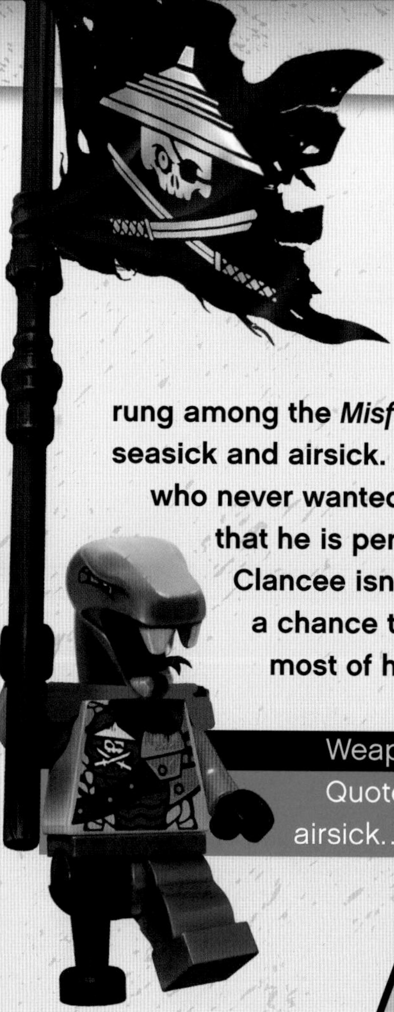

CLANCEE

Clancee is a nervous, peg-legged Serpentine who occupies the lowest rung among the *Misfortune's Keep* crew. He tends to get both seasick and airsick. Clancee is the only member of the crew who never wanted to make a wish for himself, saying that he is perfectly content to live the life of a pirate. Clancee isn't too bright, but by not giving Nadakhan a chance to transform him, he may be smarter than most of his crewmates.

Weapon: Mop

Quote: "And look at me, Cap'n, I'm no longer airsick…oops, spoke too soon."

FLINTLOCKE

Flintlocke is Nadakhan's trusted first mate. For a Sky Pirate, Flintlocke has his feet on the ground. He's willing to follow his captain anywhere, as long as he has some idea where they are heading. But he expects the same loyalty back, and that will lead to trouble down the line.

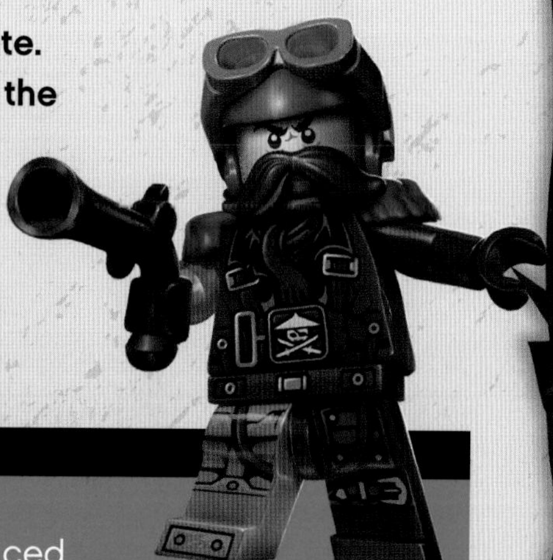

Weapon: Pistol

Quote: "I'll believe that when I believe a pirate be born to tell the truth…We've sacrificed a lot to follow you, but trust is a wind that blows both ways."

DOGSHANK

The woman known as Dogshank was once someone who complained that she was always the "second prettiest" at the ball. She wanted to stand out. Nadakhan granted her wish by transforming her into a hulking brute strong enough to use an anchor and chain as a weapon. She is a powerful fighter, but has her own unique code of honor, even when fighting a ninja. She and Nya will encounter each other on a few occasions and come to enjoy their fighting "playdates."

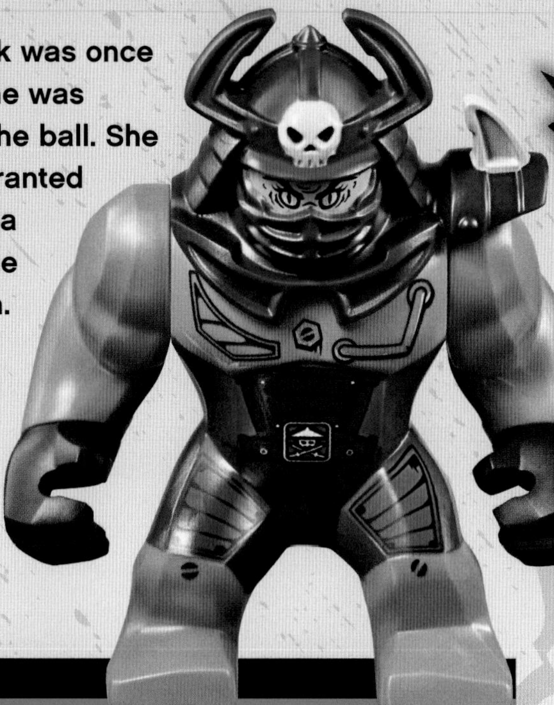

Weapon: Ship's anchor

Quote: "We fight like girls, not like cheaters. Let's see what else you've got."

MONKEY WRETCH

Monkey Wretch is the mechanical monkey who takes care of the tech and does general repairs on the *Misfortune's Keep*. Monkey Wretch was once a regular ship's mechanic. He was skilled but wanted more and more work. Nadakhan tricked him into wishing for more hands and more speed, and then gave it to him by turning him into a mechanical monkey!

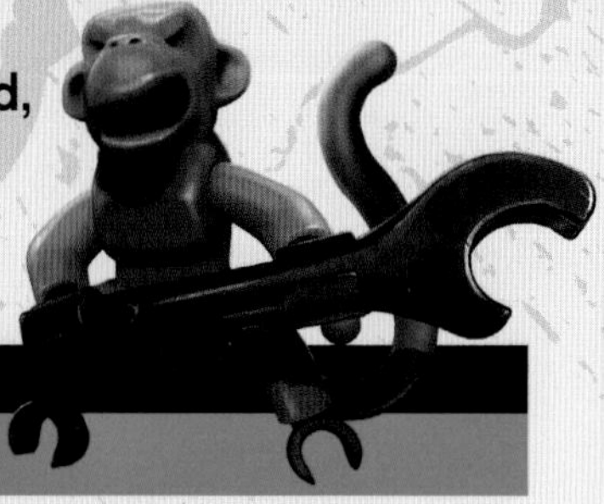

Weapon: Various tools

Quote: *"Screech!"*

DOUBLOON

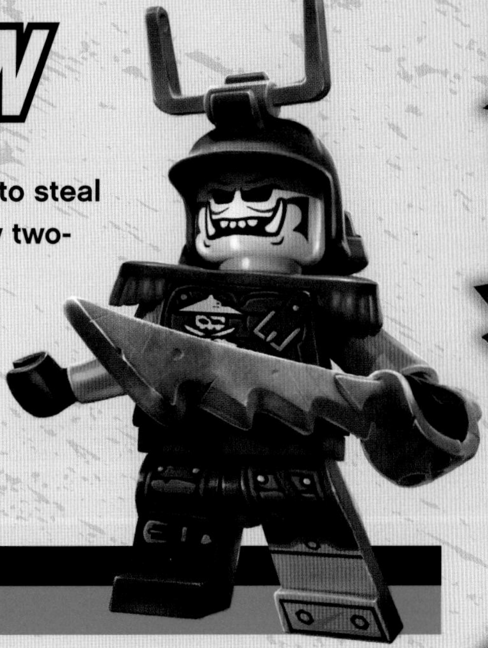

Once a "two-faced thief" who tried to steal gold from Nadakhan, Doubloon is now two-faced for real. His facial expressions are on a pair of masks, so he can look happy or unhappy. Doubloon never talks, but he is an effective fighter and now a valued member of Nadakhan's crew.

Weapon: Pirate swords

Quote: Doubloon does not speak.

SQIFFY

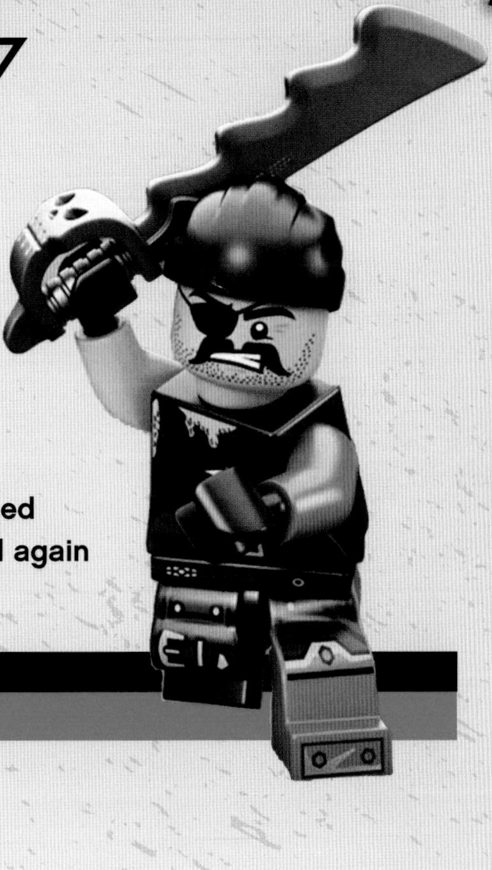

"Sqiffy" is a new recruit to Nadakhan's crew, who signs up while the Djinn is rebuilding Djinjago. His real name is Colin, but Nadakhan didn't feel that's a real pirate's name, so he christens him Landon. When a second recruit turns out to be named Landon too, Colin's name is changed again to "Sqiffy."

Weapon: Pirate sword

Quote: Giggles while he mops.

CYREN

Cyren wanted to be the greatest singer in the world, able to enrapture audiences with her voice. Nadakhan granted her wish by making her voice capable of temporarily sending humans into a catatonic trance. It didn't do much for her career—you can't get any applause that way, and no one remembered her performance afterward—but it was a help during Sky Pirate raids. One quick tune and out went the guards...

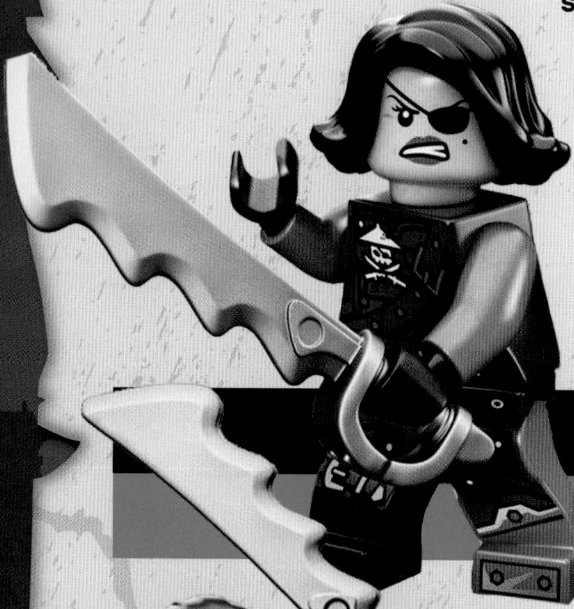

Weapon: None. Relies on the power of her singing.

Quote: "This salt air is terrible for my voice."

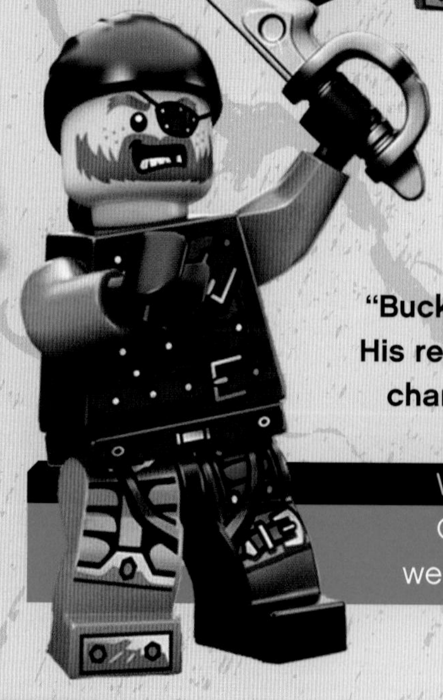

BUCKO

"Bucko" is a new recruit to Nadakhan's crew. His real name is Landon, but Nadakhan changes it to Bucko.

Weapon: Pirate swords

Quote: Likes to sing while he cleans the weapons.

VEHICLES

MISFORTUNE'S KEEP

Misfortune's Keep is Nadakhan's Sky Pirate ship. After he rescues his crew from the various realms to which they have been scattered, they refit the ship so she can fly. Unbeknownst to Nadakhan, a lantern on the ship conceals Captain Soto's map to Tiger Widow

Island. Jay spends a good deal of time as a captive on the ship, swabbing the decks. Later, the ninja stage an attempt to board the ship and rescue Jay. The ship is heavily armed with cannons for fighting off other vessels.

SKY SHARK

This sleek and powerful jet serves as an advance scout for the *Misfortune's Keep*. Piloted by Flintlocke, it's used to search for other ships and aircraft, and, if possible, disable them before the Sky

Pirate vessel arrives. The jet has some nasty surprises in sky battles. Two blunt anchor-shaped wings project from either side of the plane, capable of slicing through sail or steel. A hidden dynamite drop function adds an explosive punch against enemy vessels.

RAID ZEPPELIN

One of the most potent weapons in the Sky Pirates' arsenal, Raid Zeppelins are mid-sized ships held aloft by gasbags filled with hot air. The vessels are steered by ship's wheels, and armed with cannons mounted at the bow. Surprisingly maneuverable and dangerous in battle, Raid Zeppelins play an important role in the Sky Pirates' current success.

SKY GLIDERS

These one-person crafts are designed for rapid ascent, extreme maneuverability, and just enough power to bring down a larger vessel. There are many different types of Sky Gliders, all armed with different sorts of weapons. Sky Gliders work best when attacking en masse, striking like a swarm of insects against a more powerful target.

WEAPONS

DJINN BLADE

The Djinn Blade is a weapon that belongs to the royal family of Djinjago. As Djinjago collapses, Nadakhan's father, the king, gives it to Nadakhan. The Djinn Blade can trap spirits inside of it, thus providing power to the wielder. Nadakhan attempts to capture all the ninja inside the sword by manipulating them into making wishes that backfire.

VENGESTONE

A powerful substance used to make chains for prisoners. The vengestone chains binding the ninja inhibit their powers until Cole tricks Nadakhan into using magic to make them do just the opposite.

CAN YOU DECODE THE SECRET MESSAGE?

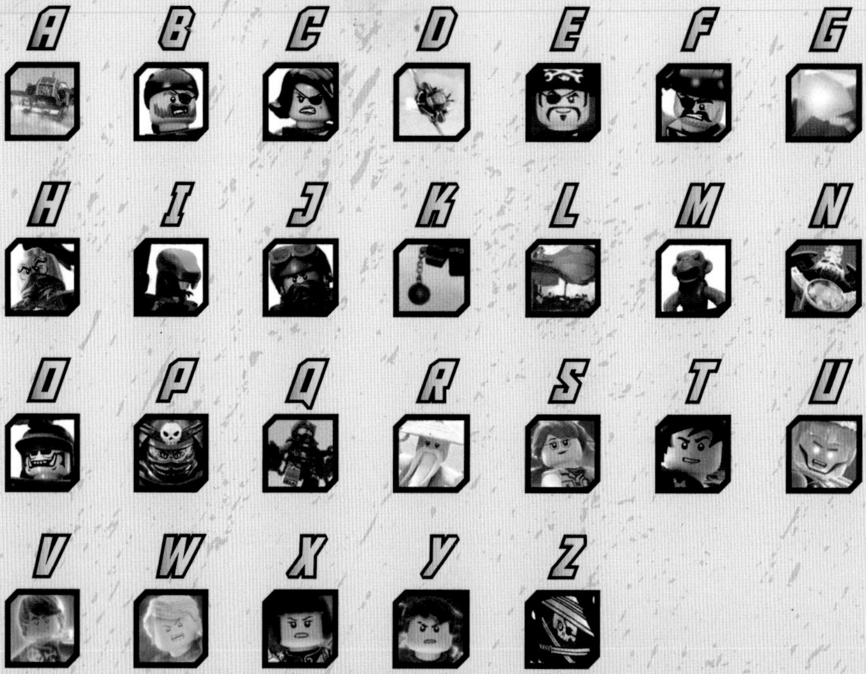
A B C D E F G
H I J K L M N
O P Q R S T U
V W X Y Z

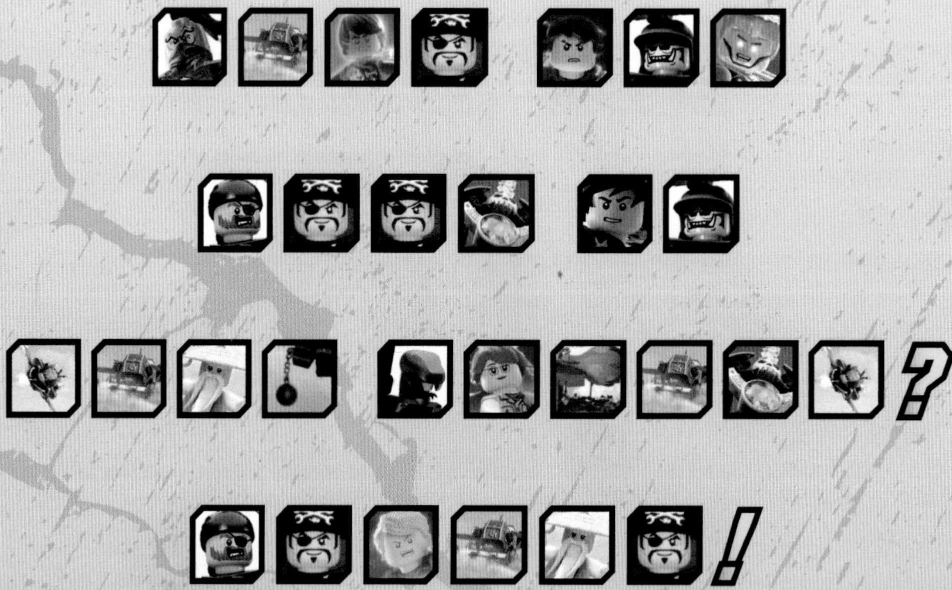
?
!

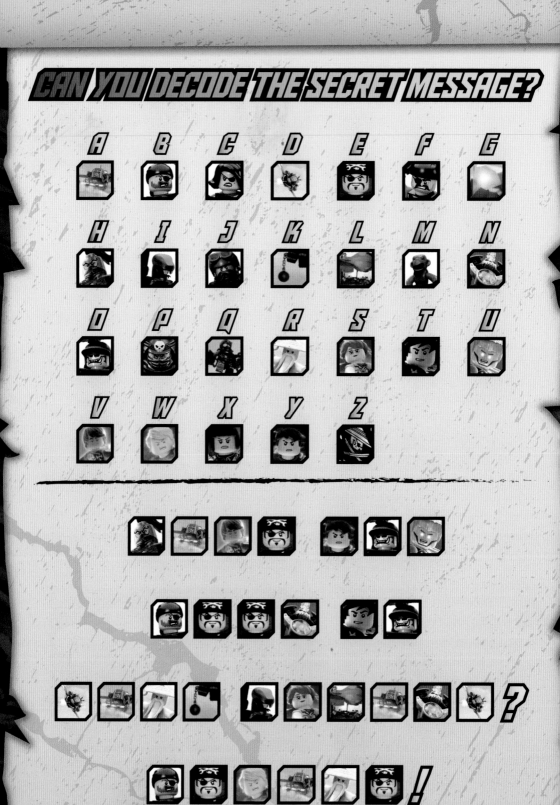

POSTER GALLERY!

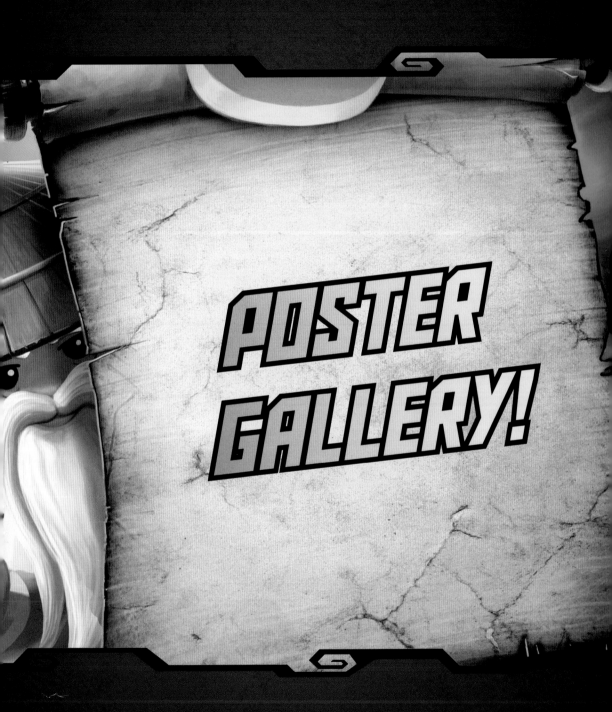

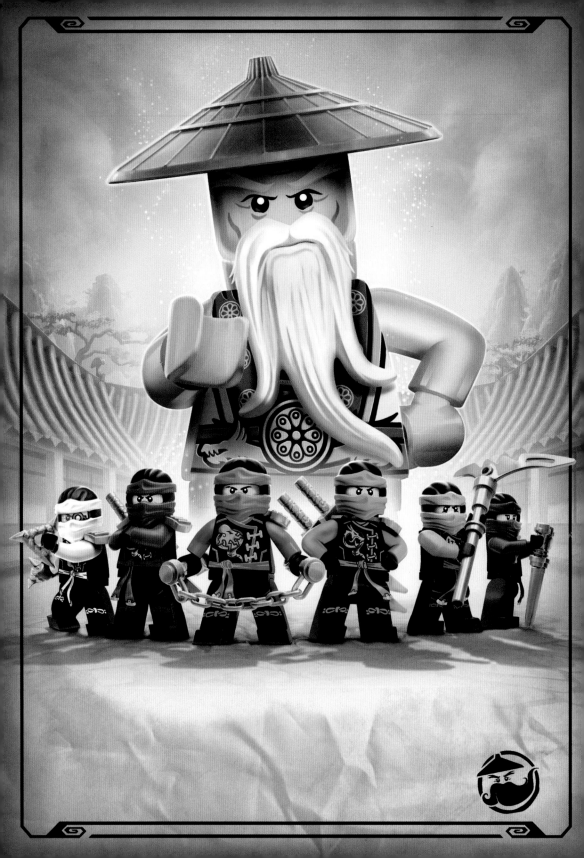

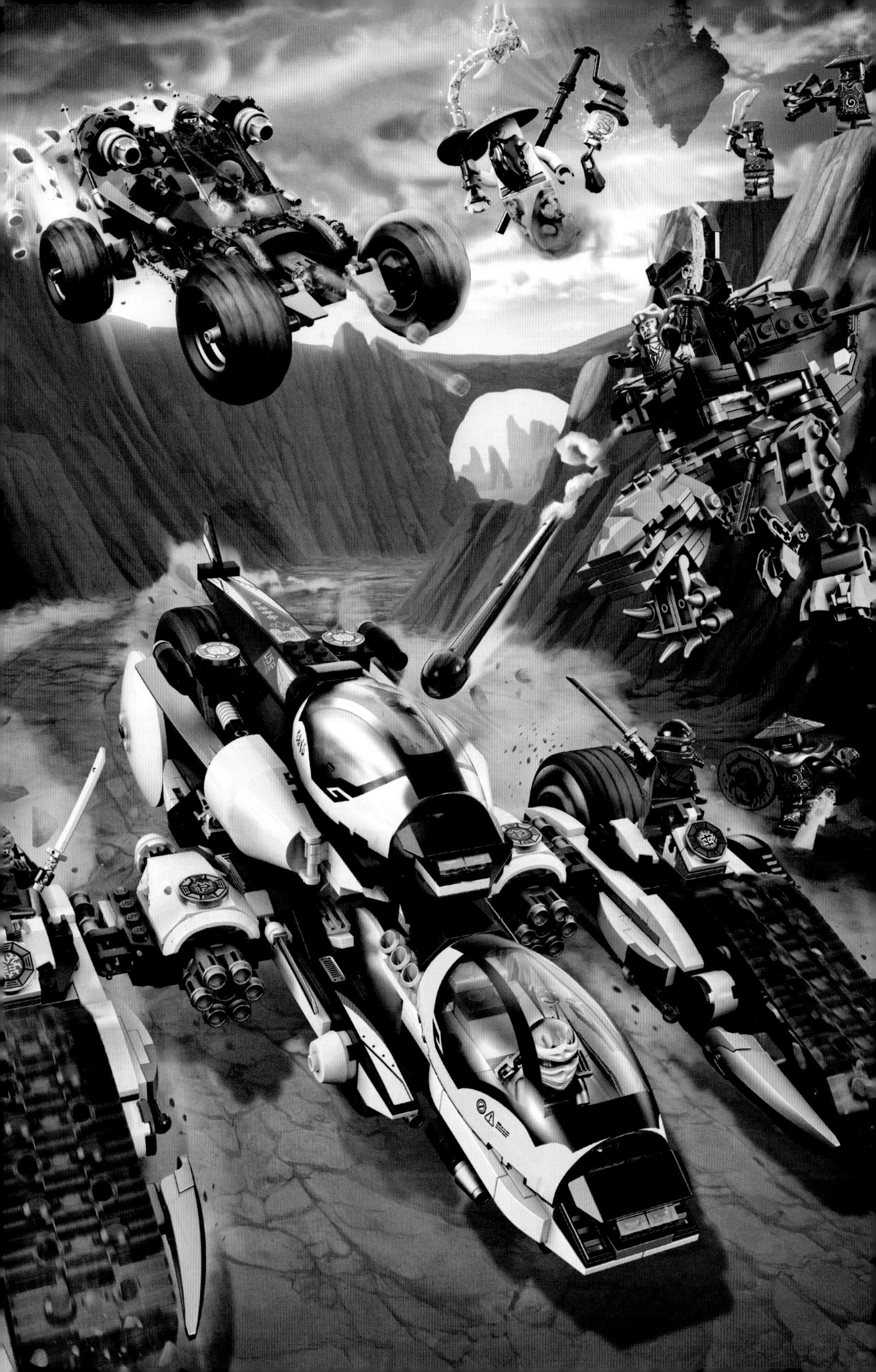

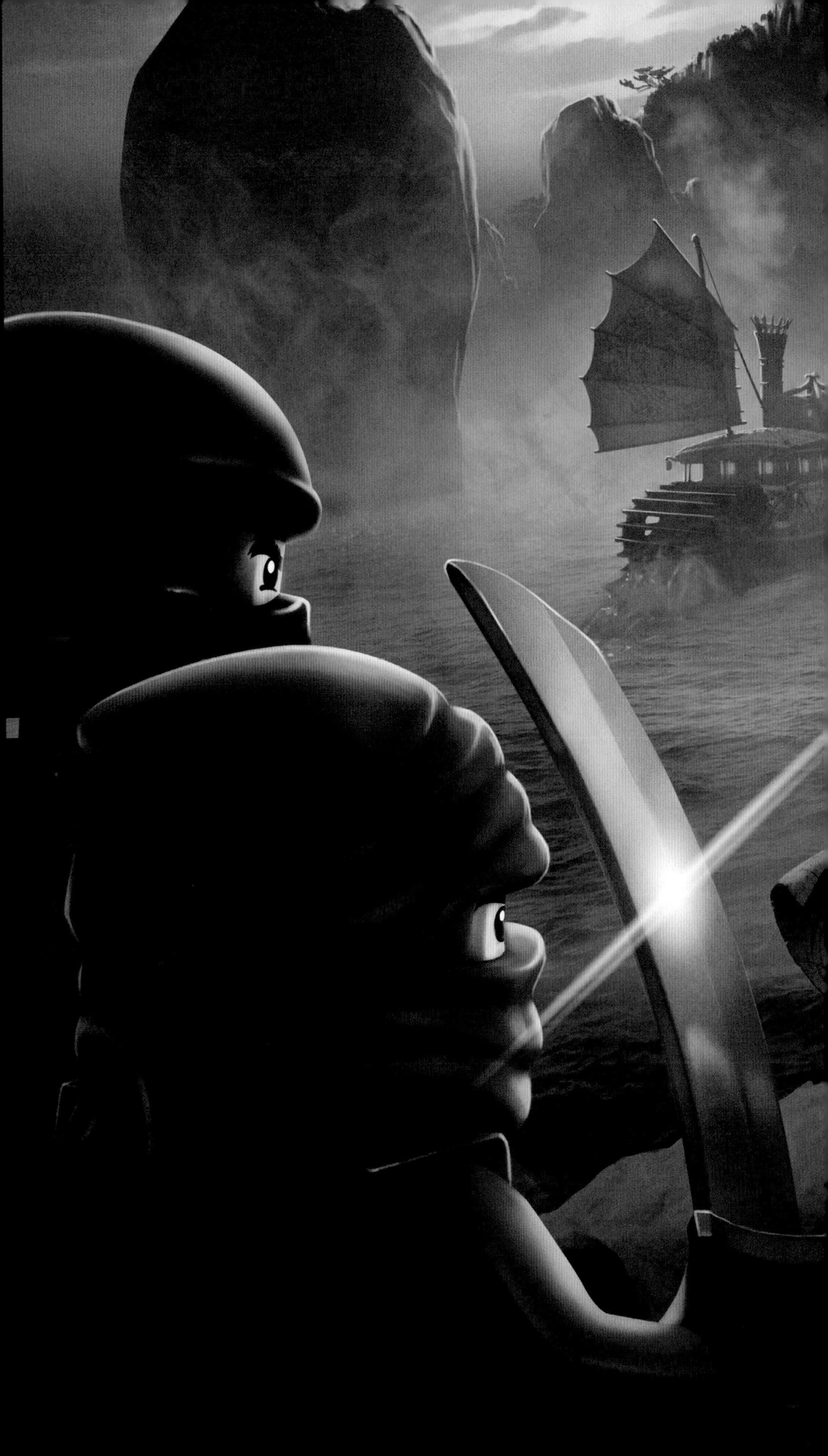

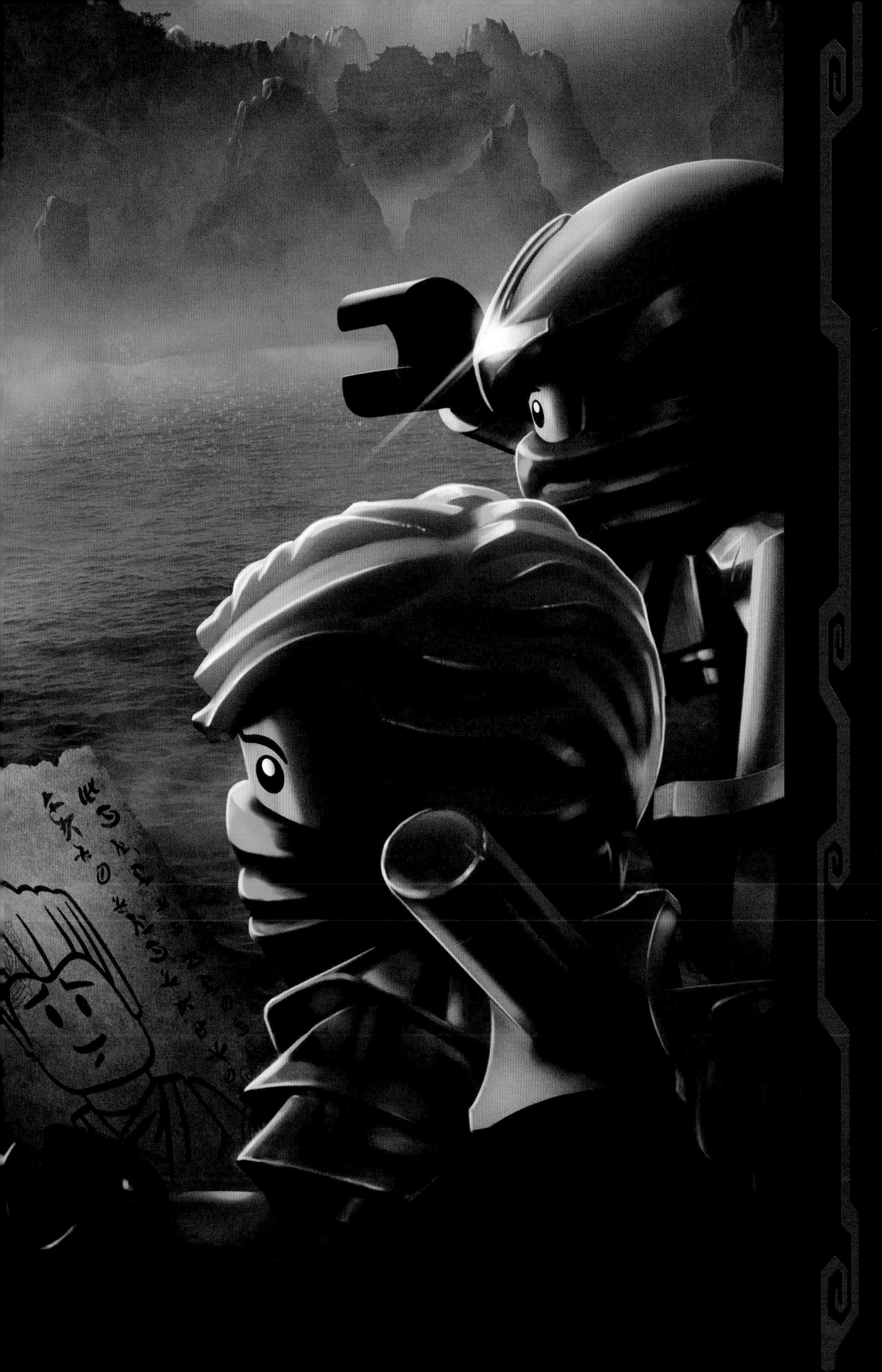

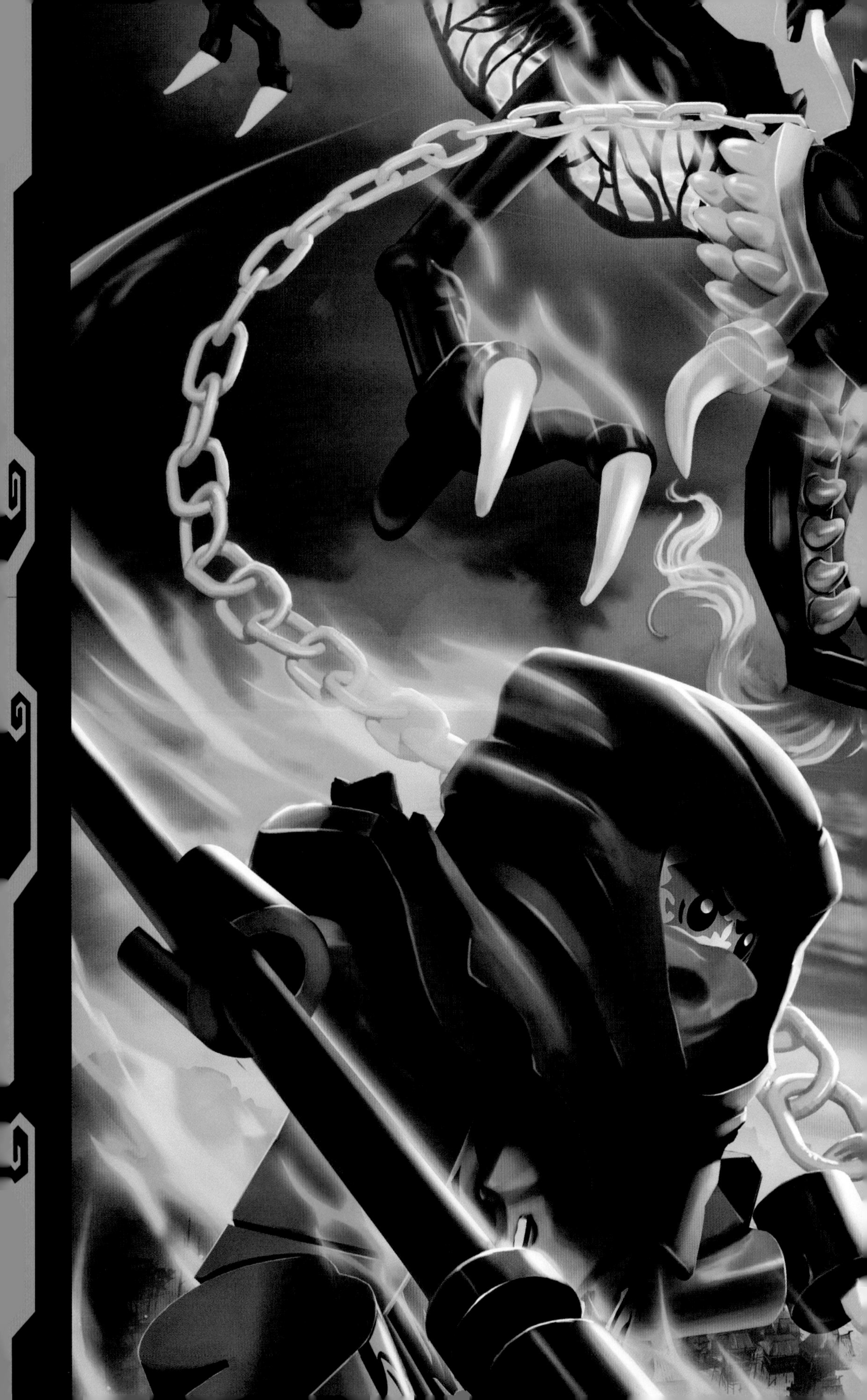

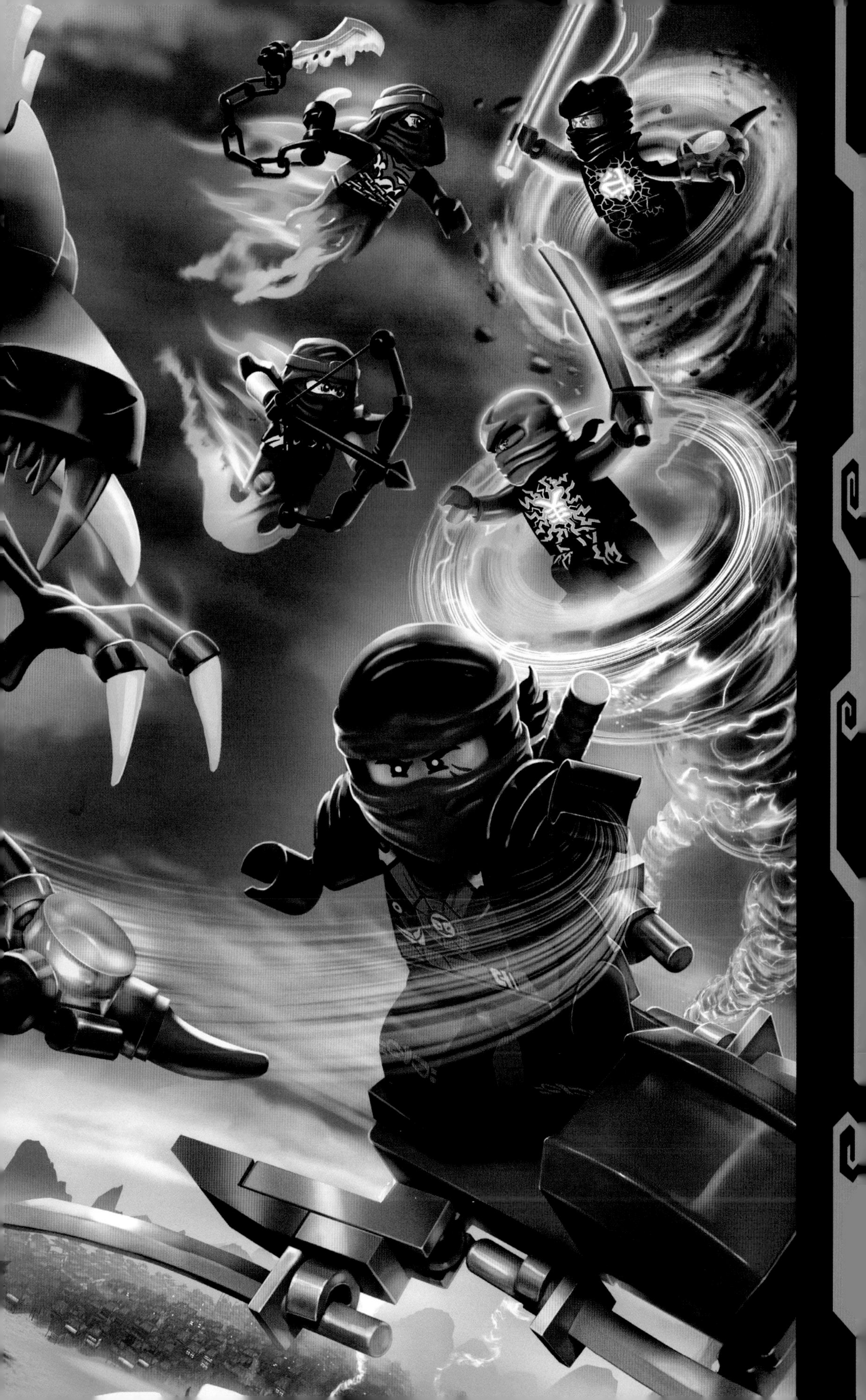

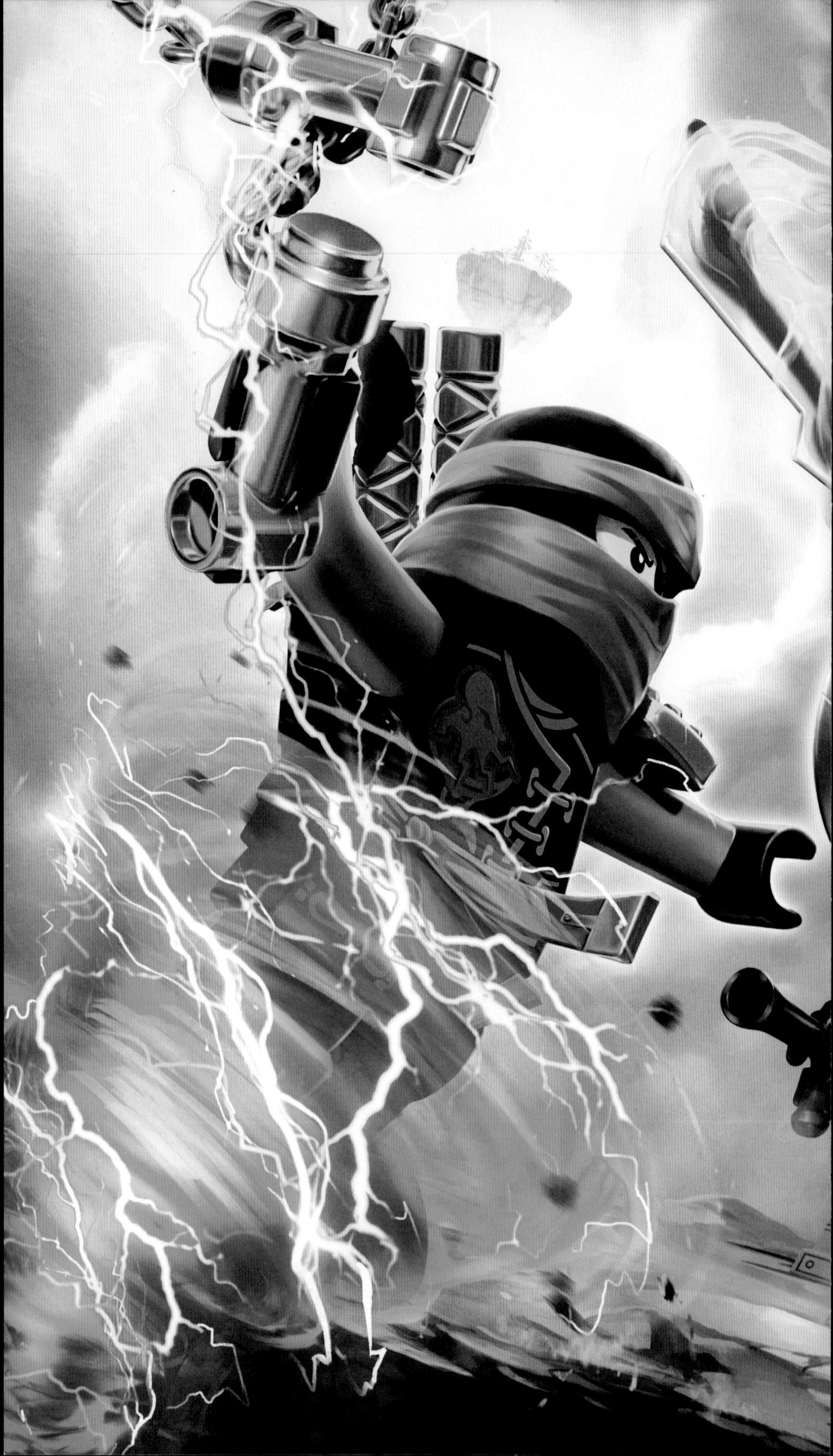

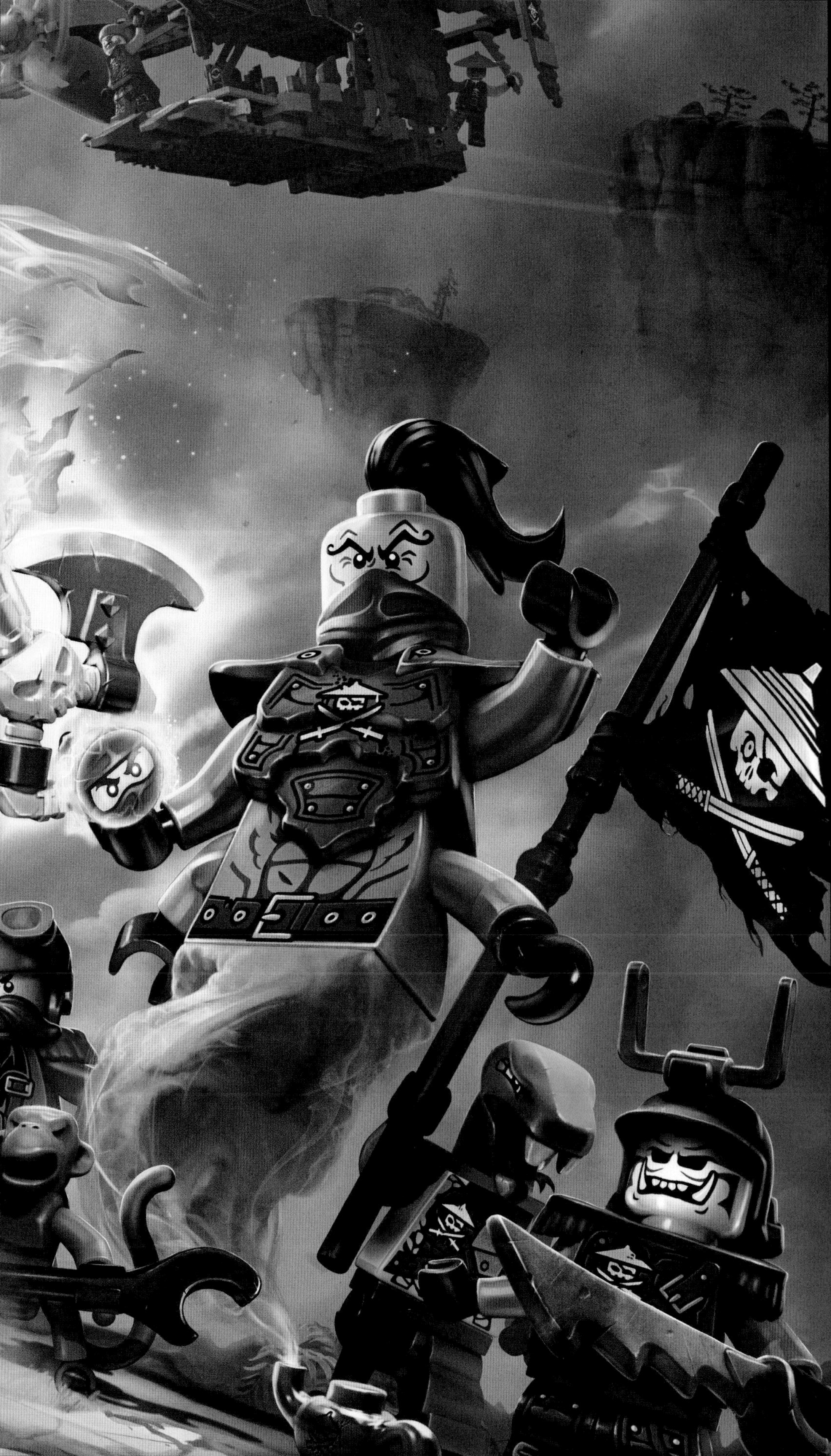

Don't miss the Dark Island Trilogy!

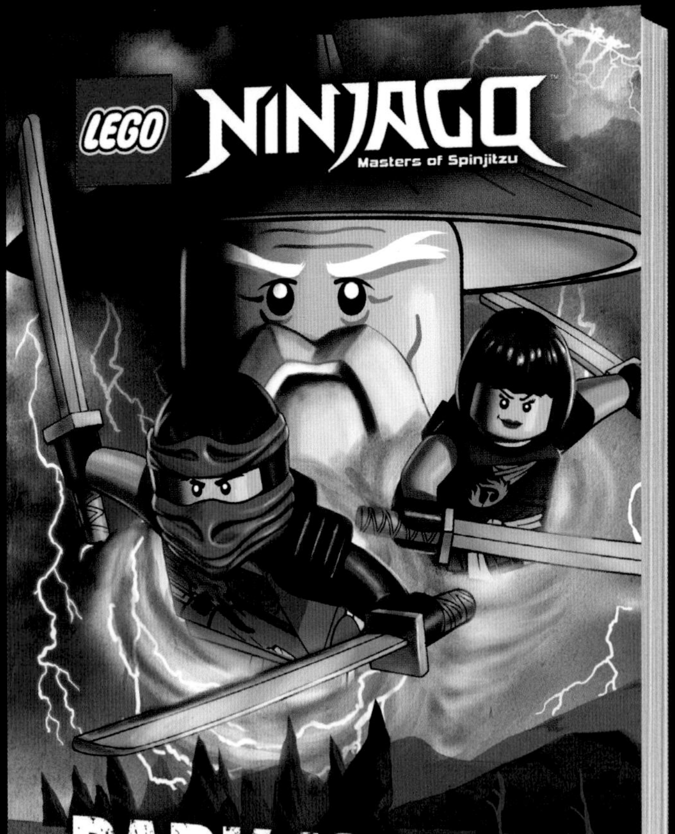
LEGO
NINJAGO
Masters of Spinjitzu
DARK ISLAND
TRILOGY—PART 1

BUILD YOUR LEGO® LIBRARY TODAY!

LEGO BIONICLE
GATHERING OF THE TOA
BONUS PAGES!
Secrets! Codes! Maps! And more!

LEGO BIONICLE
BATTLE OF THE MASK MAKERS
BONUS PAGES!
Secrets! Maps! And more!

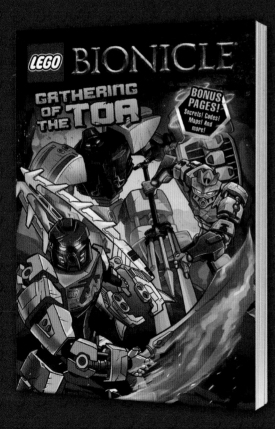

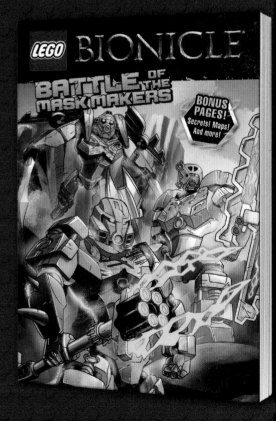

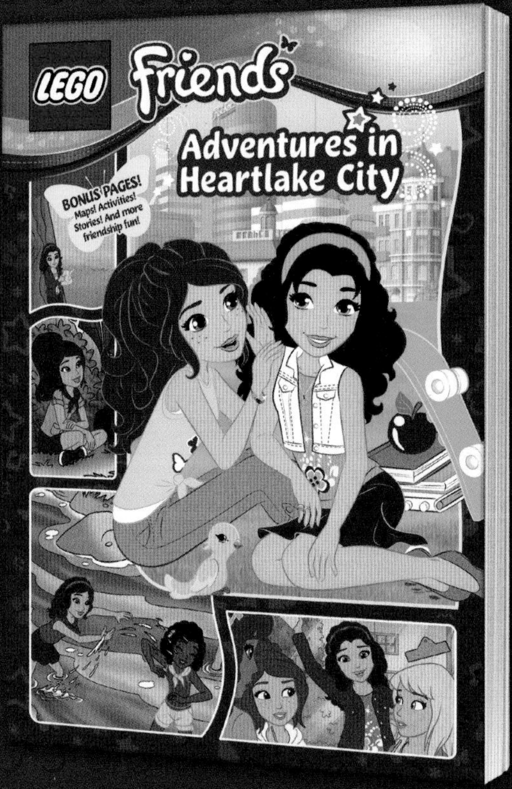
LEGO
Friends
Adventures in Heartlake City
BONUS PAGES! Maps! Activities! Stories! And more friendship fun!

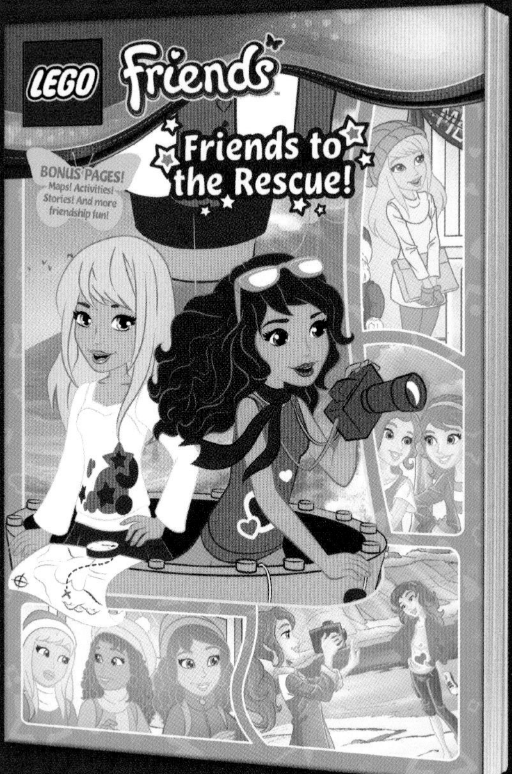
LEGO
Friends
Friends to the Rescue!
BONUS PAGES! Maps! Activities! Stories! And more friendship fun!

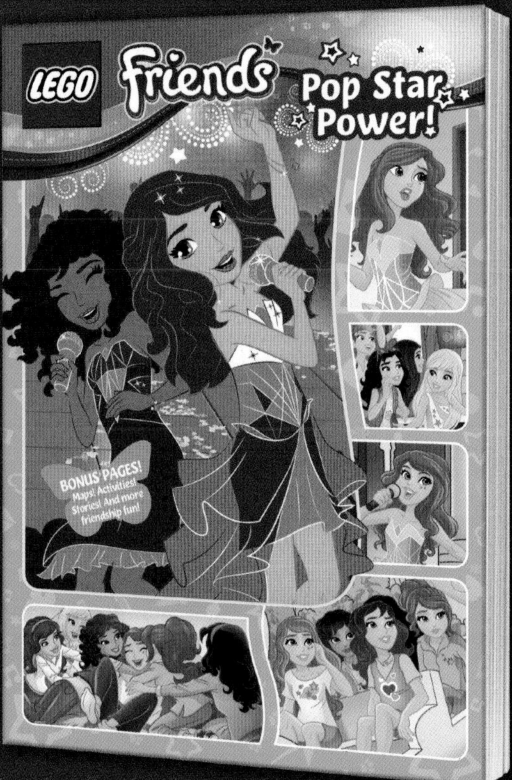
LEGO
Friends
Pop Star Power!
BONUS PAGES! Maps! Activities! Stories! And more friendship fun!

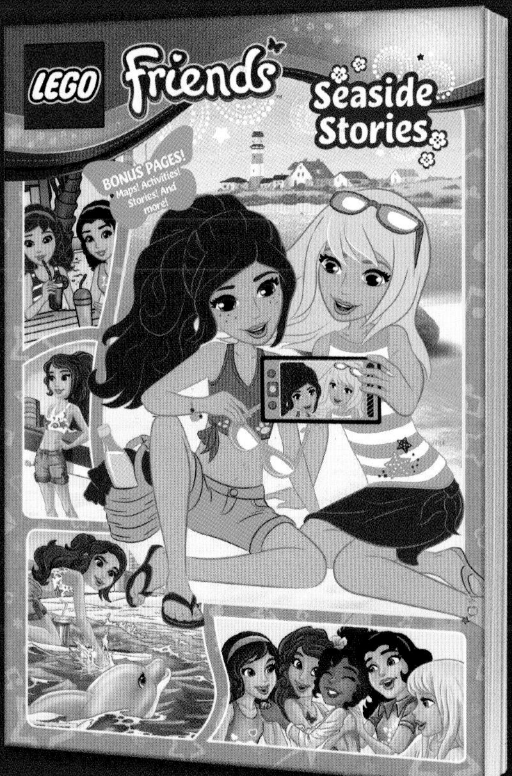
LEGO
Friends
Seaside Stories
BONUS PAGES! Maps! Activities! Stories! And more!

LEGO

NINJAGO™

Masters of Spinjitzu

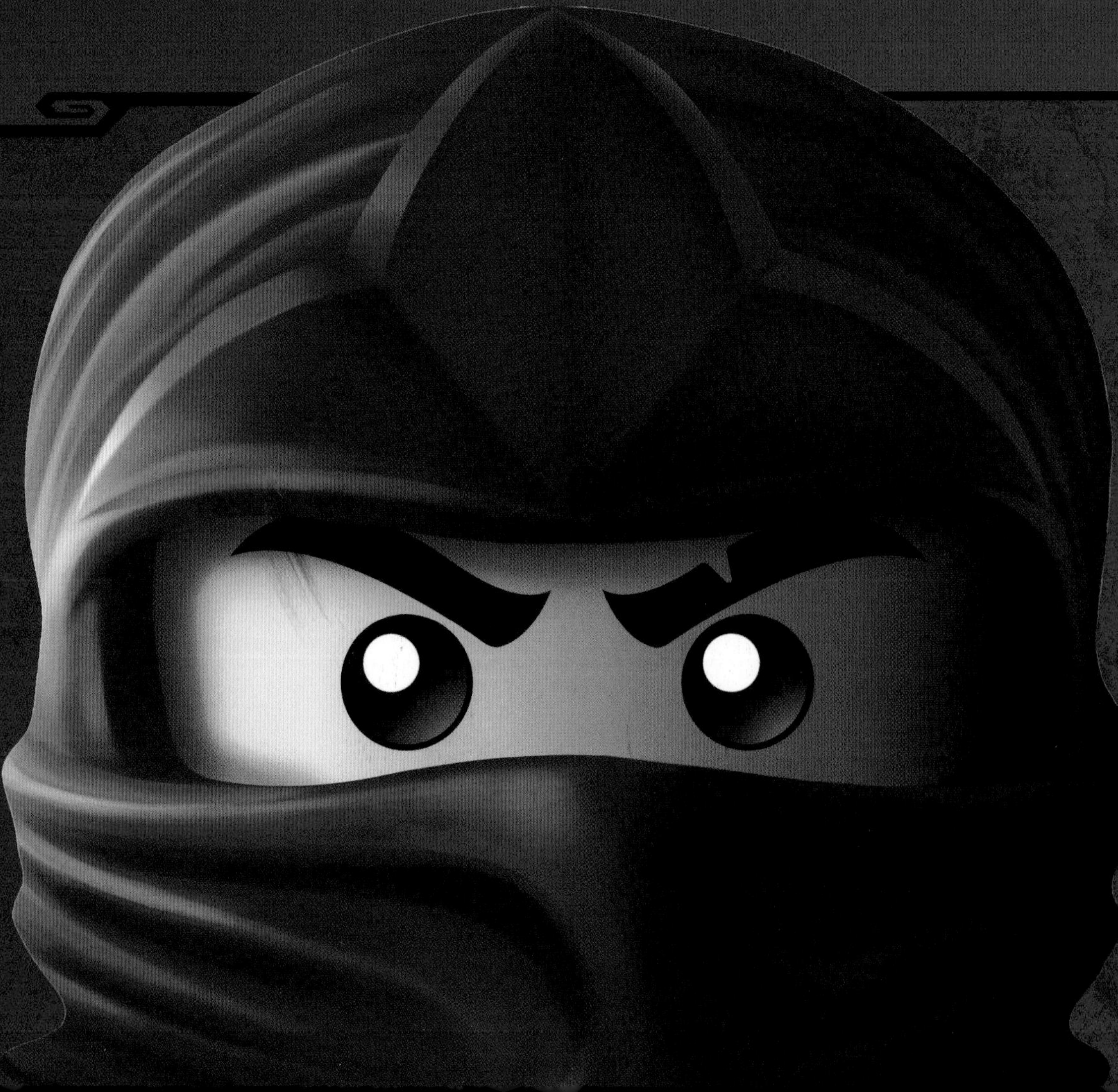